Janet A. Martin

I am fully convinced that the soul is indestructible, and that its activity will continue through eternity. It is like the sun, which, to our eyes, seems to set in night; but it has in reality only gone to diffuse its light elsewhere.

— JOHANN GOETHE
1749-1832

To know what is impenetrable to us really exists, manifesting itself as the highest wisdom and the most radiant beauty, which our dull faculties can comprehend only in their most primitive forms——this knowledge, this feeling, is at the center of true religiousness. In this sense, and this sense only, I belong to the ranks of devoutly religious men.

— ALBERT EINSTEIN
1879-1955

The discovery of extra dimensions would show that the entirety of human experience had left us completely unaware of a basic and essential aspect of the universe.

— BRIAN GREENE
2004
The Fabric of The Cosmos

THE CHRISTMAS
Swap

Janet A. Martin

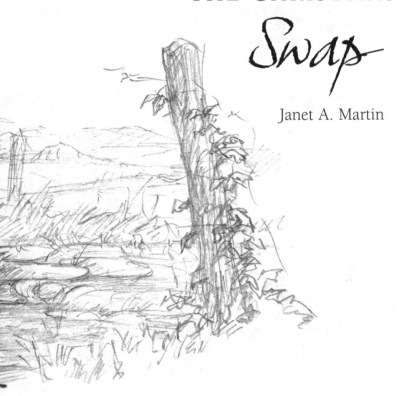

Chanticleer Imprint, LLC

The Christmas Swap © by Janet A. Martin, 2007.

ISBN: 978-0-9794251-0-3

Publisher's Note

This is a work of fiction. Names, characters, places, and incidents either are the product of the author's imagination or are used fictitiously, and any resemblance to actual persons, living or dead, business establishments, events, or locales, unless specified, is entirely coincidental.

Printed in the United States of America by
Thompson-Shore, Inc.

Published by
the American Book Company
and FirstWord Press

EXECUTIVE PRODUCERS: Tom and Lily Grace Hudson
PRODUCTION ASSISTANCE: Pat Fitzpatrick
MANAGING EDITOR: F. Charles Carmichael, PhD.
BOOK DESIGN AND COVER: Linda Berry
ILLUSTRATIONS: R. E. Lee Gildea
BOOK EDITOR: Lisa A. Allen
WEB DESIGN: Josh Robertson

For information and book orders, please visit the website
www.thechristmasswap.com

For Charles, who was there.

I am deeply thankful to the people who, from the start, believed in this work: my design editor, Linda Berry, who devoted time, energy, and creativity. To readers early on from various walks of life . . . on rural farms, in small towns, and within giant cities . . . who offered suggestions and encouragement, including George Beller, M.D., Chuck Lewis, Martha Farlow, Kimberly Ritchie, Angus and Nancy Robertson, Charles Schlessiger, J. Anderson Thomson, M.D., Linda Westby, Kathie Woods, and especially Tom and Lily Grace Hudson. It is my conviction that libraries are among the world's sacred places, and librarians, among the world's finest people. Particularly, I am indebted to librarians at Alderman and Clemson libraries at The University of Virginia, including Warner Grenade, M. Sajjad Yusuf, and V. Irene Norvelle, and to the welcoming staff members in the public library of Clinton, Tennessee, who offered a desk with a window to this author while she was visiting and writing at intervals between 2003 and 2005. I am beholden to the Virginia residents who are unabashed in their love of the rural land-scape and its vanishing way of life, and for their ardor in protecting it against ill-conceived development. It is their passion that inspired a theme in this book. Finally, I am grateful to my children, Kristen, Bradley and Lane, who along with my husband, F. Charles Carmichael, saw this book pilgrimage confidently through.

PROLOGUE

THAT NOVEMBER, the first snow had come to northern New York on Thanksgiving Day. It fell softly both within and beyond congested cities, stretching its domain toward less populated terrain, including a distinctive two-hundred-acre campus of manicured nineteenth-century grounds, skillfully planted with evergreen shrubs and towering trees. The November snowflakes hugged the rough-faced sandstone on the clustered campus buildings, enhancing their Romanesque windows and doors, and sculpting frozen white, the curve of connecting archways. Now that the snow was still, nature's iced glaze clung to two central stone towers that dominated the campus. Their pointed roofs of black slate stood poised amid the hush of pastoral surroundings as if contemplating whether or when to ram the threshold of heaven with fervent appeals of hope.

In one of the tall towers, empty, unused, and unlit, stood a lone custodian gazing at the placid frozen sight far below. It was about twenty-four hours since the first flake had fallen, and he had rolled open one of the pointed tower windows, the hinges arthritically protesting as he slowly twisted the handle. He had come to smoke a cigarette, to prolong the peace of night before resuming his hospital rounds. He inhaled slowly, tranquilly, and the tiny spark of light in the surrounding dark glowed red beside his face, and then glimmered less brightly as he exhaled. Smoke mingled with the frozen vapor of his breath in the bone-chilling dark.

He heard the heavy scrape of the iron main gate below, the one announcing the grounds for more than one hundred years now, stoutly supported by stone pillars the same reddish-brown that distinguished the other structures within this private, often tormented place. It was, this place, an institution of good intentions, conceived in the decade following the War Between the States, built in 1880 to house the souls of the mentally tortured within the enlightened environs of landscaped peace.

Below, as he watched the gate ease open before the nose of a sleek black limousine, the man heard something else. It was the sound of a door in the tower he occupied, opening and closing. His friend was coming; he knew it; he pulled on his cigarette with thin, pursed lips. He could hear the muffled footsteps measuring the flights of steps: *Shump. Shump. Shump.* Pause. *Shump. Shump. Shump.* Labored breathing. Then a voice.

"That you, Moses?" He heard his name.

"Oh, yeah."

"That time of night?"

"Oh, yeah."

"Can I bum one?"

"Jest one."

In the dark, Moses held out a crumpled pack of cigarettes along with a lighter, which he flicked as his friend leaned forward. A halo of light warmed the man's thin, dark face. The light snapped out, leaving the shine of burning ash as his friend inhaled.

"Thanks, Moses."

"Oh, yeah."

The two men smoked together quietly. The glossy limousine pulled determinedly past the iron gates below. The red taillights glided toward a separate stone building, brightened, turned, and disappeared. The purring limo engine died in the distance, leaving stillness in its wake.

Then . . .

"He's back, Moses."

"Oh, yeah. I know."

"First snow."

"Always gets to him."

"I kinda like the old guy."

"Yeah, he feeds the squirrels and the birds, even the deer come up to him once in a while . . ."

"He say some interesting stuff, uh, about the world and all. Ever, uh, listen to him, Moses?"

"Oh, yeah. But not much."

"Why's that, Moses?"

The custodian was quiet for a moment. "Well, this place—it's for crazy folks, ain't it?"

"Heh, heh, heh. Well, I guess so. But he don't seem nuts to me. Jest strange and old."

"He be old."

"How old you think?"

"No telling." Silence cloaked the dark. Then,

"What that you call him, Moses?"

"St. Nick."

"Heh, heh, heh. St. Nick. Why's that?"

" 'Cause he allus busts out 'round Christmas."

"Well, this time, uh, he done some damage, I hear."

"Only to his own kin, I bet, that snarlin', mean rat pack of greedy folks."

"They want him, uh, locked up again. Called the nurses' station on the schizo ward. Want him held 'cause, uh, they's after another court order. Say, uh, he hit the bank once more—hit their inheritance."

"Oh, yeah. But it ain't."

"It ain't? What you mean, 'It ain't'?"

"It ain't their inheritance, 'cause he ain't dead."

"Heh, heh, heh. You right 'bout that."

Moses smiled in the dark, silently watching his cigarette vapor curl in the cold. Then he spoke.

"Nobody called his lawyer, I bet."

"I 'spec you right about that, too, Moses. You goin' to?"

"He tole me to, whenever this happens. Ain't no mistake it's pitch dark and midnight and they bringin' him in here quiet and all."

"The lawyer give you his, uh, his number?"

"In my wallet." Moses stubbed his smoke out on the stone floor. He picked up the twisted butt and put it in his front uniformed pocket. In his baggy pants he reached for a mashed billfold and retrieved a business card with a hand-scrawled phone number across the back. He looked at it and sighed.

"I'll be headin' on. Gotta use the pay phone, and it's a long way from duty. Plus, I don't walk so fast these days."

"That's the truth, Moses. We both be gettin' on."

"Oh, yeah."

"You callin' the lawyer in the middle of the night?"

"Um hum."

"So, uh, when you think he'll be out again?"

"St. Nick?"

"Heh, heh, heh. Yeah, St. Nick, the man who's allus lookin' for good folks who, uh, love each other."

"He better stick to squirrels."

"Or birds . . . Heh, heh. But, but, Moses, uh, how long you think befo' he be out again?"

Moses turned to face the friend, his own weathered profile

limned by the smudged chalk of the starry night framed by the tower window. "Out?" he asked and scratched his chin.

"Heh, heh. Yeah, uh. Out."

"I'd say—well, I'd say," Moses nodded slowly up and down, thinking . . . "I'd say by the next snow."

1. Never Enough

Three states south, in Central Virginia's Peach County, snow was on the way, a white presence hoped for but as yet unseen. Rain, instead, drummed the earth, bringing down the last hanging leaves from the silver maples and the pin oaks, filling the evergreen cedars with crystalline weight, dislodging cone-laden branches from the loblolly pines. Commiserating with one another, a gaggle of crows rasped from heights in the tall Virginia pines.

On the Saturday following Thanksgiving, at the edge of a woodsy thicket, a large white-tailed doe raised her grayish brown head, her dark amber eyes alert. She stiffened in silence. The fawn, pure white at her side, stepped, then stood, his long white ears forward, his pink eyes dim-sighted, unlike his mother's. The doe moved a few noiseless steps to the right, away from the pale fawn. Beyond the cedar boughs, a mottled green mass moved, closer, closer. Too close.

Suddenly, the doe released a piercing snort. With that warning she leaped, her brown frame crashing away from the fawn, back into the thicket. The blast of a rifle filled the air, followed by snapping tree branches and a heavy thump. The mottled green mass surged. The white fawn bolted. The black crows flapped—a circle overhead—drifting to a settled clump in the pines. Back and forth, from lofty views, they squalled the news of the season.

Less than a mile away, a sleepy Jan Midland wandered into the family room of the farm cottage she lived in with her husband, Frank.

"Was that a gun shot?" she asked, twisting her uncombed hair into a rubber band.

Frank was up early, wiring his new surround-sound system to the television.

"Hunting season," he grunted. Then he pointed to a corner of the room and scowled.

"Five boxes of red Christmas balls. For what? We already have ten boxes of balls up in the attic!"

Jan gasped in surprise. The partially decorated Christmas tree, purchased the day before, had been moved from its place before the window. It stood slightly askew in its three-footed stand. Beside it, a puddle of water stained the carpet.

Jan took it all in—the wet carpet, the tree shunted aside, and Frank's unexpected protest. "Well!" she said, somewhat miffed, "Once again you are crouched behind the television. You've made a mess on the floor. And you growl at me?"

"I just wondered why we need more balls when we already have plenty to decorate a tree."

"I told you, Frank Midland," her voice climbing the scales, "that this year is our year for a theme. A theme tree! All other years we've had ghastly, blinking lights, bubbling lights, and tacky ornaments made of toothpicks and paper chains! Now, with the twins off to college, I can have the tree I want! And they can't do a thing about it when they get home for Christmas break but complain! Which, undoubtedly, they will."

"That's their job." Frank offered a limp olive branch, but Jan wasn't having it.

She shook her head. "So I went for red—red balls and white lights and farm animals!"

Frank stared, immobilized. "Farm animals?"

"We live on a farm, don't we?" Folding her arms across a body that retained much of the muscular shape of a college tennis player, Jan impatiently tapped her foot as she awaited her husband's further reaction. But he sniffed the direction of the emotional wind and ducked from sight. She glimpsed his tousled grey head swinging rhythmically side-to-side, hunting inserts and inputs, finding exports and ports.

Just like Frank, Jan thought. *Bury yourself in the jungle of a wired world.* She spun in her sock feet and headed for the kitchen area of the family room.

"I put an extension cord right here last week," Frank said, frustrated. "A heavy duty one. Orange. Did you move it?"

"Maybe. Straightening up the place. I can't remember," Jan groused, opening the refrigerator.

Frank kept muttering. "And where is that box of cables I keep?"

Jan migrated from the refrigerator, a carton of milk in hand, toward the coffee pot. Mercifully, it was full.

"How should I know? In the garage? In the doghouse? Cables, cables. They all look alike. Anyway, ever since we've downsized our living space, I don't have room for junk. Or—or! My furniture. Even"—Jan exhaled a self-pitying moan—"my piano!"

Frank groaned. "Well, for the hundredth time, as I've said, until I design and we build our farmhouse, the piano's in good hands at the Urbanes' home. Francine says it fits right in her music room, the one with the bay window."

"Oh God. To have a room just for music!"

Here come the dramatics, Frank thought. He watched Jan move back and forth, coffee pot to refrigerator—gracefully—like she once played tennis, a slip of a woman in a short tennis skirt. Those were the days . . . Frank heard the song lyrics in his mind. He watched her lean into the cold box to poke among the leftovers in plastic containers. Frank sighed, knelt on the floor, and reached for an audio cable behind the TV. His wife chattered on.

"One room in Francine's home for just music . . . and another room for just plants . . . and still another for the washer and dryer!" Jan railed as she popped open a plastic lid here and there. "*You and I* share all those functions in a fish bowl!"

Frank raised his head and bumped it smartly on the back of the television stand. "Darn!" He rubbed his forehead. "May I remind you that you wanted a farm?" He checked his fingertips. No blood. "And we bought fifty-five acres in beautiful Hunt Country, Virginia. And you knew back then—you knew upfront—we'd have to make do in this old cottage. But we fixed it up. It's nice. It's cozy."

"Cozy. True. And the coziness has lasted five cramped years."

Frank continued rubbing his forehead. "Well, we've got two kids in college now, you know?" He felt a stab of pain. *Ingratitude. How could she?*

"I'm doing my best," he said. "If you don't like the way I provide for this family, then find somebody else." Frank squinted his eyes, pushed out his chin, and put his long arms at his thin waist.

Jan recognized the "I've had it!" pose. She turned and began impatiently rinsing out leftover containers. "Let's stay focused, shall we?" she called over her shoulder. "I do my part. I work to stay in budget. But you call my decorating efforts 'clutter.'"

"It is, a lot of it."

"At the same time, I can't get things arranged before you push them aside to put your backside behind the TV—"

"To improve the sound." Frank shook his head. "But truthfully? I hate the cluttered look. You can be sure Francine Urbane doesn't have a jumble of Christmas crap, packages, tinsel and hundreds of red balls in one corner of the room."

"That's because Francine has room—lots of room—at least five corners to every room in her house!"

Frank bent down again behind the television. "No matter what I do, it's never enough. You're always complaining."

"About the TV? It's always in the center of the living room!"

Frank paused, noticed that he was breathing heavily, and looked up. Where was the femme fatale he had wed? The gay divorcé with twin boys, a beautiful woman, some said. *Slim. Athletic. Lucky guy, that Frank.*

Well, lucky-guy Frank had taken her on. And she was beautiful, but not always. Right now, she had on her bottle-thick granny glasses reflecting the morning sun. Her long brown hair dangled in loops. She was standing in a pair of green, thick hunting socks, and she was wrapped in her snowy Ritz Carlton robe (he had purchased it for her on an exorbitant courtship fling), its terry-cloth sash tied haphazardly at the middle. Now it was Frank's turn to take it all in.

Through the green branches of the Christmas spruce, Frank Midland gazed at Jan Midland. "Let me get this straight," he said evenly. "You want surround sound and lots of space?"

"No! *You* want surround sound! I want a TV that stays in place."

"In place?"

"In place."

"And space?"

"Right. And space. Someday, when we build the farmhouse."

"Well in the meantime, why don't I just move the TV to create space?"

Jan threw up her hands.

Frank stalked past her toward the front door. He opened it wide. She shivered in the blast of late-November air. The door slammed. She winced. She slumped in the rocker near the tree, cradling her cup of coffee. She sipped it and reflexively turned up her lip. *Cold,* she grimaced.

Her conscience nudged. She knew she should follow Frank and apologize, but she didn't want to. She wanted to sit in peace and drift, to gaze at her handcrafted balsa wood ornaments on the tree. She noticed how the shaken glitter specks on the animal shapes caught the morning sun from the east cottage window. She warmed as she saw how the cow's black eyes twinkled, how the rooster's red comb gleamed, how the sheep's white sequins glinted as if magically alive.

She shrugged, thinking, *Tacky maybe, but quaint.* She liked the effect. But in the next instant, she sighed. Since her nest had gone empty, the twins, Ryan and Kyle, having flown the coop to college, she had not felt the magic of Christmas. Furthermore, she and Frank, after ten years of marriage, realized suddenly, that for the first time, they were together alone. My! How irremediably they had changed!

Looking back now, giving credit where it was due, Frank had wanted to marry Jan mid-life and help raise the kids. Her boys needed a strong man, and Frank filled the role despite his bent as a contemplative intellectual. He taught the twins practical skills, how to cut trees, how to bush hog a field, how to wire almost anything.

And Frank was versatile, Jan had to admit. Recognized by his peers as an architectural innovator, he could pluck from thin air a visionary design innately in tune with a physical site. Frank Lloyd Wright, his hero, inspired *her* Frank's love for form-functioning, uplifting space that molded itself rather like children's play dough into dynamic shapes. Passive square rooms bored him. But for reasons she could not comprehend, he was fascinated with wires. While these days, Jan, by comparison, was not fascinated with anything!

Her gaze drifted to the window beyond. *Typical after-Thanksgiving weather out there*, she thought. *Everything's brown.* She pushed her foot rhythmically against the carpet, rocking while her mind coasted. Then . . .

What was that noise? She put aside her coffee cup. *Thump! Thump!* Encroaching. *Thump! Thump!* Closer. Jan listened intently as wheels rolled across the deck. And—bang! Through the front doorway. Damp air along with . . . what? Why, their vertical, yellow hand truck—*Thump! Thump!* Squealing metal rolling right in her direction.

She watched the scene unfolding in freeze-frames before her wire-rimmed glasses:

Frank pushing the hand truck through the entrance hall.

Frank positioning the truck in front of the television stand.

Frank bending himself in half over the large TV.

Frank pulling it from the corner of the room.

Frank—Frank! Breaking his back loading the television on the hand truck! Uh oh. Better stop this—NOW! Or both of them would spend next week at the hospital.

"Stop it, Frank!"

"Nope!"

"You'll hurt yourself."

"What do you care?"

"Frank, c'mon, calm down."

Frank panted. His tangled grey hair curled with sweat on his brow. "I'm going to get this stupid TV into the garage where I can wire a sound system in peace!"

"Be rational!"

"Rational? I am being rational! You get up in a bad mood. You accuse me—I'm a lousy provider—unwarranted and unfair slings and arrows—may I quote Shakespeare? And over what? Over a TV! I want it out of your space!" He lunged and lifted the television off its stand.

"There!" he grunted, swinging the TV toward the hand truck, craning his neck in the opposite direction over his shoulder. "Look! There's your fifth corner to our living room!"

Well, Jan knew when disaster loomed. The slide show she'd witnessed popped like a soap bubble in her mind. She sprang from her rocker like a startled grasshopper and put both green sock feet purposefully on the metal ledge of the yellow hand truck. Her green eyes narrowed behind her glassed eyes. Her lips stretched like thin rubber bands over clenched teeth.

Frank's face was rapidly turning red, his brain boiling. When he and Jan had married, he readily could carry the blasted TV down the stairs. Now he could barely get the TV to the hand truck, where Jan had firmly planted herself.

"Get off!" he grunted.

"No!"

"Move! I'm loading the TV!"

"You've got to unload me first." Jan vigorously tied the sash of her robe around the handle of the hand truck.

Desperate, Frank turned again and, with an enormous groan, deposited the TV back on its stand. He reared up, feeling a twinge of protest in his back. He roared, "Move!" and grabbed the hand truck. He pulled it up on its wheels toward himself— with all 135 pounds of the Ritz-robed woman he'd married at 110 pounds ten years before—right up to his nose.

"Oh," he puffed. "Uh. You've gained weight!"

"Not as much weight as that TV!" she snapped.

Frank had to admit defeat. Ignominious defeat. He could not lift his wife down the steps. Maybe she wasn't an ingénue any longer, but just maybe he wasn't the swarthy stud he used to be either. Why, he was six-foot-two, slender, muscular, and strong. And sexy, even, according to some giggling co-eds at the university. But that was when? Yesterday? Last year? Longer?

Hmm. Frank felt the eerie creep of pain down his sciatic nerve, a narrow ribbon, moving from his lower back to his left foot. What was he thinking, moving that TV himself! What a fool!

Well, fool or not, he would not concede. Frank Midland, esteemed architect. *Face humiliation? Not with his wife standing in her bathrobe tied to a hand truck! How ridiculous!*

Frank thumped the metal platform down on the carpet.

"Ouch, my tennis elbow!" Jan squealed.

"Elbow? Tennis elbow?"

"You bumped it."

"Humph," Frank said. "Your best excuse not to exercise."

"What's that supposed to mean?" Jan shrilled.

"It wasn't that elbow that caused you to quit tennis!" Frank retorted. But then a winged friend nestled in his ear and said, "EDIT!"

Yep, Frank knew he was about to step across The Line into the zone where unkind words bury themselves later to explode like land mines in the brain. He wisely deleted his next thought before speaking it.

Instead he said, "I'm out of here!" He grabbed a jacket from the hall tree bulging with coats. He bolted out the front door.

"Where are you going? It's Saturday after a holiday. The store crowds are huge. You hate crowds!"

"Not at the Circle Market! That crowd is friendly—not like *this* frosty atmosphere."

Stung, Jan slid silently into her rocking chair. Then she cried in a hoarse voice, "You just want to buy someething."

"I do! I do!" Frank clambered down the front steps. "A fifty-foot orange extension cord."

2. The View in Clearview

Frank pulled his farm pickup truck, gravel spinning, from his quarter-mile driveway onto the highway. Two miles later, he reached the shabby block and wood structure known as the Circle Market. As he wheeled into the market's parking lot, he almost collided with a Mercedes sedan. Frank stopped his truck with a jolt to let a distinguished, older man, Wilburn Urbane, gracefully ease his car into the space in front of the store. Frank found another slot and pulled on his emergency brake. He climbed out thinking, *Bill is a nice guy, but just about the last person I want to see right now.* Jan's rebuke about the expansive five corners in the Urbanes' living space stung Frank mightily. Nevertheless, he greeted the man genially.

"Hello, Bill," Frank said, extending his hand. Bill pulled off an Italian leather driving glove and shook Frank's bare fingers. Frank's cotton jacket flapped in the chilly wind; Bill Urbane's leather coat lay buttoned and flat. *Gosh, what a rich sheen,* Frank noticed, *a coat the color of cognac.* Bill seemed pleased to see Frank.

"Busy time of year," he said.

Frank noticed his face was flushed. Maybe the cold, Frank surmised.

"Why are you here?"

"Francine has the florist decorating the house this weekend for the holidays. I need some space." Bill laughed self-consciously.

"Funny you should say that," Frank nodded. "I know just what you mean. Join me for a cup of coffee?"

"I'd like that," Bill said. Frank held the door open as they both stepped inside where the air was fragrant, the temperature welcoming.

Since the late 1800s, the Circle Market had been a fixture in Clearview, Virginia, its whitewashed plank exterior adapting as the rural community developed. In the 1950s, an extension built of cement blocks modernized the front. In the rear, a soda fountain area, unchanged since then, offered round metal tables covered in red-checked oilcloth. From this area, visitors were permitted a not altogether clear view of Clearview through dingy rollout windows facing west.

A white laminate soda counter running perpendicular to the windows sported metal stools with red plastic seats. The counter stretched from the cash register to the coat rack. Behind it, old-fashioned milkshake machines whirred constantly over frozen tubs of ice cream. Above, plastic replicas of idealized banana splits, milk shakes, Coca-Cola floats, and ice cream sodas graced the pale green wall. A pair of swinging aluminum doors led to the kitchen behind the counter.

"Over there?" Frank indicated a table near the rollout windows.

"Sure," Bill nodded.

Walking toward the table, Frank raised a friendly hand to catch the attention of Flossie Atkins, the red-haired waitress, pushing forty, who had been there as a server since she first flounced into the Circle Market as a teen looking for a job. She wiggled her long fingernails at Frank and her heavy painted lips mouthed "one minute" silently as she rang up a departing customer at the cash register.

"I'm making some fresh," she said out loud, intuitively knowing his request. Frank smiled. Both men sat and silently gazed out windows, smudged with traces of smoke and grease, to the vacant field beyond.

Even in winter, Frank thought the spot was beautiful. The tawny wild grasses rippled in the wind, their camel color stippled with the darker gold of hearty broom sedge, a tall, scratchy weed which farmers cursed for its inveterate march across otherwise productive fields. Here and there a cedar sprouted, tiny volunteer Christmas trees planted by fleeting birds or animals relieving themselves of seed diets on journeys to fields farther on. On this patch of vacant land, three pin oaks—dense, mighty, and red in the fall; bare, brown, and lofty in winter—stood stoutly, reaching hefty branches toward a grey sky.

Developers were gobbling up rural country like this fast. But there were some tracts left, and conservationists like Frank and Bill wanted to preserve as much as possible for future generations. Both had invested their farms in conservation easements, which banned development. Sure, they got a tax break from the deal. But they also protected the land for posterity, both for humans and wildlife. The eleven-acre patch behind the Circle Market no doubt would go commercial someday. Frank hated the thought that a "For Sale" sign might sprout at any moment. Once that happened, instead of field daisies and tough green cedars, there'd be garish lights and drab concrete; instead of sleepy crickets in golden grasses, there would be rumbling trucks and rushing people—all the indistinguishable chaos homogenizing the identity of rural towns all over America.

Why, in Clearview, The Circle, as it was commonly

known to the fifteen thousand inhabitants, formed the center-piece of the community. Just as roundabouts defined traffic patterns in world-class cities, The Circle in Clearview beckoned residents and tourists alike. Wherever they came from or wherever they were going, everyone arrived via The Circle.

"If that vacant field were in Rome, there'd be a cathedral right on the spot," Frank spoke out loud. "Or, if it were in Washington, D.C., there'd be a monument."

"That's true," Bill said amiably.

"Of course, unlike those cities," Frank replied, "Clearview was not exactly planned."

"That's also true," Bill smiled.

Frank had written books about the region now called Peach County. He knew that its plucky settlers had followed the ridge along the Southwest Mountains in wooden wagons loaded with housewares and drawn by horses and plodding mules. The newcomers discovered the rolling terrain where fecund, loamy soil promised new lives to those adventurous enough to drop from the mule trains to settle in the blue-tinged hills.

"Drawn by the land." Frank cupped his chin in his hand. "Some of the original farms are grants from Kings George II and III, thousands of acres at a time. Thomas Jefferson was born up the road at Shadwell, in 1743."

"I've been to Monticello a few times," Bill replied. "Fascinating man, Jefferson, inventor, statesman, writer, builder, and a Virginian," he smiled.

"Folks around here say *first* he was a farmer," Frank nodded.

"Well, I'll tell you," Bill sat up straighter, "the soil around these Southwest Mountains is good for almost anything, horses, cows, sheep, corn, alfalfa, and now—everywhere—vineyards!"

"Big one going in further up the road."

"In three years, it will be beautiful," Frank gazed out the window as if the wintry vines were just beyond the Market. "I like seeing development when it's agricultural use of the land," he added.

"Instead of city-style crops like mega markets?" Bill's tone was sarcastic.

"Or mega gas stations."

"Ugh," Bill shook his head. "You don't want one of those for a neighbor."

"Nope," Frank agreed.

Both men sat nodding, as if reconstructing the past and envisioning the future of the small town. Early landowners had constructed a church, a tavern, and a few houses rising around a hub, a wagon-wheel shape of land rising to a gentle knoll. They named the spot Clearview for its wide swept views of the surrounding mountains. From the knoll, the town grew like crabgrass, spreading in all directions. Shops and businesses and homes—primitive and grand—strung out and circled back. All streets led back to The Circle. Over time, automobiles replaced horses, gas stations supplanted livery shops, and country stores evolved as convenience markets. The original church and tavern fell to history's thieves—fire, decay, and urban renewal.

Frank frowned. "I'd say since the 1960s, nobody has really thought much about the view in Clearview."

At that moment Flossie brought the men two cups of steaming hot coffee.

"Thanks, Red," Frank winked good-naturedly at Flossie.

"You're the only man who can get away with callin' me that," she drawled.

"How about me?" Bill leaned his graceful head back and smiled.

"Naw. Just Frank." She patted him on the shoulder

lightly. "Don't want it gettin' around. Took me years to grow outta that nickname from high school."

"Okay, Flossie," Bill picked up the metal pitcher of milk and cocked the top open over his coffee mug.

"I've seen an early town map showing the original buildings," Frank said, "in the Peach County Historical Society."

"Oh really?"

Frank nodded. "The courthouse on Main Street was just that central brick portion with the clock tower."

"I've noticed that the existing cornerstone says 1770," Bill added. "What else did you find?"

"There was a small clapboard church, around this knoll," Frank's eyes looked through the windows to the field, "with the whole narrow front vestibule section itself forming a steeple, its foundation rested on fieldstones."

"I bet it burned," Bill said. "A lot of old structures did, you know, heated by fireplaces."

"Don't know. But I've always meant to get a class of my students to engage in a shallow excavation to see if we could find the original foundations. That field out the window there might be considered historical. Sometimes such sites can be protected, you know, from certain kinds of development."

"How about the Circle Market, is it historical?" Bill asked.

"Obviously, this place is not. But its foundations may be," Frank said. "The tavern on the early maps, also in old newspapers, was a wooden structure where hunters bought supplies. It had a buck head nailed on the front. People would say, 'Let's meet at the buck, or why don't we stop at the buck?' So they called it, 'The Buck Stop.'"

"I like that better than the Circle Market."

"Me, too," Frank said. "But anyway, the market owner bought the old tavern and changed things, adding neon signs and the store facade, lights, and gas pumps. But he saved the buck's head. That's it over the cash register at the fountain."

"That old thing should be tossed out," Bill sniffed.

"It's moldy," Frank agreed. "Sometimes, though, I look at that dusty antler rack with that dull flat coat and those vacant glass eyes, and I wonder just how many Clearview ancestors that old buck has eyeballed over the decades."

"No telling," Bill said.

At that moment Flossie came over again. She wore her usual pale peach uniform, a knee-length skirt, a short-sleeved collared shirt, her body frame slipping from slender to sinewy with each passing year. She pulled a small tablet from her white apron pocket. She hunched her sharp shoulders, flipping pages on the order pad. She held a pencil in her hand, licked the tip, and asked, "Burger with lettuce, tomato, mayo?"

"My usual," Frank nodded. She scribbled and then looked at Bill Urbane.

"The same," he said. "And more coffee, please."

"Got it." She refolded her tablet of orders and swished away.

Frank relaxed and found himself speaking other things on his mind. "I don't know about you, but there are times during the December holidays that I just get tired."

"So do I," Bill agreed. Then he said quietly, "Sometimes I feel the season of delights becomes the season of demands." He stirred a metal spoon in his ceramic cup. "And I can't always, immediately, meet all the demands."

"Tell me about it," Frank nodded. "Everything has to be—"

"Perfect," Bill finished his sentence.

"And that's a tough one," Frank said.

"Hard to always deliver perfection," Bill agreed,

smoothing back his silver hair. He raised one hand to wave at Flossie to fill their coffee cups again. The waitress saw him and came over with a fresh pot. As she poured, both men stared into their mugs. Frank leaned over and inhaled the deep fragrance with a hint of chicory.

"But that—that is perfection," he said.

Bill laughed. "And delivered right on demand."

As the men sipped the warmth inside, outside and visible through the windows, a west wind whipped the field grasses, waving the cedars, sending tufts from the stalking broom sage whirling.

3. Three Men and a Plan

As Flossie left the men with her fragrant carafe in hand, she cheerfully filled a few coffee mugs for other patrons as if she were a bountiful Santa tossing peppermints to children in a parade. But when a damp breeze swept through the room, she paused. The Circle Market's glass door had swung wide. A tall thin man, his wiry frame slightly bent, stepped inside. He wore a John Deere cap and a mottled green hunting jacket. He looked around measuring the other people in the room and pulled off a pair of rough leather gloves.

"Isn't that Larry Layman?" Bill looked up.

"Yeah, he's a good man," Frank said. "Can do most anything. Careful carpenter. He built Jan some cabinets for our farmhouse."

"He repaired my rail fences," Bill returned.

Frank turned in his chair and waved a greeting. "Hey Larry. Want to join us?"

The man pulled off his John Deere cap and pocketed his gloves. He turned the cap bill around and over in his rough, calloused hands, the kind stained permanently with ochre Virginia clay. "Oh, fellahs, I didn't expect to see anyone this morning. Been huntin'. Haven't shaved."

"Neither have I," Bill and Frank said in unison. Then they glanced at one another and laughed.

"I'll get a cup up here," Larry said, stepping up to the self-serve coffee machine by the checkout counter. He nodded to Flossie as she passed him.

"You want a burger? They're having one," she jerked her red curls in Frank and Bill's direction. Larry nodded again. When he reached the table, he pulled back a chair and swung his legs wide across the seat as if mounting a horse. He reached for a couple of packs of sugar and dumped them in his coffee. Then he said, "Bagged a doe this morning."

"Really?" Frank asked. "Jan and I heard a shot earlier. Where did you get it?"

"About five miles from here, on the Bennington Property."

"Did you field dress it?" Bill asked, not seeing blood on the hunting jacket.

Larry nodded. "Gutted it. Loaded it in my pickup. Dropped it at Harvey's to section up. My wife, Lucy, likes the meat ground mostly. Venison spaghetti, stuff like that."

"Francine won't touch venison. Or anything else wild. In fact, she had me post our entire farm, 'No Hunting.'"

"More and more folks feel that way," Larry said.

"Jan does," Frank offered. "She thinks all deer are Bambi's cousins."

"You know something strange?" Larry ran his hands through straight brown hair. "I'm sure I'm wrong 'cause the odds are agin it."

"Against what?" Frank asked.

"I think the doe had a fawn," Larry said slowly.

"It's late for a fawn," Frank observed.

"Yeah," Larry added, "and I ain't never seen one like this. Pure white."

"You sure?"

"I saw its back, its flanks. All white."

"A white deer," Frank said. "Rare. One in ten thousand or something like that."

Bill frowned. "I've heard they have pink eyes and muzzles."

"Those are albinos. Even more rare," Frank said.

"Made me feel bad. A fawn's mother. Particularly a white fawn's mother," Larry looked into the well of his cup.

"Sad," Bill agreed. "But deer are a problem."

"Over populating," Frank said.

"I know," Larry nodded. "Still, if I'd seen the fawn first, I wouldn't have shot the doe."

All three men were silent. Larry finished his coffee and tapped his cup on the table.

"You know it's kind of strange to see y'all. I was just thinking last night. Maybe you know somebody who can help me."

"Bill knows more folks than I do. He's on the Chamber of Commerce Board of Directors," Frank said, partly in jest.

"And you're on the Clearview Architectural Review Committee," Bill came back.

"Such as it is," Frank snorted. "Hasn't met in years. But what's on your mind, Larry?"

"Oh, it's nothing fancy, nothin' like knowin' somebody important," Larry said, shaking his head. "It's just, well, I've been looking for a bike for my son. You know, a dirt bike. Not powerful, 'cause he's only fourteen. But something he can ride around on his own at our place. I thought I'd get him a second-hand one for Christmas. Trouble is, everyone wants at least a thousand, even for an old one." Larry paused. Frank and Bill stayed quiet, sensing Larry wasn't finished.

"Sometimes, you know, I wish I'd improved myself, taken advantage of the government and gone to college after my military stint." Larry leaned back a little in his chair, his serious expression broken surprisingly by a slight grin.

"But then, you know, Lucy and I just had the fever to get married. And Lawrence Jr., came along real quick after that. And then after a while, little Linda showed up. She's seven and wants a pony this Christmas. No chance of that. She'll get a doll or something. But, my boy wants a bike. He's taken on a paper route for spending money toward it. And I thought I'd let Santa Claus help him out. So I'm lookin' for a bike for Christmas that don't cost an arm and a leg."

"After kids come along, there never seems to be money enough." Frank nodded.

"Lucy was grumblin' about that very thing before daylight this morning. 'Never enough money,' she said."

"Sometimes, my friends, *enough money* isn't even enough," Bill sighed.

"Women don't think that way, I guess," Larry said.

"No, they don't." All the men wagged their heads, commiserating.

When Bill observed, "It seems to me we've all escaped the house and landed here this morning." They all nodded.

Frank brightened. "You know——and this sounds nuts, I realize——but I think women should swap lives for a day or two and see how the other half lives."

"On somebody else's budget?" Bill asked.

"Yeah."

Larry frowned. "You mean wife-swapping like the TV show?"

"Nothing untoward, nothing—well—not really swap," Frank protested.

"Like a job? Nine to five?" Bill leaned forward, squinting his left eye the way he did at corporate planning meetings.

"Sure. They'd go home at night."

Larry draped an arm over the back of his chair. "I get it," he said. "Trade places, like the song, 'Walk a Mile in My Shoes.'"

"Sort of," Frank nodded.

"You're saying live on the other guy's salary for a day," Bill stated.

"Let me explain it a different way." Frank took out a pen and began turning it around his fingers. "You know the Chamber silent auction each year, when people donate goods and services and we bid for them at the Chamber Ball?"

"When local companies donate merchandise like several pounds of nails or cases of copy paper?" Bill asked.

"And services, like Clean-O-Vac? They send someone to shampoo your carpets?" Larry added.

"Yeah," Frank said.

At once Larry became animated. "You know what I heard?" he interjected. "I heard that big-selling Western paperback writer in Clearview is offering an auction item this year that sounded just great." The other men leaned across the table. "He says the highest bidder at the ball gets to be a character in one of his books. I mean a *named* character." Larry leaned forward, drumming his fingers, satisfied at having delivered this piece of news.

"That will go for a bundle, no doubt. He's on *The New York Times* best seller list almost every year!" Bill said.

"I sure would like it," Larry drawled.

"Being a character in a book?" Frank was nonplused.

Bill teasingly opened an invisible book before them as if reading his palms.

"Once upon a time, Big Game Hunter Larry Layman announced, 'Today, I think I'll bag a deer!'"

"Wow, that sounds good!" Larry laughed.

Frank grinned. "That's it. That's the kind of thing I mean. A donation. Our wives swap a day of service or talent to a different household," Frank nodded.

"Francine lives in a worried whirl during the holidays," Bill said.

"Three weeks to go till Christmas, and Jan's already geared to hang one hundred red balls on a tree," Frank upped the ante.

Larry was quiet. He tapped the table. Then he said, "I don't expect no other woman but Lucy would want to spend time on my salary, not even for a day."

"Yeah, they all want to live on an income like Bill's," Frank jested.

"It's not all it's cracked up to be," Bill blushed.

"Money? Why it's everything!" Frank countered. "Influence, travel, things, power—everything!"

"According to Lucy, it's everything, 'cause it means lots of things you can buy for the kids," Larry nodded.

"Yes, indeed. Consider Jan. Why, on your income, Bill, she could buy fifty boxes of red Christmas balls for the tree instead of the five I gave her hell for this morning!" Frank said.

"Well, money is not everything," Bill repeated. "But to the point," his blue eyes twinkled. "How could we engineer the swap idea for the Chamber Ball Auction?" He began to stroke his chin, the way he did when considering a proposal.

"We're too late, don't you think? For this year, anyway. But I sure would enjoy it. Teach the ladies a lesson," Frank beamed.

"Better watch that," Bill cautioned. "Ladies today are women—and you know what that means."

"Jan would say I was flagrantly sexist to suggest such an

idea," Frank's self-satisfaction dissolved into a mope. He propped his elbow on the table and settled his chin in his hand.

"Might ruin my lady forever," Larry looked at Bill. "But she sure would enjoy a day spending your cash."

"I'd have to set a limit," said Bill, reality crossing his brow like a shadow.

The three men smiled. At that moment, Flossie swished beside them with a heavy tray of hot hamburgers and fries.

"Best in town!" Frank said as she set down the first sizzling platter.

"Yeah!" Larry grunted happily.

"Terrific," Bill smiled as Flossie unloaded the last plate.

"Need anything else?" The men shook their heads.

"Have fun, boys!" Flossie drawled.

The men began vigorously shaking salt, pepper, and ketchup over the steaming food. Bill picked up his hamburger and rephrased his thought.

"A Christmas Swap. For a day. For fun and for charity. Let's think about that."

The other two stared at him, Frank's eyes slowly beginning to crinkle at their edges, and Larry's astonishment wrinkling along his brow. Then, over the best burgers in town, the trio bent their heads together to hatch a plan.

4. Jan's Soliloquy

*I*n the silent house, while her husband was in town, Jan Midland stood before the full-length mirror in her bathroom after showering and washing her hair. The mirror was steamy. She reached toward her reflection and swirled the towel across the surface revealing a clear self.

She pivoted slowly, running her eyes up and down her bare torso. Her right elbow stung painfully.

"Stupid of me to jump on a hand truck." She picked up a bottle of perfumed lotion and smoothed it up and down her arms. Her fingers traveled gingerly over her right elbow. She hated admitting it, but there was some truth to Frank's accusation. Tennis elbow had not been the sole reason she gave up the game. In her mid-forties, well, she just couldn't cut it with the younger women moving up the flights. The girls were Amazons—fast, agile, slim. Jan poured lotion on her thighs and massaged them moving up toward her hips.

"These are the problem," she informed her reflection. "I have a shelf of bananas on each hip. In fact, I'm like a boatload of fruit. Look at these breasts—like grapefruits—dangling. And that belly! Where did my flat front go? It's a cantaloupe!"

She continued to stare at herself critically, feeling old,

ugly, and unloved. Where was that college athlete full of dreams? What had happened to that girl? Well, she had reproduced herself according to natural design. She had married twice, the second time, happily. She had taught school. She had raised two boys. And, during those years when the kids were small, she felt a real sense of purpose. Now, midlife she felt, well, washed up.

"What's next?" she asked her reflection. "Just grow old with Frank?"

This gnawing dejection was not new. Last fall she voiced the feeling to Ryan and Kyle in a low moment before they left for their sophomore year at Virginia Tech. At once, the twins shot back in unison,

"You're not washed up!"

"Sure I am."

Then, jabbering, they made sure that Jan heard all the tapes she had voiced as Mom the cheerleader when disappointment derailed them:

During kindergarten when the ball dropped off the T— *Pick it up! Hit it again!*

In high school when Kyle missed a touchdown pass— *You'll get the next one!* When Ryan failed to net the final soccer goal—*I believe in you!*

Tumbling from the twins' mouths, the cheers echoed familiarly:

"Nobody gets them all."

"You've got to believe in yourself."

"Keep at it."

"We still need you," Kyle said.

"Yeah, you've got to choose our wives," Ryan grinned.

"Hah! You wouldn't even let me choose your snowboards one Christmas," Jan snorted. "Remember?"

"Well, *those snowboards* had to be just right!"

"Unlike your wives?" Jan's eyebrows shot up.

Ryan shrugged sheepishly.

Suddenly Kyle kicked his head to one side. "Maybe," he said, "you should try something new, like take a computer class!"

"I'd flunk!" Jan had replied.

"Silly Mom," Ryan had said. "You've never flunked anything in your life."

"A PowerPoint class at the community college. You'll like it. It's cool," Kyle persisted.

"Yeah, and that's what I'm not," Jan had shaken her head. "Cool."

"Sure you are," Ryan nodded.

"Yeah, you're our Mom. That by itself makes you cool!" The boys laughed. And Jan had smiled and hugged them, banging their heads together playfully as if they were five years old.

After the pep talk, she had felt better, and when a flyer came in through the mail listing fall adult classes at the community college, she had signed up under the category "Computer Classes." She had been faithful to her Thursday evening PowerPoint classes, even though she kept hearing Thomas Wolfe's expression, "O, Lost!" in her head, because she felt oh, so, lost! with all those young faces in class.

Now the phrase took on wider parameters. She moaned, "Oh, Lost—Youth! Meaning! Purpose!" Accusing thoughts, like harpies flapped around her head, joined by others: *Old! Fat! Useless!*

"How can anybody stand me anymore!" Jan's mirrored expression became a portrait in anguish. She flopped the wet towel over her head and wept inconsolably over the sink.

Mercifully at that moment, the grandfather clock in the

living room sounded its mellow notes. She counted twelve chimes. Noon. Time for lunch.

She pulled off the wet towel and looked at her tousled, wet reflection.

"Well," she said wearily, "my sobbing isn't solving a thing." She opened a drawer beside the sink. "Makeup. I need some makeup. It always makes me feel better. And I'll hotrod my hair on rollers, too. That usually helps."

She dropped the towel on the bath mat as she turned toward her open closet. She rifled a row of blue jeans, the only pants that fit these days. The fresh revelation depressed her all over again. *I've got to lose weight!* She glanced back over her shoulder at the mirror, and was startled by some things—well—good.

Hmmm. The back is still taut. The shoulders are still straight. Hmmm. The arms are still slim. Hmmm. Maybe there's still hope.

"Jan Midland," she pointed her finger at her image, "it's time. It's time. It's *almost time* for lunch. It's *past time* for feeling sorry for yourself. And it is *high time* you reinvented yourself."

5. The Swap

 wo miles away from the scene of Jan's soliloquy, Frank left the warmth of the Circle Market with a full tank of gas in his truck and an orange, utility-sized extension cord for the television. He whistled to the Christmas music on the country music radio station, WCVU. He felt good. Renewed. He'd even splurged on a stocking gift for himself—a floating flashlight with a heavy-duty battery. Now he motored happily on his way to his comfortable, but admittedly small by comparison, 55-acre farm cottage on a hillside overlooking the Southwest Mountains. He breezed along in the damp air, passing the winter green of frosted cedar trees, as he gazed contentedly through the windshield.

"God, Virginia is beautiful," he said out loud. "At least this part. Thank goodness we haven't crapped up the place too much yet with the fast food, fast gas, fast buck enterprises that plague so many rural towns. Why, here," he thought about Larry Layman, "a man can still hunt without driving fifty miles to a preserve."

And the wildlife . . . well, he thought about that a minute. Yes, at times it was pesky—deer eating vineyard grapes, groundhogs burrowing in a field, rabbits nibbling your garden lettuce—but, hey, it was also renewing. Some mornings around

5:30, he'd get up to inspect the dawn through binoculars, and he'd see the sun rays sift through a shelf of opalescent clouds so beautiful, it was like the Almighty Himself had just that minute strolled by; then Frank would focus closer and spot a family of wild turkeys, their heads jutting, busily stalking the grasses; and farther beyond in the valley, he'd see a doe step carefully into view, her head high, her fawn—sometimes two—trailing through the hovering veils of cloud Mother Nature had dropped during the night.

And now, according to Larry, Frank thought, squinting right and left, *there was a statistical miracle out there somewhere: a white fawn.* He slowed, half kidding himself, that he might be lucky enough to glimpse it. But, no. Instead he glimpsed the spreading pastures of Bill Urbane's farm, with Virginia's signature embroidery—white plank fences—bordering his two hundred acres. At the entrance, an American flag furled and unfurled in the wind. Two Christmas wreaths with stiff, scarlet ribbons hung from the open, double-paneled gates. In the distance, Black Angus cattle, with impassive faces, roamed, their necks outstretched, noses sweeping the ground. In his mind, Frank could hear the snorting of their breath nudging the land, as if looking, looking, looking for still-distant spring.

Bill is a lucky fellow with all that land and cattle, Frank thought. *But I don't envy him talking to Francine about the Christmas Swap idea. Of the three of us, he's got the hardest job.* Then Frank laughed to himself. If his Jan got ticked about the confusion of wiring a TV, wait till she hears about this zany Swap scheme! Frank kept his eyes on the highway, but mentally he traveled back to the Circle Market scene. He smiled as he recalled the plan's disjointed hatching.

"They'll never go for it," Frank had said slyly to the others at the table.

"They must be persuaded. It must be in their best interest," Bill responded. He pushed away a plate on which only a French fry or two remained.

"How?" Larry asked.

"Well, if each of our wives donates a day, a swap, into our three households, that's a gift."

"Just to us," Frank muffled a yawn.

"More than that. To the Chamber it is a benefit to the chosen charity, Habitat for Humanity this year."

"I don't get it." Larry fidgeted, as if he needed a cigarette.

"We can each pledge a donation. In cash or in-kind contributions say, for what? Five hundred? A thousand dollars? It goes toward Habitat in honor of our wives."

"Nobody bids on them?" Larry asked.

"Nope. This is a pre-sold bid. In effect, it's a gimmick."

"But also publicity," Frank acknowledged.

"Right, it raises money toward the Chamber Ball, which pledges its proceeds to Habitat."

"Lucy would be proud to donate toward that." Larry rubbed his rough hand across his mouth as if chewing on the notion.

"That just might work." Frank pushed his empty hamburger plate back and grinned.

"It just might." Bill's eyes registered a promising twinkle.

Simultaneously they were convinced. The plan would succeed; conviction jumped around the table from one face to another like lightning across the Blue Ridge Mountains. The men firmed up the details.

Frank began, "I'll donate my architectural expertise, and of course, my wiring abilities, such as they are."

Larry promised, "I can frame it structurally."

"The Chamber is helping to finance the house," Bill rubbed his brow. "I can make a tax-deductible cash gift and, as a board member, arrange for your skills to be in-kind tax deductions as well."

"This is the clincher." Frank abruptly hit the countertop with his hand. "We'll get Isabel Charmin as Chamber President to arrange for publicity, announcing our gift idea through the local media."

That remark brought a shared hearty laugh. This final stroke, the men deduced, would positively ensure compliance. With the prospect of losing face if they backed out of a commitment to a good cause, their wives would not back out of the Swap.

"A sure shot," Frank had grinned.

"'Cause basically, we're all married to decent women," Larry said.

"With community spirit," Bill nodded.

Pulling a publicity stunt like this in the charitable season of Christmas seemed like a win-win situation. Furthermore, as Bill Urbane pointed out, everybody would get his and her picture in the paper; he would see to that.

But the elder man also had voiced a caveat: "We must be clear in our motive." He had leaned over his coffee cup, his cheeks flushed, his fingers, gently woven, resting on the table.

"What motive?" Larry asked.

Frank, suddenly agitated, had pulled a paper napkin out of the metal container on the table. He'd taken out a pen, force of habit, and had drawn random but elegant lines on the napkin.

"Motive? It's simple," he said. "It's a fact! Women—all women in general, our women in particular—become too intense, too busy, and they tend to ignore their husbands, and they spend too much money at Christmas!" Looking back, Frank realized his compulsive tapping on the napkin, creating agitated black blots, probably belied his professed confidence.

Frank caught Bill watching his nervous pen for a few

seconds. Then Bill said carefully, "They become obsessed and unnecessarily extravagant, I'd say."

Both men looked toward Larry expectantly. "I'd just say, too busy," Larry had drawled.

With that, they chiseled the motive down to a narrow but admittedly smudged point: From the swap the women would learn "perspective," Bill suggested.

"Empathy. Maybe gratitude?" Frank said, still tapping dots on the napkin.

"Well," Larry frowned, "Lucy may get ruined by seeing how the other half lives."

Frank sensed a flashing "Caution!" sign here. So he forced an offhanded laugh as he threw down his pen. "What the heck! Who knows what will come of it?"

Bill Urbane bolstered their resolve, "It's for a good cause. Keep that in mind."

With that, the men had shouldered their jackets and tipped their hats to Flossie on the way out. From behind the cash register, she busily rang up the charges on their store accounts, as the old trophy buck stared down impassively over her blazing red hair. She threw a glance across the room over to the vacated table to be sure there was a tip left under a coffee cup or somewhere. She saw the thin ripple of green, like lettuce, pushing out from under the paper napkin holder. She smiled.

"Thanks, boys!" she called.

As he slowed the truck to turn at his graveled entrance from the highway, Frank flexed his fingers over the steering wheel. He glanced at his sign: "Double Nickel Farm." (He'd thought that a pretty clever name for a 55-acre tract.) Then he pulled up beside the cottage. In some perverse way, he felt the humor of his impending announcement. Strategically, he considered it might be wise to apologize for his anger earlier, then he would tell Jan about Larry's story of the white fawn. After that, however, there was no getting around what would happen when he sprang the news.

"A rumble ahead," Frank shook his head. Nonetheless, he just couldn't wait to tell Jan about the Christmas Swap. At the same time though, just as surely, he was glad right now that he was not Wilburn Urbane.

"Jan can be tough," Frank said out loud, opening the door of his truck, "But poor ole rich Bill is facing Francine!"

6. Francine

"What? Silly idea, indeed! Why would I want to swap?" Francine Urbane whirled around, her attention suddenly on her husband and not on the caterer who had set out a four-layer cake on the dining room sideboard. It's frosting glistened with sugar, a glittering patina over mounded white.

"The Swap is an idea for the Chamber Ball Auction, Franny," he said calling her by his pet name. "It will make a good story for the paper. Three women change places for a day, before Christmas."

"What for?"

"Perspective!"

"Perspective?"

"Well, empathy."

"Empathy?" Francine's tone approached the level of a whistling teakettle.

"For charity," Bill entreated. "Consider it a talent exchange. The whole idea is to understand how the other half lives by stepping into one another's lives."

"The other half meaning the Laymans?" Her voice rose higher and higher. "I think that's insulting to Larry," Francine said flatly. "And I think 'perspective' is insulting to me! How many charity boards have I served on? Salvation Army, Goodwill, The Peach County Historical Society. Do you want me to continue?"

Bill sighed. This was not going well. He countered with reasoned sincerity. "You are right, Franny. Perhaps 'perspective' is unfair. But as for the Laymans, Larry's agreed to this idea. He knows he's a smart man. He has talents. He just hasn't had our financial advantages."

"I see," Francine squinted. "Now, tell me again, what do you men contribute?"

"I am giving a cash donation. Frank is donating one thousand dollars worth of architectural design time toward the Habitat house; Larry will frame it structurally."

"But that won't happen until spring! This is December, the busiest month of the year!" Francine heaved a sigh that shook her cultivated, petite five-foot-four frame. "I am so-o-o-o busy, Bill. You know Anna's coming on the twenty-first. Maybe we can do this silly swap thing later. But a-a-a-a-ah, I don't think so." She rolled her sapphire-blue eyes at her husband.

Bill watched his wife as she turned toward the young landscape design assistant dragging fresh greenery through the front door. Behind him, Anthony, the owner of Fantasy Florist, carried two enormous wreaths of deep green boxwood and peacock feathers. They were tied with stiff silver bows.

"Beautiful! Perfect!" Francine pronounced them. "Those go on the front doors. Anthony, tell your assistant that the mistletoe hangs in the entry hall," her orders sailed out like a ship captain's. "The green spruce branches fill the mantelpiece. And, Anthony? The silver three-branch candelabra go on either end, when you finish. Also, don't forget to tuck in the crystal bells. A total of eight spaced nicely. And be careful. They are from New York—Tiffany's."

She spun around toward her husband, her voice suddenly melodious. "Honey, don't you remember how we started collecting those bells a few years back? Each one engraved with the dates of the past eight Christmases."

"Nice," Bill said.

"Nice? Just, nice? Elegant!" Francine corrected him. "Perfect!"

Perfect. That was it. That's what Bill had begun to detest. Perfection. "Perfection is the enemy of the good," his father had said when Bill was in his early twenties. "You can control only so much in this life. No plan is perfect No deal is perfect. No person is perfect. Figure out what's important, anticipate pitfalls as best you can, do your darnedest to make things succeed and be content with the consequences. Nothing in life is perfect."

And to illustrate his point unforgettably, his father had strolled into the living room of his Park Avenue home where his wife, Bill's mother, sat in a chintz floral chair before the fireside, wrapped in a red flannel robe. Bill's father kissed her and then lifted his wife's left hand, her thin arm resting comfortably in his palm. He pointed to his mother's modest diamond ring. "If you examine this stone under a microscope," he said, "you'll find a flaw. A crack. But it was all I could afford when I was twenty-two. I've offered to replace it for her a dozen times with a larger, perfect stone. But, listen to this:

"You want another diamond, Ellen?" His eyes crinkled as he held his wife's fingers gently. That night, Bill had looked at his mother huddled beneath the blanket, and he knew the cancer would take her in a matter of weeks.

"No darling," Ellen gazed at her husband, comfortable love in her eyes. "I've told you many times, this is good enough for me. Always has been. And so are you, Wilburn. And so is

Little Bill." She turned weakly and smiled, her eyes lighting on her son with adoration.

Years later, on the night he asked Francine to marry him and presented his mother's ring set in a circle of deep blue sapphires, Wilburn Jr., "Little Bill," did not mention the diamond's flaw. He feared Francine would reject the ring. And him.

"Perfect!" He heard it once again in his own dining room. That word. Francine had said it again, this time directing the caterer's helper setting the immense dining room table where soon the neighbors would feast on a dinner of roast duck.

"I want it in perfect scale! Why, at Buckingham Palace the royal staff actually measures the precise distance between the dinner plates, the silverware, the crystal glasses, just to be sure the table setting is perfect."

"Franny, Honey," Bill said, jangling nervous change in his pocket. "This story—the Swap—*will make* the papers. I've already contacted our Chamber president."

"Isabel? You haven't!" Francine spun around once more, her sculpted eyebrows rising in a perfect tent toward her perfect widow's peak where her perfectly shaded chestnut hair met her perfectly sculpted porcelain face.

"I have," Bill said matter-of-factly. "So for the good of the community, I think after this party tonight, you should start making plans for the Swap."

7. Lucy Reacts

*L*arry expected Lucy to jump with joy when he broke the news. She merely stared, blinking her eyes, those lovely wide circles, soft amber, the same shade as the sun tea she set out on the backyard picnic table to brew in the summer sunshine. Every few seconds she blinked, as he tried to explain the curious exchange. When he finished, she frowned.

"Are you turned on to those other women?" Lucy asked, creamy skin as smooth as a baby's, her soft blonde hair curling in short ringlets around her forehead. Larry loved that baby face and those amber eyes, but he hated her hair these days. It was cropped and he thought that was a shame. It was wonderful hair, and naturally curly. When he met Lucy, her hair had bounced like a flowing cape around her shoulders. He could not keep his fingers out of those long golden tresses. But since the children had come, she had worn it up around her ears. "Less trouble," she claimed.

"Turned on to those women? Are you kidding?" Larry had not, since he'd laid eyes on Lucy, been attracted to another woman. So it was easy for him to answer her honestly,

"No, Honey. It's not like that. We fellahs just thought maybe it would be a good idea to change places. Or, I mean, let you women change places. And the men make a donation. For charity. Mr. Urbane says it's good publicity for the Chamber, and it will help people."

"I don't know, Larry, I really don't, where you get some of your crazy ideas. You know how hard it's been since September when your Mama broke her hip and came to stay with us."

Standing in front of him, Lucy was folding a basket of clean laundry that she piled in shaped stacks on the kitchen table. Larry watched her hands work—nimble, quick hands. "And we hoped to move her into the new bedroom as a Christmas present," Lucy continued. "Why, you've been working late nights enclosing that porch space, creating a door wide enough for her wheel chair. How can I possibly take off time right now to help charity? Charity begins at home, Larry! Sometimes I really don't know if you are living in the real world." She folded the last T-shirt in a white square and lifted the stack into the basket.

"I know it's hard living with me on what I make, Lucy. I thought you'd get a kick out of spending Mr. Urbane's money for a day."

"What will it cost me?" Lucy's luminous eyes crinkled with contempt. She continued loading the folded laundry into the basket. Unsophisticated she was, but not unintelligent. She'd been the homecoming beauty queen and Miss Peach County High School's Best-All-Around Student. She'd forfeited a full college scholarship to marry Larry. Of course, there was that complicating secret of her out-of-wedlock pregnancy with their son, Lawrence.

Larry frowned. "It will cost you nothing. Both men are gentlemen. And you know Mr. Midland since you go there once a week. It's like a temporary job. For one day, each of you girls swaps around. You will live like the Midlands and the Urbanes."

"I like living with you," Lucy shot back. "At Christmas, the most hectic time of the year. It sounds crazy," Lucy said. "Anyhow, as for you dreamin' up silly plans, I'd really rather you spent your time finding a bike for Lawrence, Jr." With that she picked up the full basket and flounced toward their bedroom.

"Awww, Sweetie," Larry called after her departing back. "I'm trying." He sniffed. Lucy said he was silly. How could he be silly, mixing with men like Frank and Bill? This was their idea! He groaned inwardly, but he knew he was trapped. He forced his voice to sound as resolute as he could muster. "In the meantime, Lucy, can I tell Mr. Midland and Mr. Urbane that you'll do it?"

Lucy paused at the door to the bedroom. "Oh sure," she offhandedly kicked her blonde ringlets to one side. "Maybe us Laymans will have a big ole party on Mr. Urbane's cash. I'll go to Sam's Club and load up on all the trays of barbecued chicken wings and peeled shrimp and bags of cookies and fresh layer cakes I've ever laid eyes on."

Larry looked at his wife, a couple of sizes wider since childbearing years. She adored sweets, particularly cakes. Any kind of cake—butter cream, coconut, but especially the Sam's Club Triple Chocolate Bundt cake. She bought one every other month.

"If you do that," Larry said guardedly, "just make sure that not too many trays are chocolate."

"Watch it, Mr. Layman!" Lucy's prickly retort came quickly. "And, mark my words. If I do this silly Swap *before* Christmas, you have to enclose the porch *by* Christmas. I mean that! You better shake a leg! Your mother moves into her new bedroom in three weeks—on Christmas Day!"

When Frank eventually broke the Swap news to Jan around suppertime that evening, she wryly suggested that a vital wire had snapped loose in his brain.

"How can somebody as brilliant as my husband engage in such cockeyed ideas?" she said. Then she flopped down in front of the television and punched the remote to a segment she had taped of *Desperate Housewives*.

"Talk about cockeyed," Frank nodded toward the television. "What a stupid show."

"Sometimes stupid fiction makes more sense than everyday life," Jan retorted. She clicked the remote button to fast-forward through the advertisements. "These TV women admittedly are desperate, but I haven't seen a segment yet where one of their husbands comes home and suggests she swap herself out to the neighbors just in time for Christmas! So excuse me, Frank, while I escape into fantasy. Somehow, it appeals more than reality right now."

Frank merely threw up his hands and retreated to his home office to grade some student designs for the next day's class. With Jan, he'd learned, sometimes it paid to delay. He'd bring up the Swap idea again tomorrow.

But when tomorrow came and went, unbeknownst to Frank, the first thing Jan did on Monday morning was to get on the telephone. Frank was in the bathroom early, showering and shaving for the day. Jan had, she calculated by the bird-call clock on the kitchen wall, exactly nineteen minutes of privacy before her husband was out, looping his tie, searching for his reading glasses, gathering papers into his briefcase, readying himself for his lecture on Jefferson's novel construction of the University of Virginia. Frank loved giving that lecture. He took the students outside, pointed out the varied columns of the pavilions, examples of Doric and Corinthian architecture. "Jefferson meant his university to be a teaching environment," he told admiring architecture students.

Even as Jan sat, now back-timing Frank's shower, she felt her breath come in nervous spurts. She pulled her white fuzzy Ritz

43

robe around herself and settled on her grandmother's antique kitchen stool. She curled her sock feet on the rungs as she nervously wiggled her toes. Determination traveled across her brow like a storm cloud. She punched numbers into the telephone receiver.

"Lucy?" she said, twisting a section of her long brown ponytail with her left index finger. "Are you agreeing to this Swap foolishness?"

"Only if you say so, Mrs. Midland. After all, I work for you."

"Well, I think the whole idea is pure male chauvinist revenge for holiday crimes *not* committed. So I have my own Christmas idea. Are you ready to listen?"

"Yes, Ma'am," Lucy said.

The next phone call Jan made was to Mrs. Urbane. "Do you need some fresh eggnog?" Jan asked.

"No, I don't think so," Francine answered, surprised at the question.

"It's the best eggnog in the county, and most people don't know it," Jan said. "If you meet me at the Circle Dairy Ice Cream Parlor this morning, I'll buy you a quart."

"Oh, my," Francine replied. "I already have a refrigerator full of grocery-store eggnog."

Jan dropped her voice a conspiratorial octave. "This is a ruse, Francine," she said candidly. "You and I need to meet to discuss this silly Swap thing in person where the men can't hear us. Those scoundrels have told Isabel Charmin, who, in turn, has told the newspaper. We can't back out."

"Oh dear," Francine said. "I had indeed hoped that Bill was teasing about Isabel. Yes, I would love to have a cup of the best eggnog in the county."

"Meet me there in half an hour?"

"Well I have to put on my makeup, and it takes fifteen minutes to tease my hair."

"Don't bother. I'm wearing a baseball cap. Be casual."
Perched on her kitchen stool, Jan leaned an elbow on the
kitchen counter and unloosened the rubber band holding her
hair. "Well," she added, thinking of the glamorous Francine,
"maybe I'll put on a little mascara."

"Hmm, a baseball cap," Francine mused into the phone
receiver. "That's a clever camouflage. Let me see. Sure! I can
make it in thirty minutes. I'll tuck my hair under my mink
cloche! Nobody will ever know it's not teased perfectly!"

"Nor will they care," Jan said.

8. Three Women and a Plan

When Jan met Francine Urbane and Lucy Layman at the Circle Dairy Ice Cream Parlor on Main Street, she accomplished two things right up front. First, she saw to it that each woman picked her favorite ice cream cone. Lucy chose Oreo Cookie Dough, for its rich, pasty taste. Francine selected Lemon Yogurt for its low calorie content compared to ice cream. Jan chose Pralines 'n Cream because she adored caramel. Then, as a second step, Jan put into words their mission. She began with a background statement:

"The notion our husbands have contrived may serve a good cause, but it's their gift at our expense. Why, who ever heard of wife swapping at Christmas? Ever hear of Santa sending off Mrs. Claus in the sleigh?"

"As if she weren't busy enough at the North Pole," Lucy smiled.

"Right," Jan said. She bit into her cone and dribbled a piece of praline. She quickly licked it. "Without her, the old boy would never make the Christmas deadline."

"But that's a fable." Francine tilted her head, her blue eyes framed by her dark fur cloche, her yogurt cone a splash of gold centered before her pretty face. "We're real."

"Exactly," Jan agreed. "And that brings me to my point. For the Swap at each other's homes, we should all be ourselves. Our real selves," she said firmly, in what once was her schoolteacher's commanding voice. "Only more so."

"Really?" Lucy's eyes glinted a soft gold fire.

"What do you mean?" Francine asked, her tongue daintily licking the soft lemon in a curl.

"You like things nicely done, right?" Jan turned to Francine.

Before Francine could respond, Lucy nodded her curls vigorously. She knew firsthand the woman's exacting standards. Occasionally she assisted the caterers at Mrs. Urbane's parties.

Francine sensed Lucy's nods and brightened. "Not just *nicely* done, perfectly done," she said. She fingered a strand of her dark chocolate hair streaked with tiny strands of silver whispering down her neck. Automatically she tucked it back under her mink cloche.

"Okay. Perfectly done." Jan recorded the distinction. "But next week, I want you to insist on everything being even *more perfect*." Then she turned.

"Lucy," she said, "you're always telling me how handy Larry is. What drives him nuts?"

Lucy rolled her eyes. She was not used to being on equal footing with these two women. It made her feel a bit shy. She bit into her doughy ice cream cone and chewed a moment, thinking. Francine thought she looked like a Christmas cherub, being so young and having that short curly gold hair.

Finally Lucy wiped her mouth carefully with a paper napkin and said, "He's no plumber. If anything leaks, he makes it worse. And he hates calling a plumber. You know, because of the cost."

"So, Francine, our mission is to make things leak," Jan said.

"How does one do that?" Francine asked imperiously.

"With a wrench," Lucy volunteered.

"Why, I've never operated a tool in my entire life!"

"It's easy, just reach under the sink and give a little twist to the connection," Lucy nibbled on the top crust of her cone.

"Bingo! A little leak!" Jan bit the bottom point of her Pralines 'n Cream cone. She waited a few seconds for the hole to drip. She pointed the leak at Francine. "See?"

Francine's blue eyes danced merrily.

"Oh!" Lucy blurted in. "His mother! She's old, you know, fragile. Like I said, I'm the caretaker. Bathing her, helping her to the bathroom, you know. Larry gets embarrassed about that kind of thing. He never even wanted to change his own children's diapers."

"Aha," Jan said, as if she had just won the state lottery. "I know how to handle that kind of leak."

"Well," Lucy added, somewhat shyly, "Larry's just real sensitive to smells."

"Aren't we all," Jan said dryly.

"Excuse me, Jan." Francine blotted her mouth daintily on a napkin. Her nails, the two other women noticed, were perfectly manicured, perfectly pink. "Our husbands know each other, and of course you and Lucy do, but I don't know you or Lucy very well. I don't quite understand . . ." She tapped her left hand on the circular table. Her nails made little click, clicks, on the metal surface. "I don't understand what we're trying to accomplish here."

"Accomplish? Well, my hunch is our husbands somehow got together and talked about how we drive them crazy—four-plus bananas—at Christmas," Jan stuck an index finger underneath her leaky cone.

The other women nodded.

48

"And that we probably don't pay them enough attention,"

"My hunch, too," Lucy said, biting into a chunk of chocolate.

"Hmmm," Francine said, placing her cone on an extra napkin. She reached for her small Prada bag on the table and withdrew a lipstick and compact mirror.

"So, my theory is," Jan said, watching Francine form a pretty pout as she spread a glistening pink across her lips, "men get disgusted because they don't know what Christmas involves. We do all the work."

"So we'll teach them." Francine put her perfect lips together into a paper napkin leaving a pink blot, perfect, like a valentine.

Lucy giggled. "Looks like their plan for us might backfire. Larry has never unfolded even a clean Depends diaper. Not once."

"So we're agreed. We'll do their plan to benefit the Habitat House. We'll spend a day in each other's house," Jan began.

"And we'll teach those husbands of ours a lesson or two," Francine chirped.

"About what a good woman each man has," Lucy raised her pointed chin.

"Sure enough," Francine sniffed. "I bet I could operate a wench."

"Not wench, WRENCH," Lucy giggled.

"A wench is a sailing tool, Francine," Jan smiled wryly.

"And it also means wild woman," Lucy grinned.

"Aha! Right! At least on the first count," Francine laughed gaily. "I spent my youth sailing off Hyannis Point. Silly me!" Her self-deprecating laugh happily surprised the others. Then Francine smiled mischievously. "Wild woman," she continued. "Maybe 'wench' applies on that account, too." She snapped her expensive bag shut. "I guess we three will learn something from this Swap, too," she twinkled. "We'll learn *plenty* about each other!"

"Christmas mission clear—shall we say—to boomerang the men's plan?" Jan asked, reaching her arm over the middle of the table, holding her dripping ice cream cone aloft.

"To make sure they never do this to us again!" Francine pulled her melting cone off the napkin and leaned it toward the others.

"To teach them men a lesson!" Lucy exclaimed, as she met the others. The three cones touched, forming a frozen three-pronged torch.

Afterward, Jan smugly watched her co-conspirators climb into their cars—Francine into her pristine new silver Mercedes, Lucy into her dented 1995 green Ford. She saw each woman set a quart of eggnog gingerly on her respective front seat. Jan felt pleased with herself. She had supplied them both.

"Drink a little eggnog every night," she advised handing out the quarts from the dairy bar, "to remind you we're in this together."

"Oh, but not too much at night," Francine squirmed. "It's very fattening." Then she blushed realizing that Lucy might take offense.

"Who cares?" Lucy laughed.

Late that night in bed, recalling the exultant pledge of female loyalty, Jan lay on her back, musing privately in the dark. *Well, well, well. Those husbands think they have a winning idea of swapping their Mrs. Santa Clauses for a Habitat House. But they failed to conceive one thing—that their twenty-first-century wives could concoct a plan of their own. Sealed with an ice cream torch!* The image, oddly, reminded Jan of the Statue of Liberty. *Hah!* She suppressed a wicked, silent giggle. *Ladies of liberty, unite!* She hugged herself with the idea. Then she rolled over on her side and listened to

Frank's even breathing. She closed her sleepy eyes, and a foggy question floated aloft in the dark . . .

    Who could say what awaited three cocky husbands in the town of Clearview this Christmas?

9. Swap Day One

On the first day of the Swap (the women had settled on Wednesday, December 1, to get the ordeal over with as soon as possible), Jan pulled onto the circular drive of the Urbanes' farm. She hopped out of her serviceable SUV, stepping onto the tiny, rounded, sand-colored pebbles that distinguished a first-class gravel road from the usual gray crushed-run variety. She arrived just in time to see a red van pull behind her with—of all things—a satellite on its roof.

Francine and Bill's dish must be on the blink, she thought. But then she heard her name.

"Mrs. Midland! Can we shoot you walking up to the house? We want to open our story with that footage."

"Footage? Story? What are you talking about?" Jan whirled around. Nobody had mentioned television.

"Yes, Ma'am," a twenty-something blond male reporter climbed out of the van holding a slim notebook in one hand and extending his other. "Morning, Ma'am. Terry Turner, News Channel 2. My video cameraman is Zeke."

"I see," Jan said. But all she actually saw was the slender back side of a young boy leaning in the red van, scrambling among a pile of cables, and reaching for a sturdy black case.

"We have contacts at the newspaper, and we heard about this story. Also, we talked to Mr. Urbane, and he said the shoot was fine with him. He says you are going to decorate a tree in his home."

"Oh, gosh," Jan muttered under her breath. Wilburn Urbane at work again.

"You'll get one take," Jan said to the reporter. "I'm in a hurry."

"It would be helpful to have two." Terry Turner fixed his beaver-brown eyes on her. "For editing purposes." Then he smiled disarmingly and stroked his blond hair back from his forehead.

What a cutie, Jan thought. *Hired for his face and personality.* For an instant she thought of him as a son, like her twins.

"Two takes. That's it."

"Thank you," Terry gushed.

Jan backed away from the home according to the cameraman's direction.

"Just act like I'm not here," Zeke said. Jan couldn't see anything but a thatch of brown hair behind a camera with an eyeballing lens in which she found her own reflection.

Meanwhile, Bill Urbane came out and volunteered to open the door, ostensibly to welcome Jan inside.

Hollywood setup shot, Jan thought. Fabricated news.

She walked the pebble drive, careful not to look at the camera, as if she had no idea there was a man—Zeke of the thatched hair behind the camera—walking backwards two steps away in her path. She also tried not to squint in the bright morning sun, as she knew it would emphasize her wrinkles.

A few paces away, Bill smiled genially and opened one side to the double front door. The cameraman spun around to catch the view of Jan stepping inside, narrowly missing one of two enormous green boxwood wreaths with spiraling peacock feathers and silver bows hanging against the massive oak door panels. Bill greeted her effusively. The blond reporter shouted, "Cut!"

"Cut. I agree, Bill," Jan said. "Let's cut this out, okay?"

"They just want footage of you decorating the tree. And your impressions of changing places. Just a short interview. A few minutes."

"Interview? Bill, this is going too far, don't you think?"

"Oh, it's fun, Jan. You're a good sport. I know that. And it's a benefit for charity. What's Christmas for anyway if you can't help others?"

"I'd rather just mail a check to the Salvation Army," Jan mumbled. "But okay."

"Speaking of a check," Bill snapped his fingers, "I have one—for groceries, tree ornaments, and any incidentals. Will a thousand cover what you need?"

"Good grief! Of course. Too much, Bill."

"Not really. Francine spent five thousand in two days decorating the tree in the living room, here." Bill beckoned Jan down the hall to where it opened into a two-story formal living room, dominated by a row of four floor-to-ceiling Palladian windows. A twenty-foot spruce was positioned evenly between the vaulted arches, and it almost touched the ceiling of the room.

"Yikes!" Jan said.

"Yours is more modest," Bill laughed. "Here, in the den." They both looked at a six-foot blue spruce. Bill chuckled. "You can buy all the red balls in China if you want. Frank mentioned you were working with a red and white theme this year."

"Yes. That's when the trouble began," Jan rolled her eyes.

There was a knock on the door.

Jan reached for it. "Uh, Terry?"

"Yes, Ma'am. Terry Turner, News Channel 2."

"Well, Son,"

Terry grimaced at the word, *Son.*

"You've got to give me time to get oriented."

"But we need to interview you. We're also talking to the other two ladies this week."

"Look, Son," Jan said using her former school-teacher's voice, not to mention her mother-of-two-grown-sons' pitch. "This is an ambush, see? I haven't agreed to an interview. But if you come back this afternoon, I'll talk, but only for five minutes."

"And we'll shoot B-roll of your decorating the tree?" Terry pushed.

"B-roll?"

"Wallpaper shots to illustrate your sound bites."

"B-y-t-e-s?"

"Like quotes in the newspaper. B-i-t-e-s. Not computer bytes."

"Oh, yeah. Hmmm. I knew that, didn't I? Well, okay."

"This Swap is to benefit Habitat for Humanity, the Chamber's Christmas project," Bill volunteered, stepping beside Jan. "Mrs. Midland is a good sport to participate."

"Oh, yes, Sir. We understand." Terry stepped back from the doorjamb. "And we'll just swing back by, say, around two? That gives me time to get back to the station to get ready for the regular six-o'clock news. Your story won't air for several days. A pre-Christmas feature, if you know what I mean."

"I don't know what you mean. But obviously, it doesn't matter," Jan grumbled. "Obviously this thing is out of my hands."

"See you then," Bill smiled and waved and closed the door.

"Well," Jan looked at the empty tree in the Urbanes' den. "This tree won't be anything like Francine's," she said.

"That's the point," Bill replied. "It's yours. Here's the check. Have fun shopping. You're fixing dinner, right?"

"That was the deal. Swap lives for a day," Jan replied. "And that includes Francine's Historical Society meeting tonight."

Bill rubbed his chin. "I had forgotten about that."

Figures, Jan thought. She looked pointedly at Bill. "I don't know how in the world I let Frank talk me into this. You guys have no idea what's involved in getting ready for Christmas."

"Maybe this will teach us," Bill said distractedly and drifted away. He sat down in his sunken leather club chair by the den fireplace. The empty tree stood nearby, against the mahogany paneled walls. The elegant man leaned his head back, white hair swept serenely off his forehead. He inhaled the blue spruce fragrance, leaned over, and pulled a copy of *The Wall Street Journal* from the mahogany newspaper rack near his chair. He opened the paper, its pages rustling, and leaned his head in toward the fold. Jan watched him settle into a private world. *Just like Frank*, she thought. *Maybe this settling skill—zoning out—is how men avoid seeing what needs doing around a house, particularly during the holidays. Frank burrows into wiring his TV sound system or his books. Bill here buries himself in the financial news pages.* She turned silently from the room and moved to the entrance hall to retrieve her coat.

Maybe the Swap will indeed teach you men something, she thought. *All of you, about women.* She tucked the one-thousand-dollar check inside her jacket pocket and pulled open the oaken front door. She brushed past the hanging deep green boxwood branches and the bobbing peacock feathers fastened with stiff silver bows entwining the enormous, the incomparable, the—gasp!—most beautiful-she-had-ever-seen, wreaths.

10. Italian Dinner and Southern History

*T*he evening of the first day's Swap, Jan could not believe how tired she was. Frank had said he'd see her at their favorite little Italian restaurant in town. She felt relief as she pushed open the door to the small central room and met cheerful table candles and the heavenly smell of garlic, fresh bread, and minestrone soup wafting from the kitchen in the back.

La Frutta always played true Italian music, often engaging Italian operas with which she and her husband subtly sang along. Tonight, both were quiet and exchanged smiles laced with fatigue. She joined him at a small table with a floral fuchsia and green tablecloth. A single, fresh red camelia bloomed from a bud vase next to centered condiments including fresh mozzarella cheese and a decorative bottle of olive oil. Frank stood up and leaned over the table, careful not to bend too close to the solitary candle burning in a small hurricane lamp near the camellia. He pulled out the chair for Jan as she settled her coat over the back.

"So how did it go?"

"It's still going. Francine's day does not stop at five."

"Ah, yes. The Historical Society meeting tonight."

"At seven thirty. And I have to go to that, after I have

already decorated their family room tree, done a television interview, and fixed the Urbanes' dinner. I think I could just fall into that vat of minestrone soup bubbling back there in the kitchen and drown from exhaustion."

"You wouldn't like that. Tomatoes in the hair, you know, noodles in the eyes, okra swimming around," Frank said adroitly. "Besides, I've ordered a bottle of Chianti. I'd suggest you have a glass before you plunge into the soup."

Jan smiled. She always did like Frank's sense of humor. "Furthermore," she sighed, "Francine handed me some papers as I went out the door. A leaflet of sorts and a description. Some house the county wants to tear down to build a road. She wants me to make a presentation. She said she didn't have much time to research."

"Much time? No time! Hand you the stuff this afternoon to present tonight?" Frank frowned.

"It's just to get things started. The county won't move on this for six months. I'm supposed to get an initial reaction from the Historical Society board to help them assess whether the house is of historical value or just an old wreck of a place."

"You have a picture?" Frank asked

Jan handed him her sheaf of papers just as their waitress brought them the Chianti in a straw bottle along with two wine glasses.

"You look. I'll pour," she smiled. Frank nodded and glanced over the photocopied pictures and newspaper clippings about the old two-story house.

"Mansard roof," he said. "That means circa 1870s, Second Empire style. But the house looks older. What's the name? The print is blurred."

"Hickory Hill," Jan said. "You can see all the old hickory trees towering over it."

"Yeah. That also means old. Hickory is a tough wood."

"The house was built by a general on the Southern side in the Civil War, I think Francine said."

"Four over four floor plan, wide central hall. Hmmm, fairly typical. Likely Greek Revival." Frank ran his hands through his curly grey hair. "Wait a minute. Where is this house?"

"Off Highway 16, south of town."

"That's the old Helsley place," Frank said. "Who wants to tear it down? And why?"

"Is it historical?"

"I'll say. I recognize it now. Covered up by weeds and a mile or two from the road. Built in 1855 or thereabouts, sitting on a thousand acres."

"You know something about it?"

"Yes I do. I can promise that you will go to your meeting tonight fully armed with facts," Frank arched back in his chair. "But first, I think we should order dinner."

"Should I take notes, Professor?"

"Not yet, my dear. Just take note of what you'd like."

"Clever," Jan said. "A man with a plan. I'll make ordering easy."

"A first!" Frank feigned shock.

Jan glanced at her husband and raised her chin slightly. "I'll order the fried calamari as an appetizer to share, and I'll split a house salad and take less than half of whatever main course you want."

Frank's dark eyebrows shot up. He looked at his wife and said, "That's all?"

"That's all." Jan was denfinite. "It's part of my new invention."

"Invention?"

"Reinvention," Jan replied evenly. "I'm reinventing myself."

"Don't go too far," Frank said, raising his wine glass. "I fell in love with the old you."

"You'll like the new me even better," his wife said, lifting her glass, also.

"So, what do we toast to?" Frank swirled the light red wine, catching the candle light beneath it.

Jan clinked her glass with her husband's. "Fresh starts."

Francine started meetings on time. So, when Jan hurried in a few moments late, she received the disapproving arch of the Historical Society president's right eyebrow. But Jan held up her sheaf of papers significantly to say silently: *I've got something on this!* Francine understood. She turned to an elderly gentleman with a white goatee who vertically unwound himself from his chair with the help of his cane.

"Madame Chairman, you have asked my committee to track the sales of property that may have historical significance to Clearview and surrounding Peach County. I think I should tell you that we have heard rumors about the Helsley Farm south of here. We have also heard some news about the Bennington Property, closer by."

"Mr. Tufton, I have the Helsley Farm covered," Francine said, glancing at Jan. "But please, tell us about the Bennington Property. Surely it's not for sale?"

"No, Ma'am. But the Bennington land brings with it a surprise. It seems Old Colonel Bennington had a vengeful streak in him. After he died a few months ago with Alzheimer's disease, his family divided up his personal effects and turned over his papers to his lawyer. The attorney found a handwritten version of the will, post-dated by two years to the official version written ten years before and filed with his office. In the handwritten will the Colonel divided his land, not in three equal parcels as he'd done earlier. Instead, he left the first daughter the front seven hundred acres. He left the second daughter the back seven hundred acres. And the third daughter he left seven dollars."

"Seven dollars!"

"That's the daughter who married Hiram Venald, Stephanie Bennington Venald!" Jan blurted out.

Murmurs erupted.

"The developer's wife?"

"He's no developer. He just buys land and sells it."

"He's a low-rent horse trader, if you ask me."

Francine delicately tapped a pen on the antique desk in front of her. "Our purpose is to know about these things," she reminded her audience, "so that we can be a watchdog of historical properties. Also, so that we can be sure the county zoning board makes informed decisions. Do you have any further information, Mr. Tufton?"

"No, Madam. I just heard this news. Bennington's attorney is a friend of mine." He looked around the room as if garnering the importance such association might convey. Some people nodded pleasantly. Others sat stone-faced. "And besides," the gentleman raised his eyebrows, turning back to Francine, "as you have probably guessed, Stephanie Venald is contesting the will. Likely, the matter will take years to resolve."

"Keep us informed, Mr. Tufton." Francine smiled. "Good work." The man nodded appreciatively, leaned heavily on his cane, and resumed his seat.

Jan thought she would be called upon next. But instead, she got to see Francine, the administrator, in action. One by one, with courtesy and tact, the graceful president called upon knowledgeable citizens in the community. The meeting ran like a Japanese train schedule, on time and as predicted.

This woman is a powerhouse, Jan thought. From the back

of the room, Jan watched how the petite brunette smoothly delegated special agendas, kept speakers focused, and drew out issues of substance for the group. Preoccupied with Francine's demeanor, Jan was caught off guard when she heard her name.

"Jan Midland, a guest tonight, has a special report on the Helsley Farm," Francine said, and she sat down. All heads turned expectantly. Jan stood up, wavering a second, as she thought her legs would give way.

I can't do this! she screamed silently. Then she reached for the wooden back of her chair, stepped around it, and walked to a slate blackboard that ran the full length of the back of the room. With a hand that trembled slightly, she picked up a stick of chalk and wrote HELSLEY FARM ~ 1855 ~ 1100 ACRES. Then, unexpectedly, she felt her fingers relax, and her composure settle in place. She turned, looked just above the heads of the assembled group. She opened her mouth to recite the facts that Frank had provided earlier at dinner—but unexpectedly, the facts became fluid—in the form of a story. She began,

"Once upon a time, long before our great grandfathers first glimpsed the Blue Ridge Mountains of Virginia, before the first shell exploded at Fort Sumter, South Carolina, when cotton was still king in the South . . ."

In a succinct six minutes, Jan neatly tied up the narrative in a bow. She concluded with,

"So, the Helsley property not only represents history, it conveys a way of life that is adaptable to change. With its main house, its outbuildings, its vastness, and its views, with a slight re-surveying by the county, it can remain intact. And by keeping it intact, my friends, we have a sustainable property—whether a camp or a campus—that adds economic and scenic value to Clearview and Peach County." A burst of reactive applause surprised her.

Wow! she thought. *They must have liked it.*

Francine's eyes twinkled as she entertained a motion to close the night's meeting. "Mrs. Midland had only this afternoon to prepare her report," she told the listeners. "But she has done splendidly, wouldn't you agree?"

More applause circled the room.

"Well, gosh, thanks," Jan blushed. Her mind groped to explain the small moment of success. "Uh, once upon a time, I was a teacher."

11. Swap Day Two:
South Beach Carbs and Computers

"Mr. Midland, along with my regular cleaning chores, what do you want me to do for the Swap?" At nine in the morning, Thursday, December 2, Lucy set down her plastic bucket of supplies—toilet brush, Lysol, spray furniture polish, and clean rags—on the kitchen counter between Frank and herself.

She was chewing gum. Frank hated the habit; it reminded him of his architectural students at the university, the non-blinking variety, reminiscent of young heifers in the field. Frank always suspected the kids in class were hung over, struggling to stay awake, and wanting Frank to entertain them.

Right now, Lucy had the same watchful expectancy. She chewed. She stared. She waited. Fortunately, scratches sounded at the back door and Frank said, "That's Lamont. He wants in."

Lucy reached for the door and opened it. The lugubrious Bassett hound lumbered in.

"Hey, Lamont," she greeted him. The pup's woebegone eyes searched one face, then the other.

"Blessed be dogs," Frank exhaled quietly. "They breaketh the ice." He bent down and rubbed the dog behind his ears. "Hey, Ole Boy. Time for the ole breakfast?"

"He sure is growing." Lucy said. "Every time I see him."

"He's grown."

"Yes, Sir."

"No, I mean he's an adult, almost five now," Frank corrected himself.

"He's still growing." Lucy looked at Frank with those amazing eyes of hers, the color of, of, hmm, resin? *Yes*, Frank thought. *Pine sap.*

"Growing sideways, like the rest of us grownups," Lucy giggled and shifted her wad of chewing gum with her tongue.

Frank blinked. "Well, that reminds me," he said, "Jan is still asleep. 'Twas a late night at Mrs. Urbane's Historical Society meeting."

"Yes, Sir?" Lucy put her hand on the bucket of supplies.

Frank reached for a notepad near the telephone. "But what she says in her note here is that you can make up the chocolate chip cookie dough. Use the recipe on the back of the bag of chips. Then she wants you to press out that store-bought refrigerated sugar dough and cut it into shapes—I don't know, into stars and trees and Santas—whatever cookie cutter shapes she has. Then she wants you to bake all the cookies, decorate 'em any way you want. She says you like to bake. She'll freeze them until Christmas when the twins get home."

"Mrs. Midland's right about baking. I love to do that stuff!" Lucy exclaimed. "Really, I just plain love to cook!" Then she blushed. "Almost as much as I love to eat! 'Course that's beginning to show, like Lamont, around my middle."

"It shows around all of us after a while," Frank said. He looked down briefly and spoke to the Bassett. "Right, Lamont?" The dog made a garrulous and enthusiastic "Woof!"

Lucy giggled again.

"Jan's boys taught him to do that," Frank said. "Good dog! Right Lamont?"

"Woof!"

"He's got that down for sure," said Lucy.

"Yes, he does. Okay, let's get busy." Frank reached for his billfold. "Here's a check for two hundred dollars. It's got to cover what you fix for supper. And cookie makings and any cleaning supplies you need. And also the grocery list; it's short, okay?"

"Yes, Sir," Lucy said. "I'll go to the Food Deal. They have the best prices. What do you want tonight?"

"That's your call," Frank said. "I've been on the South Beach Diet, lately, watching my carbs."

"What?"

"The South Beach Diet—cutting out the bad carbs."

"Mr. Midland?"

"Yes?"

"What are carbs?"

"You know, Lucy. Carbohydrates. Carbs is a trendy word for pasta, potatoes and rice, and sweets like cookies and cakes. Carbs—carbohydrates. Get it?"

"I do. You don't want to eat those things?"

"No. Well, I'm trying to cut them out where possible. But tonight it doesn't matter, Lucy. You fix what you like to fix. We'll eat it," Frank said.

"Mr. Midland?" Lucy looked confused.

"Is something the matter, Lucy?"

"Mrs. Midland said she had a class tonight."

"Oh, right. So do I, as a matter of fact. My Tuesday/Thursday seminar. It's Thursday, right?"

"Yes, Sir."

All day long, Frank muttered to himself. *Must be losing it.* Out loud he said, "Okay, Lucy, no matter. Just leave dinner in the oven on warm. I can promise you it will get eaten."

"Yes, Sir." Lucy inadvertently popped her wad of bubble gum.

Frank winced and walked toward the front door. He pulled his jacket off the brass coat stand. "I'm off to the university. Have a good day."

"Yes, Sir, you too," Lucy said. She closed the door behind him and turned to walk toward the kitchen.

"Funny," she said to herself. "If carbs mean pasta, potatoes, rice, and sweets—well, sweets—like he said—include cookies. Wonder why Mrs. Midland is cooking so many sweet carbs?"

She looked at the Bassett who had settled on his brown plaid pillow in the corner of the kitchen near a gas-burning wood stove piped into a brick wall. The flame danced behind a shield of glass, its black iron doors flung open, its radiant warmth filling the room.

"Don't make sense, does it Lamont?" Lucy asked. "I mean the carbs." From the corner, heavily lidded canine eyes opened. No vocal response.

"Right, Lamont?"

"Woof!"

Lucy giggled, imitating Frank. "Atta boy!"

From the next room, Jan awoke to the smell of sugar and cinnamon. For a while, the fragrance had mingled pleasantly with her dreams of holidays when the kids were small. How much fun it was when they invited their friends for their annual Cookie Bake Day! Armed with candy sprinkles, red and green crystals, and prepared frostings, the children decorated sugar cookie dough, baked their gooey creations, and left her kitchen a yard sale of sticky beads and powdered sugar, with the aroma of cinnamon everywhere. (Her twins called it "Elf Dust!") Everybody had a great time, and when the mothers came to pick them up, the children presented them with take-home bags of cookies tied with a bright ribbon. Jan smiled. She opened her eyes and looked out the bedroom window at an overcast December sky. She rolled over to squint at the clock at her bedside.

"Good grief!" she gasped. "It's ten o'clock!" She grabbed her robe.

"How could I sleep so late? So much to do—homework for my PowerPoint class. All those workbook exercises! They take hours."

She opened the bedroom door and called toward the kitchen. The sweet breeze of Elf Dust blew in her face.

"Lucy, the house smells wonderful!" Jan shouted. "I'll be there in a few minutes. Oh! And, Lucy, are you going with me to my class tonight?"

"Yes, Ma'am," Lucy called back. "But I don't know nothin' 'bout computers."

"That makes two of us, Lucy!"

In the community college classroom over a bank of computer monitors, about a dozen students in the PowerPoint class that evening leaned toward illuminated screens. The sound of fingers pecking and voices murmuring sounded like chickens in a coop to Lucy. She took her seat next to Jan, after noticing how young most of the students seemed. It was a little intimidating—all these kids typing away like they'd been born with keyboards attached to their umbilical cords. Tentatively, Lucy put her hands on the keys. She had taken typing in high school—and made an A—but she had never typed on a computer keyboard before.

"Wow," she said. "Don't have to press so hard."

Jan smiled. "Bet you learned on a manual typewriter."

"Yep," Lucy smiled back.

"Heads up!" The instructor, a dark-haired man with the disciplined posture and the precise manner of an accountant, pointed a long pencil at a pull-down wall screen. He bent over a computer monitor before the screen and pitched his voice across the students' heads.

"We have here, pictures which we will illustrate with type. The beauty of PowerPoint is that it combines slides with lecture into one seamless performance, controlled and paced by the speaker. Look at how we organize these pictures into a story—or lesson—with visible narration. Everybody ready? Let's go."

Jan scowled. "Just like the Kentucky Derby. I'm late for the starting bell, behind the other horses, and I'll never catch up." She looked up first at the wall screen, then down at her computer screen. A few seconds elapsed between each glance, and she was lost at the starting gates of commands and executions. She glanced over at Lucy who was squinting at her screen. The younger woman took hold of her mouse and moved it around, tracking the curser on the screen.

"Well, if that don't beat all!" she smiled.

The class took fifty minutes, but to Jan, it flew by like five. And now the professor was assigning a project! Oh no! A three-minute PowerPoint presentation by each student, due next week! Jan groaned.

"Lucy, as part of the charity Swap, you got to help me," Jan hissed to her right. Lucy glanced back, registering surprise.

"Why, Mrs. Midland—"

"It's Jan! Don't call me Mrs. Midland in here—"

"Jan," Lucy began again. "Like I told you. I don't know nothin' about computers. In fact, there's only one thing I do know about."

"What's that?" Jan's voice held a hint of panic.

"Why, cleaning house."

Jan's face fell.

Lucy added, "And I don't have the foggiest notion how a computer can do that!"

Driving home from class, Jan and Lucy were quiet, listening to a classical music station on the radio. The dark night enveloped the automobile as if in a tunnel, the headlights focusing only a few feet of road at a glance. Jan took her foot off the accelerator to let the car slow on its own. She saw her own mailbox and the gravel drive on the right. She made a slow turn, the tires audibly registering the surface change from asphalt to gravel. Suddenly there was a scattering of three or four blurred dark shapes leaping to clear the headlights.

"Watch out!" Lucy squealed. Jan hit the brakes.

"Deer," Jan said. "They're all over the place."

"Scared. Hunting season." Then Lucy sat bolt upright in her passenger seat. "Look!" she pointed. "See the white?"

Jan peered through the windshield to catch the disappearing flank of a small pale deer.

"It's the white fawn!" Lucy exclaimed. "Larry told me 'bout it! Solid white, an albino."

"Frank told me about that! I've never seen one," Jan said. She stared into the darkness.

"Larry killed its mother. He didn't see the fawn. Felt so bad about it."

"Awww." Jan sat a moment, her foot on the brake, the car stilled, idling, She reached for the radio knob. The music was a favorite, Pachelbel's *Canon in D*. She continued to look through the windshield, but the white fawn was swallowed by the dark. "Well, accidents in hunting, like everything else, happen sometimes," she said vaguely. "But I'm glad the fawn is still alive."

"Kinda magic, don't ya' know?" Lucy said. She leaned her head back against her seat.

"A pure white baby deer." Jan nodded quietly. She had only the briefest glimpse, but with the silvery light reflecting its shape, the creature seemed to be not just a deer, but some new animal creation, lit from within, as if inhabited by an ancient god.

But then, maybe, Jan mused, she was simply carried away by the moment. She heard the sweetness of Pachelbel's violins as she watched dust motes in the dark dance in her headlights. "Rare. Beautiful," she leaned her head back against the driver's seat. "Yeah, Lucy, I'd say that's magical."

12. Swap Day Three: Francine Takes Charge

*O*n Swap day three, Friday, December 3, Francine Urbane pulled her Mercedes toward the Laymans' modest red brick bungalow on a side avenue perpendicular to Main Street. The day was overcast, and the temperature hovered at an unseasonably warm sixty degrees. Unusual for December, but not unheard of, it was one of those pearly-cloudy days in which the sun seemed to be sleeping late but would arise soon.

She turned the ignition key off and sat in the dirt driveway looking at the domestic winter scene through her windshield. She was about to step into the Laymans' world and to clean house. She shook her head. Cleaning was not her field of expertise. Why, she had hired that all out years ago! She drummed her fingers on the steering wheel. Before her gaze, multicolored lights swung from the giant oak that shaded a brick front porch. The house was built probably around 1910. Its four wooden columns on square brick platforms had been replaced recently, along with some of the trim around the windows. But the new wood had not been painted.

Her eyes moved upward to take in more lights, the crinkly variety with tiny strings flailing loose to simulate frozen icicles. These hung from the roof under the gutters. *The gutters need painting, too,* Francine said to herself. *In fact, everything that isn't brick on this house needs painting.*

She scanned the front yard, a patchy mix of crab grass and fescue, mostly yellow from December's chill; then she gasped, her gloved hand flying to her mouth at a most incongruous sight. Before the hood of her car, pecking the grass, arched forward and erect, stood a pair of pink plaster flamingoes—tropical birds purchased in some far-flung Florida paradise—souvenirs, no doubt, of the couple's honeymoon fourteen years before. Francine slowly smiled. "Flamingoed," she said.

Pink flamingoes had been a joke when she was a student at Smith College in North Hampton, Massachusetts. During spring break one year in the late sixties, she and her girlfriends headed to Florida beaches—Daytona, Fort Lauderdale—anywhere the boys were, as Connie Francis had sung, and they found them—flexed, bronzed, and lounging in the sun. The Smith girls came back in love with life and lifeguards, but also laughing about the quintessential bad taste they encountered for the first time in their young lives—the Florida bungalows with pink flamingoes posed on the front yards. Francine had bought one of the hideous birds on a whim, and she and her housemates planted it outside the room of the girl who notoriously kept the messiest quarters. A tradition was born. The pink flamingo traveled up and down the residence hallways like an ocean tide. The dishonor earned its own status as a figure of speech. "I saw you were flamingoed today," people teased victims who inherited the stain of disdain. The remark usually prompted an abashed smile and a blush.

Today, Francine didn't blush. But she did continue to smile. *Well, there is no accounting for taste. Those horrid birds are probably pets by now, not to be removed. But, on the other hand,* Francine reasoned, *no one can argue with the tasteful appeal of a*

*fresh coat of paint. I may be rusty at cleaning, but a paint job? That's
something I can handle.* With that, she climbed from her car, just
as the sun sent a small ray through the clouds.

Larry wasn't home, but he'd left a note on the
mildewed back screen door.

Welcome, Mrs. Urbane. The handwriting was rough, on
a torn sheet of child's notebook paper, taped with a piece of
masking tape. She opened the door and stepped inside.

Blinking in the shallow hallway while her eyes adjusted to
the interior light, she was struck immediately with an impression:
the three bedroom home was immaculate. Spotless! She straightened
her shoulders. *Thank goodness! That angel Lucy had spared her from the
dreaded job of cleaning!* Francine noticed that the winter green oilcloth
on the kitchen table boasted a white poinsettia in a ceramic Santa
bowl. As she closed the door, Francine saw a rough-hewn end table
at the entranceway with a small manger scene. The A-frame doll-
house of a barn housed a plastic painted Mary, a Joseph and the
Baby Jesus arranged just so, among tiny plastic cows and chickens
and sheep. Inside the manger, someone had stashed pine straw and
leaves to add earthy realism to the display.   •

I bet their children did that, Francine thought. She put a
French-manicured finger to her soft white cheek. *I wonder where
Bill's and my nativity set is? The hand carved one from Italy?*

In the corner across the central room, which with the
kitchen doubled as living space, a wood-burning stove danced
cheerily. It was then that Francine saw something jump. A cat!
A huge, fuzzy tabby thumped down from a bundled blanket on
a rocking chair, causing it to sway back and forth. The feline
laced its way across the pine board floor in greeting, its tail a
bronze plume.

Francine wasn't much for cats. Some dogs, she liked.
She and Bill's King Charles spaniels—hand picked—had been

flown all the way from England. She felt the cat rub her boot. Well, this cat seemed civilized enough. She leaned over and said, "Hello."

"Hello!" An elderly voice responded and this time, Francine jumped. Why, that lumpy shape across from the empty rocker near the fireplace was a tiny person. An old woman! She sat in a wheelchair, her knees covered with a crocheted blanket. Apparently, she had been dozing when Francine walked in. Her greeting had awakened the elderly woman.

"I'm Mrs. Urbane," Francine said, walking over with a smile.

"And I'm Ida Rose Layman," the woman smiled back. Her silver hair was piled in a little topknot. Francine noticed she had a hand-knit red scarf around her neck.

"Pretty," she said as she leaned over and fingered the scarf's texture.

"Hit's a little rough, a stitch dropped here and there," Ida Rose offered apologetically. "But hit's Linda's first crochet project. I helped her, even though my arthritis makes it a little hard."

Francine looked at the woman's gnarled fingers. She dropped her eyes to the woman's feet and saw the characteristic upturned twisted shapes, caused by severe rheumatoid arthritis. She wore fuzzy, red bedroom shoes. Francine instinctively sympathized.

"Do you know why I'm here?" Francine asked.

"The Christmas Swap. To help the poor," Ida Rose answered brightly. "Nice thing for you folks to do."

"Yes, well, did Lucy leave me a note? I mean, as to what things she wants me to handle while I'm here?"

"Why don't you look over there on the kitchen table? I believe she wrote down something before she left."

Francine turned and walked back to the oilcloth-covered table. There she found the other half of the torn sheet of notepaper.

Dear Mrs. Urbane, Francine read. *The $10 is for your lunch. Mamaw Rosey likes Campbell's chicken soup. Fix what you like and do what you want. You can just sit with her if you want. For supper, I'll get chicken at KFC on my way home. Don't worry about fixing nothing. If you really need something to keep busy, it'd be nice if you swept up the sheet rock dust Larry made working on the porch last night. He was up till 2 this A.M.*"

"Hmmm," Francine said. "Construction in progress." She looked up at Ida Rose who was watching her. "Larry is adding on to your house?" she asked.

"This is Larry's house and Lucy's. I live here now, because of my hip. Done fell and broke it."

"Oh, I am sorry," Francine said.

"Hit's better," Ida Rose demurred. "Don't hurt so much now." Then she said brightly, "But if you want to open that door, you'll see my new room."

Francine strode across the living room and opened what once had been the back door. There, large sheets of chalky sheetrock held by fastening screws clung to the ceiling and walls. On one side, a pair of glass sliding doors led to the backyard beyond to let in the sunlight. It spilled gloriously into the room. Francine realized that Larry had completed the sheetrock part of the task. But trapezoidal scraps and chalky dust lay everywhere.

"This room," Francine began, her finger again to her cheek in thought, but Ida Rose interrupted her to finish her sentence,

" . . . will be my new home on Christmas Day." The old woman beamed.

"Why, that's just a few weeks away," Francine said. "There's a lot of work to do yet. Somebody will have to get busy!" Then, like a sunburst, she had an inspiration. *She— Francine Urbane—could be that somebody!*

She stepped from the new room back into the living room. Francine's nose wrinkled in a friendly childish manner, the way it always did when she was amused. She looked at the cozy little woman near the fire and telegraphed a conspiratorial wink.

"Miss Ida Rose," she asked, "just where does Lucy keep the phone book?"

13. Larry's New House

That afternoon, as Larry Layman approached the turn off Main Street that led down Sunset Road to his home, he couldn't help but reflect on how nice it was to roll down the truck windows in early December. He had the radio on, WCVU, rejoicing with the disc jockey's sing-song remark about "sixty-five f-i-n-e degrees outside," and Larry was humming—off-key a bit, but no matter—to a song about c-e-l-e-b-r-i-t-i-e-s and how some country guy wished he were famous, just so he could feel special. Larry liked that song. He didn't have much use for celebrities . . . folks who were considered important—not 'cause of what they did—but just 'cause other folks knew their faces.

He pulled his old carpentry truck into his rutted drive-way, glanced forward, and abruptly hit the brakes.

"What is goin' on?" He thrust the truck into park, leaned toward the windshield, aghast at what he saw: three other vehicles . . . a shiny silver Mercedes SUV, a white van marked "Best Paints" on its side, and a dark blue pickup truck with tools hanging all over a frame in the truck bed. His eyes nearly fell out of his head.

"What the—" he began. Then he noticed something else that just blew him away: men—lots of men—coming from the back of his house with buckets of paint. And, Whoa! He hadn't seen those guys on the other side of the house with brushes just a'strokin' his gutters with white paint. And, *What's this?* Two more men in coveralls pushing their way out the screen door to climb ladders propped against the walls of his front porch.

How many are there? "Five? No, eight!" Larry kept on counting as he scrambled from his truck.

They were dressed in white, mounted on extension ladders, painting a fresh coat of white up and down the square wood supports stretching to the roof from brick columns on the porch. He strode around the side of his home to see men with long-handled rollers leaning up and down, stroking paths of oily white on the unfinished siding of his newly enclosed porch.

He walked quickly toward the door opening just in time to hear the startup roar of an electric sander and men's voices shouting above the noise. He stepped inside and hollered at three men busily spackling nail heads on the sheetrock walls.

"Whoa!" he said. "What's going on here?"

"Mrs. Urbane hired us," a wiry fellow in blue jeans shouted as he cut off the electric sander. His brown hair was coated white with flecks of sheetrock dust. "She called us over here."

"She did what?"

"She called us and said come today or not at all. So, we came."

"So did we," a painter stuck his head in the back doorway.

Larry took off his John Deere cap and turned it in his hands to settle his jangling nerves. "Oh, my. Oh, my," he said, taking long strides toward the kitchen.

He found Francine underneath the kitchen sink with, of all things, a wrench in her hand!

"Mrs. Urbane," he said. "Excuse me, Ma'am, but can I talk to you?"

"Hey, Larry. Oh, I'm so glad you're here. You know, I've tried to twist this ring thing down here and I don't have the strength. I do believe you have a leak in this pipe."

Larry dropped to all fours and crawled beside Francine. She pulled back and handed him the wrench.

"I'll be dad gum," Larry said. "I can't keep that leak fixed for nothin'."

"Well. I didn't think so, judging by the soggy wood under that loopy shaped pipe," Francine said matter-of-factly. "So I've called a plumber."

"What? A plumber? You called a plumber?"

"Yes, I most certainly did," Francine said.

Larry straightened up to his knees and stared. "But Mrs. Urbane, plumbers cost sixty-five dollars an hour." Francine folded her legs, sheathed in slim black pants, Indian-style, and leaned her head against a kitchen chair under the kitchen table.

"Poof!" She waved her hand in front of her face as if suddenly she were a fairy godmother. "Poof! —As much as one platter of catered peeled party shrimp," she sniffed. "Believe me, Larry, I can handle that!"

"But you can't!" Larry protested. "You can't. I have to! That's the deal."

"Whatever do you mean?" Francine blinked her blue eyes rapidly, that nervous manner she'd had since she was a girl.

"The deal! The swap! You have to manage on *my* salary. I'm not supposed to live on *yours*. I can't afford these men!"

A puzzled dawning traveled across Francine's milky brow. Larry's face was growing redder by the minute. She folded her bow-shaped lips together, running her tongue back and forth across them. She needed a moment to think. What was this man saying? She squinted. Suddenly she understood. She sat up straight.

"Oh, Larry, Larry. I'm sorry. I guess I got it backwards. I was trying to help, you know, help fix things."

"Well, I know, but it ain't a help to spend money a man ain't got," Larry said.

Francine's blue eyes registered helplessness. Larry stared at her face for a second, and then he glanced down at the wrench in his hand. He felt his head was about to blow up. So, to save face—his and Francine's—he crawled back under the kitchen sink.

Just then a horn sounded in the driveway to the rhythm, "shave-and-a-hair-cut." Francine scrambled up from the floor and peered out the kitchen window over the sink.

"They're here!" She clapped her hands in delight and ran out the screen door.

Before Larry could wedge himself out to follow her, he could hear Francine. When he reached the doorway, he glimpsed disaster. Francine, waving those manicured fingernails, was directing a television crew—television for God's sakes—to videotape the painters at the front railings, more painters on ladders at the gutters, and a third group of painters finishing the rear siding.

When Larry caught up to her outside, she whirled and grabbed his arm. She called to Terry Turner, the reporter, and to Zeke, the cameraman, "This is the owner! Mr. Layman is a carpenter. A very fine one! He's building his mother a new room out of the back porch for Christmas Day! But, also, he's volunteered to frame the Habitat House the Chamber is sponsoring this year."

Francine glowed at the camera, as she clung to Larry's plaid shirt. She hoped she would photograph as well on TV as she generally did in the newspapers. And she was grateful she'd undergone three series of Botox shots to make her look younger.

As of last January she'd begun the treatments—not fun! It took a lot of courage to have ten or so shots in your forehead every three months. But she'd done it. Hadn't told Bill, though. He just kept saying, "Darling, you must be sleeping better these nights. You're looking rested, less worried lately."

Her lips curled, thinking of the clever subterfuge. How satisfying. Now, when she needed it, an unwrinkled brow was at hand. She turned toward the expectant Terry Turner and said, "Would you like me to tell you what Mr. Layman and I are doing here?"

"Please," Terry answered. "Roll, Zeke," he ordered the cameraman.

During her lifetime, Francine had acquired some prodigious public relations skills. Beauty constituted part of her technique. She did photograph well. Plus she knew how to arrange photo opportunities and how that skill could rake in the dollars. Now, as the video camera light glowed red, Francine relaxed within her reflection on the camera lens and spoke just as though she were Barbara Walters herself.

"You get the issue before the public," Francine enthused, "and you'll find that most people are good-hearted and the issue here is," she bubbled, "why, just as Larry's mother Mamaw Rosey said—helping those in need!"

When Terry Turner heard that line, he scribbled the name in his slim notebook. Then he held up his hand to pause the camera and asked Francine who Mamaw Rosey was. "She's right inside that house, a beautiful little woman, a little diamond named Ida Rose Layman. She looks just like Mrs. Santa Claus!"

"Well, we'll shoot her," Terry said, stroking his shock of blond thick hair away from his forehead. "But first, Mr. Layman," he spoke directly to Larry, "we'd like you in the wide shot of your house standing beside Mrs. Urbane. Could you smile?" With that question to Larry, Terry surreptitiously sent his left hand in repeated circles behind his back, signaling Zeke to roll.

Larry scowled at the reporter. *Smile? How could he? This woman had just spent thousands of dollars he didn't have. In a matter of hours!*

Terry, pencil poised over his notebook, sensed something was wrong. More importantly, he realized he was not getting the shot he wanted. The homeowner not only appeared tough, he was actually hostile. So he asked, "Mr. Layman, do you think these men are doing a good job painting your house?"

"Well," Larry said as both he and Francine instinctively turned to watch the painters. The sun lit their profiles from behind, a mellow haze like pollen in spring. Terry held his breath.

"Well, yes, I think these men are doin' a fine job on my house," Larry said.

"G-o-o-o-o-d," Terry Turner drawled unctuously. He turned to the cameraman and mouthed the word *wide* at Zeke, who adjusted the lens. Whirr! A perfect wide shot, subjects on the left looking at the construction site, stage right. Zeke pulled his eye from behind the lens and nodded at Terry. The reporter grinned. He was satisfied. He had his sound bite and his shot.

The only thing left was to get little Mrs. Santa Claus to say on tape that the Swap was "to help those in need," a phrase the twinkling Mamaw Ida Rose, in the wheelchair by the wood stove, happily provided the "handsome young boy," as she called him. The camera dutifully recorded the tiny little woman with the radiant smile.

Moments later as he watched the red satellite van pull out of his driveway, Larry, stood silently, as frozen as the flamingoes in his front yard. Then he turned to Francine with a scowl. "Mrs. Urbane," he said. "Don't mean no disrespect, but I think this situation's got turned around by mistake."

"Well, Larry, you may be absolutely right," Francine agreed with conviction. "Sometimes I do take charge more than I should." Then she smiled. "However, I think something can be done. We can talk to my husband. Bill is good at situations like this. Bill will straighten things out."

14. What Next?

"Straighten things out!" Bill Urbane raised his usually calm voice. The word, *straighten,* spit like a dart, right into Francine's astonished face. "You've probably spent a half-year of that man's salary! He knows that! It hurts his pride." Bill had poured himself a scotch. He placed his half-full glass under the ice dispenser of the refrigerator door.

Francine held a raw chicken in her hands over the kitchen sink. Her graceful fingers swabbed the bird cavity with sea salt and garlic, plus a little savory and sage. "Well," she turned toward Bill, dropping the clammy bird in the sink. She grabbed a kitchen towel on the tile counter. She rubbed the cloth vigorously as her face clouded up like a threatening afternoon storm. "Well, Wilburn Urbane, you don't have to shout at me! I got us some great television publicity today! And, and—even though my head went a little off track because I got excited, my heart—my heart, Bill—my heart was in the right place!" She hustled from the kitchen down the hall to the powder room and slammed the door.

Bill watched distractedly as the dispenser dropped three half-moon ice cubes into his half-filled tumbler—*splash, splash, splash.* "Problems, problems, problems," he muttered. Then he took a sip of liquid comfort and sighed.

When Frank told Jan at dinner that night the news of Bill's dilemma with Francine and the faux pas at the Laymans' home that afternoon, Jan, to his dismay, sailed off into gales of laughter. She playfully pushed a sprig of fresh mint down deep in her glass of iced tea with her finger, and she just hollered with glee:

"Whatcha' gonna do now, Frank?" she teased. "You guys—you and Bill and Larry—-gonna penalize the well-meaning, prominent, ultra-ladylike Mrs. Urbane?"

"Hmmm," Frank said staring beyond her irritating smirk, "This revolting development could jeopardize the whole worthwhile project. I think Bill's right. We fellows better meet again at the Circle Market."

15. For Sale: The View in Clearview

The men had settled by phone on meeting around twelve-thirty for lunch the following day at the Circle Market.

Frank left home early to run a few Saturday errands. As he popped in and out of his truck during the morning, he noticed that the temperature had dropped noticeably since the day before.

Wonder if a cold front is coming in? He pulled up to the Market and climbed out of his truck. As Frank stepped inside, his lean, tall frame straightened as he observed Flossie, finishing up a bit of Christmas decorating. In honor of the season she had fastened silver tinsel garlands over the windows. She had strung multi-colored lights around the front door frame, and she'd tied the trophy buck's eight points with red ribbon and sprigs of fresh mistletoe.

"Mistletoe," Frank smiled. "Aha!"

"That way, I jest might get a kiss or two," she giggled at Frank. "You say you got two more coming?" She picked up a pencil to scribble on her order pad lying on the counter.

"Yeah. We all want hamburgers, please, Flossie, lettuce, tomato, onion, the works."

"All the way, *ATW*," Flossie wrote.

Frank gazed at her irregular scrawl. A good-hearted

person, Flossie; she lived alone with her aging mother and had never married. Rumors flew that at least once there was a significant man in her life. She'd taken him home to her daddy, and the old guy had not approved. Later, Frank had heard, she ran off with some other man and stayed gone about six months. The Market nearly folded without Flossie's hamburgers and chicken salad. But after a trip to parts unknown, Flossie returned on a Monday. She'd been at the Market ever since. Her dad eventually died of a stroke, or "meanness," as some folks said. Flossie and her mother stayed in the family home. Frank and everyone else in town were glad about that. People like Flossie, dedicated and cheerful, were a vanishing breed.

"Anything else?" Flossie was looking at him, the pencil poised.

"French fries. Coffee," Frank answered, noticing her red curls peeking from under her cap. *Unusual color. Wonder if she uses a rinse?* He thought distractedly. Then his eyes drifted toward the wall behind her curls to the old tavern namesake, the glass-eyed trophy buck. *Kind of regal in a sad way*, he thought, *an eight-point deer, symbol of the untrammeled rural landscape, in which his kind roamed freely across open pastures, their white tails like flags, waving right and left.* And now, he had heard that there was a pure-white fawn near his own farm. "Rare and beautiful—magical," Jan had told him after catching a glimpse of it Thursday night. Frank hoped he would get to see it before some hunter got it. Not a vanishing breed, deer— just the opposite—too many. But somehow Frank felt sympathy for the wild creatures struggling to live in a wilderness leached by commercial development each passing day.

Frank took his customary seat at a table near a window overlooking the vacant field behind the market. There it was. Frank's stomach lurched. There was the stark sign he had been warned about by an ominous phone call from Isabel

Charmin that morning. A moment later when Wilburn Urbane walked up to Frank's table, he stripped off his leather coat, and without even saying hello, he blurted out, "When did that sign go up?"

"What sign?" Larry Layman asked breathlessly, coming close behind Bill.

"The 'For Sale–Rezoning' sign," Frank said. "Have a look."

Bill and Larry leaned toward the window. Bill stroked his hair back from his forehead. Larry repositioned his cap and began unbuttoning his hunting jacket.

"I'm afraid, my friends," Frank continued, "that prime spot of real estate has attracted interest. I got a phone call from Isabel at the Chamber first thing today. Since I'm chair of the Architectural Review Board she felt I should know immediately that the developer wants to sell it to a filling station."

"Ugh," Larry grunted.

"Surely not!" Bill exclaimed.

The men settled down in their chairs and continued to stare out the tinsel-festooned window. Somehow its gaudy cheer framing a For Sale sign seemed incongruous.

"A gas station? We already got two on the Circle," Larry said.

"What kind?" Bill asked.

"The worst. One of those Crane's monstrosities, with the red and black poles and lighted signs and a hundred pumps and a pickup store—"

"Greed!" Larry growled.

"Horrible!" Bill's mouth wrinkled as if he'd bitten into a grapefruit. "That's the focal point of the town, fronting the circle as it does. And we just landscaped the Circle last fall! Francine headed the committee, picked out that sizable red maple—not cheap—— I can tell you. She hired a man with a truck and a tree spade to plant it. Then she and her Clearview garden committee oversaw the bulb planting around its base."

"I know," Frank said. "Jan donated some heirloom daffodil varieties we found on our farm. But—the sale could go forward. Crane's Petroleum is willing to pay a lot of money for three acres of that eleven-acre tract."

"Who's the developer?"

"Take a guess." Frank's face wore a wry smile.

"Not Hiram Venald."

"The very man," Frank nodded.

"Sleaze is written right in his name." Bill shook his head in disgust.

"Sludge, too." Larry lowered his voice. "I did a job for him once. Cheated me out of a bunch of lumber. I paid for it on order, he returned about a fourth of it, got credit toward his personal account, but subtracted it from my invoice. So I guess you could say I bought him some lumber, only I didn't know I bought it."

"Sounds just like him. Did you confront him?" Bill asked.

"Didn't realize it 'til a year later when I was doing my accounts for income tax. Same thing happened to a friend of mine. He figured it out and told me how Hiram done it to him, too."

"What a jerk." Bill stroked his hair. "But zoning," he began, "Frank, won't there be opposition? Surely?"

"Oh, there surely will be, once it hits the papers. Isabel predicts a called meeting of the zoning board, and, of course, my architectural committee, before Christmas. Hiram wants to start construction in March."

"No way!" Larry protested.

At that moment, a chilling wind blew the red-check tablecloths in the dining area. A few paper napkins fluttered across the tan linoleum floor. Conversation halted throughout the room. The three men looked up to see a compact male about five-foot five, wearing a black leather jacket, with a black rawhide cowboy hat, and black leather boots with two-inch heels.

"The devil hisself," Larry said under his breath.

"Hello, boys," Hiram Venald flagged the men. He stopped at the self-serve coffee counter and poured himself a cup. He took a gingerly sip, and through the coffee steam, he winked at Flossie.

"Same old rust water, good and strong." He lolled against the counter, grinned at the waitress, and loud enough for everyone to hear, quipped, "How you doin', Red? Lookin' good as usual, Sugah."

"Mister Venald, I've told you many times, my name is Flossie."

"It was Red back in high school," Hiram jeered.

"Well, I outgrowed that name," Flossie said.

"Okay, okay. Hard to forget the past." Hiram's smile faded. He reached into his pocket and pulled out a wrinkled pack of Camels. He picked up a Bic lighter from the shelf of purchasable items next to the cash register. He flicked it and lit a cigarette.

"You can't smoke in here no more," Flossie said curtly.

"The hell I can't. I own this place," Hiram told her.

"Mr. Venald, you know it's a town ordinance that forbids it," Flossie said.

"Well, guess I'll have to buy this town and change the rules." Hiram cut his eyes at Flossie up and down like a moving elevator. Flossie began edging toward the swinging metal door that separated the retail section from the kitchen. She put her hand on it and paused.

"Well, you can't buy everything in Clearview. If'n you do, I'll move away," she said.

"Wouldn't we all?" Larry echoed under his breath.

Hiram's eye roamed from Flossie to the threesome near the window. "Now, boys," he said, loudly. He dropped his cigarette to the floor, twisting it with the toe of his shiny black boot. "You've have seen my sign, I see, 'cause you're lookin' at it right out the window. So, listen up, my friends. That sign is a promise! This town is gonna grow and we'll all be rich someday. Why, one of the largest oil companies in the entire country is interested in our little town of Clearview. In fact, the oil men want to develop that spot you see right there. Just like winning the lottery! What a kick-start it'll bring to this area!"

"And the quality of life we'll lose," Bill spoke up.

"Why Bill Urbane, you and your farm, you'll benefit. Your acres will hike in value. We're gonna be a D.C. suburb someday. This town's gonna grow, boys, whether you like it or not."

"It's the beauty of the town, not only the distance from the big city, we want to retain, Hiram," Frank offered, "Controlled growth is one thing, cancer is another."

"What's that you say?" Hiram jerked his head up.

"Some development is as bad as cancer," Frank said evenly.

"It can kill a town," Larry joined in.

"That's a matter of opinion, boys," Hiram said, reaching for his cup on the counter. "But I can see now who'll be among the foot draggers to progress."

"Progress is a matter of opinion, too, Hiram," Bill spoke politely. "We want Clearview to attract people who appreciate the rural lifestyle and its history."

"Who appreciate its beauty," Frank said.

"Quality folks," Larry couldn't help but add.

Another gust of the cold air wafted in from the front door. Hiram looked around as he tossed his Styrofoam cup into the trash.

"Quality folks," he ran the phrase over his tongue as if

fleshing out its meaning. His eyes darted at the fellow who had brought the wind throught the front door. As was his custom, Hiram sized him up instantly in a pithy phrase: *a homeless old bum.*

The newcomer did look old, maybe seventy-five, maybe more, it was hard to tell. He stood about six feet tall. He wore a black overcoat, frayed at the sleeves, tied with a mismatched belt, and pocked with what looked like moth holes. A red wool scarf around his neck disappeared into the front of his coat. He wore a black felt hat that emphasized a pair of scraggily eyebrows snarled over a thin nose. The man breathed heavily. He bore his weight grudgingly, as if carrying a pot-bellied stove. His face was ruddy with cold. He showed several days' beard across his cheeks like patchy snow. For a few seconds, he stood blinking. Then he looked around and began removing a pair of ratty wool gloves.

"Quality folks," Hiram repeated within earshot. The old man looked at Hiram briefly, and Hiram thought he saw a flash in the old man's eyes. But, the stranger nodded politely, then coughed slightly into his hands.

Oh, great, thought Hiram. *A tubercular, homeless old bum.*

As the man shuffled by, Hiram gestured with a hitch-hiking finger behind the man's back while silently mouthing sarcastically, "Quality—like him." Then Hiram kicked his squashed cigarette butt on the floor toward the coffee counter and hustled toward the door as he waved offhandedly.

"Merry Christmas, boys."

The three men shared a collective sigh of relief.

"Smells good in here." The stranger eased himself onto one of the red counter stools. Flossie peeked from the swinging door between the serving area and the kitchen. She came back out after Hiram was gone. Automatically, she rang open the cash register to charge his cup of coffee and the Bic lighter to his account. From behind the machine she looked up at the old weathered man.

"Would you like to see a menu?"

"Yes, Miss, I would." He looked beyond Flossie's red curls, his gaze traveling upward to rest on the trophy buck hanging on the wall.

"Why, hello, Old Buck."

"Why, how'd you know that name?" Flossie asked.

"Why, that is his name," the gentleman huffed genially.

Flossie giggled. "Well, it sure is," she said. "He's what the old tavern, the one that sat on this very spot, was named after–The Buck Stop. 'Course the new owner, 'long time ago, changed the name to Circle Market. But that guy," she said, tossing her red curls toward the deer, "he's been around for sixty years or maybe even longer."

"His coat needs a little care," the man said.

Flossie looked up at the buck. "Yeah. I need to dust him," she remarked. Then she turned toward the hot chocolate machine and fizzed hot steaming cocoa into a ceramic mug.

"I put some mistletoe on him," Flossie said, talking as she worked. "Just for fun. 'Course he don't know it, being dead so long."

"Good souls never die, do they, boy?" The fellow winked at the vacant eyes of the deer.

Flossie rolled her eyes. *Some kind of kook,* she thought. *But he seems harmless.* She turned her head back in the stranger's direction.

"A little whipped cream?" she asked.

"A lot," replied the old man still staring at the trophy buck.

"All we got's instant—like you spray out of a can," Flossie was apologetic.

"Fine. Cover the top of the chocolate, will you, Miss? And don't be a bit shy."

"Enough?" Flossie drizzled a spray of white around the cup rim.

"Almost," smiled the old man.

Flossie brought the circular cream to a cone. "Enough now?"

"Just right."

"Good! Can't fit no more in!" Flossie grinned.

The stranger gave an appreciative grunt. He glanced briefly at the three men at the corner table. He pulled off his coat and turned back toward the counter.

At an angle, Bill studied the old fellow's face, framed by a thick shock of white hair as he pulled off his hat. The old man's eyes were dark, almost blackish blue, but at the same time they wavered with light, as the moon wobbles in a bucket of rainwater. Frank and Bill and Larry continued to observe the old fellow as he unwound his red scarf.

Underneath his tattered overcoat, he was dressed even more oddly in a grey business suit and vest that resembled something from the thirties. Larry saw that the man's dress shirt looked frayed at the collar and the cuffs.

Bill noticed the necktie similar to his own grandfather's and thought the stranger was a study in contrasts: proud but disheveled. Obviously poor, but clean.

Frank surmised ruefully, *Maybe he's a broke architect.*

An old drunk, Larry figured silently.

Some eccentric old businessman who's beginning to lose his mind, Bill thought.

All three men glanced from the stranger, then back to one another and then, as if on cue, they turned their eyes to gaze silently out the smudged café windows. At that moment, balancing a tray, Flossie unloaded their order of hamburgers and fries.

"Pass the ketchup, please, will you Mr. Midland?" Larry asked.

"Sure," Frank said, munching on a hot fry with seasoning salt. "I guess we have a matter to talk about here."

With that, the topic of interest deftly changed.

"Yes, we do have a matter to talk about here," Bill nodded toward Larry. "Francine feels really bad about what she did."

Larry sighed.

"So, I've thought about it, and I have a couple of ideas," Bill said, his tone resolute. "The first is a gesture to put the Swap on an equal footing again. The second deals with a project I have in mind at my place."

"I'm all ears," Larry said.

"Me, too," Frank bit into his hamburger.

In the corner, the stranger sipped his chocolate. His white mustache wrapped the mound of whipped cream as he slumped contentedly over the fountain counter in what appeared to be an unheeding trance.

16. Isabel Charmin's Secret Weapon

"That's hitting below the belt, Bill!" Francine announced, her eyes igniting as blue flames. She put down her brandy snifter on the coffee table in the den. "The biggest event of the year and all kinds of local media taking pictures, and I'm dressed in rags?"

"It's a gesture, Franny. I'll donate the money saved on a new gown toward the paint bill for Larry's house. And I'll hire him for a project or two around here."

"I won't stand for it!" Francine was livid. "It's a hideous idea!" And abruptly she stood up and left. She left a cozy fire in the den. She left her husband sitting snugly next to her on the sofa. She left the comfort of a first-rate cognac. She marched down the hall of her home and banished herself with a slam of the powder room door.

Bill sighed. He had purposefully waited until after dinner Sunday evening, when things were quiet, and the two of them could relax and listen to some Aaron Copeland, and watch a comforting fire dance in the grate in the den. Now his plan to break the news gently was shattered by the not-so-gentle bang of a door. Furthermore, he felt the situation might get worse.

His premonition proved correct.

When Francine came out of the powder room, she went straight upstairs where she stayed in their bedroom for almost twelve hours. She gave Bill the silent treatment until, until—he couldn't believe it—until ten the next morning, when she said goodbye and slammed the front door. Bill had never seen such unremitting fury. Early that morning, Francine had silently arisen, put on her immaculately matched clothes in her private dressing area, teased her hair to a perfect bouffant, and purposefully put on her makeup with the skill of a starlet. Obviously, she knew what she had to do, although Bill had not the faintest clue what it was. Now, over a cup of coffee he had brewed himself, Bill heard the gravel pebbles (which had cost him a fortune) spinning all to heck into the bordering bushes as his wife's car roared out of the front drive.

Within the tidy center of town on Main Street, shop-keepers were engaged in Monday morning tasks, sweeping November's residual leaves from the windows, festooning them with welcoming December displays of figurines and fake snow. Francine pulled right up to the curb before the Chamber of Commerce building. She reached for her small black purse in the passenger's seat, then she swung two form-fitted pants legs from the front seat of her Mercedes onto the street. Next, she slipped a quarter into the parking meter before the brick Williamsburg-style structure and strode straight through the open door of the president's office, bypassing the assistant. She flopped down in the seat before a large woman settled behind an expansive mahogany desk. On its corner sat a ruby red poin-settia nestled in a gleaming silver bowl.

Classy, Francine thought, looking at the arrangement. She'll understand.

"Isabel," she said, unwrapping her black cashmere scarf

from her full-length black suede coat. She sat silently for a moment, watching the woman's left hand peel pages from a stack of papers and place them aside, while at the same time, her right hand gripped her fountain pen, which scratched the woman's florid executive signature across the page. The hand-writing was recognizable to many because of its characteristic brocade of curls and swoops. It announced what everyone knew: Isabel Charmin was a force to be reckoned with. She was not just large, she was grand. She had what people call "presence," even "charisma," some said. Her commanding frame moved through any room like a street-sweeper. She wore her dyed black hair straight back, clasped into a full bun at the nape of her neck. She penciled her brows razor thin. She favored the reddest lipstick. Not many people crossed Isabel Charmin; and if they did, generally they lived to regret it. She demanded loyal-ty; she did her homework; she noticed details; she remembered names. No surprise that she became president or chairman of almost any organization she chose to join.

A born leader, Francine observed. In fact, not long ago, Jan Midland had told Francine that very thing.

"I'll bet," said Jan, tossing her ponytail for emphasis, "that within twenty-four hours of birth, Isabel was unanimously named president of her hospital newborn nursery by her screaming infant peers." Francine had laughed and said, "Little do people know, that forbidding presence has a heart of gold."

Today, Francine was waiting to call upon Isabel's heart. So she sat respectfully. Then as Isabel raised her dark brown eyes briefly, Francine scrunched her mouth up like a wet dishrag and began what amounted to a rehearsed speech.

"You know, Isabel, that I go a long way toward helping people." Her voice wavered at first, then picked up momentum and strength. "Why, I have served on three community boards to help this town of ours. And I've made donations to parks and other worthy projects both under my name and anonymously. Now, at this moment, I feel like I'm being shamed. A victim, that's what I feel I am."

"I heard about the latest glitch." Isabel looked down and licked her scarlet lips as she finished signing the last letter with her fountain pen. She placed it with finality in its onyx and gold base in front of Francine. On its front, Francine spotted the engraved words, *President, Chamber of Commerce*.

"Glitch? Oh, well, Isabel," she squirmed. "I misunderstood the Swap terms, and I saw a need, and so . . ."

"And so you painted Larry Layman's entire house."

"Not the entire house. Just the wood trim . . . and the front columns, and the gutters." Francine fanned ten perfectly pink nails before Isabel in a gesture that politely said, "Whoa!"

"And the new porch addition," Isabel raised one thin eyebrow.

"Yes, it was wood, too. I just painted the wood, except for the aluminum gutters, which were included, of course, and a base coat for the sheet rock." Francine lowered her hands and drew her nails across Isabel's desk, as if to show her the sections of Larry's house. "Anything wooden, mostly, really, connected to the structure." Francine sat back in her chair and watched Isabel for a reaction. Since arriving, she had not pulled off her black coat. Now she fingered the top button as if not knowing whether to leave or stay.

"To the tune of six thousand dollars," Isabel continued, still with an eyebrow arched.

"Something like that." Francine waved her right hand as if swatting a gnat.

"And you're supposed to pay it back?" Now, Isabel raised both penciled eyebrows in dual arches, revealing parallel ripples above her bold brown eyes. Francine saw immediately that Isabel could vastly benefit from her doctor's recipe of Botox shots to her forehead. Furthermore, because, post treatment herself, she couldn't frown effectively, thereby visibly expressing her own indignation, Francine just narrowed her eyes to slim slits.

"Pay it back? No! Well, yes! In a manner of speaking!" she said. "But it's a totally meaningless gesture. It's just a mean, mean thing, meant to embarrass me!"

"Tell me about it," Isabel said.

Francine unbuttoned the top suede button to her coat, and she hunched her normally squared shoulders toward Isabel to do just that. She would tell her about it, yes, she would. She had the ear of The Force . . . The Force to be reckoned with!

"For the Chamber Ball, you know," Francine began in a wheedling tone, "where we make the announcement about the donations. I'm supposed to wear a gown—just like I usually do, like we all do. But to compensate for my mistake—but of course even though it would hardly cover the painting costs—I'm supposed to purchase a dress at a charity store," Francine shivered, "like the Salvation Army, or Goodwill. Specifically a store that accepts donations. Oh, it's horrid, horrid! The very idea!" Francine had slung her black suede coat inside out, over her chair, by now. She sat perfectly erect, her soft dove-grey wool pantsuit jacket covering a lavender silk blouse with a cascading bow lying tastefully across her grey wool lapels.

"Indeed," Isabel sat up straighter.

Encouraged, Francine rushed on, without even pausing for a comma.

"I want to know something," she said flatly. "And you have the answer."

"I do?" Isabel made a tent of her fleshy palms.

"You do," Francine said firmly. "The Chamber is giving

a certificate of occupancy to somebody who needs a home. Who is that person? I want to know just who—just for whom—I am being humiliated!" She batted her mascara-coated eyelashes and opened her eyes wide. Had it not been for the mighty effects of her own latest onslaught of Botox, her forehead just might have been as corrugated as Isabel's. For a half-second, Francine felt better, but only for half a second. What happened next completely flummoxed the elegant visitor. She sat frozen in her chair, staring at the august Chamber president. What was going on here? Francine cocked her head in bewilderment. She stared, fixated, at a scene unfolding like one of those old-fashioned animated frame films:

Snap-Scene! Snap-Scene! Isabel's bulbous chest began to chug up and down in a rapid, voluptuous, mighty tremble. Francine blinked, unbelieving.

Then—there came a sound: *Blur! Blur!* Like a gurgling drain, Francine heard something unrecognizable, something totally out of place, something unspeakable, welling forth from that black-haired, pencil-eye-browed, oversized human tent in front of her behind that behemoth mahogany desk.

What was it? A giggle! A giggle? Could it be? Incredible! Isabel—her friend, her *good friend*—was laughing at her? Surely not! But—wait—surely, yes! The woman's shoulders shook, her hands clapped together, her heavy head of hair leaned back and the woman just—to Francine's utter amazement—she just *guffawed.*

"Well, I never in all my life!" Francine began and she flopped her manicured hands down on the desk again to help herself up on her way just—just—just absolutely out the door!

Isabel stopped her. She dropped her plump palms on top of Francine's fingers and said in spurts—still laughing— "Wait, Honey, just a minute." Laughing, laughing, she heaved heavily. "Just, just, let me get hold of myself."

Isabel reached near the telephone with one hand for a Kleenex tissue to wipe her tearing eyes, leaving her right hand on Francine's as if to hold her down so she couldn't button up her top black suede button, wrap her black cashmere scarf and leave. The impulsive gesture gave Francine a few seconds to reflect on what everybody in Clearview knew and *did not know* about Isabel.

If you weren't more than half blind you could see that the Clearview Chamber Madame President was a generously—very generously—sized woman, maybe a size eighteen, maybe a twenty. Her weight carried power and prestige. You could tell she liked that fact, but it had its down sides. On the one hand, she didn't like being fat, but on the other hand, she couldn't see going through her life hungry. So she had spent her adult years melding opposites, finding figure-enhancing outfits, while at the same time, enjoying those lovely sweet Peppermint Patties with her coffee every morning and with her decaf every night. People often said, because of her size and those nonetheless flattering styles, it was just no telling how much money Isabel poured into her clothes. But she never confided in a soul. Isabel liked mystery. She entered any event parading like an enigmatic queen, dominating the crowd, not only with expansive girth but also with exquisite taste.

But today, Isabel had displayed egregious taste, in Francine's opinion, by laughing at her. Right in her face! But as the moments passed and she remained silent, Francine could see Isabel slowly moving toward her customary presidential composure.

"So according to new terms of the Christmas Swap," Isabel said, dabbing her eyes, and finally able to speak without a bosom-shaking giggle, "you have to buy a dress from the Salvation Army?"

Francine noticed that Isabel still wore a smile. It made the wealthy woman terribly cross. "Yes," she huffed. "And probably most of them won't even fit." Francine's mouth assumed a perfect pout. "Those castoff sizes are usually much too big." She glanced up at Isabel.

"Excuse me. No offense," she said.

"None taken," Isabel replied genially. "How about the Junior League Thrift Shop? They take donations. And rich women, generally the donors, often run small. Is that legal according to the terms of the Swap?"

"Hmmm. Hadn't thought of that. Good idea," Francine said. "High-class clothes for cheap." Then she had a horrible thought. "But the donations are by my peers!" she moaned. "It would be terrible to show up at the Chamber Ball in a dress donated by the likes of Mrs. Fielding Taylor or Mrs. Jefferson Marshall or"—here she shivered again—"that sleazy developer's wife, what's her name? Uh, that Mrs. Hiram Venald."

"Stephanie Venald," Isabel said, then she stayed prudently silent for a second.

"Horrors! I'd never live it down!"

Accompanied by the audible rustle of fabric, Isabel leaned her frame, swathed in an elegant drape, back in her oversized chair. She began to chuckle again.

"What are you laughing at now?" Francine snapped. "I think you are being extremely rude!"

"Well, I guess I am, dear. I'm trying to make up my mind. To trust or not to trust you. So, I guess I'll trust. It's time to introduce my secret weapon," Isabel said conspiratorially.

"Secret weapon?"

"Yes," Isabel said, heaving her hips from the chair and waddling toward a closet in her office near the file cabinets. Francine could hear her pantyhose brushing, thigh against thigh. She watched the woman's shadow, a heaving bovine, travel across the opposite wall as she walked past the window.

"Huge," Francine involuntarily shook her head with the impression.

Isabel turned the closet knob, swung open the door, and reached inside. She pulled out a brilliant midnight blue, satin gown with a blue velvet sash. Dark sequins sewn with tiny, black pearls lay in a spray across the back neckline of the gown. The dainty decoration flowed around to the front of the dress, drifting in gradual spaces as the bodice led the eye in a soft V closure that stretched toward the velvet-covered waistline. A few jeweled sequins here and there adorned the wrist cuffs, and, like the spray at the neck, they caught the afternoon sun like baguette diamonds.

Francine gasped. *The brilliant flecks, the deep blue velvet sash!* Why, Francine could just see it—that sash alone would slenderize Isabel's frame by at least two sizes. But also! O, glorious night! The sequins and pearls would distract the eye from Isabel's ample middle, while at the same time, they would flashingly reflect the antique lights from the lobby, the Alistair Hotel's massive crystal chandeliers! Once again, Isabel scored another triumph for another year! She would be the belle of her own Chamber Ball!

Francine gingerly reached trembling fingers out to touch the gown as if it were too beautiful to be real. "That is gorgeous, Isabel!" she exclaimed. "Where ever did you get that?"

"Through the mail," Isabel twinkled.

"Bloomingdales? Saks? Bergdorf Goodman? Surely not a catalog dress!"

"Nope," Isabel corrected her with satisfaction. "The local mail."

Francine tapped her rose-colored fingertips to her papery white cheek. "Now, you tell me about it," she said narrowing her eyes, which had become a fiery blue, once more.

"I have a secret—"

"Weapon! You claim," Francine said encouragingly

"Yes. A secret weapon," Isabel said. "A seamstress designer!"

Francine's eyes grew round.

"And—stay in your seat, Honey," Isabel pointed a hefty finger at her friend. "She is the same person that the Chamber has chosen to receive the Habitat House. But you have to keep that a secret! We announce it in the newspaper tomorrow, and we celebrate it at the Chamber Ball on December 22nd. I'm telling you, between now and tomorrow, you cannot tell a soul."

"You can trust me," Francine said, nodding. "But, why does she get the Habitat House? Terribly poor?"

"Poor. Worthy. Hardworking. Out of luck." Isabel answered. "She's a widow. She lives in a trailer. Her car's broken down. It's hardly worth selling for parts. The trailer park is booting her out, because she doesn't have money for rent."

Francine squirmed.

"But here's the kicker," Isabel continued. "She has a son. And the boy, who's about fourteen, has cerebral palsy. The medical bills, along with everything else, have plunged her into the horrible pit she's in."

"Awful. Awful. Awful. I'm so glad you found her!" Francine exclaimed.

"Yes. I am, too. She is a good person and a diligent soul. And gifted. She can turn a rag into a Cinderella's gown. But no matter how fast she sews on sequins," Isabel fingered the elegant bodice of her midnight blue Chamber Ball dress, "the medical bills mount up faster."

"I can't stand it!" Francine said. "Why, something like that could happen to me, I mean if Bill died or became incapacitated. And if my Anna had a terrible disease, oh, I just think I would die. I nearly *did die* a few years ago"—but then Francine stopped mid-sentence.

Isabel waited in the silence. She'd heard a rumor about the prominent, elegant Urbanes, formerly of Boston, Massachusetts. At national chamber conventions she attended annually, when the Urbane name was mentioned, people hushed and shook their heads sadly. But Isabel had never, nor would she ever, ask Francine if the story she had heard were true. So, after a prolonged pause, Isabel inhaled and said,

"Well, this woman is not going to die. She's determined to rear her son and see him walk one day. Because he is talented, too."

"How? How can anybody with CP be talented?"

"Check out tomorrow's paper," Isabel said. "But until then—that's twenty-four whole hours from now, Francine—you can't tell a soul. I haven't even told the TV people. That blond male bimbo, Terry Turner, loves to scoop the newspaper. This time he'll have to land in second place. I'm partial to newspapers," Isabel added. "Their pictures of me are more flattering."

Francine smiled. She suddenly felt such relief! Oh! Such relief. And, at that instant, the overwhelming fun—pure fun!—of sharing a secret with Isabel just all-of-a-sudden turned over Francine's own giggle box. She threw her perfectly coiffed head back, tossed up her manicured hands, and just hooted with helpless, raucous laughter. Isabel joined right in with her. When, after several minutes, they both grew quiet, Isabel assumed her place in charge.

"But now you promise, Mrs. Urbane," Isabel said with that wagging finger before Francine's wide blue eyes, "you won't tell a soul. For twenty-four hours! No one. Not about my designing seamstress, and not about her Habitat House!"

Francine shook her pretty porcelain face sideways. "Not a soul," she repeated. She picked up her black suede coat and buttoned it up over the lavender silk bow of her lavender silk blouse. She wrapped her black cashmere neck scarf daintily around her neck. Then she leaned over and he picked up her black leather purse—small, smart, Prada after all—and shouldered it smoothly as she spun around to leave. "I won't tell a soul," she smiled over her purse strap, as she touched her cell phone snuggled in her coat pocket and waltzed out Isabel's door.

17. Women and Secrets

Jan heard the phone ring as she clambered down from the attic steps with a large, dust-covered box containing the front door Christmas wreath. She clumped the box on the primitive antique kitchen table creating a dust explosion, which she waved impatiently away. She reached for the jangling wall phone.

"Guess who the Chamber Habitat House is going to!" The voice in her ear was Francine Urbane's.

"I have no idea who gets the Habitat House. I thought it was a secret." Jan leaned her head toward the receiver.

"It is a secret!" Francine crowed. "But I know it! Just heard it! She's a secret weapon—a seamstress who is fabulous!"

"How do you know?"

"Can't say."

"Okay, you know. So?" Jan frowned with impatience.

"So? Well, you know how I am supposed to wear a castoff dress to the Ball?"

"Silly idea. Men can be merciless," Jan's nose wrinkled in disdain.

"Well, I'm going to find a dress and let that seamstress turn it into Cinderella's gown."

Jan laughed. "You know, Francine, there's one thing I've got to say about you! You've got spunk! Why, I would be positively mortified to have to buy a dress at Goodwill!"

"You know there's another option," Francine lowered her voice. "The Junior League Thrift Shop."

"Yes," Jan said. "On the Main Street Mall."

Then suddenly, Jan experienced one of those brain flashes like a firecracker in the night.

"Francine!" she exclaimed. "I've got an idea!"

"What? You do?" Francine said.

"Yes! *All three of us* should wear charity gowns to the Chamber Ball! That takes the heat off you, Francine. And it shows we're all good sports—not just shallow celebrity-seekers playing charity in a corny swap idea conjured up by our three corny husbands! I bet Lucy would do it! She's been part of the Chamber Ball publicity."

Jan leaned against the kitchen wall; she reeled her memory back to the day Lucy had swapped to her home for extra duties. Jan had asked,

"Did that local TV crew catch you stamping out cookies here this morning?"

Lucy had backed away from loading the freezer with containers of newly decorated Santas and reindeer and stars. She had responded with,

"Humph! Yes, they were here. I thought they'd never leave. That blond reporter fellow kept loading up my chocolate chip dough on his finger and puttin' it right in his mouth. Cameraman did the same thing. I told them to stop it, or there'd be nothin' left."

Jan giggled involuntarily into the phone.

"Everybody in town today has the giggles," Francine harrumphed in her ear.

"Just remembering Lucy fussing at the TV crew," Jan said apologetically. "She's really an awfully good sport about things."

"But Jan, would she wear a Goodwill dress? I mean, I don't want to insult her."

"I'll call her."

"Tell her I know someone who can make them over like new."

"Depends on the cost. That's all. She'll worry about that," Jan said.

"Tell her not to worry about the cost," Francine said.

"Watch it, Francine! That's how you got in trouble in the first place," Jan corrected.

"Okay, okay. Tell her we'll do some ruthless shopping and we'll get something just right."

Jan translated that in her mind, *Francine says, she's good at finding great-looking inexpensive things that will make us look fabulous.*

"We'll have Isabel's seamstress gussy our things up. Good publicity and you should see what she did for Madame President!" Francine crowed.

"I'm sure I will see it if it's her ball gown." Jan had an intuitive hunch.

"It is her ball gown," Francine said. "But it's a secret."

"Yeah, I know about women and secrets," Jan snorted. "I'm surprised you haven't told me her name."

"Well, I don't know her name."

"Well, well, well! That's probably why you haven't told me."

"Yeah, you're probably right," Francine purred.

"Well, I gotta go. Are you coming to help me decorate tomorrow?" Jan turned toward the table and opened the flaps of her attic box while still cradling the phone. She wrinkled her nose at the sight of a skein of dusty pinecones shaped as a wreath. The thing needed a definite facelift—some holly, fresh cones, or at least a new wreath bow.

"Your house? Yes, that's our Swap deal." Francine tapped her cell phone with her pink fingernails. "But don't expect me to cook. Decorating I can do. And my caterer's bringing your dinner, don't misunderstand. I'm just in a dither these days. What would Frank like?"

"Anything Italian. But don't worry about Frank. He's got a seminar at the university on Tuesday night. And—" Jan paused.

"Yes?" Francine asked.

"You and I, uh, you and I are dining out."

"Why do I sense a secret?"

"Because there is one."

"And?"

"And, I'll tell you about it tomorrow."

"Why not now? I told you a secret!"

"Tomorrow." Jan was firm. Then, as an afterthought she said, "Oh, Francine?"

"Yes?"

"Let's go thrift shopping Wednesday. Why don't you see if you can find out the name of the seamstress?"

"We'll all find out in the newspaper tomorrow. But I'll find out where she works from Isabel," Francine added.

"Bingo."

Jan hung up the receiver and reached for her phone directory. She dialed Lucy's number, but got no answer.

"Good Lord," Jan muttered. "I'm fooling with ideas about charity dresses, and what I need most is an idea for a PowerPoint presentation." From her backpack for class on the floor near the refrigerator, she pulled the laptop Frank had purchased for her at the university bookstore and opened it on the kitchen table. Meanwhile, she pulled out a chair to sit while staring blankly at the blinking cursor. "Ideas, where are you?" she asked the screen.

There was a scratch at the back door. Jan recognized it as Lamont's signal. She got up to open the door, and in wandered the Bassett hound along with—surprise!—Lucy Layman.

"Hello," Jan said. "You're not due until Thursday."

"No, Ma'am. But I thought I'd better come today for a minute."

"C'mon in. Coffee?" Jan asked. "Actually, I just left a message for you." As she pulled out two coffee mugs from a cabinet, Jan posed the idea of the three women wearing used ball gowns.

"If the dress don't cost too much, sure, I'll do it." Lucy said.

"I knew you would," Jan smiled. "And Francine knows just where to find quality for cheap that will look great."

Lucy nodded her head. "Know about the great." Then she shook her curls, "Don't know about the cheap. She sure spent a fortune painting my house!"

"Well, she's learned her lesson. She meant well. Now . . ." Jan poured hot coffee from a carafe into the two mugs waiting on the table.

Lucy pulled out a chair and flopped her generously sized handbag beside it. She leaned over to rummage in its contents and removed a large manila envelope. Quietly, she laid it before Jan.

"What's this?"

"An idea for your computer project," Lucy said, blushing. "It ain't much."

Jan turned over the packet, shook it mischievously, winking at Lucy, and then she reached inside. She pulled out several four by six pictures of—what?

"Good Lord!" Jan exclaimed, "What are these? Piles of clothes strewn on the floor? A toilet bowl ring—gross! A shower black with mildew—Yuk! A kitchen splattered with spaghetti noodles and tomato sauce in the sink. And, aaaaagh! A coffee table with beer cans and cigarette butts inside a half-eaten bowl of popcorn? What in the world?" Jan wrinkled her nose and glanced at Lucy.

"My job," Lucy stared back evenly. "Them college kids. I clean a lot of their apartments. Last week, after your computer class, I figured I'd take some pictures before I done my work this week."

"Blackmail," Jan laughed.

"No, Ma'am." Lucy said. "Just an idea. A teachin' idea."

"I get it! I get it!" Jan slapped her palm on the table. "PowerPoint pictures we can scan. And then?" Jan brought her eyebrows together.

"Then you can write some words to teach 'em how to clean up their places."

"Hmmm." Jan frowned. "Sounds dangerous. If we insult those kids, they might strangle us with their computer cords. We need a face-saving gimmick."

"Like, 'How to clean fast'?" Lucy asked.

"Right. How to clean your place in—how long, Lucy?"

"I spend about two hours in a two-bedroom apartment. But I put through a load of wash or more—change sheets and towels."

"One hundred twenty minutes." Jan said, drumming her fingers.

"Yes," Lucy said, her chin jutting out. "I'm thorough."

"Well, let's figure two kids to a two bedroom."

"Two people could do it in an hour."

"You got it, Lucy. Here we go. Our PowerPoint presentation is, 'Clean Your Place in Sixty Minutes.'"

"Got to be systematic," Lucy said guardedly.

"Right on." Jan stood up and reached for a legal pad in her back-pack. "You dictate, Lucy. I'm taking notes. Step one?"

Lucy didn't blink. "Strip the bed sheets. Collect the dirty laundry from all over. Dump it on a sheet and tie the corners together. Drag it to the washing machine. Take your soap and quarters with you, if you need 'em. Separate white, light, and dark colors."

"Whoa! I'm writing as fast as I can!" Jan said.

Lucy took a sip of her coffee. Then she continued, "Load in the sheets first, 'cause they need to go back on the bed. Punch 'Start.' You got twenty minutes wash time and thirty minutes to dry."

"Next?"

"Pile your cleaning supplies in a bucket. Head for the bathroom."

"What kind of supplies?"

"Aw, surely them smart kids know that," Lucy frowned.

"Not a chance. What's in your bucket, Lucy? Clorox for mildew? Pine Soil to disinfect? Windex for mirrors?"

Lucy stared at Jan. "Looks like I gotta snap another picture, if you're serious 'bout the bucket," she said.

"Never been more serious in my life," Jan said. "This may be the most important computer lesson those college kids ever get!"

18. Frank Beats the Blues

rank felt one of those many small angers that multiply with age, and he was ashamed. He likened it to gnats hovering in his face. He was disgruntled. He knew he had no right to feel this way, his predicament was his fault, but he was annoyed anyway. For another night, he faced an open refrigerator with leftover choices of fried chicken, mashed potatoes, corn, macaroni and cheese, biscuits, and fried okra.

"Carbs and fats," Frank spoke out loud. "Alone. Jan's gone off with Francine. Where, she would not say. Women. Baffling creatures." Why wouldn't Jan tell him where she was going? Come to think of it, she had gone somewhere last Tuesday night, too. And she never said where.

"Hmmm," Frank frowned. "And she's left me to eat this junk again." Frank blew his nose. Tonight he had cut his architecture seminar short. He had a miserable cold and, he was convinced, a fever, too. Now he faced congealed grease. "Gross."

At the sound of his voice, Frank heard another noise, the click of toenails across the wooden kitchen floor. The hound, Lamont, ever on the lookout for a morsel, entered the room on the prowl. Frank glanced down.

"Of course, the stuff is good, Lamont, old boy," Frank

continued his soliloquy. "And I did tell Lucy last week to fix anything she wanted. But you'd think she would have listened to my
carb lecture. Potatoes, corn, macaroni, bread—why, I did, didn't
I?— explain very clearly that potatoes, pasta, and rice were off limits? I'm a professor, for God's sake. Didn't I make it clear?"

Lamont wagged his tail, looking at Frank with a mix-
ture of affection and anticipation. Frank felt a little ungrateful in
the atmosphere of hope set by the dog. He busily loaded most of
the leftovers into the microwave and hit the two-minute button.
"Well, she left off the rice, ole buddy," Frank said to Lamont.
"But she baked biscuits! And I love biscuits. Especially open-
faced and toasted. Come to think of it, we love biscuits, Lamont.
So how can we resist them?"

The canine's mouth hung open, his tongue rolling to
the side as he salivated.

"Yes, well, you're in luck. There are two biscuits, and
you get one of them, Lamont. Not that your waistline needs it.
Nor does mine. And, anyway, these are several days old." Frank
tossed Lamont a cold lump into his empty doggie bowl by the
back door. Next he removed the warmed leftovers and slid others into the microwave, punching the timing button once more.
"There is one bright spot, however, provided by the lovely Mrs.
Urbane," he said. *"Tiramisu . . . delivered to our door this afternoon . . . the most divine dessert Jupiter ever created for Roman
mortals, including me."* Frank smiled with satisfaction.

He hummed a tune. He stopped. What was it?
Oh yes . . . Pavarotti. Frank paused to think. *Yes, he could name
it.* Proudly, he announced to the genial lug at his feet: "*Nessun
D'Orma* from Puccini's opera *Turandot!* I heard it driving back
from the University!"

Lamont wagged his tail slowly.

Ah, the richness, the command, the range of the human

voice! Frank regaled in the magic of his own imagination. Then he sneezed again, retrieved a crumpled handkerchief from his pants pocket, and vigorously blew his nose.

"Where is that CD? Pavarotti?" Frank walked to his stereo/television configuration and cued up his selection. "Listen up, Lamont." He returned to the kitchen.

Frank was a man who loved opera. As a youth in the sixties, he had hitchhiked around Europe. When he arrived in Italy—Milan, specifically—he felt he had come home. Sometimes he convinced himself that his surname, Midland, was a corruption of Milano, or something close. It was common during waves of immigration from Europe for induction officials to misspell or intentionally change the names of newcomers to America, particularly those landing at Ellis Island as Frank's great-grandparents had done. The Midland name, he had always meant to research.

"Milando del Milano," he sniffed through a dripping nose.

He knew they came on a ship with a few beat-up trunks, almost no money, and they squatted together in New York with relatives, sharing the advent of new lives. Family stories suggested they had little, if anything, to eat. Later, a branch of the Midlands migrated south to Georgia, where Frank grew up.

As he reminisced, Frank set the leftover containers on the countertop.

"So, facing all this food, why am I complaining?" He reached into the cabinet for a plate. "I should be grateful, not complaining," he continued, looking down again at his dog. "I, am, perhaps, a descendant of the great, but unrecognized, courageous, but unremembered, Franco Milano—Hah! Alias Frank Midland! Italian! Why should I whine? I should be proud! And strong!"

"Right, Lamont?" The dog, unheeding, licked biscuit crumbs, his identification tag vigorously clanking against the side of his metal bowl.

"Right, Lamont?" Frank said again.

The canine turned and gave his owner a baleful look.

"Woof!"

"Ahchoo!" Frank sneezed. "Amen to that. Atta boy! Can't forget our tricks just because the twins have gone to college," Frank said. Then he frowned. *Anyone coming in and overhearing this conversation would probably lock me away in the nearest loony bin,* he thought. He turned his attention to the flatware drawer.

While he gathered the utensils, he glanced at the unread newspaper Jan had flung nearby against the back-splash before she left this morning. He started to pour himself a glass of sweet tea sitting in a pitcher nearby, but he hesitated.

Where is that open bottle of wine? He and Jan had not finished it last night, had they? Hmmmm. In the refrig? No! It was red, better at room temperature, and Frank—alias Franco— remembered that it was an Italian wine. "Aha! A nice Chianti!"

Briefly, he considered the effect of red wine on his overblown sinuses. But he squashed the thought with how much better he'd feel. Why, he couldn't feel any worse! He uncorked the bottle.

"We shall drink these grape carbs instead of sugary tea carbs, Lamont," Frank boasted, "in honor of my ancestors who had little to eat! We shall celebrate their lives by downing this food with

Italian wine, and we shall be grateful!" Frank poured the reddish-purple liquid into a large wine glass, lifted it to his nose, and inhaled.

"Aaaaaaah," he said, his spirits lifting already. He felt the Bassett nudge his leg. "Life is mostly attitude, Lamont. Remember that, old boy," he said, sipping. "And my attitude is beginning to improve . . ."

With that, Frank loaded his food to the kitchen table where he grabbed the newspaper, and sat down to read while he ate. The headline for the local story in the upper right two columns caught his eye.

"Clearview Chamber Honors Seamstress and Son," Frank read, as he looked closer. *The picture . . . yes that is the ample frame of Isabel Charmin. Who is that beside her? Hmmm.* Frank stared at a petite young woman—skin and bones next to Isabel.

"Of course," Frank mused, "most people would be petite next to Madame President." The woman who Frank took to be the seamstress had a gentle face, carrying a plain, understated beauty. Next to her a thin, pre-pubescent boy in a bulky chair sat with his hands mid air. His face had that "Oh!" expression as if caught unawares. But obviously, the boy knew his picture was being taken. Frank took a bite of toasted biscuit. He sipped his wine.

Something's not right with that boy, Frank thought. *What is it? He's seated with a tray wedged right to his chest. A highchair? A wheel chair with a tray? Oh, I see. His hands are splayed and his elbows are bent. That rigid chair must be holding him in place. I bet that boy has cerebral palsy.* Frank scanned the newsprint and confirmed the diagnosis.

As a spontaneous experiment, Frank held his wine glass beside his face, his graceful thin fingers on the stem. He could not help but notice how still, almost perfectly steady, he was able to hold the wine, the surface of which barely stirred.

What must it be like not to be able to control your hands?

"CP. Terrible disease," he spoke out loud. Frank leaned back to reflect on the photograph beside his dinner: *So, this is the family to benefit from the new Habitat House I've designed. Hmmmmmm.*

As the minutes ticked by, a transformation occurred in the Midland kitchen. Whether from sinuses lulled to sleep by wine, or from the rise in his blood sugar due to the same, or the felicitous taste of hot fried chicken, or the memory of noble ancestors either fictional or real, or perhaps the sudden realization that he was helping real people in a small but significant way . . . Whatever it was, Frank's previous disgruntlement, he discovered, not only had faded, it was gone.

While Frank ate dinner alone, several miles away, his wife, Jan sat with Francine Urbane at the Blackbird Café in downtown Clearview, over iced tea and a Cobb salad. The Blackbird was comfortable; it combined cozy dining with a welcoming bar; beer was brewed on the premises; crisp salads and chunky sandwiches were the main fare. In front of them, a bartender rinsed glasses, drying them and hanging them upside down in an overhead wooden rack.

"I enjoyed your decorating help today," Jan began. "The Italian hand-carved animals you brought over, and the plaid red and green ribbon you fashioned, why, those simple touches transformed our old dusty pinecone wreath into something special.

"And the jingle bells! I love bells on a door. So cheery!" Francine bubbled.

"Amazing what you can do with florist's wire, wooden spikes, and imagination," Jan smiled.

"Imagination is more important than knowledge." Francine brightened. "Einstein said that!"

"Smart guy," Jan said. "Imagination is the mother of discovery."

"Who said that?" Francine's eyebrows rose.

"Jan Midland," Jan laughed.

"You have a zany sense of humor," Francine shook her head.

A familiar musical trill erupted in the corner of the room, and both women turned reflexively toward a television set on the wall behind the bar. The women watched the animated lead-in for the local evening news.

"Isabel Charmin told me the Swap story would be on tonight," Francine said. She fingered the lemon slice perched on her iced tea glass and surprised Jan by biting into it.

"How can you stand that?" Jan asked. "Biting a lemon?"

"I'm tougher than I look," Francine twinkled. "Sometimes I eat them with salt."

Jan shuttered. "Getting to know you has been one discovery after another."

Francine cleaned out the pulp with her teeth and bent it backwards.

Jan watched and said, "So you think our news man Terry Turner will show all three of us? "

"Well, for a town the size of Clearview, a Christmas story about three women trading places is rich fodder." Francine dropped her lemon rind into her half-drunk tea.

"So, yes, I think he'll show us."

Jan pushed her fork around playing with the salad remains. Listening close, she noted, "Here comes the tease . . . " Sure enough, there was Lucy Layman baking cookies in Jan's kitchen. Terry Turner, dressed in a red Patagonia vest, stood camera front-and-center, holding a cookie in his hand. He began,

WHILE BAKING COOKIES IS A NORMAL HOLIDAY CUSTOM, LUCY LAYMAN IS COOKING UP NOT ONLY THIS

KIND OF DOUGH, BUT ANOTHER KIND, TOO. (Here, Terry swapped his cookie for a one-dollar bill, which he flashed in front of the camera.)

"How corny!" Jan snorted.

"Ssssh!" Francine said.

THIS YEAR, Terry continued, TO BENEFIT THE CHAMBER'S AWARD OF A HABITAT HOUSE, THREE LOCAL WOMEN ARE TRADING TALENTS BY SWAPPING PLACES . . . AND THEIR HUSBANDS ARE FORKING OVER THE DOUGH.

"This is terrible," Jan muttered.

"Look! There's Bill!" Francine squealed.

"Ssssh!" Jan retorted.

YES, Bill said in an interview, his handsome face ruddy against a backdrop of snow, WE CONCEIVED THE IDEA TO HELP WITH THE CHAMBER HOLIDAY AUCTION. OUR WIVES HAVE BEEN WONDERFUL SPORTS AND WE'RE . . .

"Wonderful sports!" Francine sniffed. "I'd say so!"

"Right on," Jan answered. "Look, Francine, see? There I am decorating the tree in your den. Oh, God, I have *got* to lose twenty pounds!" Jan moaned. Then she pointed, "And there you are, Francine. You look great, just directing those painters up a storm!"

"I'll say," Francine returned. "It definitely caused a storm."

"You ladies made the news," the bartender shined up a fluted glass with a clean white napkin.

"Such as it is," Jan said carelessly.

"She didn't like the way she looked," Francine offered.

"Camera adds ten pounds, so they say," He turned a glass upside down and threaded it along the overhead rack. "But I thought you both looked great."

"I knew there was something I liked about you," Jan smiled.

They turned back to see Terry Turner walking toward a stand of pine trees. He loved walking transitions; you could just tell.

YET, WHILE PEOPLE LIVE THEIR BUSY LIVES THIS
WINTER, MOTHER NATURE HAS INTRODUCED A SUR-
PRISE. WE HAVEN'T SEEN IT, BUT A LOT OF PEOPLE HAVE
. . . A WHITE FAWN . . . WE GO, NOW, TO, THIS WEEK ON
THE STREET.

Jan and Francine saw a sampling of man-on-the-street
interviews with Clearview residents. First, an unshaven farmer
pushed back his baseball cap and leaned toward the TV microphone at Turner. "I seen it. It's pure white."

Second, "I thought I shot it," offered a man in hunter's
fatigues. "But I missed." He wagged his head in front of Terry's mike.
"It's not good—albinos breeding. Affects the healthy population."

Last, a woman loading her toddler into the front of a
grocery cart, said, "I saw it driving past the Bennington Property.
So pretty, a white baby deer."

Jan nodded, remembering.

For a wrap, Terry pivoted closer to the camera. SO
THERE YOU HAVE IT, FOLKS. A LITTLE MAGIC IN
CLEARVIEW FOR CHRISTMAS. IF YOU SEE THE WHITE
FAWN, GIVE US A CALL. WE WANT TO SHOOT IT—Here
Terry gave his most engaging grin—BUT ONLY WITH A CAM-
ERA—FOR OUR CHANNEL 2 VIEWERS!

"What a clown." The bartender wagged his head.

"Ditto," Jan said.

"Small-town news," Francine agreed.

As Turner signed off his broadcast, the women paid
their bill and left the restaurant. Walking toward their cars,
Francine turned and said pointedly to Jan, "You *still* haven't told
me where we're going next."

19. Thrift Gowns

Lucy thought she'd died and gone to heaven. On the afternoon of December 8, while her companions browsed the rows of merchandise, she slid plastic hanger after plastic hanger along parallel dress racks. She couldn't believe her eyes: the most beautiful gowns for the cheapest prices she had ever seen. Who would have guessed what treasures lay in an old dry goods store on the central town mall? The hand-painted sign on the glass, a simple "Thrift Shop," had never beckoned Lucy before. She thought the store was for poor people. And she, Lucy, was too proud to consider herself poor. Why, she and Larry were hard-working up-and-comers. That's what Larry's mother, Ida Rose, always said. She put it this way:

"Just because them Union devils came through these parts during the Civil War and burned our homes and torched our fields, don't mean we got beat. Not our kind!" The old woman held strong feelings of regional pride. "Look around you!" she told Lucy's children. "You don't see no Laymans down on their heels standing on corners looking for handouts. No, Sir, we're good workers!"

And, Lucy mentally added, as she whisked through rack after rack, *good shoppers.*

Lucy was a connoisseur of T. J. Maxx, Wal-Mart, and K-mart—anywhere you could get a bargain. She had a laser eye for quality at bargain prices. She thought she'd seen everything Clearview had to offer in terms of discounts. But never before had she been to the Junior League Thrift Shop.

Tall shelves reached toward a hammered tin ceiling that soared two flights above. Tall wooden ladders hinged on railings provided access to sweaters, bathing suits, and other seasonal merchandise. The tall second-floor windows sent rafts of streaming sunshine onto the shoulders of dresses and suits and gowns, the kind of merchandise that Lucy had only glimpsed by window shopping or watching TV. As Lucy walked row after elegant row, the old wooden floors squeaked their own melody. Lucy felt that the antique boards were singing to her, revealing apparel secrets, step by step.

"Happy?" Jan laughed, watching Lucy whisk from one hanger to the next.

"Good merchandise," Francine smiled knowingly.

"Yes, Ma'am," Lucy said. Then she paused. "But, there is one problem."

"What?" The other women spoke in unison.

"The sizes. All these society women sure are small."

Jan twisted her ponytail with her fingers. Francine blinked her eyes. Both were silent.

Lucy began fingering the hangers again. Then she stopped.

"Why, aren't these two prom dresses the same?

"Oh, I bet those are Liz Marshall's girls' dresses. I know she just hated to give those away," Jan said. "But the twins have grown tall. Just look at that—strapless silhouette gowns with pink Chanel jackets to match. Gosh! I'd have been sick to part with them. Makes me wish I had twin girls as well as my twin boys. The gowns are just beautiful!"

126

"Pink is my favorite color," Lucy sighed wistfully. "But one of those dresses wouldn't half cover me. Really a shame."

"Lucy," Francine interjected. "Half cover you . . . well, that's an exaggeration . . . but you just gave me an idea. You think we could piece those dresses somehow?"

"Ma'am?" Lucy asked puzzled.

"Put them together."

Jan caught her drift. "Bingo, Francine," she said. "The designer seamstress!" Jan pulled out one gown on its hanger. Then she reached for the other one. "Buy them, Lucy! Buy them," Jan urged, holding up both flowing dresses like a flagman, squinting at the hanging price tags. "They are only fifteen dollars each!"

Lucy looked at the women curiously.

"You think a seamstress could really sew those two dresses into one to fit me?" She asked. Her almond eyes, flecked with gold, looked like a wondrous child's, her flaxen hair framed her face in tiny ringlets.

Jan pushed the dresses up against Lucy, nudging them close to her face. "The soft pink shade on you is exquisite, Lucy!"

"Larry always says, it's my best color," she blushed.

"Why, it's just perfect!" Francine nodded merrily.

"Clever girls, we three," Jan noted with a spontaneous little clap of her hands. Her ponytail bounced just like a cheerleader's.

"You know," Francine brightened. "I was just thinking that. Our ingenuity is turning our husbands' stupid Swap idea into fun. What a surprise!"

Lucy took the two pink gowns and hugged them against her chest. "One pretty dress from two," she said in her perky drawl. "Larry always says there's more than one way to skin a cat."

And then Lucy, bright with anticipation, spun on her heel, "Does this store sell things for men?"

20. Frank's Vision

Frank picked up the ringing phone in his kitchen with a brisk, "Midland," as a greeting. Then he leaned his head back and spoke a little more genially.

"Hello, Isabel. How are you? Fine." He paused a minute to listen.

"The blueprints? Well, it's a new version of the Habitat House. Generally they build the same one over and over. But I made some changes." He paused again. Isabel Charmin's voice in his ear matched her frame—throaty, hearty, and hefty.

"No, it won't be more expensive. Just distinctive," Frank reached for a pencil and pad on the kitchen counter. Unconsciously, he began his habit of doodling.

"The picture for the presentation? You mean the colored poster of my drawing? Yes. It will be ready. An easel? Sure. I have one of those. I can bring it. Sure, Isabel. A splendid occasion. We'll be ready."

He scratched down the word *easel* alongside his scribbling.

"One more thing? What's that Isabel? The land behind the Circle Market? You are kidding. That fast! No. Called Architectural Review meeting, yes. Called general public meeting, no. Hiram Venald insists? No! He can't insist! Wrong!

People won't come to a called zoning meeting the week of Christmas, and, as a result, the town won't be adequately represented. Postpone it!" Frank fidgeted more and wrote *eleven acres* on the same notepad with the word *easel*. He murmured and shook his head silently. "Hmmm. Don't think it's a good idea but, well, you're the boss. Bye, Isabel."

He sighed and placed the telephone receiver back on its cradle on the wall. "Obdurate. That's Isabel. Stubborn as they come. Her way or the highway." Frank talked to himself as he wandered around the kitchen. He opened the refrigerator. Cold salmon, pink, inert. It lay wrapped in a plastic sandwich bag in the transparent meat drawer. Very unappealing. But, well, it occurred to him that he could put it on a bed of lettuce. Use some Ranch dressing—although that added a bunch of calories. He began pulling out leftover lettuce, mushrooms, cilantro, and the salmon, wondering how his South Beach-style lunch would match his dinner that day. Dinner. Ah, Thursday night. The faculty club. His seminar tonight, the last before the exam next Tuesday, December 14. After tonight,

O Dread! Grading papers, final grades to be turned in.

Then, O Joy! A blissful two-week holiday break.

He scratched his curly grey hair. This morning Jan had rolled out of bed and claimed the first shower. She mumbled something about her PowerPoint class and putting pictures to computer text. He was rather amazed. Jan had begun to speak computer language. But on the other hand, she seemed gone all the time, meetings at night, and she was busier than ever.

From the wall, the startling peal of *pituk-ituk-pituk* ripped into his thoughts.

"Silly, stupid bird-chirping clock," Frank glanced at what he called, the twelve o'clock bird—the rosy-red Summer Tanager—just as its peal faded. Jan had found the clock in a rummage sale and put it on the wall last summer. Now, every hour, day and night, a different bird piped up with a recorded message—its own song. Frank had begun to tell time by birdcalls. Then he became obsessed and bought a book about birds, so he'd know something about who (meaning what species) was keeping track of his hours. Summer Tanager—*Piranga rubra*— the twelve o'clock bird. Frank shook his head. Sometimes, he thought he really was going nuts.

It wasn't just the clock that irritated him these days. His wife did, too.

Because of Jan-speak, he had learned still another way to tell time, even beyond the birds. "Afternoon" meant anytime up until evening. "Evening" began at twilight. "Night" began when the sky turned to "pitch."

"So how about sundown?" Frank had asked one late summer evening six months before, as he and Jan were grilling tuna steaks outside on the front porch landing.

"Sundown is a whole 'nother dimension." As she spoke, Jan crossed a pair of long, tanned legs leading high up to a pair of shorts. She twirled a glass of golden chardonnay in her fingers, lifting it into the light of the sun, which was melting like lemon ice cream behind the Blue Mountains beyond. "The moment a girl becomes a woman."

"So, 'sundown' means 'teenager'?" Frank came back.

"Sundown," Jan corrected, rolling her eyes up and down his tall frame in a wash of mysterious allure, "means 'day's end.'" She swept her rich brown ponytail lightly across her shoulders, bare around the seams of her narrow-strapped T-neck, and she smiled. She tilted the last sip of golden wine to her mouth and the glass coruscated in the gasping flashes of the fading sun.

"Mama Mia!" Frank had said, picking up the tuna with

a metal spatula to see if the fish was ready to flip. "You marry a woman midlife and you have to learn a whole new language!"

Jan had laughed. But Frank had not. He merely leaned over the smoking grill and deftly turned the tuna one more time to perfect those little charcoal-black cross hatches on the fish that lets you know a chef has paid attention. He had reflected then on what had occurred to him many times over the past decade. *You marry a woman with kids and it's you—You!* Frank said to himself—*who changes the most. You! Have to change shape just to fit into a ready-made family. A tribe.*

So true. For years, until his early forties, Frank had been a reasonably contented bachelor. As a professor, his students looked up to him, his colleagues called him "Dr Midland"—doctor of philosophy, that is—a hard-won title of respect. He dated fellow professors, no one terribly appealing. Students, according to university policy, were off limits, although surreptitiously he did take a Ph.D. candidate out to dinner occasionally. Frank was known for his dignity and intelligence. Frequently he was quoted in articles about historic structures featured in *Architectural Digest*. All in all, life was not bad.

Then one summer evening (that is, after twilight, and maybe after sundown as well), he backed into Jan, literally, in the local Barnes & Noble bookstore. She had crouched over, looking for a book about Jefferson-inspired homes in Virginia and he had bent low in the opposite direction, when he noticed a title on a lower shelf written by a former colleague of his at Princeton. They both backed up to read the titled spines, and their backsides collided. How embarrassing! They had risen up, turned to apologize, and then she blurted out, "Haven't I seen your picture?"

He shook his head, confused.

"Yes! Just now. In this book!" She reached up and pulled

from a shelf the coffee table collection of designs he'd compiled of eighteenth-century homes. She turned it over and pointed to his picture. Frank stood before Thomas Jefferson's magnificent central campus building, the Rotunda. He looked like the confident professor he was—his left hand holding a tweed jacket slung over his shoulder, his right hand clasping some rolled blueprints. His expression was a mix of debonair erudition and casual warmth. Frank had always thought it was his best photograph ever.

"You're an architect!" Jan had accused, thumping his picture on the back of the book, as if he were the most brilliant man she had ever met.

"Yes," he said slowly.

"So what's the best book on Jeffersonian architecture?" she asked breathlessly.

"I'll have to think," he said. And he gazed at the row of titles, beginning to enumerate the merits of one over another. This pert woman, about five-foot seven, slender, obviously athletic, and also obviously quick-witted, engaged him with her fuselage of questions. He had a thing for bright women.

After a few minutes and with a couple of books under her arm, Jan had suggested they get some coffee. "And let's split a warm chocolate chunk cookie in the bookstore café, shall we? So-o-o-o good!"

And Frank answered, "Good idea," and that good idea had led to his present situation as a university professor with an adopted family including a wife, two male children—twins—and another male—a dog named Lamont. Frank didn't know to this day why he'd married her. It's just, well, she was pretty, she was alone, she had a formidable backhand on the tennis court, she had a vibrancy about everything, she loved books, particularly ones on architecture, and she had the utmost admiration for . . . well . . . for him!

Recently though, that admiration seemed to have dwindled. Frank could pinpoint the change to the time the twins had left to begin their four years at Virginia Tech. Jan had become aimless and, worse, peevish. She had been a grammar school teacher when they had met. But five years into the marriage, she wanted to quit teaching to try her hand at a florist's shop. Frank had said, "Good idea." And it had been—for a while. But after about two years, Jan became disenchanted. "The results," she said, "don't last—well, except in snapshots—weddings, birthdays." A day or two after she created the beautiful arrangements, she whined, the brilliant blooms faded, the petals dropped off, the leaves shriveled, and the masterpiece stiffened as brown desiccated stems. "Their destiny? The trash heap," as Jan ruefully phrased it.

After the florist venture, Jan said she wanted to be a full-time soccer mom. After all, she reasoned to Frank, she had just a few years before the twins would leave home. She wanted to be there with orange slices and Gatorade in a stack chair on the sidelines, rooting for the twins, or traveling on the yellow school buses to away games.

Frank said, "Good idea," and it had been a good idea—despite the loss in income. But it was only good until the twins left the soccer fields and headed off to college. Then, everything soured. Jan's vibrancy vanished. And her respect for Frank morphed into irritation. She began to nibble Oreo cookies, among other things, and gained weight. Tennis made her breathless. She grew not only peevish, but also depressed.

This December, to tell the truth, Frank ultimately had faked enthusiasm for the Christmas theme idea and all those blasted red balls at first (after that fateful Sunday morning), just because Jan seemed finally excited about something. He loved seeing that glint in her lovely green eyes, like sunlight dancing in the sea.

But there had been that quarrel over the television, which was, Frank realized, symptomatic of deeper issues. And afterward, the three men, he and Bill and Larry, had gathered at the Circle Market and come up (implausibly) with the Christmas Swap. Hah! What an idea. Basically, it sprang from revenge. All three of them were chafing under the domestic whip that day. Dumb jocks, all of them. What a stupid, dumb, ridiculous idea!

Frank grunted in self-disgust as he leaned into the refrigerator to rifle the contents of the cold storage drawer. He pulled out some packaged lettuce and placed it on a plate, his thoughts tumbling out in a jumble like the greens.

He heard a familiar click, click, click, click. Four paws for a total of sixteen toenails rasping across the hardwood kitchen floor.

"Hello, Lamont," Frank spoke companionably to the Bassett. "How about some salmon, ole boy? I know you like the skin best." Frank looked down and Lamont gazed soulfully at him with his droopy brown eyes, his low-slung black, white and tan body only centimeters above the floor, his long tail wagging.

"Where's the Ranch dressing?" Frank asked Lamont, who came closer to inspect the inside of the refrigerator as he opened it once more. "You like that stuff, don't you boy? I'll give you some. We've got to watch it though. This dressing and our evening wine are expanding both our midsections. Right, Lamont?" He laughed as the dog barked. Then he slumped heavily under the antique harvest table.

"Cheer up, fellow. You know the twins are coming home soon from Virginia Tech?" The Bassett rolled up a pair of bloodshot eyes. "Yes, indeed." Frank nodded. He had received two e-mails during the week, one from each boy. Both began with "Frank—"

They never called him Dad, but Frank didn't mind. He

had never pretended to take their father's place. Of course, that would not have been hard to do; the man had left a note fifteen years ago—"I'm gone"—and vanished.

"Nobody knows where he is. Never could keep a job. Always running from creditors," was the truculent way Jan summed him up. Frank had wondered what kind of man would leave his family, the same family he had felt privileged to adopt. "Even despite their warts, even yours, Lamont," he said. Frank sat down at the head of the table to eat his lunch; the pup nestled at his feet. Frank squinted, trying to remember precisely the electronic message from each twin.

Ryan had written, "Frank— you'd love living here. The whole town is wired. Fiber optics everywhere."

Kyle, his younger brother by seven delivery-table minutes, had scratched off, "The VT girls R hotter than the U."

Cocky guy, Frank thought. Kyle used to drool at the beautiful girls at UVA when he ate with Frank in the small faculty lunchroom on the University Lawn. Now that same boy claimed he'd met the "hottest blonde" at a cyber-café in Blacksburg.

Frank was summoned back to the present by the chirping of the one-o'clock bird—the Brown Streaked Song Sparrow— *Melospiza melodia,* he recalled from his prior obsessive research. He listened a moment after and heard Lamont's gravelly snores from under the table.

Finishing up his solitary lunch, he felt, what? Melancholy? Hmmm. More precisely, lonely, yes, lonely, even with the Bassett asleep at his feet. Frank sipped a bottle of spring water and settled in his ladder-back chair. He had a stack of student projects to grade; they waited in his home office on his desk. He had a guest lecture to write, but that wasn't due for two weeks. So he sat and stared absentmindedly at his surroundings. On either side of the solid oak table that had welcomed the boys' friends over the years, plank benches stretched like church pews. Frank cocked his head and gazed at them, considering—a new angle, a new what? It was then that his gaze migrated to the television set in its ugly, cheap rolling stand across the room. Suddenly, his mind wanderings coalesced like loose hemp coming together as rope. A vision!

"Aha! Aha!" the architectural professor roared, and the startled Bassett hound scrambled up. Frank jumped from his chair. He strode to the television. The dog followed.

"Ah hah!" Frank shouted again. "Lamont! Jan will be amazed! I have found it! I have found it! The fifth corner to our cottage living room!"

21. Anniversaries

"You know what tomorrow is?" Bill Urbane asked his wife as she walked in the front door. She put her car keys down on the little antique table in the slate hallway and turned to look toward the welcoming kitchen of whitewashed cabinets.

"Yes," she replied. "It's Friday, the day I get my hair done."

"Humph," Bill said. He leaned against the kitchen sink and folded his arms. He watched his wife as she unwound her scarf and took off her black suede coat, draping them on the mirrored antique hall tree near the front door. In a couple of strides she was beside him. She pressed her cheek next to his and made one of those kissing sounds women make in the ear.

"Cold cheek," he said.

"Warm heart," she smiled and put her finger on his chin. Then she turned and walked over to inspect an oblong dish on the central marble preparation counter. The dish was covered with Saran wrap, a casserole Jan Midland had prepared for the couple's dinner the week before. Francine had frozen it until that morning, when, before leaving the house, she had put it on the counter to thaw. Now she picked up a corner of the transparent wrap covering a Pyrex dish, and she daintily sniffed the fragrance. "Hmmm. Sherry," she smiled. She noticed that Jan had sprinkled the creamy noodle dish with a little paprika and a light dusting of parsley. "Red paprika and green parsley— Christmas colors. I bet this is perfectly delicious." She turned to her cabinet of silver hollowware.

Bill cleared his throat as if to remind Francine of his presence. "The date, tomorrow?" He leaned into the liquor cabinet. It was six o'clock. Time for a cocktail.

"Tomorrow? What is tomorrow?" Francine pulled out a silver chafing dish to cradle the casserole once it warmed in the oven. She placed it next to the chafing dish, noting with satisfaction the sheen of the scrollwork.

"December 11. My mother's birthday," Bill said.

Francine stood quietly for a moment. *Of course,* she thought. *Of course, I know what day tomorrow is. Ellen Urbane's birthday. Ten days before the Solstice.* She closed her eyes momentarily then straightened up, her glance moving to the centerpiece she had created for the counter. There, for Christmas, Francine had placed a family heirloom from Ellen Urbane, the gold and white Royal Derby soup tureen. Francine never hesitated to appreciate its classic, ornate square shape, unusual and lovely. She had filled it this year with remarkably full, pink poinsettias.

Now, she looked at her arrangement and sighed. "Darling, I know."

From the liquor cabinet Bill walked to the glass cabinet that held their wine glasses and crystal goblets.

Francine silently eyed her husband as he reached inside for a glass. Then she picked up her potholders and placed Jan's casserole dish in the oven.

"Well, how can we *not* carry those anniversaries in our hearts? Loving is what makes us human," she offered. To Bill the remark sounded hollow, her conviction laden with sadness.

"I don't know about that," Bill replied, a hint of sadness in his own voice. "Not only humans are loving. Dogs are loving. The King Charles spaniels love us. You suppose they'd miss us after we're gone?"

Francine shivered even though the kitchen was warm. She knew they were treading on dangerous ground. Bill, overall, was a fairly even-tempered man. But during the winter months she had her own leaden memories to deal with, so when Bill showed symptoms of The Grouch, as she called the impending mood, there was the real possibility that he was falling into despondency, and she might not be able to pull him out. She tried a tactic that often worked with Bill, and sometimes even herself, when she felt despair descending: She changed the subject of conversation.

"Well, I don't know, Honey. But I miss their bright puppy faces right now!" She said with forced gaiety. "And it's cold outside. I saw them a little while ago when I drove up. Why don't you let them in? I love it when they curl under our feet at dinner."

"All right." Bill stared vacantly at the glasses in the cabinet. "I'll do that in a minute."

"I've simmered some fresh green beans in the crock pot," Francine chattered, moving from one counter to the next. "All we need is a tossed salad." She turned toward the refrigerator. She reached inside for some carrots and a selection of lettuce varieties. Then she fingered a couple of winter red tomatoes stacked with white onions in a hand painted Lenox bowl not far from the poinsettias on the center counter. Beside the china bowl of tomatoes, several twenty dollar bills covered with a silver tablespoon lay neatly stacked on the counter.

"Goodness! What is all this money sitting here?" she exclaimed.

"Change," Bill replied. "Something I haven't seen in a long time." He turned and raised a grey eyebrow knowingly at Francine. "It came in a Christmas card from Jan Midland." Bill stepped back to his liquor cabinet and poured three fingers of deep amber Woodford Reserve whiskey into a crystal old-fashioned glass.

"Well, well, well. You'll probably see even more change tomorrow," Francine observed with a tinge of frost. "Lucy Layman's your next swap. And I happen to know she's very, very frugal."

"'Cause she has to be." Bill lined up a second glass and began to fill it.

"Exactly," Francine said. "And she's got not only the two children to care for, but Larry's mother as well. Poor thing. I don't know how she does it."

"Well, you've certainly helped her out by painting her home place all crisp, white, and new," Bill grunted. "But of course, her husband, Larry, is in knots, worrying about the cost. I've got to deal with that."

"Sorry, Honey. But I misunderstood. You know how I am with projects: I take charge."

"Taking charge is *not* the idea—changing places is. Like I have told you, Francine. Sharing perspective, understanding—that was the original concept. Now, it has grown, turned into a community Christmas benefit, which may—incidentally—just be a very darn good idea."

"Well, well, well!" Francine returned, cold as an icicle.

Her mood shifted abruptly, catching Bill off guard. He watched her ferociously tear into the salad making, whirling the salad spinner, ripping at iceberg, green leaf, Boston, and romaine leaves, as she carelessly tossed them into a crystal bowl. She kept talking.

"Christmas benefit aside, I'm beginning to be a *l-i-t-t-l-e b-i-t* tired of feeling like the Wicked Witch of the West, just because I've tried to help the Layman family. This Swap wasn't my idea. But I believe I have been a good sport." Francine sniffed a little as a tear rolled down her cheek.

"Oh, Franny, don't cry." Bill unaccountably wondered if she was still in menopause. Surely not. But, well, she hadn't cried so often in many years, since well, five years ago, three years after his mother died. But that was understandable. Bill brushed the more recent memory from his mind and reeled time back further . . . back . . . back . . . when he first beheld the creamy-skinned, dark-haired beauty with the brilliant sapphire-blue eyes. Of course he fell for her at first sight. She was twenty then, and they met as undergraduates, when she was at Mary Washington near Fredericksburg and he was a fourth-year at the University of Virginia, in Charlottesville. She walked into Bill's fraternity house on the UVA Grounds during a mixer. She was so thin; he thought she had floated on the breeze through the door. She radiated such translucent beauty, he gasped out loud, to the amusement of his fraternity brothers who had anticipated the reaction and positioned Bill to be first greeter at the house door.

Years later, Wilburn Urbane had yet to catch his breath. The first impression had lasted for more than three decades. He remembered how she used to cry every time he put her on the train to travel back to her campus. But then, his mother had been one to cry easily, too. Sensitive. Yes, endearingly, Franny had his mother's sensitivity. So, Bill knew at this moment in the kitchen, he had stepped over the line. But he needed a short buffering moment before he could apologize. So he took a sip of his drink and walked to the back door. The King Charles spaniels, one with a brown head and brown spots on his long furry back, another with black markings, came bounding in, sashaying their long tails into the kitchen.

"It is hard to be sad with happy puppies in the kitchen." Bill leaned down and petted them quietly. He noticed how they quickly scuttled toward Francine and clustered expectantly around her feet.

"They love you," Bill said genuinely. He walked over and put his arms around his wife and kissed her milky white forehead. "And so do I."

Francine put her dark hair against Bill's shoulder. "I'm trying, Bill. I know I'm fortunate that you're such a good businessman. And I am s-o-o-o-o glad you are." She wiped the tear off her cheek. Then sniffing, she reached for some buttermilk in the refrigerator and began to whip up a homemade salad dressing.

"Whew," Bill said under his breath. But then,

"Bill?" Francine raised those lovely eyes toward him as she worked.

"Yes?"

"You can be sure it had occurred to me earlier today, what Friday is."

Bill nodded silently. He kept nodding slowly and turned. He walked from the kitchen into the hallway, his footsteps measuring with his long stride the close-knit stitches of the Oriental runner, predominantly red and gold and blue. He passed through the doorway to his richly paneled drawing room, generously sized, lavishly furnished, the two-story Christmas tree towering before tall windows. He settled down in his favorite wing chair before the marble fireplace. The dogs followed and flopped at his house shoes, a comfortable pair of shearing-lined suede moccasins. He stared at the dancing flames within the hearth, listening to its rhythmic crackle, thinking of Larry Layman and his hesitant words to him about Francine earlier.

"Mrs. Urbane meant well," Larry had said. "But ain't no way in hell I can pay for what she done to my house."

"Well, Larry, I've been thinking about the matter. And I have a suggestion. Let's meet at my farm tomorrow, after the women get busy on their days," Bill said. "You bring Lucy over here for her Swap day at our house, and you and I will go outside and talk over the idea I'm considering. Would that suit you?"

"Yes, Sir," Larry said. "But I've got to pick up boards at the ByWay after I drop off Lucy at your place. Can we meet around one? I'll come back by."

"Sure," Bill said. "I'll be here."

"Thanks, Mr. Urbane."

"Bill," he had corrected. "Call me Bill."

"Yes, Bill," Larry replied. "Sir."

Bill listlessly stared at the fireplace. He smelled the promising aroma of nutmeg and Sherry, the turkey tetrazinni bubbling invitingly. He could hear Franny moving back and forth, setting the dining room table, the silver clinking as she counted out two knives, two forks, two spoons. The linen drawers slid open and snapped shut as she pulled heirloom crocheted placemats and white, crisply-pressed linen napkins. Next weekend, Franny would set the table for three, Bill thought, their tradition with Anna, home from Smith for the holidays. But, never, never again would Francine set it for their original family of four.

Bill rubbed his leonine forehead wearily. He sighed. He sipped his expensive whiskey, inhaled the opulent atmospheres around him, and looked down at the elegant sleeping dogs at his warm feet. He shook his head sadly.

"Even with it all," he told the snoozing spaniels, "life's not fair."

22. Coffee and Whiskey

Dawn crept in on frozen fingers, lacing the windows of the Urbane home with flakes of snow. The tranquility of the landscape outside was no match for the frenetic atmosphere inside. Francine was in a dither. She had scheduled a Friday morning hair appointment, but after an early peek through the lacy curtains of her bedroom window, she had bolted from bed and urgently dialed the number to the beauty salon. As she had feared—she got a recording.

"Gosh! Just the machine. It's telling me the shop hours," Francine wailed.

"It's only eight o'clock," Bill said grumpily as he contemplated easing himself down the winding staircase from the master bedroom. He tied the sash of a silk bathrobe around his waist, which was still fairly narrow for a man in his sixties and still in proportion to his six-foot-four frame. But this morning he didn't feel slim, and he didn't feel tall. He felt like a hunchback, all slumped over. He had definitely overdone it last night with the Woodford, and he had a colossal headache.

"Drink some coffee," Francine said, dressed already and skirting down the steps. She kept talking over her shoulder to her husband all the way to the kitchen. "Honey, I'm not worried about getting to the beauty parlor. My Mercedes can go any-where! But how about Myrtle! She drives in from Blackstone County, over those hills. I'm sure she doesn't have four-wheel on that wreck of a car she drives. Oh, and I just have to get my hair done today! The grey is beginning to show. So tacky. And I can't stand the length. It's dragging on my collar!"

Bill gingerly followed Francine down the steps. When she paused her chattering, he said, "Wait till eight thirty. Then call back." At the foot of the steps he turned into the first floor powder room to search the medicine cabinet there for some aspirin. He shook three white tablets into the palm of his hand and leaned back, throwing them down his throat. Then he moved toward the kitchen.

"I thought of that," Francine said. "But I think I'm going to leave now. I don't care if I have to drive all the way to Blackstone County for Myrtle to do my hair! Oh, I never should have waited this long. Too busy. Just too busy."

"Don't you owe the Midlands a dinner as part of the Swap?" Bill asked, remembering the delicious tetrazinni from the night before.

Francine's reply came quickly. "Oh, swipe, sweep, swap! I'm tired of the whole silly idea. As if I don't have enough to do at Christmas!"

"You promised."

"And I keep promises. I took care of that detail." Francine waved her hand at Bill, and then she reached for a scarf to cover her head. "I think Jan's supposed to go to Larry and Lucy's house today." Francine began fumbling with the ends of the black scarf, tying it under her soft chin.

"Yep," Bill said, pouring dark rich coffee into a mug from the heated carafe.

Francine rattled on as she darted about preparing to

leave. "Jan did do a nice job on that tree in the den. Royal blue decorations. Silver bows. Cute. Of course, it's not my style, a little too country for me. But Jan likes that look; you know she's very knowledgeable about antiques."

"Mmmm," Bill said, rubbing his brow.

"She collects American primitives."

"Primitives," Bill scowled. "Circa 2002. I bet they're all made in West Virginia, distressed with authentic dents and scrapes by ex-coal miners wielding clubs and chains."

"Oh, Bill, you are such a skeptic sometimes."

"I'm a businessman. I can sense a potential market like our spaniels sense a squirrel."

"Well—glad you mentioned that—feed the pups their breakfast, will you? I'm in a rush." Bill shuffled in his house shoes over to get a glass of water. He could hear Francine's low-heeled pumps clattering from the Italian-tiled entrance hall to the mirrored coat tree, across the polished oak floors of the kitchen, then squishing on the dining room Aubusson rug and back again to clatter across the tiles. She was mumbling phrases, "Scarf, gloves, keys, purse, umbrella." He heard the front door open.

"I'm gone!" Francine called. The front door slammed.

Bill was alone with his headache in the quiet, looking very much forward to some relief from the aspirin. *How long does it take? Thirty minutes to get to your bloodstream?* He couldn't remember. *Seemed like about that long.* He wandered haphazardly around the central kitchen counter and moved toward the living room where the previous night's fire smoldered. He grabbed a split log from the brass stand of wood on the marble hearth and tossed it on the coals in the grate, a spray of sparks greeting the new piece of wood as if welcoming a latecomer to a party.

So pleasant, Bill said to himself. *But I can't linger. What was the task of the day? Oh, yes, gravel for those low places in the*

main driveway. But that won't happen in the snow. But, there was
something else—yes, Larry Layman said he would come this after-
noon. And his wife's coming here this morning, I guess, if she can get
here. He sighed, his temples throbbing, *God, when will those*
aspirins take effect?

Bill noticed his mother's red blanket wrapped around
and under the regal living room tree. Red, blue, green, and gold
packages fringed its circular edge. Unaccountably he shivered. It
had been an icy day eight years before when they had buried his
mother within days of her final birthday. In a bone-chilling
wind, the mahogany casket swayed slightly on the steel supports
above a frozen square hole below. Although the gaping hole had
been discreetly draped with green astro-turf, the disguise was no
comfort to the disconsolate only son of Ellen Urbane.

Above the soft-spoken murmurings of the Episcopal
priest, Bill's grim thoughts rattled loudly: *My mother is in that
box. Soon to be dropped forever alone, underground.* He shivered
again as across time his panoptic memory traveled to the funeral
scene. He had taken it all in—the blanket of red roses, the
bowed respectful heads of loyal friends, the pall bearers with
their gloved hands folded, the studied solemnity of the funeral
director, the shiny brass handles on the mahogany coffin. Bill
bowed his head, his eyes clinched. *Niceties aside,* he thought,
death is still death.

As the priest said, "Amen," Bill had raised his eyes
toward his father. It was the only time ever in his life he had
seen his father weep. Bill suddenly realized how old and beaten
his father looked. All the money in the world had not protected
him from losing—too young at any age—the woman he adored.
To cancer. Insidious, disgusting cancer.

After that day, Bill's father lasted barely twelve months.
He died of a stroke and they buried him also in December, as

they had Bill's mother. Then, worst of all, three years later on the shortest, darkest day of the year, Bill and Francine's own s— . . . But here, Bill's thoughts veered protectively off course. His generous heart rebelled against an unjustifiable loss whose pain never lessened.

Until the last decade, Bill had enjoyed the festivity of Christmas, particularly the music, of course, but also the food and the decorations. Now, artificial gaiety left him cold. And, while the holidays brought his much-loved daughter, Anna, home from school, the month of December also ushered in anniversaries of ineffable sadness.

After the accident five years before, Bill and Francine had agreed—at Bill's insistence—not to speak the boy's name. He lived only in memories, in pictures, and in newspaper clippings in a bureau drawer. He had died December 21. And now, every year, Bill was glad to see the date go by, the winter Solstice, swiping the calendar like a shadow, ushering in the celestial edict that sunny days would lengthen, that dark winter nights would wane, that the anniversary days of death were past.

Not too many days until the Solstice. Bill automatically glanced at the mantel clock, as it chimed nine strokes. He looked at the stoic little clock face for a second, and then his gaze traveled around the warm paneled room. His eye fell on a familiar patch of red underneath the magnificent tree that Francine had asked the decorator to create. He put his coffee mug on the side table, got up, and walked over to the tree. Since his mother's death, Francine thoughtfully wrapped the red blanket—soft cashmere, his mother's favorite—as a tree skirt. He leaned down and eased the blanket from underneath the tree, leaving the colorful packages in a circle. He wrapped the comforting red warmth around his shoulders and walked back to sit by the fire. The Woodford Reserve still stood on the stand next to his chair where he had left it the night before. The bottle was half full.

"I wonder how that whiskey would taste in my coffee?" Bill thought. In college, he remembered, that's the way he and his friends used to get past a hangover. They just started drinking again.

"God, I wish I were young again," Bill said out loud. "And I wish my mother and father and —and—" he paused to let silence finish his sentence. He pulled the blanket close around his waist in the wing chair. He put his slippered feet up on the needlepoint ottoman. He watched the refreshed fire dance in the hearth, he stared at the snow-specked window-panes, and he drank.

23. Snowfall

"Well, darn!" Francine said as she pulled past the parking spaces before the Uptown Hair Boutique on First Street. There, a "Closed" sign hung on the shop door behind the gauzy-curtained glass. Francine was not surprised. After all, she had just traversed the highway, powder covering ice, which led to this urban wilderness. Only the Circle Market seemed moderately normal with a few hearty souls in snow boots pumping gas and stomping in and out the glassed front door.

Driving down Main Street, Francine had seen very few car tracks in the snow, but she did notice pristine streets with glistening storefronts and signs with icicles hanging in pointed frozen drips. Street lanterns curled forward, festooned with green wreaths and red ribbons. She couldn't help but conclude that Mother Nature's pixilated moods would not delay Christmas.

"Only my hair appointment!"

She saw people attempting to get to work, but mostly in vain. Cars stalled here and there, tilting and twisting like dinghies on a stilled white sea. Some of them lay askew in the drainage ditches. A few drivers had bailed out of them. Francine slowed to pick up some pedestrians, but they waved her on.

Many grinned as if enjoying the challenge of hiking in drifts, while simultaneously reporting their fates to friends by cell phone. She must have seen twenty people with their heads bent over their ears, summoning help from home, or she supposed, gleefully calling in late to work.

Francine reached into her purse and pulled out her own small flip phone. She kept her eye on the road, slowed to ten miles per hour, and scrolled down to "Beauty." Yes, the shop number came up, but—clever Francine—she had also programmed Myrtle's home number. There it was. Francine pressed the "Call" button.

"Yes'm," Myrtle said. "No, Mrs. Urbane, I can't get to you. Can't get to the shop. But if you can get to me, I can cut you and do your color and wash and set. But I can't get out of the park."

"The park?" Francine asked.

"Yes'm, the trailer park's perched up on a hill at the intersection of Highway 14 and Route 34. We've got a foot of snow."

"Well, darn, darn!" Francine said, exasperated. "Okay, I'll make my way slowly. Every minute of every day until Christmas Day is programmed into my schedule, including my appointment with you before the Chamber Ball."

"Yes'm. I understand," Myrtle said. "It's a busy time of year."

"But with these grey roots showing, I can't wait another week."

"Like I said, Mrs. Urbane, if you can get to me—"

"Give me the directions to your trailer, please Myrtle." Francine interrupted. "Real good directions. Otherwise I'll get just perfectly lost."

On her way up Highway 14, Francine called Jan.

"I'm driving to Myrtle's place in the hills. Her shop in town is closed," she said.

"Did you ever find out where that seamstress lives?" Jan sat at her kitchen counter on her grandmother's stool, making a "To Do" list. She twisted a strand of her long brown hair, privately suspecting that Francine had not given a thought to the seamstress since their Thrift Shop expedition on Wednesday. Sure enough, Francine paused and mumbled vaguely into Jan's ear, "The seamstress. Oh, for heaven's sake. It just slipped my mind. And now, with all this snow . . ." Francine's voice trailed.

"Did you call? Jan asked.

"I didn't call Isabel at the Chamber," Francine interrupted. "Today, she's not there. The town's virtually empty. We got about a foot of snow and ice, you know."

"I know. And more expected next week. Makes me worry about my twins driving home from school. 'Course the Toyota 4Runner has four-wheel drive."

Francine shut her eyes tight and leaned into the cell phone. "Are you there?"

"Yes, Jan."

"You have the dresses? Remember, Lucy and I put all three—er—four—in your trunk."

"Goodness! Where has my mind gone? Yes! They are still in my trunk."

"You'd better hurry. The Ball is less than two weeks away."

Francine did not like being second-guessed. "I know, and I'll handle it," she said more crisply than she intended.

"Did Lucy make it to your house?" Jan asked.

"I don't know."

"Well, Larry has a truck. He might bring her."

"Bill's there."

"You should watch out for Lucy's fried chicken if you value your trim waistline. She'll likely prepare it for you tonight. Four hundred calories a bite."

Francine dodged. "I'll eat her turnip greens. She makes wonderful greens."

"With fatback," Jan said. "That's what makes them wonderful. Calories, calories."

"Yeah, anything good costs calories," Francine agreed. "But anyway, I'm off to get gorgeous. I'll get back to you later."

"Monday I go to the Laymans'. With Larry's mother and the two kids, I guess I'll have my hands full."

"Oh, she's a cute little old lady. Ida Rose, don't you just love it? So Southern."

"Well, that Southern stuff we have in common."

"Don't spend more money than what is left on the kitchen table," Francine cautioned.

"Right, Mrs. Urbane," Jan said. "We know how much trouble you caused by spending a fortune!"

"Larry's wounded pride," Francine quipped. "I got carried away seeing things that needed doing. But Bill's onto that ticklish situation. He's good in a crisis. Now that I think about it, he's meeting with Larry today. Bill will smooth things out."

"Well, good. If anyone can smooth things out, it is Bill Urbane." Jan signed off.

24. Lucy Cleans House

Lucy Layman tugged a wool cap over her yellow curls. She gave her husband, Larry, a parting smooch on his unshaven cheek as the windshield wipers swished light snow back and forth across the front glass of his idling truck. Then she hopped from the four-wheel-drive pickup.

As Larry pulled away, she stepped gingerly across the snowy, pebbled driveway, noticing small footprints heading in the opposite direction. *Someone's out early*, she thought. She picked her path trying to reach the frozen flagstones that led to the heavy carved front door of the Urbane farm home. She knocked, then she squeezed the heavy door latch and let herself in.

She and Mrs. Urbane had formulated an altered plan for the Swap, which Francine had conveyed by phone. Francine had suggested that Lucy clean her home for one day and get paid for it, thus salving Larry's wounded pride. Then Francine had made a second suggestion.

"In the spirit of changing places, Lucy, I'd like for you to have a 'girl's day out' and pamper yourself, the way I occasionally do," Francine said. I want you to be my guest at the Clearview Country Club Spa, and do whatever you like—exercise with a trainer, have lunch, a massage, a salt rub, a soaking bath, a manicure, a pedicure, whatever."

Lucy gasped.

"Yes, and also Lucy, I have authorized a two hundred dollar gift purchase—your choice—from the spa."

"Oh, I couldn't," Lucy began.

"Oh, you could and you can!" Francine exulted. "Lucy, please do it! I know how hard you work. And you know the saying, 'Woman's work is never done.' It will give me so much pleasure to give you a day off."

"Oh! Mrs. Urbane, thank you!" Lucy could only imagine such movie star decadence. She looked forward to it with unquenchable enthusiasm.

Meanwhile, in the stillness of the Urbane residence, she wondered if anyone was there. "Mrs. Urbane? Mr. Urbane?" she called. "It's Lucy. I'll start in the kitchen."

Slumbering in his chair, Bill Urbane did not hear Lucy's galoshes squeak across the Italian tiles. He was not aware that she removed the wet shoes after a few steps and placed them neatly underneath the antique hall tree. He didn't hear the rustle she made hanging her coat and hat on the hooks framing the furniture piece from which more than an hour ago Francine had removed things to head out the door. He didn't know that Lucy skirted through the dining room and into the kitchen, moving quickly to the dishwasher to unload it, the usual way she began any housekeeping day.

Lucy clinked glasses and stacked porcelain plates. "Pretty china," she noticed. "Why, I bet that's real gold in the design." She flipped over a plate. She read, "Royal Doulton, England."

"Ooooh. I better be super-dooper careful," Lucy said out loud, handling the plates more gingerly.

Next she moved toward the washroom with a handful of dirty dishtowels. She saw some soiled clothes in the bin, which sat below a laundry chute from the second floor. She loaded the dark colors and some powdered soap, and she started the washing machine.

"I suppose I should strip the sheets and check the upstairs bathrooms for dirty towels," she said to herself, moving in her efficient circle up the steps along the wide carpeted hall. The guest bath off Anna's bedroom was clean as a whistle.

"All ready for their little grown-up college girl," Lucy mused. "Pretty pink hand towels." Lucy turned to look into the bedroom. "And a pink plaid dust ruffle and a pink chenille bedspread." She warmed at the sight. She knew Anna liked pink. It was her daughter Linda's favorite color and Lucy's, too. She thought of the pink dress the seamstress might make out of those two prom gowns Lucy had found at the Junior League Thrift Shop. "Pink must be every girl's favorite color at some time in her life," she said quietly. "Guess I never outgrew it."

She left Anna's room and walked briskly down the dove-gray carpeted hall and went into the master bedroom suite. The towering canopied poster bed was unmade, the covers a tangle of lavender solids and purple prints—comforter, sheets, blankets, and pillows tossed hither and yon. Mrs. Urbane's shimmering silk nightgown, a soft lavender floral print, was slung carelessly around one of the posters at the foot of the bed. Lucy picked it up and inhaled the lingering fragrance of lilac. She fingered the silk dreamily and then efficiently hung it up in the closet. She pulled up the bedcovers and topped them with the goose down comforter in its frilly violet striped duvet.

"Ummmm," Lucy gave into impulse. She flopped down into its foamy softness. "Wonderful!" she sighed.

After a second or two, she slid backwards, stood up,

plumped up the duvet, and went toward the master bathroom. There she picked off the towels, askew on their racks, and removed the wet cloths slung over the shower rod. She noticed that only one bath towel had been used. But then, her husband, Larry, often bathed at night when he had finished with farm work, rather than early in the morning as most men did. "Guess Mr. Urbane did the same thing, too, today," she said to herself.

She opened the linen closet hamper chute and pushed the damp towel and cloths into the square hole, listening as the load swooshed into the bin in the laundry room below.

"Better not forget to collect the powder room towels in the downstairs hall." She talked to herself as she passed dozens of framed family portraits and descended the stairs. She peeked in the living room with its towering tree of silver ornaments. She smelled smoke from the fireplace. Then she was startled by a sound—a loud rhythmical snoring. She looked around the corner. There was Bill Urbane, wrapped in a red blanket, his head bent over against the side of the wing chair, an empty glass obviously dropped from his outstretched hand, a pool of brown liquid on the rug. Lucy tiptoed toward him and saw the empty bottle of what must have been expensive liquor on the small table near the fire.

Lucy was sensitive to smells. And the smell most noxious to her was that of alcohol. It was the singular cause of the heated arguments in her home. After years of pleading, last September she had finally told Larry that it was either "AA or the Highway" with her and the kids. Larry knew this time she really meant it. He had started Alcoholics Anonymous that fall. Shortly after, he began the construction converting the porch to a bedroom for his invalid mother. Without drinking every night, all of a sudden Larry noticed that he had more hours in the evening. Furthermore, he needed to keep busy during those hours to keep himself from drinking.

Lucy looked at Mr. Urbane wrapped before the chair in a soft red blanket. Unaccountably, she felt sorry for the gentleman. She moved closer, reached out, and tapped him on the shoulder.

"Mr. Urbane?" she said. Bill repositioned himself in the brocade chair, still wearing his slippers. He had crossed one over another on the needlepoint ottoman. His hands clutched the red blanket. He coughed, turned on his side, and resumed snoring.

Boy, does he reek! Lucy thought. *Expensive or cheap—all liquor smells the same. I guess I'll let him sleep it off. Larry can help me with him when he comes at noon.*

She left Bill in somnolent peace.

25. Trailer Park

Francine held up the mirror to look at the back of her hair. "Nicely done, Myrtle," she said. "Perfect."

"Glad you like it," Myrtle said. She had been afraid she could not please the exacting woman, particularly in these surroundings—the living room of her trailer—likely the size of a bathroom in Mrs. Urbane's house. Even though Myrtle had equipped the space with a salon sink and a mirror near the kitchen counter, the cramped environment was not the place to show off this lady to her most elegant advantage.

"Feels good not having that hair down my neck," Francine said admiringly. "And those grey roots peeking through at the scalp, are all covered up," she smiled with satisfaction.

"Yes'm. It's all hidin' or lyin' on the floor now," Myrtle observed.

Francine changed the subject, "While you were working on me, I couldn't help but notice the little tree on your counter there close to the sink."

"Oh that little fake thing. I pull it out every year. It's small, fits my trailer and all, and my grandkids like it."

"But I was particularly taken with the skirt. The tree skirt. All those darling appliqués with sequins. Why, it's truly elegant, Myrtle."

"My neighbor done that," Myrtle said. "I'm real proud of it. She knows I like snowmen. So you see she's done different kinds of snowmen and sequins."

"I see. You should be proud of it. Very clever, your neighbor."

"I have a picture of her. She's in the paper this week."

Myrtle took two steps from her living area into the kitchen and reached for a paper clipped with a magnet to the side of the refrigerator. She handed Francine the article. Francine unfolded the half page spread, which showed a young woman over a sewing machine with her young son—behind a table? In a wheelchair? Francine couldn't tell. She quickly glanced at the cut line below the picture.

Local Woman, Son, To Get New Home for Christmas. Francine inhaled involuntarily.

Another picture showed Chamber of Commerce President Isabel Charmin grinning before a small audience of people, probably the local press. Francine experienced a dawning: *This—this woman—this Evangeline Holmes is Isabel's secret designer-seamstress!*

"The Habitat House lady," Francine gasped, and she looked up at Myrtle.

"Yes'm. She'll be moving soon. I'm glad for her. And her boy. He's not right. Got cerebral palsy. But he sure can draw. See that?" Myrtle turned again to her refrigerator. There, a gauzy scene on artist's sketch paper revealed the Blue Ridge Mountain skyline in mists of pink and grey and blue.

"He done that for me. I love the mountains 'round here," Myrtle nodded.

"How can he do that with CP?" Francine marveled.

"Don't know. Eva says he kin hold pencils and chalk,

and the shaky moves his hands make, that's his technique. You kin tell, it looks like feathers or somethin'."

Francine bent closer. "Almost the look of finger paint, but delicate," she agreed.

Myrtle nodded. "Eva—she goes by that more than Evangeline—anyway, Eva says it's a miracle gift. God done give it to her boy, Tom."

"You say she's your neighbor?"

"Yes'm. Couple of trailers down the way."

"Incredible," Francine batted her eyes quickly. "I wonder if—"

"You want to meet her sometime?" Myrtle had returned to her makeshift salon where she put away the blow dryer. Then she dropped the used combs into a cylindrical clear tank of blue sterilizing solution.

"Meet her? Yes I do! Why, this very minute! Actually, I have four dresses in my trunk I want her to look at. They need some magic!"

"She's good at magic. And she'll be glad." Myrtle dropped the used hairbrushes into the sink for scrubbing later on. "She takes in work that way. She's kind of got a miracle gift herself. The sewing, I mean."

"I'll say!" Francine hastily wrapped a scarf over her richly brown bouffant hair. "Let's call her right now."

"You mean it? Now?"

"Absolutely now."

"Well, we gotta just go. Eva don't have no phone. She's real hard up. Medical bills. No money. That's why the trailer park is kickin' her out. She ain't made rent in over two months. At least not all of it. My husband and me helped her some. All we could, anyway."

"That's so kind of you, Myrtle. Gosh Almighty!" Francine shivered. "Throwing someone with a child out in the dead of winter—in the snow!"

"You ready to go?" Myrtle pulled on an old jacket.

"Ready," Francine said, her scarf in place, her black suede coat buttoned tight.

An hour later the elegant Mrs. Urbane put her Mercedes SUV in gear and pulled slowly away from the snowy landscape. Francine noted how the snow softened the harsh lines of flimsy square boxes of homes stacked one after another in the trailer park. She eased down the graveled driveway and onto the paved road, still covered in white. She looked straight ahead, her Italian leather gloves gripping the steering wheel. Francine had one thing on her mind.

Not the pretty woman's thin frame.

Not her sad expression converting to joy at Francine's delivery of dresses.

Not the clean, cramped quarters where the woman lived with her son.

No, not any of these things, save one:

The boy.

"God in heaven!" Francine said out loud, more in exasperation than as a prayer. She gripped the steering wheel tightly. She leaned toward the front windshield, suddenly strangled by irremediable pain.

"God! Oh, God! Is death ever better than life?" Her voice rose to a scream. "There is that pitiful young man—still a boy—trapped in a flailing body! What is his future? Why should *he* live? But he does. He lives!" Francine pounded the steering wheel with her right fist. "He is alive!"

She drew in a ragged breath. "And my boy is not! Not! Oh, God! Not!"

Francine surprised herself. After five years. Anger, still. More than anger, she felt rage. Tears, a waterfall of anguish, blinded her eyes for a second, spilling across her lower lids, down her cheeks, washing into her mouth. She could taste the salt. Her eyes burned. She clenched them shut. In that second, the car slid abruptly on an ice patch. She swerved the steering wheel to regain traction on the road, but the car might as well have been a child's toy bobbing in a bathtub. The vehicle careened, spinning in a half circle into a snow bank.

"Oh," Francine cried in a small, distracted voice. Immediately she felt a rush of calm. She realized that she was all right. Nothing broken, except maybe a headlight. Her hair was still in place; the car was still running. She knew that she could get away from the snow bank. Just a small ditch she'd landed in, and she could handle it. Determinedly, she put the Mercedes in reverse, backed out and sat, just sat, beside the road. Then she ramped the gear into park, and cut the engine. She grew very still and stared numbly at the forest around her filling with snow. It drifted silently to cling against naked dogwoods sculpting their branches with crumbly ice. More flakes sifted against the windshield as light as powdered sugar, each tiny point melting from the leftover engine heat, a unique evanescent design . . . Poof! Poof! Poof! The flakes landed, then vanished.

"Life," Francine said, her voice ragged.

He would have been twenty-four next week. Five years before, Francine and Bill's precious boy, driving home from his freshman year at Amherst, died on December 21.

"Oh, oh, oh," Francine groaned. A swirl of thoughts, a collage of his face, a baby smile, boy's grin, a lost front tooth;

her laughing teen, a shock of brown hair over an unfurrowed brow. A youth! Never a man, not really. Not given enough time.

In the solitude what escaped from her was a primal cry. She unleashed the forbidden word, the one she had cried in whispers in her private showers when the water rushed down onto her head and over her shoulders, blotting out the sound— the name that she and Bill had agreed never to speak to one another in their new home in Virginia—the name she saw sculpted in stone in the snowy graveyard behind an eighteenth-century church in Boston.

"Andrew. Andrew. Andrew! Oh, my darling, perfect boy. Broken all to pieces." Her breath came in gasps. She stretched her gloved hands above the steering wheel as if pleading for the snowy flakes to stay their descent. "If only you had lived. I would have cared for you every minute of every day. Just like that trailer park mother cares for her son! I loved you, oh my dearest. If only, if only, you had lived!"

Francine felt a fresh wash of tears on her cheeks, drawn tight by the salt of tears shed before. She clinched her dark gloved fingers as fists against her grief-stricken face. She bent her covered head forward against her knuckles. She sobbed and sobbed, surrounded by the stillness of the sifting snow.

26. Larry at The ByWay

*I*n the lumberyard at Hank's ByWay, Larry's construction boots crunched across saw-dusted cement floors until he paused before a stack of boards that caught his eye. From a small selection in the corner, he leaned over and eased out a piece of walnut. He ran his rough stained hand across the grain as if it were the soft, new leather of a baseball glove. "Boy that burl is purty," he said to himself. Then he turned to Glenn, the lanky owner, who walked up and looked over Larry's shoulder.

"You got any more of this?" Larry asked.

"Sure do. But I pulled most of it for my wife. She wants some cabinets."

"So does Mrs. Midland," Larry said. "And I think this wood might just fit right in their house."

"How much you need?" Glenn asked. He was chewing on one of those wooden toothpicks he'd picked up at a diner checkout counter.

"Enough for a television cabinet with room for speakers, wires, DVD player—all that stuff," Larry said, still rubbing the board.

"You know the dimensions?"

Larry reached in his pants pocket and unfolded a piece of paper with numbers. "Yep. Won't take much," he said, looking at his pencil marks.

"I could let you have some," Glenn said. "You could put the best burl on the front."

"Just what I was thinking," Larry said. "But I want all good walnut."

"Good walnut is all I sell," Glenn said, shifting the toothpick. "But walnut with a burl like that just comes in every onc't in a while."

"Well, this is purty," Larry agreed. "And I hope you'll give me your neighborly price."

"I'll do my best," Glenn nodded. "Neighbors is my best customers. And, after all, it's almost Christmas."

Larry pulled out a thin wallet from his back jean pocket. He retrieved a credit card. "Yes, it is," he said. "Almost Christmas."

"Looks like Santa has come already. You got a new jacket?" Glenn fingered the sleeve of the heavy wool jacket Lucy had found for Larry at the Junior League Thrift Shop.

"New? Lucy picked this thing up. I told her it don't suit me. Too nice for the work I do. Got this woolly fabric. Snags every hitchhiker and brier in the woods. Not my style. And it's too big in the shoulders and too long in the sleeves. But I wore it this morning, just so her eyes would dance."

"Funny how a woman gits to us," Glenn said.

"Men are fools for 'em. But then, I guess that's the way it's supposed to be."

"Nature's way," Glenn grinned.

Larry heard a motor sputter to life and looked outside Glenn's metal warehouse to the yard, which contained what must have been an acre of stacked wood. A heavyset man in an odd hat operated a forklift, gingerly moving stacks of wood systematically into the storage facility.

"Who's that?" Larry asked.

"I got me some extra help," Glenn said. "He came in lookin' for seasonal work."

"Oh, I recognize him now. I saw that guy at the Circle Market a couple of weeks ago," Larry said. "Took him for a homeless type."

"Kinda strange. Don't say much," Glenn said. "But okay. Strong even though he's got some years on him. Said he could operate any kind of machinery. I put him on the lift. I want those boards inside afore the heavy snows come this winter."

"Better hurry. We've already had a couple."

"Yeah."

"He drives that thing pretty good." Larry pulled out his pack of cigarettes and offered one to Glenn.

Glenn took it. "Thanks. Yeah, he knows what he's doin'." He waved at the forklift operator. "I'll get him to load your walnut," Glenn said.

"That's it!" Larry pointed at the back of his pickup truck.

The forklift operator turned slightly with the load, leveling it in such a way that Larry could pull the boards into the bed of his truck. The lift stopped and the man cut the motor to idle. "Let me help," he said, climbing down from the lift cab.

"Thanks," Larry said.

The men worked silently a few minutes, pulling, positioning, and stacking the boards.

"Getting colder," the old man said.

"Yeah. Should snow again pretty soon, now. Temperature's down into the twenties."

"I like it," the other man replied.

"You look like you like it. But you need something warmer than a sweatshirt," Larry said.

"Got an overcoat. Not good for work like this."

"Nope. You need something like I got."

"Nice jacket."

"I don't like it," Larry said. "Too big."

"Maybe you'll grow into it," the man chuckled, his belly jostling.

Jolly guy, Larry thought. He reached for his wallet to tip the man. He flipped through the dollar section and realized he'd forgotten to stop at the bank the day before. No cash. "Dad gum," he said. He reached in his jacket pocket for his checkbook, and realized it wasn't in the usual place. "Wrong pocket, different jacket," Larry muttered. He hated not to tip the fellow. Then he stopped with a thought.

"Look. Would you do me a favor?" He unzipped his jacket and pulled it off. "Would you try this on?"

The old man looked at him, his dark eyes curious.

"Go on. Try it on," Larry said.

The old man shrugged. He slipped on the black woolly garment, zipped it, and ran his thick fingers up and down its thick front. "Nice jacket."

"Yes, and it fits," Larry said. "Take it, if'n you like it."

"Thank you, but I couldn't."

"You don't like it?"

"It's nice."

"Take it."

"You're fooling me."

"No, I'm not. I mean it. My wife picked it up on a whim last week, and she knows it don't fit me. She'll be glad I gave it to someone who can use it. If'n you want it, it's yours."

"That's very kind. But can't you get your money back?"

"Nope. It's from a thrift shop. All sales final."

"It's worth some money."

"Look. You'd be doing me a favor," Larry said. "Can you use it?"

"Well," the old man frowned silently.

"I mean as a gift," Larry nudged.

"A gift?" The man's white eyebrows shot up. "Why, everyone can use a gift!"

Larry grinned. "Well you got one." He climbed into his truck. "Merry Christmas."

"And you, too, Mr. Layman," the old fellow waved.

Larry started the motor and pulled out the ByWay fence gates. "Glenn didn't do nothin' but point the man to my truck. Wonder how he knew my name?" The carpenter shook his head and pumped up the volume to his country music station as he headed down the highway.

An hour later, as Larry unloaded the boards carefully into the open barn shed behind his home, his mind went into overdrive. Boy, was he ever going to be busy over the next few months! Moving his mother in by Christmas, then framing the Habitat House, alongside other tasks he'd already promised. And now, on short notice, he was crafting a piece of cabinetry for the Midlands as a Christmas present for Frank's wife. He'd told Frank on the phone this morning that he could not finish by Christmas Day; in fact, all he could get done were the box frame and the components' shelves. The rest would have to wait until January. Frank had said fine. He hadn't quite decided how he wanted the cabinet doors to work, but he had a good enough idea for Larry to begin, and he wanted walnut. Larry always liked a customer who knew his woods. It meant the fellow appreciated Larry's craftsmanship. He wiggled out a cigarette from his shirt pocket. *Glad I got rid of that woolly jacket. That old guy seemed to really take to it. Fit him,* too. Larry walked over to his truck and reached in the back cab for his old hunting jacket. He slipped it on, reached for his lighter in the customary pocket, and flicked it. Inhaling, he jumped in the driver's seat, started the motor, and backed out of his driveway. *Funny how a man's body works.* Larry leaned his head back and flicked his cigarette ash out the cracked window of his pickup. Just thinking about Lucy's tuna sandwiches and smelling that new lumber reminded him: he was hungry!

27. Secret in the Old Barn

Bill Urbane slept soundly, his snores filling the living room. Lucy kept the fire going and checked on him from time to time. She ran the vacuum cleaner upstairs thinking that might wake him from a distance. He didn't stir. She carried laundry back and forth down the hall to and from the kitchen. Bill slept.

I'm glad he's snoring, Lucy thought. *Otherwise, I might think he was dead.* But as the little chiming clock on the mantel struck eleven, Bill awoke with a start. He put his hands on his head.

"Oh, what a crashing headache," he moaned.

Lucy heard him, and she made sure to make a clatter of pots and pans in the kitchen sink. She ran the spigot, hoping he'd hear that, also; then she cut off the water and opened the door to the dishwasher. In that few seconds of silence, she heard a protracted groan, followed by a heavy thump.

She ran into the living room to find the distinguished Wilburn Urbane in a slovenly heap on the floor, having leaned forward and fallen in front of his chair. His eyes rolled up at her, as he lay crumpled like a towel on the rug.

She cried out, "Mr. Urbane!"

"Water," Bill gasped a bit sloppily. "Just bring me some water and some aspirin."

At that moment, she heard Larry's truck spin into the gravel turnaround. She sighed with relief and ran to the door.

"Larry!" she shouted, as her husband swung his long legs from the truck. "Help me!"

After a shower, Bill felt better. His face, however, burned—a flaming red, scorched with booze and shame—as he walked down the steps to his own kitchen. There, Lucy ladled out some vegetable soup in china bowls alongside a large plate stacked with plump tuna-salad sandwiches with fresh iceberg lettuce peeking from the sides. Bill and Larry sat at the kitchen table and ate the soup and sandwiches in virtual silence. Then they got up, thanked Lucy, and left through the back door.

Not looking at each other, they walked toward the weathered gray barn on the back of Bill's farm. It was an odd structure, primitive and yet elegant in a way. The old-time set- tlers as a group built these barns in one day, pegging milled boards against round poles. The main struts formed a slanted structure somewhere between an A-frame and a saltbox. This building was large enough to house a couple of tractors. But Bill had chosen to build a new structure for the John Deere equip- ment he had accumulated over the years.

Amazingly, he had never been inside the old barn. During the last household move, the one from Massachusetts, he had been on a business trip in Europe. He had left Francine to direct the movers to pack everything. When he arrived at the farm in Virginia, he asked what she had stored in the pole barn out back.

"Stuff," she replied, dismissively. "Just stuff."

Last winter Bill had noticed the doors to the barn had begun to weather badly and to rot along the bottom, a condition encouraged by lingering snow piles. The lowest board ends had begun to break, forming a jagged fringe of splinters. The sagging hinges created a lopsided look, the doors tilting toward each other. On this particular day, Bill's plan was to get Larry's advice on how to best repair the structure and then give him the opportunity to easily earn back the money that Francine's careless benevolence had cost him. Of course, he'd make Larry a generous deal; Francine had tallied up quite a bill on the man's house that fateful afternoon.

"I'd sure appreciate it if you could repair these doors for me," Bill began as they stood before the barn. "Just fix the hinges. Straighten up the doors so they will function and not drag the ground. Also, I want to know if I should do anything about the rot on the lower half of the boards here," Bill added, slightly kicking a scraggly panel in a section near the doors.

"Better catch the rot before it gets too bad. Lunch for termites and beetles."

"Yeah, I would think so. Can you repair that?" Bill asked, suddenly glad he had thought to put on a cap. The day was partly cloudy and chilly.

"I can do that," Larry said putting his gloved hands in the pockets of his jeans. "And I'll figure out about them low boards. What's inside?"

Bill paused. "Why, I really couldn't tell you."

"Is it locked?" Larry asked.

"Don't know that either. Don't think so," Bill said. "Francine told the movers to put the extra stuff from our home in Massachusetts in here. I've no idea what she's stored inside."

Larry reached up and pulled an old, frayed rope that

led through a hole to the other side of the door. The rope was lightly encrusted with ice crystals, but he yanked it strongly and heard the scrape of a board lifting against wood from inside.

"Neat," Larry said. "The old timers knew how to make do with nothin'."

"Guess this barn is old," Bill said. "Our farmhouse was built in 1895."

"This building's older," Larry said, tugging at the huge wooden door. The barn door squeaked as Larry half-lifted, half-dragged the old board frame to reveal the interior, a black hole, smelling of mildew and damp and still as a tomb. Inside, the contents were obscured by the contrast of light reflecting off snow outside.

Both men stepped inside the barn, wiping dusty cobwebs from their faces, noting shapes of furniture, chests of drawers, wardrobes, end tables, limned by cracks of pale white light from between the wallboards in the back of the barn. Much of it Bill recognized, even in the dusty dimness. It was a collection, things his parents had left Bill that Francine had not particularly cared for, or that wouldn't fit in the Virginia farmhouse. He felt a haunting draft of wind and stopped where he was. The ghostly residue of years gone by reached inside his jacket like clawing fingers of ice.

Larry kept walking. Bill heard the workman's worn boots stamping the frozen earth floor. The steps suddenly ceased.

"Well, I'll be!" Larry said.

"What is it?" Bill asked.

"Somethin' shiny," Larry said, and Bill slowly walked in his direction, easing himself around furniture he had not laid eyes on in five years.

Leaning against the far wall, something caught the glint of the sun that suddenly had broken through the clouds outside.

Smears of light and years of dust coated the chrome handlebars. The frame sat on two flat tires. Rust sprinkled the red and silver frame like cedar sawdust.

"It's a bike!" Larry exclaimed. "You've got a dirt bike?"

Bill said nothing. Larry turned around and saw him put a shaking gloved hand to his forehead. The older man's eyes squinted with an unspeakably sad expression that the younger man could only begin to read. Then, as Larry silently waited, there came a shudder as Bill Urbane spoke,

"That bike belonged to my son."

28. The Accident

The boy had died instantly. Bill and Francine knew that, because the driver of the cement truck had perished violently as well. The police said neither driver had a chance on the icy highway, the blizzard obstructing any view of one another. It was a bad, blind curve. The cement truck slid outside its lane, swerving on the icy turn. The Jeep, right in the way, was crushed against the snow-covered highway railing.

The impact was severe enough to total the smaller vehicle and demolish the driver's side of the truck. The impact actually hurled the Jeep's radio-CD player as a solid block into the back seat.

Their boy, Andrew, had installed the player himself the summer before, not using all the screws in the package. Bill could almost hear his own voice from the fluid distance of memory . . .

"How about these?" Bill had asked his eighteen-year-old son, holding up the remaining screws in a cellophane package.

"Aw, Dad," Andrew had run his fingers through long, auburn, rumpled tresses, like Francine's, which fell across his brow. "That thing's not going anywhere."

"Will it rattle? I hate rattles."

"A Jeep always rattles," Andrew laughed. "But I won't hear it. My music's always too loud!"

"Yeah, I guess that's true," Bill had said ironically and inwardly thought, *Youth, too great to waste on the young.*

At the site of the wreck, red police lights frantically whirling, ambulance lights hopelessly blinking, the demolished Jeep—a crumpled deadly accordion—was hooked to the tow truck. The wrecker people had retrieved the disc still inside the player. Amazingly it was intact within the preserved block.

"I'm bringing you music for Christmas," Andrew had phoned early that day from Amherst. "It's the coolest recording of carols I've ever heard. Different. All kinds of instruments. New arrangements to the old songs. The best is number eleven."

"What song is it?" Francine had said into the extension telephone.

"Patience, Momma—you'll hear it," Andrew laughed. "It will be a surprise—Santa and all that," the boy laughed again, his voice the sound of bells on a clear night. "See you in a few hours."

"Be safe," Bill had cautioned. "It's slippery according to Weather Channel reports. Snow and ice everywhere. Hard to see. Go slow."

"I'll be safe. I've got my tunes. Love you guys," he rang off.

On the shortest, blackest day of the year, and the longest, darkest, night of his life, Bill had stood in the cold and held the CD in his hand. A disc. A slim flat disc. Was this all that was left of his only son? Angrily, he pitched the thing into the dirty snow as the ambulance pulled away, carrying their boy's fractured body, leaving Bill and Francine in the wake of its powdery black exhaust. But Francine reminded him through tears, "Andrew was bringing that to us." She went to where it lay

in the track-riddled snow. She brought the disc back to
her husband.

He glanced at it. *Mannheim Steamroller,* he read its title.
What a silly name for a musical title! he thought. He slipped the
CD in the pocket of his overcoat. Later, he locked it away in
Andrew's bureau drawer, and he shut the door to the boy's room
for the last time.

After the accident, Bill left the States for business in
Europe. Previously, he and Francine had discussed retiring to
Virginia, and they had researched and found a two-hundred-acre
farm. As Bill left, Francine called the movers. They left Massachusetts
with their daughter to begin a new life. Younger than Andrew, Anna
had one year remaining in high school before she went to college.
Bill had instructed Francine that he didn't want to see Andrew's
things in the new home. And he never wanted to speak his son's
name. He couldn't stand it. He didn't even want to speak it himself.
The pain would not go away. At times he felt he couldn't breathe. He
wished to die. He had horrible dreams. Thoughts of suicide. *Maybe,*
he conjectured, *just maybe he'd exercise that option.*

On that trip he negotiated a deal that made him more
than five million dollars. He would have traded every penny to
have his son back. Instead, he simply walked into a Virginia bank
the week he returned from Europe. He paid his first and last farm
payment on the same day in cash. The rest of the money he invested in bonds and stocks. A talented hedge fund manager netted Bill
a 60-percent return on tech stocks in one good year. Bill and
Francine gave to selected foundations. Unfailingly, despite the gifts,
the couple's wealth grew like the Biblical descendants of Abraham,
hither and thither, far and wide. . . .

"Does it work?" Larry's voice floated into Bill's con-
sciousness as if filtered through a thick hiking sock. Bill shook

his head groggily. He couldn't breathe. His chest felt crushed. His head throbbed.

"What?"

"The dirt bike. Doesn't seem to have rusted too much." Larry pulled off his work glove and ran his bare hand over the handlebars.

"I have no idea whether it still works or not."

"You mind if I look closer?" Larry leaned over to inspect the motor.

"Pull it out if you want."

"Naw, no real need to. I see what I need to know. Mice been eatin' on the wires." Larry leaned over to look closer at the bike engine.

"Those varmints did that to my tractor last year," Bill replied. His words came as croaks. It was difficult to speak. He felt like a zombie, almost as if he were not inside his own body.

"An easy fix," Larry said, looking up at Bill. "If'n you was to want to."

"Want to?" Bill asked, as if suddenly back from another world. "I remember now. You wanted to give your boy a bike for Christmas."

"I been noticing your fences sagging 'round the north end of the property . . ." Larry began. "Or I can pay you straight up. Name yer price."

"How much work realistically can you do, Larry? I need a lot done," Bill swallowed. "And you've got a lot on your plate—barn doors, fences, Habitat Houses, your own home . . ." Bill's voice trailed off.

"I kin do a lot, now that I ain't drinkin' no more," Larry said.

Bill was silent. Then he spoke, awkwardly, "For a while after I lost my boy, I lost myself. Then I started AA. But I stopped going. I guess you can tell," Bill sighed.

Larry stubbed the toe of his boot several times in the hardened dirt of the barn floor. He spoke cautiously, respectfully.

"It meets on Tuesday nights at the Elks Lodge. You know where they play Bingo on Wednesday? Well, Tuesday's AA night. You'd be surprised who's there."

"No," Bill said. "Candidly, I don't think I would be surprised. But anyway," he shrugged, "you think this bike would roll if we pushed it toward the door? The tires are flat. But would you like to see it in the sunshine?"

"I sure would," Larry said, barely able to contain his excitement.

29. The Devil's Wife

"How about spaghetti? I'm good at that," Jan asked Larry's boy, Lawrence, Jr. It was December 13, just twelve days before Christmas.

"We like Ragu." In the doorway to his room Lawrence eyed the visiting Mrs. Midland with visible skepticism as she stood in the kitchen area of his home.

"Bottled stuff?" She involuntarily shuddered. "Oh, I make sauce from scratch."

"What's scratch??"

"All the ingredients, you know, green pepper, hamburger meat, a little celery, a splash of wine."

"Mama don't allow no alcohol." Lawrence shook his head.

"Well it cooks out. The alcohol. It just flavors the sauce."

Mamaw Rosey spoke up from beside the wood-burning stove.

"Better not use alcohol."

"Okay," Jan said, duly informed. "I can use Worcestershire sauce." She glanced down at the table. Larry had left a twenty-dollar bill for the day. Jan sighed. *How can I feed this family on that?* She thought a moment. *Maybe I'll buy Ragu and add a half-pound of hamburger and some canned tomato sauce. I guess I could buy a pepper and maybe some mushrooms, and, of course, Worcestershire sauce, too.* She opened the refrigerator. *But also they need milk,* she said to herself. *I'm going to have to be careful or I'll pull an over-budget faux pas, just like Francine.* She shut the refrigerator door.

"You have a paper route, don't you?" She turned. She hoped to soften the scowl on Lawrence's forehead.

"Yes'm. *The Clearview Clarion.* I ride my bicycle."

"I see," said Jan. "That's pretty good, to be in business for yourself at the age of fourteen."

"Savin' for a dirt bike." Lawrence shoved his big hands into his pockets. He was at the stage where he'd grown tall, his hands were a man's, but his facial hair was nonexistent and his features had yet to assume the confidence and seriousness of an adult. Jan remembered when her twins were that age. Now they were twenty.

Time flies, she thought. She smiled at Lawrence.

"Well, I hope you get that dirt bike."

"Yes'm, that'd be nice." He stared fixedly at her, as if sizing her up as someone who could keep a secret. Jan passed the test.

"My sister, Linda, wants a pony for Christmas," the boy volunteered. "My mom and dad told her she was too young. Only seven, you know. But she done climbed up in Santa's lap right there in the mall—big as she is—you know and asked him."

"For a pony?"

"Yes'm. She still believes." Lawrence rocked back on his heels when he said that. He leaned his head back a little, rolling his eyes, as if confiding in Jan.

Jan folded her arms and eyed him conspiratorially.

"Believes?"

"In Santa Claus."

"I see."

"I ain't told her."

"Well, you're a fine big brother. You are a man who can keep a secret, I see."

"Yes'm."

The bell tones of Mamaw came from the sofa on the other side of the room. She was busily crocheting something; Jan noticed a red and black scarf, or a blanket? Something, anyway, trailing over her knees. She was surprised the woman had followed the conversation so closely. But she had. She spoke in a voice steady as a the striking of a clock, "He is a fine boy, yes indeed, keeping our secret. We think Linda ought to have one more Christmas. Believin'."

"Well," Jan said, picking up the grocery list. "In that case, I'll keep the secret, too." She folded the list and shoved it in her purse. "I'll head out now to shop, and I'll pick Linda up at school. You want to come, Lawrence?" She slipped on her coat and opened the back door to the home. Impishly she paused, holding the door slightly open.

"Maybe there's something you should know about me," she glanced back at the pair in the den.

"What's that?" The boy stopped, shouldering his coat. He stared at Jan. Mamaw Ida Rose stilled her crochet needles.

"Well, I'm over forty," Jan tossed her head. "And I still believe in Santa Claus!"

Jan took a right on Main Street. "I'm hitting the grocery store first. And from raising my boys, I know how dull that is." Jan said, looking at Lawrence in the passenger seat.

"Sure is." He shrugged.

"So where can I drop you off? What's your favorite store?"

"Universe One," Lawrence promptly replied.

"The music store off Main Street?"

"Eighth Street."

"On our way," Jan said.

Jan pushed her cart through the grocery store, cussing the crowds. She was due in ten minutes to pick up Lucy's daughter following an after-school activity. But good grief! The Christmas shoppers had slammed the store. She scowled. She was not ready for Christmas. With the silly Swap confusion she hadn't finished buying her family gifts. Why, even Lawrence was ahead of her, shopping at Universe One.

When she dropped the boy off at the music store, he surprised her with an uncharacteristic smile.

"Thanks," he said climbing out.

"I'll hurry," Jan called after him.

Lawrence turned and said. "Don't. Please. My mom never gives me enough time in here."

"That's what my boys would say, too." She waved at Lawrence, who didn't notice. Already he was through the door.

Now in the cashier line, Jan tapped her foot. Her gaze traveled over the racks of cheerful display magazines lining the checkout lane, *People, Martha Stewart Living, Family Circle.* She flipped through the Christmas edition of the last one, noticing the happy people—mothers, children—smiling over cute cookies and charming Christmas decorations.

"However in the world do people have time to do all that stuff," Jan said aloud. "I know! They don't! What we have here is the conspiracy of appearance! People appear to do these things. Then they buy cookies that simply look homemade."

The checkout clerk looked at Jan sleepily and murmured in a monotone, "Twenty-seven, eighty-five."

"Ooops, over-budget," Jan groused. She dug into her

184

black leather bag for her billfold to supplement Larry's twenty dollars. *Wonder if Lucy could have made it under twenty dollars?* Jan asked herself. *I better give that woman a raise this Christmas.* She counted out the change for the cashier, scooped up two plastic bags, and quickly left.

Going just a shade above the speed limit, Jan rounded the Clearview Circle and passed the Circle Market. The sign Frank had warned her about was staked into the hard wintry field. She slowed and rolled down her window, letting in the frozen air. She squinted, "For Rezoning. 11 Acres. Petition: Commercial-One. Hearing December 20, Clearview Courthouse."

Commercial-One. C-1. Jan had to think. *Oh, gosh,* she felt a stab. *That's the highest commercial designation—like filling stations and grocery stores and car repair shops.*

"No! No! No!" She shouted at the sign. She and Frank had hoped the town would save that picturesque spot . . . the little knoll rising, why it would be a lovely place for a church, a courthouse, even a school. She peered closer. Sure enough, as Frank had described, "For details, call Venald Realty."

"Creep!" Jan said out loud. "He'll sell to the highest bidder, even if it's for a landfill right in the center of Clearview! The town must stop it." She hit the accelerator.

At Clearview Elementary, she pulled next to the curb and watched as Linda Layman walked down the sidewalk, her red book bag bouncing against her back, her golden curls bound up in long braids. The felicific vision eclipsed for a moment every negative thought weighing on Jan's mind. She sat and watched as if witnessing the innocent dawning of the day.

"What must it be like to have a little girl?" Jan leaned back contemplating what a girl would entail: braiding the hair, packing lunch for the back pack, hemming a skirt, finding the pink tennis shoes under the bed—all the things Lucy must do every morning to get this beautiful child off on her school day. "Really special," Jan smiled. "And having two boys is really special. And, happily, mine are coming home next week, just as surely as this cute thing is heading home for the holidays."

Linda was carrying something rather proudly in her gloved hands. It looked like a bundle of yarn.

"Whatcha' got, Honey?" Jan asked, leaning across the seat to open the passenger door.

"For Mama!" Linda said with a shy smile that showed baby teeth except for the front two, which were missing.

"See?" She held up the mangled red yarn, which, on closer inspection, Jan realized was a knitted Santa face with black beads for eyes, pink beads for a smile, and white beads for a beard. "It's a surprise."

"Why, look at that. Did you make it?" Jan smiled.

Linda nodded. "It's a door badge. You hang it on the door."

"I see," Jan said. "So Santa makes sure to stop at your house?"

Linda nodded again. "The teacher says mine is good," the girl said with pride. "Mamaw taught me about crochet."

"Oh, I remember," Jan recalled the old woman wearing a loosely knitted scarf around her neck to keep warm by the fire at home. "She taught you to do this?"

Lucy nodded again, her braids going up and down on her small chest like pulleys. Then she settled back in the seat and sighed contentedly.

Well, Jan thought. *The door badge Santa is not Family Circle quality but it's lovingly homemade. I guess these kinds of projects are more important than I thought when I was teaching grammar school.* Jan watched the child carefully fold the Santa and tuck it in her book bag.

"C'mon, Honey." She started the car. "Let's go get a chocolate milkshake at Horton's."

"A chocolate milkshake?" Linda's eyes grew wide. "Can we have it with vanilla ice cream?"

"Oh, you mean a black and white? Sure, Honey. You got it. And we'll buy one for Lawrence, too."

"He likes vanilla."

"Vanilla it is. We'll order his to go. He's at Universe One."

Linda's eyes widened knowingly.

"So," Jan babbled on, "we'll sit in a booth, play one of those juke boxes they have, you know, at each table, and we'll split that shake, just like we're teenage girls."

Linda smiled widely and looked up at Jan. "I want to be a teenager, just like my Mama was. She was the Peach County Homecoming Queen when she was sixteen."

"I know that, Honey. People in this town have told me." Jan assured her. "And I must say, I've also heard—and now I see for myself—that you are every bit as pretty as your Mama. Why, I was just saying to myself as you came walking toward my car, how very special it must be to have a little girl like you!"

Linda nodded, still smiling. "So, now we're going for a teenage milk shake?"

"Yes, we are."

And that's just what they did. They became a pair of juke-box-playing, soda-sipping teens in wooden booths with high backs joined to tables where youngsters for generations had carved their initials. It would all have been deliriously happy, except that as Jan poured the last dollop of creamy ice cream from the tin shake cylinder into Linda's Coca-Cola glass, who should slide by but Stephanie Bennington Venald—high heels, tight skirt, too much lipstick, and a pancake of makeup for a face. Mrs. Seven-Dollar-Inheritance herself. Jan felt a stab of disgust as she saw the woman wearing a fake leopard skin jacket, weaving her way toward the booth table where she and Linda had been having such a good talk about ponies and schools, shoes and songs.

"Who is this?" Stephanie asked.

"Lucy Layman's child, Linda," Jan made the introduction.

"This is Mrs. Venald," she told the child. Linda looked up with her mother's long-lashed almond eyes. Jan glanced at the child and thought, *sometimes the right features come right on down the chain.*

Linda kept her lips encircled on the red and white straw in the glass as her lids dropped, and she resumed her attention to the shake.

"You're babysitting Lucy's child? Funny. I thought it went the other way with domestic help." Stephanie's black eyebrows rode imperiously high over lashes caked with mascara. "I guess turnabout's fair play."

A snooty remark as usual. Jan hid her disgust with her napkin. Then she forced herself to look up and smile.

"It's part of the Swap—" Jan began. Then she paused, thinking better of it. Stephanie had an uncanny knack for smudging anything with the grime of sarcasm.

"The what?"

Obviously Stephanie had not seen the television story about the three women's changing places. So Jan left it simple.

"I'm just helping Lucy out today," she said. She pushed her empty glass away.

"I see that," Stephanie drawled.

"I saw Hiram's realty sign near the Circle Market." Jan diverted the conversation. She didn't want Stephanie to sit down, so she made it clear that they were almost ready to leave the drugstore. She picked up the bill on the table.

"His sign?" Stephanie shouldered a large black bag. "Oh, yes," the woman pursed her mouth. "Hiram's been approached by an important developer in the Northeast. We agree completely with what he has in mind. We think the Circle is a grand location for a Crane's Station."

"For a what?" Jan virtually bolted from the booth.

"Your husband didn't tell you?"

"One of those ghastly red-and-black neon twenty-four-hour fill up things that blocks out the stars for miles around and attracts all kinds of noise and clutter? Oh—I hate those! Hideous—with metal legs and lighted signs like eyes—O-o-o-o-o-h! Odious things! They look like spiders—like——steel tarantulas!"

"Well!" Stephanie huffed. "Better get used to the idea! Hiram knows a motivated buyer when he sees one. And Crane's is that. And, as you no doubt know, Hiram is always a motivated seller! So this is a deal in the making." Stephanie drew her mouth into an even thin line. "Like I said, better get used to the idea. 'Cause Crane's is comin' to Clearview."

"Not unless it passes county zoning." *A Crane's station——right at the centerpiece of the town. No! No! No!* Jan's brain screamed. Then she reassured herself out loud, "My husband is on the architectural review board. Of course, it will have to be approved."

"Oh, it will be approved. Yes, indeed. We have it on good authority." Stephanie nodded her pancake face.

Floozy! A cheap dumbbell, Jan cursed privately, crumpling the milkshake ticket in her hand. She reached down beside her seat in the booth and gathered her coat and bag.

"Well, Stephanie," Jan began, glancing over at baby doll Linda, who had by now reached the bottom of her glass with the characteristic gurgle of a straw, "nothing against you and Hiram personally," Jan slid from the booth to stand up, "but I very much hope you are wrong. And I fervently hope the zoning petition fails."

"It won't fail," Stephanie sniffed and turned on her narrow three-inch heels, leaving Jan to watch her wavering strut down the drugstore aisle.

"Who was that?" Linda asked, handing Jan her small pink coat as she scooted out the drugstore booth.

"The Devil herself," Jan said.

"Really?" Linda's amber eyes were wide.

"Not really the Devil, Honey," Jan said. She grimaced privately. *Just the Devil's floozy wife.*

For its window logo, Universe One, adopted the saying, "All the Best Tunes in Town," and Jan felt the description was apt. All kinds of people liked to linger there—teenagers, grammar school kids, Boomers, and rap enthusiasts. She expected to find Lawrence somewhere in the younger sections. But surprisingly he was near the seasonal classics wearing a pair of headphones, obviously lost in another world.

Jan touched him on the shoulder. He turned and looked at her.

"Are you about ready?" she asked.

He did not answer; rather, he took off the headphones and reached up to put them on Jan. She fit them snugly to her ears and listened. A haunting melody, a startling composition of a familiar Christmas carol, spun through her mind, the smoothing sounds of French horn and violin. She closed her eyes. Amazing. This boy had picked out such music!

"What is that?" She removed the head phones and looked at the boy. He silently held up a plastic bag with the store logo smeared across it in yellow and black. "All the Best Tunes in Town."

"You bought it?"

Lawrence grinned. "It's a gift. A surprise. Mamaw Rosey loves Christmas music."

Jan laughed. "You know what, Lawrence?" she cried. "You're an okay kid! I mean a *really okay* kid! Anybody would love that music. It's a great gift!" She ruffled his hair, and he dodged and grinned.

"Let's go," Jan said. Your sister's waiting in the car with a shake. Vanilla." She rolled her eyes knowingly.

"The best." The youth ran his tongue over his lips.

"She said you'd like it," Jan winked, feeling lighthearted as a kitten.

Later that evening after fixing the Layman's dinner, however, Jan felt less lighthearted due to creeping tentacles of guilt accompanying her on her way home.

As she drove slowly through the dark, Jan reasoned with herself. *Well, Lucy knows about it. We all agreed at the Dairy Parlor. Still. It was a dirty deed. Not my style to do something messy and mean. Even to help a husband appreciate his wife.*

She could imagine Larry entering his back door, going past the mudroom sink.

"And the stink!" Jan said out loud. "Changing adult diapers is certainly different from changing children's." Jan had been kind to the apologetic Mamaw and cleaned her up cheerfully when she'd had an accident. She put the Depends diapers in a plastic bag and loaded the entire bag into a plastic diaper pail, as instructed, to be carried to the trash. But she did not tie the bag shut, nor did she replace the pail lid.

Larry Layman "always comes in the back door," Lucy had told Jan. "And he always says, 'What did you do today?' Like it was nothin'. I think Larry needs to get the idea of what I do. You know, and with him being sensitive to smells and all, I think that will teach him."

"Well that stunt should teach him to appreciate Lucy," Jan murmured as she put on her blinker signal and turned into Double Nickel Farm. "Just as Frank seems to appreciate my cooking after a few nights of Lucy's carbs and chicken grease."

30. Lady of Leisure Lucy

*T*wenty-four hours after Jan swapped into her household, Lucy Layman found herself floating in a whirlpool at the Clearview Country Club, surrounded by six or seven other women, none of whom was wearing a stitch. At first, Lucy had been mortified by the unselfconscious nakedness. As she watched the women toss aside towels to enter the pool, bobbing next to her in the pulsing water, and then dripping without robes as they went toward the showers, Lucy felt like two people: Lucy the Prosecutor, and Lucy the Defense. Her mind seemed to divide itself with each half talking to the other.

Lucy Prosecutor said, "Why, you looked up to these women when they were girls in high school. They were so pretty and skinny. Now, look what's happened to them—some of them as sleek as seals; others as flabby as hippos."

She observed her own wrinkles as she floated up and down, the warm jets of water massaging her limbs. She said privately, "Well, I've sort of let myself go, too."

Lucy Defense: "But these women have had advantages. Money. They can exercise anytime on those bicycles upstairs in the workout room—gosh they took my breath away! And that treadmill, like hiking the Blue Ridge Mountains, that wavy line just a-goin' and a-goin', up, and up jagged hills till I thought I'd drop, but I was afraid to jump off! Thought I'd kill myself!"

Lucy Prosecutor: "But you know, don't you? Maybe you don't need those fancy machines. You could walk the block around your house. You could meet Lawrence, Jr., halfway on his paper route. That would be a mile. And really, Lucy, you could walk to the market when you just need a few things. You really don't have to use the car every time."

As the warm water swirled, Lucy abandoned the interior dialogue as she let herself drift deeper and deeper, up to her chin, her head like a human beach ball on the water surface. She sighed and closed her eyes. Hypnotized, she listened as the women talked.

Oh, such talk it was . . . women talk . . . about men . . . and children . . . and the pace of living . . . and the price of shoes. . . Women talking, one subject flowing into another like colored swirls of finger paint on slick paper. Overlapping, around and again, talking . . . talking . . . Lucy drifted. The talk shifted. Lucy heard a new word. She thought she heard a woman say, *Hippo-suction*. She opened her eyes.

"Yes. It's the truth. You just suck it out. It works. Presto! The fat is gone."

"It's dangerous though."

"Naw. All the movie stars do it."

"Even Jane Fonda."

"No!"

"Yes!"

"And to think I nearly killed myself trying to get skinny like she is with her exercise videos. Worked out every morning for a month!"

The voices turned into giggles, reminding Lucy of the girls these women had once been.

"But don't you have to go under?"

"Anesthesia?"

"Well, I did, but course I was having my hips liposuctioned—or is it liposucked? What's the past-tense of lipo?" Gales of laughter erupted.

"Well, anyway, I had my hips done, my thighs done, and my tummy done, too."

"All at once?"

"Gosh, you really shrank yourself!"

"I was desperate. I couldn't get the weight off."

"Not even with exercise?"

"Nope. Now, my cleaning lady did it. She looks great."

"You have a cleaning lady?"

"Yes. She's a diamond. But she doesn't have any days open." The woman's tone became suddenly wary, as if protecting her life savings.

"Too bad. I could use a good helper."

"Yeah, wish I could find a cleaning lady." The tension in the pool became palpable.

Lucy began to wave her arms in the water slowly as if treading, she rose up to chest level in the water, her interest piqued by the direction of the conversation. She kept silent.

"You just can't get good domestic help anymore."

"They don't stick with you. Somebody's always out-bidding you."

"Or they don't show up. I must have tried out a dozen."

"Or they steal."

"Yes, that's always a risk."

"Well, I pay more than minimum wage. I don't want them stealing, but also, I want them to come back. I pay twelve dollars an hour."

Gasps floated in ripples over the water. Then another voice said,

"I pay a flat rate of fifty dollars."

"For how much time?"

"Takes her about four hours."

"Wow, that's a lot."

"Well, she gets the job done each week, and I don't have to run the vacuum cleaner."

"I hate cleaning bathrooms."

"Dusting is the worst!"

"Excuse me," Lucy ventured, and everyone's head turned in her direction. "I'm a guest today." Lucy twisted one of her wet, blonde curls. "Mrs. Urbane gave me a gift certificate."

"Oh, Francine, she's a doll."

"So generous."

"A classy lady."

"Well, I agree with you," Lucy said. "But what you were saying about cleaning people, I find a little confusin'. You say you ladies pay a good rate and you can't get dependable folks to clean your homes?"

"I add gas money on top of that good rate," said a hefty woman to Lucy's right. The floaters began to illustrate their frustration with arms gesticulating, splashing,

"They don't show up!"

"They don't stay!"

"A lot of them don't really know how to clean!"

"My, my," Lucy said wading through the rolling water over toward the steps. She reached for a stack of warm, white towels. She draped the rich, deep pile modestly around her flushed, pink body as she stepped from the heated pool.

"This has been nice," she said. "And I wish you ladies luck. You have given me an idea. A good idea. Because you see, I know some people who need to work. I mean they already work, but it's factory work. Some of them work at the chicken factory down the highway, cuttin' and packin' raw chicken parts." Lucy noticed that a few women reacted with shivers, even in the pulsing hot tub.

"Now that's hard work . . . smelly and dirty," Lucy stood, as if saying something new to her audience, "but cleaning, also, is hard work . . ."

All floating heads nodded.

Lucy felt encouraged. "But factory work is not pleasant, not like being in nice homes like you ladies have." The women looked at one another in agreement. That was true, indeed.

"So, it seems to me, if somebody trained the women who wanted to leave the factory and made sure they were dependable, and bonded them to insure their honesty, well . . ." The women in the pool kept nodding.

"Well," Lucy continued, "that might just be a business. A business I could run." Lucy blinked her almond eyes. She reached over to the stack of folded white terrycloth to grab another towel. She began to dry her dripping curls.

"If you started this business, what would you charge?" The hefty woman's voice floated from the pool.

"Well, factory women make more than minimum wage!" Lucy wanted to set the standard.

"Oh," another woman said.

"What's minimum wage these days?" Another voice.

"Well, I'd pay more than minimum wage. I don't know what it is, but if you, Maryanne," the large woman turned to her friend, "pay twelve dollars an hour and you think it's worth it—"

Maryanne nodded, "It's worth it, Susan," and Susan turned back to Lucy and finished with the flat statement, "For good help, I'd pay."

"If somebody showed up consistently, I'd pay too," came another voice.

"And ran the vacuum and cleaned my four bathrooms, I'd sure pay." Another head echoed.

Lucy stopped towel rubbing her hair. From the swirling whirlpool she heard nothing but babbling encouragement popping to the surface like bubbles in champagne. She felt giddy, rejoicing in the musical round of two beautiful words:

"I'd pay."

"I'd pay."

"I'd pay."

31. For the Love of Chocolate

*F*rank Midland loved the grounds of the university at
night: its centerpiece, the historic Rotunda, modeled
after the Pantheon in Rome—its brilliant windows lit
from within, overlooking the connected buildings of Thomas
Jefferson's Academical Village, a balanced composition around
an elegant quadrangle known as The Lawn. A corridor of lights
linked faculty pavilions and colonnades, their buildings inspired
by the Italian architect Palladio. The Rotunda was originally a
library; it represented Jefferson's bold departure from the signature church central to earlier colleges in America. From the
Rotunda steps, Frank could hear, far down graduated tiers of
grass, the plaintive strains of melodies wafting up from Cabell
Hall facing the Rotunda from below. Every year Christmas con-
certs were scheduled in December, before the student vocalists
and symphony musicians left for winter break. Frank could hear
the orchestra tuning up.

This Tuesday, December 14, he had collected his final
exams at six that afternoon, and wished his architecture students
Happy Holidays. Within three days, he told them, he would
have the exams graded and their semester grades posted online
according to the last four digits of their social security numbers.

Meanwhile, he advised them, to go home, forget school, dismiss stress from their minds, and spend time with their families. That's what he intended to do.

He stood a moment, shifting his briefcase and buttoning his coat higher around his neck. His advice, for the first time in his life, sounded hollow. *Spend time with your family. That's what I intend to do.* Frank had no family but the one he had adopted. His parents had both died. And now, his family of choice, well, his wife mostly, seemed distant. Furthermore, for the past four Tuesday nights when he had called during mid-class break, she had not answered her cell phone. It made him nervous. He began to think the unthinkable. And he had begun to do incautious things, like ask Francine Urbane where she and Jan had gone the Tuesday night they had met for dinner together. Francine had listened and then brushed him off. "After dinner at the Blackbird," she said, "Jan went her way, and I went mine."

At that, Frank had gone silent. But in the middle of the same night that he'd queried Francine, Frank had been unable to sleep. He had gotten up, poured a glass of milk, and noticed Jan's cell phone charging on the kitchen counter. He hesitated, hating himself. Then he had flipped open the phone and spotted a new number. It appeared several times on her incoming calls. He had written the number down and tucked it in his coat pocket hanging in the closet, the pocket that housed his gloves. He reached for the gloves now and unraveled the small square of paper. In the outdoor lights of Cabell Hall, to the strains of *The First Noel*, he read the unfamiliar string of local digits. Should he call it?

Earlier that afternoon, he had suggested that Jan come to the concert on The Lawn. "After my exam," he said, "we can go for hot chocolate on the Campus Corner. We can talk about a million things the way we used to do, over hot chocolate with a mound of whipped cream." But she had rolled her eyes and said,

"Can't do it. Can't do whipped cream."

And he had said, "Okay then, how about coffee?"

And she had said, "Can't do it. Not tonight."

Frank pocketed the phone number. He began to walk down The Lawn to his valued faculty parking space behind one of the Pavilions toward Cabell Hall. He could smell the wood smoke from student rooms, cozy fires built from stacks of firewood provided in neat bundles beside brick walls. It was a nice amenity to rooms that had no bathrooms, only communal toilets and showers reached by treks outside, retrofitted in quarters that once stabled the horses of university students in Jefferson's day. Frank nearly ran into one young man bolting out his door in a raggedy bathrobe, carrying a pail stocked with toothbrush, soap, and shampoo. The fellow looked up and laughed, swinging his towel over his shoulder. Frank said, "Happy Holidays," and walked on briskly, the music of carols from Cabell Hall following his steps.

Lately, Jan had seemed different to him. She stood sometimes, lost in thought, in almost a pose, her head to the side as if seeing things that were not there. She kept trying on the same old pair of jeans, and then taking them off. She began to hum, a low, constant hum. So irritating! And what she hummed were classical melodies. Jan! Classical music? No way! He had tried to get her interested when they first married. She said Mozart was okay; she couldn't handle the others.

The other day, he could swear, he heard her humming Tchaikovsky. What could have turned his wife onto Tchaikovsky? Or who? *Who* was the pronoun that worried Frank.

On his way home, the professor approached the town circle where the neon lights of the Circle Market beckoned yellow and green. He reflexively looked at his gas tank and decided, yes, at less than half full, he might as well stop. After filling at the pump, he decided he was hungry, and not wanting to go home to an empty house, Frank looked for a parking place in the queue of cars before the market. Not a vacant spot in sight.

"Crowded tonight," he reflected. He eased his car around the corner of the market to a darkened graveled space that separated the structure from the open field next door. He entered the front glass door. At once, the smell of coffee and burgers and the sight of Flossie wiping her hand on her brow as she hurried from customer to customer cheered him. She glanced up at him.

"Full house?" Frank said. She nodded and indicated a spot at the end of the counter. Frank picked up a local paper on his way to the counter and put it down in front of him.

"Excuse me," he said to a solid pair of shoulders in a heavy black jacket to his left.

"Certainly," said a gravelly voice. Frank looked up. "Why, hello," he said.

"Evening," the man replied.

Frank flipped his paper on the counter to the headlines below the fold. "I hear you're working at the ByWay," he said.

"That's news?" the heavy-set man chuckled.

"In this town? Are you kidding? Anything's news. Look here, a front-page story about a two-headed pig born on a farm not far from here."

"Strange things happen."

"Sure do. Have you seen the local TV news reports on the white fawn?"

"Nope," the old man said.

"Well, supposedly there is an albino deer near here. I know people who have seen it."

"Hmmm."

Frank took this for interest, so he rattled on casually,

"A guy named Larry Layman, for one. He told me you were working a forklift at the ByWay."

"Nice man."

"Yes, he is that. He saw the white deer while hunting on the Bennington Property." Frank left out the part about Larry's killing the mother of the fawn. "And then my wife saw it at the foot of our driveway one night. She said it was simply magical. But that's Jan's way of expressing things."

The old man smiled. "I believe in magic," he said and shifted his robust frame on the stool.

At that moment Flossie put before the fellow a generous mug of hot chocolate mounded with whipped cream.

"This is the only kind of magic I know," she said grinning through teeth that always had been a little wide for her narrow face.

"And what is that?" Frank's eyes crinkled.

"Kitchen magic."

"I'll have some of that, then," Frank said. "Just like his chocolate. And —"

"Your usual burger?" Flossie whisked her tablet from her apron pocket. Frank paused. "Chicken salad with lettuce on wheat toast."

"Got it," she said, spinning around.

"Trying something new?" his counter companion asked.

"Something new," Frank sighed and once more thought of his wife. "The usual things aren't working so well," he reflected, and he glanced down at his newspaper. Frank found the story about he upcoming Chamber Ball. The talent auction hoped to realize twenty-five thousand dollars toward the Habitat House charity this year. As he read silently, Frank could feel the old man raising his arm, sipping the cocoa, and he could smell its rich aroma of chocolate mingled with cream.

Let's split one of the chocolate chunk cookies. They're wonderful when warmed, Jan had said at their first encounter in the bookstore years before. She loved chocolate. But tonight—tonight—she did not want chocolate with her husband. Not tonight. Frank bent lower over the newspaper as if to blot out his consternation. And then, out of the blue, he heard his wife's voice.

"Two bottles of water, please." Jan handed a few bills to the young boy helping Flossie with the cash register at the Circle Market. He was new and efficient. He did not linger with customers nor engage in small talk. He handed Jan back a few coins, and she smiled and said "Thank you" and was gone.

Frank looked above the edge of his newspaper. He felt as if a two-by-four had smacked him in the chest. Jan didn't see him seated as he was at the corner of the counter near the back. But he saw her. She was dressed in a two-piece crushed velvet jump suit the color of cranberries. New suit? Frank watched her spin with her bag of two bottled waters and bounce out the front door. Then he followed her with his gaze as Jan climbed into her car parked cattycorner behind the solid row of vehicles before the building.

He twisted on his seat to get off the stool as if to follow, but at that instant Flossie put down his hot chocolate and chicken sandwich before him. So he sat there, dumbly, and watched farmers and town folk coming and going, eating and buying, and laughing and talking. He sat there and watched his pretty wife, shiny brown hair pulled high in a ponytail, lean forward to start the ignition, and he watched her drive away.

Frank bit into his sandwich and found it too mushy. He sipped the chocolate and found it too hot. He wiped his mouth in irritation, while he felt the old man's gaze upon him. He looked up and saw a question in the blue-black eyes buried within lines of kindness in the bearded, weathered face.

"That was my wife," Frank said, feeling ridiculous.

"I thought you knew her," the man said.

"Maybe I do and maybe I don't," Frank said, and then he was ashamed. He slapped a twenty dollar bill on the counter and got up without speaking. He walked by the cash register with the fresh-faced boy standing there behind hundreds of incidentals, chewing tobacco, cigarettes, lottery ticket machines, and small boxes of chocolates. Impulsively he picked up a tiny yellow two-piece box of Nunnally's and waved it at the boy.

"It's covered in my money on the counter," Frank told him.

Flossie came through the aluminum swinging doors from the kitchen and registered surprise that Frank was leaving without eating. The boy turned and asked,

"Is the chocolate covered?"

Frank held up the small box for Flossie.

"Sure it's covered," the waitress said, palming the twenty dollar bill as she walked toward the boy.

"Gotta go, Flossie," Frank said into her startled face. "Something's come up."

"Don't want yer sandwich to go?" She called.

"No time," Frank huffed. He ran outside and stood before the glassed doors, glancing right and left. Far down Main Street he saw the rear lights turn bright red as Jan braked for a stoplight. He bolted around the side of the market and jumped in his car.

From his seat at the counter, the elderly stranger caught a glimpse as Frank zoomed past the market windows into the dark. He shook his head over his mug; then he buried his white mustache into the melting mound of whipped cream.

"Do I want to do this?" Frank asked himself, trailing the vanishing taillights of Jan's car. Do I want to know what she has been so careful to hide?" He shook his head. Then he saw her left blinker flash. The car slowed near the railroad trestle that divided the town. It turned left and sped along away from Main Street. Frank slowed without putting on his blinker and made the same turn.

Jan followed the road, which twisted and turned, skirting past houses, a small neighborhood park, the baseball field, the community swimming pool. Frank stayed several paces behind. He saw her right blinker signal. He slowed. He made the right turn behind her at a crawl. He squinted at the street sign on the passenger side. This part of town was remote to him. What did it say? Old Ch— Street? He couldn't read it, the lettering rusted and bent as it was. When he returned his eyes to the road he realized Jan had disappeared. He felt a stab of panic.

"Where did she go?" And that brought him up short. Where, indeed, did she go? Not only tonight, but also a week ago, and the week before, and a month before? Frank felt nauseated. Hunger, maybe, but the coil in his stomach riled angrily, and instinctively he pulled to the side of the road. He hit the window button and leaned out, gasping for air. The chill made him sneeze. He fumbled with the glove compartment, then his coat pocket, hunting a tissue, a handkerchief, something for his nose. And blowing his nose there in the car, he heard the night stirring around him in wind and leaf rustle and music.

"Music?" Frank held his breath. The twinkling of piano keys drifted from somewhere in the branches overhead. What was it? The melody, so familiar. A whiff of high notes trickling down, ending in a swirl.

"Sugar Plum Fairy! *The Nutcracker Suite!* Tchaikovsky!" Frank sat a moment, the music playing in his mind. Then he eased his car off the shoulder of the road and crawled forward, listening, listening.

He slowly motored through the dark, his headlights fanning two upcoming bends in the road, passing a small brick house on the left, a small steepled church on the right. Frank drove by the church and the music began to fade. He backed up and turned into the gravel driveway divided into irregular spaces by old oak trees. He could hear the music inside. The church windows, tall, narrow, and pointed—obviously old glass—wavered with light, reminding him of flickering candles. He shut off his car engine and sat a moment. Then he opened the car door.

Feeling like a foolish peeping Tom, he crept to one of the windows, wedging between flanking boxwoods as tall as himself. He cradled his face on either side and peered inside.

"Huh!" he said, and then ducked down between the bushes. He couldn't believe it. How odd! Within the old church the chandeliers were left in place, but the pews had been torn out. Near what must have been the altar, at an upright piano a grayish little birdlike woman pumped the keys. And on the high step with a cane in her hand was another woman—lithesome, tall, imposing, her hair in a silver-black pompadour, stamping the rhythm with her rubber-tipped wood cane and calling out words in French!

Glissade, glissade, arabesque! Glissade, glissade, arabesque!

Back and forth, their arms waving like garlands, their toes curled, their bodies swaying rhythmically together, in black leotards and gauzy black skirts, the ballerinas flitted across the sheen of highly-polished hardwood floors. In shell pink tights and rose pink shoes, they twirled and bent and bowed like children's tops. In the midst of them, Frank found his wife. For the second time that night he felt stabbed in the chest—this time with relief. It rushed him so suddenly, Frank inhaled a sob. He wriggled from between the boxwoods and ran to his car. He sat there disbelieving his own emotions. Unexpected tears brimmed in his eyes.

His dear wife. His crazy, dear wife. That is why she tried on jeans to check their fit. That is why at times she stood erect, her neck arched, her gaze reflective. That is why she folded her hands in a low arch, fingers laced, while her husband intoned on one topic or another. Frank had thought (a) *she was obsessed with weight,* (b) *often she was not listening to him, and* (c) *she was bored by his topic of the moment but politely trying to stay awake.* Instead, she had been measuring her weight-loss progress and also practicing in private what she had learned secretly in ballet.

He felt ashamed; then he succumbed to an unrecoverable wash of tears. His Italian father had wept at sappy television shows, sentimental movies, and operas on the radio. Frank had inherited strong emotions. What he felt now was the weighty mix of relief and joy. *It is not too late!* He thought. His wife was working on—what had she told him that night in *La Frutta*, their favorite Italian restaurant? "The new me." And he had said automatically, "I fell in love with the old you." But he was wrong. What a fool! "The old you." Dolt! Frank flat fell in love. Irrevocably, heedless and headlong. He had fallen for Jan—all the Jans—old and new, bright and crabby, twins' mother and schoolteacher. Jan was his partner. Jan was his life. And blind, supercilious jerk that he was, Jeepers! He only saw it, now!

Leaning against the steering wheel, Frank retrieved his handkerchief from his tweed jacket pocket. He wiped his eyes and blew his nose once again. He gave a huge sigh and turned from the oak-sheltered driveway. He pointed his headlights toward town.

"No class next week! Holidays begin. See you in January!" The imperious voice of Madame Adrienne followed Jan as she opened the front door of the church studio. The blast of arctic air seemed to freeze on her perspiring face and neck. Her dark red jump suit top unzipped over her black leotard; she fingered a pair of woolly gloves in her pants pocket.

"Oh, delicious cold!" Jan said to a companion alongside.

"Yes, but better get warm," the other dancer answered, wrapping her coat and hustling to her car in the tree shadows created by light from the tall church windows. Jan exhaled a cloud of vapor and whimsically looked up beyond the tall branches, her eyes enveloping the swirl of overhead stars. She sighed with quiet contentment. The moon was filling toward full. She walked toward her vehicle humming *The Nutcracker* melodies that had recently stirred her feet. A little smile played at the corners of her mouth, and her heart was light. She watched her ballerina classmates hurrying to their cars, the vehicles sputtering in the cold, trailing oily-smelling exhaust as they pulled from the pointed window lights in the church, leaving the parking area virtually deserted. Then she heard a voice,

"Can you help me?"

Jan started. There in the parking area, half-lit by the moon, she saw the familiar silvery hair, the broad shoulders, the tweed coat, and the rugged smile—a man leaning against his car. Frank was holding two thick paper cups in front of him. He cocked his head to one side and said,

"I am the Handsome Prince in search of the Sugar Plum Fairy."

"Hah!" Jan snorted.

"Okay then, I'm an architect in love with a ballerina who loves chocolate. Would you be the one?"

At this, Jan smiled. Then she frowned. "Have you been following me?"

"The truth?" Frank said, putting gingerly into her

gloved hands a cup of hot chocolate. "Tonight, yes. For ten years, yes. Hell, I guess I'll be following you 'til the day I die."

"Well, then you know my secret." Jan cradled the chocolate, inhaling it dreamily.

"And I'm proud of you. And, actually relieved." Frank's eyes found hers.

"Why?"

"For all the reasons any man married to you would be relieved."

Jan squinted. "You know, Frank?" She said, her head cocked to one side. "You are an architect, true. But you're also a romantic." And suddenly her irrepressible laugh slid up and down as if scampering across a xylophone. Next, to his surprise, she stood on tiptoe and kissed his lips.

"Yes!" She exulted. "I am the one! You have found me! I am the ballerina who loves chocolate!"

"Good," Frank nodded, "because I brought us a small box of chocolate candy and a huge chocolate chunk cookie."

"Oh!" Jan gasped. "Is the cookie warm? You know they are wonderful when—"

"Warm," Frank said, and he put his long tweedy arm around her and nestled her in his warm car for a small chocolate picnic beneath a half-wafer moon.

32. Isabel Cuts a Deal

*I*n the small-town world of Clearview business, Isabel Charmin was universally considered not a woman, not a man, but a titan. Her crafty intelligence, her laser intuition, and her incisive reasoning skills put enemies on guard and allies at ease. As a result, aligning Isabel to one's side achieved half of any battle involving the community.

It was for this purpose that the one person in town with the delusory notion of being Isabel's equal sat idling his car at a parking meter on Main Street as he smoked a final hand-rolled cigarette and stubbed it out in the ashtray. Adjusting the rearview mirror to check for tobacco strands in his teeth, Hiram Venald reached for the door handle and slid his chubby frame onto the sidewalk. He glanced high above his head, to the masonry doorsill that proclaimed in carved letters, "Clearview Chamber of Commerce." Inside, Hiram well knew, was the behemoth he and others called *The Force.* He pursed his lips and feigned a confident whistle, preparing to impress the prim secretary in Isabel's long-term employ. He stepped inside the building. Before he could say "Hello," the tiny woman bent in a customary curl over her keyboard, looked up, and automatically hit the phone button for Isabel. "He's here," she said and bent back over her keys.

"Well, if it isn't Mr. Venald," Isabel boomed, swinging her office door open wide.

"A pleasure, Isabel," Hiram said, instantly uncomfortable in the presence of a woman taller and wider than himself. He leaned over and kissed the fleshy hand she proffered him to shake.

"Now what can this outlandish gesture mean?" Isabel laughed. "Charm, Hiram, will get you nowhere with me."

Hiram replied with a "Heh, heh," without smiling a whole lot. "You can't blame me for trying, Isabel, now can you?"

"Have a seat," she said, indicating a modest armchair before her mammoth desk. She wore a black cherry silk dress, which rustled around her shape and sent the overhead lights bouncing in chaotic reflective darts from her bosom and thighs as she circled the desk square to sit down herself. Fluttering like a hot-air balloon in an immense puddle of ruffles she eased into her executive chair. Hiram preferred not to sit. He began to pace back and forth, trying not to cringe before the powerhouse; however, she consumed much of the room.

Isabel's eyes followed his pacing with bemused affection, the same look she saved for her Jack Russell Terrier, when he barked for dinner without obeying her commands. So, now instead of saying, "Have a seat," she ordered, "Sit, Hiram."

Hiram sat.

"I'm listening," She picked up a pen from her desk and twirled it, a few thin gold bracelets clanking together around her right wrist.

Hiram wished he could smoke another cigarette. But a sign posted over an antique brass spittoon on Isabel's wood file cabinet read,

"SPITTERS AND SMOKERS WILL BE SHOT!"

So he wrung his hands and cleared his throat, pitching his voice in a placating tone.

"You called me," he began. "I'm prepared to listen to you, Isabel." He flattened his mouth. "You said there was a problem with the zoning meeting next week. The one, may I remind you? You granted me a few weeks before?"

"Before I had all the relevant information," Isabel replied matter-of-factly. "Since that time, it has come to my attention that the owner of the Blackstone Trailer Park is evicting a woman who happens to be the Clearview Chamber of Commerce Habitat for Humanity honoree this year. And this owner is a man I know . . . "

Hiram rolled his eyes. "Well—" he began.

Ignoring him, Isabel went on " . . . a man who has asked many favors of this Chamber and this Chamber President. You know of whom I am speaking?"

Hiram's throat constricted. He hated this way of talking—the sly phrases—"of whom" and "come to my attention" and the vague metaphor of himself as "the man I know."

"Isabel," he sighed. "I own the trailer park—true. I am a businessman. And I am a fair man." He cleared his throat. "But my park manager has brought to my attention that the tenant is two months behind on her rent. By contract, Isabel, she's out." Hiram rose from his seat and began pacing before the chairman's desk.

"Hiram," Isabel said in a voice not be confused with a growl, "Hiram, Stay!"

Hiram stayed and returned to his seat, his lips pursed, his eyes straight ahead.

"So, this same man," Isabel continued, "who has asked favors from this chairman, has directed said manager to evict the tenants, my Habitat honoree along with her paralyzed son, on December 31st, right smack in the dead of winter?" The Chamber President's voice jumped an octave.

"She's six hundred dollars behind in rent," Hiram retorted.

"Six hundred," Isabel repeated. "And how much are you selling the land that you are requesting a called meeting for, Hiram?"

"Two million," he muttered.

"What did you say, Hiram? Speak!"

"Two million! But, Isabel, no landlord can put up with losing rent for more than a couple of months. It's not good business."

"Well," Isabel replied, "I am *not* asking you to put up with losing rent for two months, Hiram."

Hiram brightened. "Oh, good." From his pocket he pulled out his cigarette paper container and his pouch of tobacco, which he laid on Isabel's mahogany desk.

Isabel stared at him coldly. " Can you read?" She asked, pointing a black-cherry fingernail at the sign above the brass spittoon atop her filing cabinet.

"Yeah," Hiram said folding his hands in his lap. "Seeing the ciggies close just calms my nerves, that's all. What about the two months?"

"I'm not asking for two months, Hiram. I'm asking for *eight* months. I'm asking for relief until we get the Habitat House built. And I figure six months construction and a two-month grace period means eight months, beginning January 1."

"You can't do that!" Hiram brought his fist down on his tobacco pouch. "You can't! You can't! That's blackmail!"

"Hiram! Control yourself!" Isabel stood up accompanied by the relieved rustlings of a thousand smashed wrinkles of silk. "Or I shall insist that you leave!"

Hiram reached for his cigarette case and tobacco pouch and pocketed them. Then he leaned back in his chair. He cleared his throat twice. Time for charm again.

"Please, my dear lady, why don't you sit down so that we can reason together?"

Isabel eyed him like a wary hen. She sat down slowly,

her dress crinkling around her, darts of light glancing from her generous frame.

"We can reason," she began, not taking her eyes from his, "but in the end, Hiram, in the end, you *will* see things my way."

"Why should I?" Hiram demanded, losing his composure again.

Isabel had regained hers. "For two million reasons, Hiram," she said evenly. "No meeting in December, no zoning change. No zoning change, no sale."

"That's black—er—bribery."

Isabel made a tent of her fingers, her nails entangled like thorny blackberry branches sprouting blood-red fruit. She watched Hiram begin to drum his knuckles on her desk. She leaned toward him, the pink flesh of her forearms oozing across the wood like toy putty. Her tone was casual.

"Hiram, the other day, I saw your wife Stephanie in the grocery store. We both wanted a cantaloupe, and she was thumping every single one, so I noticed her hands. On the left hand, third finger, I spotted what must be a two-carat diamond ring."

"Aw, Isabel, c'mon. It ain't and you know it," Hiram slipped back into to his small town vernacular. "But it is almost a carat, and I'm proud of it."

"Well, Hiram. I just have to ask you, was that ring a bribe?"

"Isabel! How insulting! I gave that to Stephanie before we married."

"Why, Hiram?"

"So she'd marry me."

"So she'd do you a favor?"

"No. It was a gift, a heartfelt gift!"

"But you got something, right? You got Bennington's youngest daughter, right? Old Bennington, the man who owns thousands of acres of land?"

"Well, he's dead now," Hiram said. "The slime ball."

"Yes, I heard about his last will and testament and his leaving Stephanie only *seven dollars*. But that's beside the point right now."

"What is the point?" Hiram's visage grew dark.

"The point is, you're about to make a record two million dollars on a small tract of land. And you want to throw it over for several hundred in trailer rent?"

"Go on," Hiram muttered.

"Well, Hiram, you're smart; so consider this: Chamber members, whom you know, are giving money and time to sponsor this Habitat House. A landowner, whom you admire, is donating the lot. Volunteers are ready to swing hammers and drive nails. Meanwhile, Habitat is giving the future homeowner an interest-free mortgage. She, herself, is sewing curtains for use in other Habitat homes. All this gifting to the common good of Clearview. Yet, at the same time, Hiram Venald is wrenching every last penny out of a widow with a crippled son!"

"Oh, C'mon, Isabel," Hiram whined. The Chamber president's plump lips kept moving, her words pricking the reptilian conscience seated before her.

"This house is a hand up—not a handout, Hiram. The mortgage is based on ability to pay. Already, despite penurious circumstances, Eva is giving back. Giving is empowering, Hiram. You should try it sometime. Maybe right now!"

Hiram squirmed.

"So I trust that you see the wisdom of a heartfelt, and tax deductible, Habitat gift of eight months rent and the pledge not to evict Evangeline Holmes and her son, Tom."

"Ugh."

"And since this is the season of gift giving, I'll reciprocate. I'll see to it that you get the gift of a zoning meeting before Christmas, wrapped up in the red bow of opportunity for you to

216

make enough money to buy out old Bennington's daughters or to purchase another large farm in Peach County."

Hiram's eyes bulged. He blushed, purplish crimson traveling up his bull neck to his jowly cheeks. He felt as if his head would explode. Then, he inhaled slowly, his belly rising.

"Eight months, tax deductible. I'm beginning to see things your way, Isabel," he smoldered.

"Good," Isabel said. She pushed back her desk chair. She reached in her center drawer and withdrew a sheet of type, which she slid smoothly toward the developer.

"Because, I happen to have a little document here for you to sign that says you agree to what you just now agreed to."

Hiram shook his head and pulled out a pen.

"And—" Isabel continued. Hiram finished his signature scrawl and looked up with a scowl.

"And what?"

Isabel matched his glance with an ingratiating smile.

"And—I was just wondering, Hiram, if you have a flattering picture of yourself that I might borrow for the next few days?"

When Hiram reached his ranch-style home that night, he found Stephanie Bennington Venald watching the six o'clock news. Her hair was teased into a beehive; her lips were coated a coral color; her teal pants stretched like rubber bands around her bony hips. She looked at him and raised her stemmed glass as a toast—a four-olive vodka martini encircled by her coral acrylic nails, one finger brightened by a chunky diamond ring.

Hiram registered the ring. *A bribe? What gall! That Isabel Charmin! Even though there was some truth to what she'd said about his wife, her father, and the Bennington land. What gall!*

"Hey there, Honeykins," Stephanie called. "Come look at this on the TV."

Hiram walked into the den of his spreading domain and glanced at the television set. A local story about the mysterious white deer had just ended, delivering all viewers to the advertisements. Stephanie hit the "Mute" button of the remote. Then, she twisted her olive stem in the clear drink.

"You know, Hiram?" she said, arching her neck, appearing to her disgruntled husband that she was a full three inches taller, due to the hair. "In this country, Indian princesses way back in the early days, well, they used to all crave a white buck dress to get married in."

"Well, you're already married." Hiram grunted.

"I know that, Honeykins. But you know, I thought about it, I thought, now, wouldn't a white buck skirt—straight and tight, like leather—be just the thing on me!"

"Nobody can find that white deer."

"Somebody will. I just know it. And they'll kill it. And somebody's wife will show up downtown this Christmas wearing a very cool, very white buckskin skirt."

Hiram snorted. "Well, if you want it so bad, why don't you post a bounty sign around town? 'WANTED. REWARD—WHITE BUCK—DEAD OR ALIVE!'"

"Honeykins, there you go! Smart businessman!" Stephanie brightened and sat up straight, her hair as stiff as a pineapple. She clinked her fingernails against her glass.

Not so smart. Outsmarted by Isabel, The Force, Hiram thought sourly. He strode to the open bar near the kitchen and reached for the Dewar's. He shook his head as his wife's voice prattled on.

"I knew you'd think of something! 'WANTED. REWARD.' Brilliant! Now, Hiram, help me with this. How many dollars do you think I should offer on that sign as a reward?"

33. Hank's Edition

Within the brick walls of *The Clearview Clarion*, Hank Bissell was finishing a turkey sandwich from the Circle Market when the wall phone in the paste-up room roared its heightened bell tones. The sound was necessarily loud to be heard above the rumbling of the newspaper presses in the back room, a blast of vibration that daily shook the building's foundations and rattled its walls. *The Clarion* was a two-floor operation, and the presses and layout rooms were at street level, reeking of ink, clanking with machinery, and covered with papers in stacks hither and yon. Hank swallowed his last bite, reached for the wall phone, and said, "Paste-up."

"Hank!" The voice was commanding. Hank recognized it: the Chamber President's.

"Yes, Isabel?"

"Is the article ready?"

"Of course," Hank said. "You issued the marching order, right?" Hank chuckled and listened to the squawk in his ear. "Yeah, got the photo, too. Came in this morning. Hiram Venald's picture is below Evangeline's. The story head reads, 'Trailer Park Owner Shows Compassion at Christmas.' Everything's set for Sunday the 19th."

Another squawk pounded Hank's eardrum.

"Yes, Isabel. I think you will be pleased," Hank smiled and replaced the phone on the wall receiver. He walked over to the paste-up area where his design for the weekend feature rested on the layout table. His eyes traveled to the lead article and the picture of a beautiful young woman, her arms around her son. Both gazed out a window into snowy light, which cast their faces in gauzy profiles, supple and soft. The picture had a dreamy quality to it, and Hank wondered—because it didn't happen often these days—if his own awakened emotions had traveled down his arm to his finger when he pressed the camera button.

Two days before, at the direction of his publisher, a friend to Isabel Charmin, Hank had visited the trailer park. In addition to shooting backdrop photos to portray the starkness of shaky aluminum houses on concrete blocks, he had photographed the Holmes family. He took pictures of the mother Evangeline, first, inside her home and then outdoors. In each locale, her plaintive beauty nearly struck him blind. Because of that, when he focused his lens on the boy at his wheelchair desk, all Hank could think about was, "What a shame . . . the boy's beauty is like his mother's except it's all twisted." The photographer was overcome with unexpected yearning: *How he wished that he could do something for the boy!*

Meanwhile, after watching Hank work, Tom struggled to pull some loose papers and a sketchbook from a shelf at wheelchair height beside the built-in kitchen table. The table folded against the wall with a pull-down pole, and the mother set it up creating a wide surface for Tom. Hank noticed her sewing machine stationed just a few inches away, and the thought of these two industrious artists working side-by-side touched him.

"So this is your work?" He smiled at the boy. Tom

raised his head awkwardly and nodded vigorously back and forth. "Well, let me see." Hank cast his experienced eye over charcoal sketches, watercolors, and a few chalk renderings of scenes in the boy's world. With long sensitive fingers, Hank sifted through sketches of sunflowers in full bloom, mountains ruddy in fall, and twisted dogwoods with grey tight-budded fists in winter.

Hank screwed in the macro lens of his camera and began to photograph the pictures that might illustrate the story of the seamstress and her son. Evangeline waited respectfully beside him as he worked. In the poised silence, his shutter made the whirring *click-buzz* of instants frozen in time. After Hank finished, the woman placed a bound, over-sized sketchpad on the table near the finished drawings.

"Thought you might want to see these," she said quietly.

"Okay with you, buddy?" Hank glanced at the boy in his stiff wooden chair. Again Tom began his mechanical nod.

The photographer flipped the book open and gasped. Here, the bright, curious expression of a raccoon blinked from the page. There, a quail rose in a startled flush. On the following page, a turtle warily raised his head. After staring for several silent minutes, Hank deduced, as strange as it seemed, that the lifelike movement suggested in the static drawings came from Tom's inability to control his limbs. The effect was the same one Hank achieved with the help of very expensive camera equipment—that of athletes in motion—freeze-frames in flight.

"These are very, very good, son," Hank said with genuine awe.

"Thaaaaaank yooouuu," Tom stretched his vowels wide, and his mother bent quickly to wipe some drool from his gaping mouth. Tom shook his head, annoyed. He flailed his arms as if to brush her away. He threw his thin legs apart, his feet scraping suddenly out from the rungs of his chair. He gripped the arms of his wheelchair and scrabbled his way closer to the notebook; he reached for it and flung it on its back.

"Sorry, Tom," Hank said. "Didn't mean to pry."

But Tom was reaching a spinning hand between the back cardboard cover and the final page. With a grunt, he knocked open the back cover. This time, Evangeline gasped.

From the page emerged a feathery sketch of a deer, a chiaroscuro of the pure white fawn stepping from shadow.

"This is astonishing," Hank said. "I've heard the stories about the white fawn and some of the local sightings of it around here. Have you heard those stories, too?"

Tom stretched his sideways, crooked smile. Hank couldn't tell if the smile meant "Yes" or "No."

"They are quite rare. They're albinos," Hank went on. "They have characteristic pink eyes. Sometimes, I've heard, they have birth defects, misshapen feet, and oddities like that. Typically, they don't live too long—you know—disease gets them or hunters, who can easily see them in the woods. My newspaper has done stories of people who have seen it. But I can't verify it exists." Hank was silent a moment. Then he asked the boy,

"Have you seen him?"

Tom awkwardly nodded his head.

Hank turned toward Evangeline. "Have you?"

The seamstress shook her head, No. Hank noticed that side-by-side, their view of the woods surrounding the trailer would be the same. If the boy saw it, why hadn't his mother? "Is he kidding?" He glanced down at Tom, "Are you kidding me, buddy?"

Tom turned his head left, then right.

"You've seen him."

Another nod; this time, a lunge.

"You believe the white deer exists," Hank grinned.

Tom dragged out a multisyllabic, "Yeeeeeah."

By then, Hank had begun to wrap up his gear. He had said, "Well, I wish could. Seeing is believing to a photographer. If I'm lucky enough to snap it, I'll get you a picture, okay, Tom?"

The boy nodded clumsily, and Evangeline Holmes smiled in her mysterious way, and Hank had been struck by the impression: *a modern-day Madonna and child.*

Now, placing the final photo in layout, Hank heard the printing drums slowing down in the room behind him. *Ready to go,* he glanced at the picture once more. *Today's nativity scene— played out in poverty, sadness, and greed.*

The only saving grace in Hank's mind was the knowledge that Isabel Charmin was directing this Christmas story, and if *compassion* was the word she wanted to headline a story above the sleazy Hiram Venald, then that's what she'd get. Hank wished he knew just how Isabel had engineered such uncharacteristic kindness out of the town scoundrel. Over the years Hank had photographed many people in the community, and, invariably, when the name of the developer Hiram Venald came up, everyone seemed to voice the same expression—"Ugh!"

"Well, at least Hiram is below the fold," Hank said to himself. "And Evangeline and Tom are above it, front and center." He picked up the wall phone and reached the production room. Inside, a canyon of giant drums rumbled to a standstill. Hank shouted at the man near the drums, "Front page is ready to roll!"

34. Wired Magic

*A*round the white picket fence surrounding his farm cottage on Friday, December 18, Frank Midland walked purposefully, his keen eye looking forward and backward, measuring the scallop of the Christmas tree lights connecting his fence panels in a garland. Were they level? A guy couldn't afford to be haphazard about this sort of thing; each drape should be the same number of inches from the ground. Otherwise the neighbors on distant hills would gibe him unmercifully about it.

He almost had the scallops right. A little tweak here and there, looping the tiny clear specks, like allineate glow worms, at the supporting four-by-fours, why, that would do it. Just a few more sections to go. He picked up the glittering strands at his feet and began another panel of fencing.

Every year he decorated the picket fence with garlands of lights. The effect was wondrous, Frank thought, in its own small way as exciting as the annual lighting of the great tree in Atlanta, atop Rich's department store, located downtown at the corner of Alabama and Broad Streets. As a child Frank had gone with his parents on Thanksgiving Night each year to see the lights blaze suddenly in a brilliant burst and to hear the celebratory carols sung by hundreds of voices from the assembled choirs on each tier of a lighted bridge. He never forgot the glory of it all. And so each year, inspired by the memory, he wired his stereo speakers to reach outdoors, and he lit his white fence to create a wonderland of low, reachable stars.

Call him a sentimentalist, but that was Frank. So now, though he had raised only two children starting at the age of ten, Frank was looking forward to "busting a gut," as the boys would say, to the happy instant he would cross the few yards from the picket fence to the gravel driveway where he could hug those stepsons of his, those rascally, terrific twins. Meanwhile, he busied himself creating his own boyhood memories.

Looping here, leveling there, lost in concentration, Frank gently stretched his lights. He worked silently, hearing his own breathing. And then, he heard? Or felt? Breathing other than his own. Frank froze. Somebody or something was watching him. Hardly moving his head, Frank glanced up. About ten feet away, he saw the image Jan had described to him, the same one the television had reported: a white fawn. The animal nudged a crop of brown broom sedge poking through the snow. Frank had read that deer, particularly albinos, often were near-sighted; most of their sight registered movement. Frank did not want to move; he did not want to startle this wondrous creature.

Why, I can see its spots, white circles on a white back, he thought.

The deer stepped forward, stopped, and raised its head, staring at Frank.

Pink eyes, Frank noticed. *Rare indeed.* He felt himself take a shallow breath. He looked toward the feet, thinking, *Often they are cobbled, disfigured.* And sure enough, he could see that the hooves were oddly shaped.

In spite of the distortions, Frank felt privileged to be a

silent witness. For a man who had spent his life studying masterpieces, who had seen Europe's magnificence—visited the Vatican, climbed the steps of the Pantheon, stepped inside the towering vault of St. Peter's Cathedral in London—this natural composition was no less awe inspiring . . . *an imposing study in white: white deer, white hills, white sky,* Frank thought. *Surreal.*

The fawn blinked, and then averted its head. In an instant, it sprang away and bounded into the cedars at the edge of the woods. Frank exhaled. What had startled it? Then, he heard something.

From far away, then closer and closer, Frank recognized a sound—an engine he had worked on—in fact—himself. Throwing loose gravel in their wake, the twins were roaring up the hill in their red Toyota 4Runner, the radio blasting from open windows—despite the frigid temperatures. Frank shook his head in a mixture of disgust and amusement. But superceding these feelings, excitement strangled his throat. Frank could hardly get himself untangled from the light strands over his arms fast enough to meet the car. He literally leaped across a mound of coiled, lighted wires between him and the driveway.

"Whoa Frank! Wiring again!" Kyle hollered, leaning out the passenger side window, as the car screeched to a stop.

"Bet you run outta lights again this year," Ryan cut the motor.

"No! This year the man—the man!—bought the lights—me!" Frank beat his chest with his thumb. "I know how to estimate lengths. Unlike you blockheads."

The boys jumped from both sides of the 4Runner. They pumped Frank's hand and swung their arms around his back in a bear hug. Frank developed a sudden wrench in his chest, and tears clouded his eyes.

"Well," he straightened his arms back to look at both of

the grinning young men. He reached in his pocket for a hand-kerchief. He wiped his eyes and then self-consciously blew his nose. "Now," he said, "now, your mother will feel it's finally—really—Christmas."

While Frank was greeting her twins, Jan was hurriedly returning from the outskirts of Richmond, less than an hour's drive from Clearview. She had been on a photography mission. Given the outcome of Jan and Lucy's PowerPoint presentation at the community college class on Thursday night, Frank suggested that Jan put pictures and facts to strong advantage in the zoning hearing on December 20 to defeat Hiram Venald's sale of proper-ty adjoining the Circle Market.

Cruising along, Jan listened to Christmas carols on the radio and let her mind roam. She could hardly wait to see her sons. She remembered how she had stood before young people the same age as her twins and rolled through her PowerPoint program, "Clean Your Place in Sixty Minutes!" in a speedy three minutes. She zipped through a montage of the messiest dorm and apartment rooms imaginable in quick succession right before their astonished eyes. Then she introduced Lucy Layman as her project collaborator and "Domestic Consultant." Lucy rose uneasily before the group. But then, the first question melted her jitters like boiling water on candle wax.

The question came from a brown-eyed boy with curly hair and a mischievous smile who raised his hand asking, "Why would I want to clean my apartment if I can hire you?"

"Because I'm busy. My week is full," Lucy shot back. "And if your place is a wreck, and you have a girl over, she won't last long." A ripple of laughter sailed around the class-room. Another student, a young woman with red hair, timidly raised her hand.

"This isn't about cleaning a room, but I wanted to know something. I work in a blood lab and we wear white coats. Even though we're careful, 'cause of AIDS and all, sometimes, I get blood on my lab coat. And I can't get it out. I've tried Clorox—"

"Hydrogen peroxide," Lucy corrected. She nodded her head emphatically. "That'll make them spots just disappear."

After that bit of advice, young hands began popping up all over the room. Question, answer. Question, answer. When the bell rang to signal class change, the students erupted in a spontaneous burst of applause. As they filed out toward the hall, the professor conveyed a hearty "Good presentation." Then he shook Lucy's hand. "Useful information!" Lucy beamed.

When Jan deposited Lucy at her driveway after class that night, Lucy leaned in the passenger window. "Well, now I know it's true."

"What's that?" Jan clasped the steering wheel.

"That sayin'—a picture's worth a thousand words."

Jan laughed. "Right. And your pictures of messy apartments sure set the stage."

Now, a week later, Jan was about to employ a similar technique. From a distance she saw the edge of a metallic roof glinting in the morning sun. The huge gas station reared its threatening presence like a steel knife within the staid winter surroundings of green firs and scattered snow. Canned music rasped from speakers.

Whenever she encountered these man-made "tarantulas," Jan felt revulsion. This time, she swallowed her feelings and pulled into the filling station. She inserted her credit card and set the pump handle to fill slowly. She withdrew a small digital camera from her coat pocket and in quick succession began snapping pictures. Here a pump handle; there, a fluorescent light. *Click! Click!* A metal pole strafing the clouds. An oily spill splashed on concrete. *Click! Click!* The backdrop of wilderness. *Click, click!* A mélange of signs, buildings, and traffic.

"The promise of chaos to come," she muttered. Then she replaced her camera in her pocket, put the gas pump in its metal socket, and climbed into her car. Forty-five minutes later, she pulled the car to the top of the hill at Double Nickel Farm just in time to spot Frank and her twin sons engaged in a riotous snowball fight. Eagerly she reached into her coat pocket for the camera.

Click! Click!

"A thousand words," Jan grinned. "Now there's a picture!"

35. Hiram Prepares to Fight

The afternoon of December 20, the view in Clearview revealed cumulous clouds moving across the Blue Ridge, and everyone knew that the major snow of the season was on its way. Hiram Venald looked out the window of his realtor sales office on Main Street. At this time of day, a shadow generally fell across the blinds covering his storefront window. He found it a tiresome pall. The overhead train viaduct, the one that crossed over Main and divided the town, lay west of his office. The long daily shadow reminded Hiram of his roots, which during his lifetime he had heard referred to as "shady" more than once. Hiram knew what it meant to grow up on the wrong side of the tracks. He also knew what it meant to buy on the right side of the tracks. He'd done that, too, and in the process he had elevated his social position right up there beside the genteel and the wealthy among the town's citizens, including folks like the Midlands and the Urbanes.

Now he was about to pull a notch ahead of them all, with only a high school education to match Frank Midland's Ph.D., and a hardscrabble deal to approach Bill Urbane's business savvy and inherited means. With the sealing of the Crane's deal, Hiram would be rich enough to take on any notion he had a mind to—from a cruise every year to a career in local politics.

"Not bad." Hiram fingered his bow tie, catching his own reflection in a mirror near the window, the one in which he regularly checked his tie knot when leaving the office. He also checked his teeth for leftovers from the day's lunch at his desk and any chocolate M&M's he'd smuggled from his secretary's desk drawer. "Not bad," he nodded to himself, noting his dark hair rimming his shiny head. He was glad his hair was still black around his ears, even though his top was bald. Also he was glad his expressive bushy eyebrows held not one single strand of grey. He smiled at his image and repeated, "Not bad for a guy who started out selling fresh fruits and vegetables by the side of the road."

That was the admirable truth about Hiram. He had gotten ahead by getting up early. At four every morning from the time he was sixteen years old, he was on the road to Washington, D.C., for a one-day, turnaround trip—travel time, six hours. He delivered fresh produce to Clearview before everyone else. And what he selected in those early years garnered the short, chubby boy a reputation as "Green Thumb" Venald—not for growing quality vegetables and fruit—but for picking them from the vendors' farm harvests at markets not far from the nation's capital.

Hiram liked the nickname, and used it as a logo. He hired a friend to paint a huge "thumbs up" sign, the thumb egregiously green, which he propped alongside his "The Freshest and The Bestest" boast on his first roadside stand near the Clearview Circle. One roadside produce stand begat another, and another, and finally Hiram developed the idea for "Green Thumb" farmer's market specialty stores in Clearview and other Virginia towns like Hinesburg and Limburg. Before long, the shrewd, small man not only profited from the sale of produce, but also from produce stores he financed, and ultimately from the sale of real estate on which the stores sat.

Over the years, Hiram's instincts for knowing when produce was ripe translated into successful property hunches. Hiram could smell ripeness. And he had just known in his olfactory glands that the eleven acres around the Circle Market would sell soon enough. He'd had a difficult time financing it several years back, but now the deal was poised to take flight.

"What time is it?" Hiram questioned himself in the mirror, speaking aloud.

"Pay off time!" He grinned broadly. He could hardly contain his excitement, and he began to chuckle.

"Money will soon sift down like the oncoming snow!" He gloated as he straightened his tie knot squarely at his bulging neck.

He walked over to the coat rack and pulled on his overcoat and hat. He still had plenty of time. In fact, he was early; the courthouse clock tower had yet to strike its five deep melodious chimes. He'd be the first one in the zoning room on the second floor of the building. The Crane's representatives were driving in from Washington, D.C. Hiram would grab a sandwich at Horton's Drugstore, and maybe some hot soup. Then he'd be at the courthouse by six thirty. The zoning hearing began at seven. The timing felt ripe. Hiram could smell it, along with the dampness in the December air. He glanced out his office window one last time. The wind had picked up its pace, and lacy snowflakes, the promising size of quarters, had begun to fall.

As he hustled to the luncheon counter inside Horton's Drugstore, Hiram noticed the same portly old man he had spotted a few weeks ago when he ran into Bill Urbane, Frank Midland, and Larry Layman at the Circle Market. "The bum," Hiram had called him. Tonight he noticed that the fellow was in a jacket—not the coat he wore the first day he came to town—one of those Al Capone flared, calf-length winter things from the 1920s.

"Hmmm," Hiram paused. "Wonder if the guy's as poor as he seems?" Then he spotted the same moth-eaten gloves rammed halfway into the man's jacket pocket and the ratty red scarf hung haphazardly around his thick neck.

"Nah," Hiram mumbled to himself, "he ain't got money. If he did, I could smell it."

But one thing did catch Hiram's attention. The old fellow sat at the counter engrossed in the flimsy local newspaper. On the counter beside him he had a cup of hot chocolate on which the waitress had just piled a dollop of whipped cream. And significantly, Hiram could not help but notice, the man's face was plunged deep into the front-page zoning article about the Crane's station, the one which featured Hiram pointing at the rezoning sign. Hiram stalked up and tapped a pudgy finger on his picture before the old man's face. Underneath it, the cut line read, "Developer Venald Seeks Zoning for D.C. Firm."

"That's me," Hiram said, and then he extended his hand in greeting as the old man looked up. "Hiram Venald. You're new to town, aren't you, fellow?"

"Yes, I am." The wizened gentleman still had not shaved since the first time Hiram saw him just after Thanksgiving. He slouched as if weary, but his handclasp felt strong. It enveloped Hiram's hand like a pitcher's glove.

"Big hands," Hiram said.

"Big heart," the man returned and leaned back with a knowing smile. It made Hiram a little uncomfortable, but he couldn't figure out why.

"Your name?" Hiram asked, thinking—*this guy's a real kook. But at least he doesn't smell bad.* Hiram was sensitive to smells. He could spot a rotten melon when everyone else thought it was in its prime. This old guy was clearly beyond his prime. Seventy? Eighty? Hard to tell. He was tall, maybe six feet three, broad at the shoulders, and Hiram remembered he stood up rather straight. He was round and stocky, but not flabby; rather, what Hiram's folks called "big boned." He seemed robust, as if he did outside work on a farm, maybe with livestock. Hiram fleetingly thought that maybe the old guy was looking for farm work.

"My name? Just call me 'Pap,'" the old man answered Hiram, holding his gaze.

"Like Papa?" Hiram asked. "Papa? Like Papa Hemingway?" Hiram snorted at his own joke. "Like *The Mamas and the Papas*?" Then he felt a little silly.

"Like, whatever you want," the stranger replied intently.

"I tell you what I want." Hiram's mood shifted. He thumped the paper now lying before Pap on the fountain counter. "I want that property to go C-1 Commercial." The developer tore off his overcoat and hung it on a wooden rack standing where the counter met the wall of the room. He straddled the stool at the drugstore fountain next to the newcomer.

"Tammy? You got any chicken salad?" Hiram called to the middle-aged woman washing dishes by hand behind the counter.

Horton's was the same place it had been since the 1940s. It was, shall we say, retro before retro was cool; that is, absolutely unchanged by the decades. To the delight of its patrons like Jan Midland and Linda Layman earlier that week, the place didn't have muzak. It offered the individual jukeboxes at each booth with song selections still priced at ten cents a pick.

Tonight, however, the jukeboxes were silent. Muffled patron voices were joined by the clank of dishes washed in a deep metal sink, the sizzle of burgers on the blackened grill, and a plug-in radio still operated with turn knobs, which Tammy habitually kept near the cash register. She tuned it to the local radio station, WCVU, which played Christmas carols over scattered static.

Tammy had worked in this very kitchen setup for ten years, maybe twenty. Nobody knew. Also, nobody knew if she had a last name. Everybody just called her "Tammy." She was simply a fixture, and, Hiram noticed, an aging one. Her silvery hair was getting a bit thin on top as she leaned over the soapy sink. She pulled out a final white ceramic plate, the kind seen in diners in small towns across America. Hiram drummed his fingers on the counter as he watched her rinse the plate leisurely under the running water. She put it in a rack of dripping dishes. Then, for the first time, she glanced up at Hiram.

"Finally!" he said.

"Dishwashing by hand takes time," Tammy said evenly as she leaned against the deep metal sink. "'Course if we had one of them mechanical washers like I been asking you for, for years now, I might move a little faster."

Hiram ignored the remark. "Chicken salad?"

Tammy nodded wearily. "Got some left. Jest a few minutes. Any chips?" She dried her water-swollen hands on a dishcloth.

"A few chips," Hiram said, reading the menu posted on a blackboard overhead. "Just a few. What's the soup for today?"

"Chicken vegetable."

"Same thing every day," Hiram knowingly elbowed the old man sitting beside him. "This place is a dump. But it's going down. It's part of the eleven acres backing up to the Circle Market."

"Something attractive going up in its place?" the stranger asked.

Hiram inhaled. "Depends on how you like the color green," he said, thinking himself rather clever. Hiram loved a good joke, and he thrived on puns, mostly his own.

"Greed?" the old man asked, holding his ear toward Hiram.

"Not greed," Hiram shouted, emphatically, "Green!

235

Money! It's a joke. I kind of joke a lot. Part of my charm, folks tell me." Then Hiram held up his right hand folded as the gesture, "Thumbs up."

"I see," the old man said, and those curious blue-black eyes glistened.

Hiram felt the old boy still didn't get the money part of his zoning petition. *Maybe he's a little deaf,* Hiram thought. So he leaned over and shouted in his ear to make him understand, "It will make money for the town."

"And what will it cost the town?" Pap asked reflexively leaning in the opposite direction.

At that moment, Tammy put down Hiram's sandwich on the counter before him. For once, the developer felt relieved to have an excuse not to talk. The hair on his neck felt suddenly prickly. He scowled. *Why in the world,* he wondered, *if he could spot fresh, ripe produce and promising ripe real estate from afar, could he not glimpse a tree-hugging liberal environmentalist sitting right next to him?* He was sorry he'd ever said hello to the old bum. *Who was he, anyway? Pap. What kind of name was that? A drifter, a homeless person, a God knows what—maybe a criminal or a bona fide kook escaped from a lunatic bin somewhere.*

"Cost to the town?" Hiram repeated, turning his scowling face away from the old man to lean over his full plate. "Nothin.'" He picked up his sandwich with his right hand; then he grabbed a handful of potato chips with his left. He crammed the chips into his mouth. "Nothin.'" He chewed rapidly like a rabbit. "Not a thing.'"

36. Zoning Matters

The buzz of mumbling voices permeated the air in Room 104 of the Peach County Courthouse Building, the setting for all zoning meetings. The room was warm, heated by old-fashioned steam radiators. Every once in a while you could hear the comforting clank and hiss from thick iron pipes. Inside, the metal seats filled with the rounded shapes of citizens; outside, the windowsills filled with triangles of snow.

Everyone hoped the called zoning meeting would go quickly, so they could all go home. Hiram Venald wished they had all stayed away in the first place. But they hadn't, he was sorry to see. The townsfolk had turned out. He kept craning his neck around, taking the count. There were about seventy people at first; then more stomped their shoes in the hallways, pulled off their coats, and found their seats inside. Ten minutes before the zoning meeting, the count zoomed to one hundred. Then a school bus pulled up, followed by more cars, and the room swelled to one hundred fifty.

At one minute to seven, people kept coming. Hiram began to get flushed; he felt his blood pressure rise; he pulled out a well-used handkerchief, wiped his brow, and dabbed the beads of sweat, covering his upper lip.

"Everybody but everybody is here," he noted. "The whole damn town!" He stuffed his crumpled handkerchief in his pants pocket. "Except the people who *should be here!* Where are the zoning supervisors? Where are the Crane's Company representatives from D.C.?"

Just then, the three Clearview zoning commissioners walked in ceremoniously to arrange themselves, standing erect around the smooth laminated table facing the rows of metal seats. As they filed in, the crowd grew silent. In the center of the trio Isabel Charmin, chairman of the zoning board (as well as president of the Chamber of Commerce), held a judge's gavel in her plump right hand. Hiram noticed the familiar skein of thin gold bracelets softly clanking together. He made a mental note. A thin gold bracelet didn't cost much. Maybe he would get his wife, Stephanie, to give Isabel an early Christmas present, depending on how things went tonight. He nodded at Isabel and caught her eye.

Isabel crimped her eyes in recognition and minimally acknowledged his presence. She had scheduled this meeting only after Hiram had caved in to her demands in their private negotiation. She was still reluctant, but she could not find a reason other than convenience not to schedule it, as the rulebook wasn't clear whether the chairman could arbitrarily deny a called meeting because it happened to be during Christmas week. So, she had filed Hiram's signed promise not to evict the Holmes woman inside the Chamber safety deposit box. Then she had put the called meeting on the docket, phoned her fellow commissioners, and posted flyers in select buildings and on a few telephone poles around town.

Tonight, in a tailored black pantsuit with a wide white collar over her jacket lapels, a pair of gold and onyx earrings, and her shiny clinking bracelets, Isabel imposingly raised her gavel as she assumed her most officious expression. Next to her on the left, elected zoning board compatriot Frank Midland, architect and university professor, stood quietly with his hands folded in front of him. To Isabel's right, Tim McCauley, Clearview mayor, smiled and nodded to people in the crowd as he stood genially before them. As the citizens continued to stare, Isabel glanced at the antique Regulator clock on the back wall. She leaned over the table with the judge's gavel, and smacked it on the surface with the self-importance of someone who knows she's directing history.

"Hear ye, hear ye, fellow citizens," she said. "We are gathered together on this chilly December night to hear everyone's opinion on the proposed zoning of eleven acres fronting the town circle. Y'all know the spot—the Circle Market (not to mention, Horton's, too)—sits on part of it."

There was a rustle and murmurings from the crowd as two male latecomers, obviously flustered, their overcoats shouldered with snow, wedged themselves into the back of the room. By now, townspeople had lined the walls and were clustered several rows thick in the back, holding their coats over their arms. Hiram stood up from the front row and motioned vigorously for the latecomers to come forward. He gestured to two seats beside him, strewn with his coat and scarf and hat. He'd had a devil of a time saving those seats! As the men walked down the center aisle between the two sections, the audience of citizens stretched their necks to watch. One man was tall, about six feet four; the other, probably five foot nine, carried a briefcase. In the curious silence, the sound of footsteps echoed across the polished floor.

Hiram made it a point at this instant to get one final estimate on the number of people, which he guessed had risen to one hundred seventy five. As he scanned the room he saw neighbors and acquaintances, enemies and friends, and—Hell's Bells and Glory Be!—Pap, the bum, standing in the back, his eyes glittery, his gnarled hands folded over his black jacket, his red scarf around his neck. As Hiram's glance passed over him, the old fellow nodded toward him. Looking away quickly, Hiram privately grumbled, *Probably considers himself a citizen of Clearview. Just what we need—more indigents to care for. I'll be sure he doesn't raise his hand to vote. Only registered voters can cast votes in zoning matters.* Hiram made another mental note to remind Isabel of just that.

As the men from Washington removed their overcoats, Hiram rose to introduce them; first, he pointed to Mr. Tufts (the tall man with a ruddy, rough face, the kind of complexion that reminded Francine Urbane of those medical textbook pictures of smallpox victims). Tufts stood unsmilingly, agitatedly twirling a yellow number two pencil.

"And this is Mr. Brighton," Hiram said.

The second man, thinning hair blown in all directions, was already seated, his open briefcase on his lap. He strained his head around and raised his hand to wave. Hiram took this early opportunity to tell the board what he'd been thinking. He reminded the gathering that only town citizens registered on the voting polls were eligible to vote. And he suggested that the people lining the walls and crowding the back of the room should be made to leave. "Breach of the fire code," he said, pointing to a sign above the supervisor's table. The sign read, "Maximum Capacity, 150."

But Mayor McCauley overruled the motion.

"Hiram," the mayor said, "if this meeting stretches too long, we'll consider moving to the auditorium downstairs. For now, we'll stay put. This is a public meeting, open to the public, all of it. But," he added for the educational benefit of the gathering, "Hiram's right about the vote. You've got to be a Peach County resident and registered to vote in Virginia."

Hiram took out his handkerchief and mopped his forehead. He referred to the men from D.C. as "these fine gentlemen who wish to invest in the great little community of Clearview." He kept running his handkerchief across his shiny head and intoned expansively about the proposed filling station, Crane's, and how it would bring an estimated $3.5 million in revenue over the next two years. It would be a "tasteful and valuable addition—one that would fuel [he thought *fuel* was a great word in context] growth to benefit all of us."

Isabel stood. "Any response to Hiram's opening statement?"

"Yes, Madame Chairman." Jan Midland rose from her seat. She walked to the front of the room, winked at her husband, and stepped to a laptop computer positioned on a rolling stand. The stand was wired to two monitors, which faced the audience. She hit a key before her, and the haunting music of Pachelbel's *Canon in D* filled the room like incense.

Accompanying the tranquil music, Jan showed scenes familiar to everyone of the landscape many referred to as a rural neighborhood. She had picked them for effect—a patch of summer black-eyed Susans, succulent grapes dripping in September's morning light, the pink and blue line of the Blue Ridge at twilight, a rainbow arched above a green pasture with fresh fall hay rolled up like fat gold coins.

Then abruptly she shattered the mood with drums, chains, and harsh heavy metal music, while visually she projected jarring scenes to punctuate the beats: a vaulting red pole, an oil spill, a smear of black paint, the onrush of speeding cars, glaring signs—"Buy! Sale! Cheap!" and fragments of a filling station a pump here, a handle there, and bold red and black letters spelling "Crane's."

Abruptly, soothing music returned as a doe stepped from shadow into sunshine from behind a pink dogwood in bloom. She was followed by a spindly, spotted fawn. Then, with a crash of symbols, a Crane's station supplanted the wildlife, and the television screens abruptly went black.

Not a word was spoken in the presentation. But the message was unmistakably clear. The crowd—stunned to silence—dissolved into quivering murmurs. Isabel rapped her gavel. "Any questions?" she asked.

Lucy Layman raised her hand from the back of the room and was recognized by Isabel. She twisted a curl of her short hair for a second, and then she threw back her shoulders, looked at Hiram Venald, and asked,

"What about them giant pin oaks on the property? There are three of them and each one is more 'n a hundred years old."

"Unfortunately, they will have to go," Hiram said quickly. Some people in the audience hissed and others booed.

"But we'll plant more trees, more oaks. Progress has its price," Hiram said, his palms turned up.

More hisses.

"We'll have none of that! Isabel stood suddenly, an atavistic presence like an Old World pilgrim in her white collar and black suit. "We're all here to listen to each other respectfully." She shook the gavel for emphasis, clinking the gold bangles at her wrist. The outburst quieted to an uneasy stirring. Hiram Venald smiled at Isabel, an overture she ignored.

Bill Urbane rose. "For all of us, here, I believe I can accurately say that the Circle is the focal point of our town. It is the route we take every day to get from one place to the next. A filling station would be a waste of that site. Already we have two gas stations nearby. This eleven acres, which once housed a primitive church, is the view all comers to Clearview have in common. And I believe, Frank, there are some legal, historic restrictions to the plot, are there not?"

Frank got up. "Unfortunately, no."

Bill's eyebrows shot up.

Frank assumed the explanatory demeanor of a professor. "At times like this," he said, "one might hope for an endangered animal or reptile or a significant historical or archeological find on the site. And we have considered having the site excavated. But, Bill, to answer your question," Frank turned toward his friend who had resumed his seat, "our petitioning papers have not been recognized yet by the National Register of Historic Places. We have no restrictions presently against development. Including Commercial-One development."

A murmur scuttled like a watchful lizard along the rows, as people leaned together, moved apart, and shook their heads.

"Darn shame."

"Someone should have acted earlier."

"Downtown will be ruined."

Frank stepped from behind the table and pulled an easel with cardboard props in view of all present. He felt more comfortable beside a prop.

"Old drawings, like the ones on this map," he said, pointing to the first rendering, "show that the site once supported a church dating back to the 1700s. You can see the outlines of the structure," he shifted the cardboard, "and this copy of a newspaper clipping shows that the building burned in 1847." Frank folded his hands. "But our ability to excavate the land has been held up by lack of funds. So, as I mentioned, we have no protective designation and no historic landmark registration. Only the historical authentication that these records reveal."

Jan startled him. "But what about underground? If a church was there, couldn't there be a graveyard there?"

"Could be," Frank answered his wife in the dignified tone he used to address a curious student. "And that would halt development, at least until something could be worked out. And if a historic designation came through, that could complicate things."

The men from Washington leaned toward the drawings and Xeroxes of newsprint. The tall fellow with the pockmarked face scratched his head with the eraser end of a pencil and leaned toward his frowning companion, who began rifling papers. Frank heard the short man whisper, "A graveyard could be expensive to relocate, even if it could be done at all."

"But the truth is," Frank soldiered on, "we simply don't know what's there. Many people around here have buried their folks around old churches. In times past, they also buried them in family plots on their farms. Some of us have graveyards right in our backyards."

"So you have petitioned the Register?" Bill Urbane stood up again, "but you have received no answer, correct? No one has denied your petition?"

"No denial, no acceptance. It's a matter of timing," Frank answered.

"Timing?" Bill's expression was quizzical.

"This zoning request got to us first," Frank said.

There was a collective sighing and groaning from the audience.

"Now wait just a minute!" Hiram jumped up in his two-inch heeled cowboy boots. He waved both his stubby arms, prompting his suit jacket to fly open over his round little belly. "I can't believe such childish whining and groaning as is going on in this room," he railed at the assembly. "That land has been setting around for centuries. Anybody could have bought it. But they didn't! I did! So let's quit this bellyaching and get to the point." His right hand, curled like a pistol, shot toward the ceiling. "The point is we're here to get approval for construction. I own the site, the people from Crane's are prepared to buy, and I'm prepared to sell. So let's get on with it!"

Hiram sat down abruptly in his squeaking chair; then he popped right back up like a Jack in the Box. "Furthermore, I suggest, Madam Chairman," Hiram pointed at Isabel, "that you limit discussion to one minute per person so we can move forward. Otherwise we'll be here all night."

"Suggestion noted," Isabel shook her well-coiffed head with a hint of disdain, "but we want people to speak their minds—briefly. I'll limit each person to three minutes." She glanced at the clock in the back of the room. The brass pendulum measured the hour, unhurried.

"Hmmm," she said out loud. "No second hand." She turned toward the mayor seated at her right. "Tim," she asked, "do you have a second hand on your watch?"

The mayor smiled. "I do indeed." He pulled up his sleeve and ostentatiously noted the time. A spontaneous clank of steam pipes startled the crowd. Then, accompanying the noisy heat, one by one the citizens began to stand and speak.

The thin black hands of the Regulator clock inched around a parchment face, as in three-minute increments of opinion, the age-old tug-of-war began: civilization versus nature, profit versus beauty. Within overcrowded Room Number 104, arguments rose and clashed like thunderclaps across the Blue Ridge Mountains. They rumbled on and on . . . quality of life versus convenience, the past versus the present. After an hour, the men from Washington stood exhausted from answering questions, Isabel's forehead bore the perspiration beads of overheated stress, Frank was sighing repeatedly, and the mayor had rolled up his shirt sleeves, taken off his watch, and centered it before him on the table.

The Washington men huddled with Hiram, who grew increasingly red in the face. Finally he jumped to his feet again, whipping his arms aside like a football referee. He faced the crowd. "Time out!" he shouted. "Enough! I own this land. I have owned it for five years. And now—now! It's time to develop it. I have basic development rights already. It's zoned C-2 right now. By law, I can put up something like a restaurant or a grocery store. Like I said before, Horton's Drugs is there already. I can tear it down and build a new joint. Listen up, friends and neighbors. I can do that! Nobody can stop me! Tonight, I'm just asking to upgrade the zoning a notch to help this town!"

"To fatten your own wallet!" an unidentified voice shouted.

"To ruin the Circle with crass commercialism," called another.

"Yeah—a hideous gas station!" came a third.

Hiram's tone turned nasty. "Yeah, well, you've all just seen that cheap slide show. Nothing but pure environmentalist propaganda! Metal and steel and a bunch of deers and sunsets and stuff like that. But nowhere! Nowhere! Did you see those three little C's—the three 'C' words that will mean a lot—a lot!—to every last one of you?"

"Hiram!" Isabel called.

But, Larry Layman was on his feet shouting louder than the chairman.

"What the devil do you mean, Hiram?"

Hiram flashed his left hand, fingers splayed, picking them off one at a time with his right. "I mean convenience, cash, and commerce! Three very important 'C' words. Yessireee, very important to this, our little ole backward, nose-picking community of Clearview!"

A wail of hisses circled the room.

"Hiram!" Isabel stammered. Hiram ignored her.

"Now listen here, people, and listen good! If you want to stop me, you won't! I've got a C-1 precedent, just one notch more commercial than Horton's, with the Circle Market just a settin' there on the acre next to the other eleven for sale. I can develop that acreage 'most any way I want. Put up 'most any kind of structure, like I've said. Cut those three old oak trees down tomorrow, if I have a mind to. It's mine! The land is mine! And I can sell that land to whoever meets my price! Nobody can stop me, ya' hear? If I don't sell this land to these fine gentlemen from Washington, I'll sell it to somebody!"

"By when?" The voice from the back of the room was obviously elderly, but strong. There was a rustle in the crowd as the old stranger raised his hand. Mid-air the man's fingers trembled slightly, but his posture was straight and tall.

"Damn that old bum," Hiram cursed under his breath.

"By when? By when? When will I sell it?" Hiram shouted through scrunched lips. "I'll sell it by—oh, what the Hell— by Christmas Day!" The developer had his handkerchief out again, mopping his wet brow and the top of his shiny head. The room went silent. Then everyone heard the elderly man say,

"Less than a week away."

"Brilliant, yeah. Correct. I'd say just about five days," Hiram sneered.

The room stayed tense as if all occupants waited to exhale. At that moment, Bill Urbane stood up.

"Madam Chairman," he said, raising his right hand, "you have heard Mr. Venald say, in effect, that even if the zoning request does not pass tonight, he will sell his property to the Crane's people or to someone else by Christmas Day—"

"For the same price these guys here will give me." Hiram's face wore the mottled mix of indignation and rage.

"And how much is that?" Bill asked.

247

"Two million dollars," the taller Washington gentleman said, tapping his left palm with his pencil.

"Gosh! No parcel under two-hundred acres has ever gone for that amount in Clearview." Bill was surprised, along with his neighbors. People rustled. They whispered, their mouths opening and shutting like a choir mid-chorus.

Frank sat forward in his chair, a deep line between his brows. Mayor McCauley picked up his wristwatch and put it back on his arm. Isabel's generous frame fluttered. She had known the amount, of course, but hearing it in the public meeting was discomfiting. She picked up her gavel and tapped it lightly.

"Let's calm down, folks," she said.

The crusty stranger in the back raised his hand again. Isabel recognized him.

"Yes, Sir?"

"By what time on Christmas Day?" he asked politely.

Hiram was back on his two-inch cowboy heels again.

"This is crazy," he said, waving his arms. "He's crazy! Can't you do anything, Isabel? You're supposed to be in charge!"

"What do you mean? He's under his three minutes," Isabel snapped.

"He don't live here, Isabel, he just drifted in a few weeks ago!" Hiram began to bleat under the Pilgrim visage of the chairman.

"He's speaking, not voting!" Isabel came back.

"Oh, whatever!" Hiram mopped his head. Then he spun around to face the back of the room.

"What time? By *noon*, you old fool! By noon on Christmas Day!"

That remark got Isabel's broad back up once and for all. She sprang up, flapped her arms, and smacked her gavel smartly three times on the table.

"Stop! Stop! Stop! Sit, Hiram! We have got to have respect! We have got to come to order! Mayor, you know the Robert's Rules of Order. What do we do?"

"Is there a motion on the table?" The mayor rose. He felt overheated by the long meeting and the rising temperature in the room. Nervously he began twisting his watchband.

Bill Urbane stood up. "I believe Hiram sort of made a motion by saying that he would sell his property to the Crane's men or someone else for the same amount of money, if they get it to him by noon on Christmas Day," he said.

"Right, Hiram?" the mayor asked.

Hiram nodded. "But otherwise, at 12:01, one minute after noon, I'm selling it to Crane's, and one day you folks will wise up, and you'll thank me for bringing progress to Clearview."

Tim McCauley listened. "Well, that's not exactly a motion," he began slowly. He bent his head to one side as if to appraise the situation afresh. He gave his watchband another twist. Then he folded his forearms across his chest and addressed the crowd.

"My friends and neighbors, we don't really have a proper motion on the table, but I believe the situation we face—in a nut-shell—is this: If Crane's buys the property, the company can peti-tion this board every year for re-zoning. Eventually, the way things generally go, they'll get it. Zoning boards change their minds. Citizens aren't always vigilant to protest. Folks get tired or com-placent. Time marches on." He turned back to the front and asked the D.C. men, "Do I understand correctly that you are prepared tonight to pay Hiram Venald two million dollars for the property?"

"We are, yes, subject to an inspection that indicates no archeological restrictions or environmental hazards," the tall man from Washington spoke up.

"Wait!" Hiram popped up, a flapping penguin of protest. "That's the first time you mentioned an inspection! We've not discussed any provisions!"

"And you also neglected to mention that historical structures once stood on the property." The man with the briefcase waved his papers at Hiram with an expression that silently added, *you jerk*. But he followed with, "The past *can affect* the present."

"It can't!" Hiram screeched. "It won't!"

Tim McCauley put his hands up, "Calm down, Hiram. Anybody buying the property would want an inspection. For one thing, a lending institution, if they use one, will require it, survey lines and such." He turned to the Crane's representative.

"But, to address tonight's situation, you are ready to put your money on the table for the parcel, whether it's zoned C-1 or not?"

The Crane's man took an envelope from his vest pocket and leaned his thin frame across the space between the row of chairs and the zoning board table. He placed the small, fat package right before Isabel.

"That's twenty thousand dollars cash in earnest money," he said.

Isabel picked up the envelope, opened it, and removed the wad inside. She fanned herself nervously with the green bills.

"That's mine," Hiram blustered.

"Not yet," Isabel huffed.

Frank said, "Dramatics aside, here. I'd like us to be clear. Is Hiram saying he *won't* sell the property if the C-1 zoning petition fails tonight?"

"No! No!" Hiram shouted. "I'm gonna sell it regardless! Crane's can get around any archeology stuff. And any zoning prohibition, too. Hell, at the end of the day, I'm not sure this dinky little Clearview zoning board has any real legal authority. With the Circle Market being C-1, like I've said, the precedent is set. That's an eleven-acre parcel I'm selling, and there's a Commercial-One structure on an adjacent acre. Granted, the market's grandfathered 'cause its roots go back to the old Buck Stop tavern. But anyway, the whole parcel will go C-1, sooner or later."

"But, you have said, have you not? That you will sell the property to anyone by Christmas Day who will pay you two million dollars?" Bill Urbane stood, along with the other men and a few women who wanted a better view of the action. With some people standing and others seated, the room resembled a human chessboard.

"Hell's Bells and Glory Be! How many times do I have to repeat it? Sure! Yes!" Hiram yelled. "To the Crane's men here or to somebody, to anybody with two million greenbacks, even to Santa Claus himself!"

"Cash? Cashier's check?" The elderly stranger's voice sounded genuinely interested. The audience erupted in laughter.

Hiram unloosened his tie. His eyes darted like ink jets in the wizened fellow's direction. His words came sloppily, as if through spittle, and no one could mistake the sarcasm.

"Cash—yes!" Hiram spat. "Cashier's check—yes! Gold coins—yes! Gold bouillon—yes!"

"How about the trees!" Lucy bolted from her chair.

"Whoever gets the land gets the trees, for God's sake! What's wrong with you people?" Hiram shot back.

"He said he would cut them down," Lucy flopped back in her seat and glanced at Larry, whose jaw twitched as his hands turned his John Deere cap.

Bill Urbane whispered something in Francine's ear. She picked up a new, red Chanel bag on the floor next to her chair and began running her fingernails through its interior pockets. Meanwhile, Bill stood and spoke boldly.

"Well, my friends, I am no Santa Claus, but I am a proud member of this diamond of a community we call Clearview." Francine touched Bill's hand with a slim leather checkbook. Bill took it and held it aloft. "And because of that, I will put up a matching pledge donation of one million dollars to be held in escrow by Isabel Charmin as Chamber Chairman. If you folks think you can chip in, and we can generate the money to meet Mr. Venald's price, then together we will save this prominent historic spot for a higher use. Not to mention saving the quality of the town for our children and grandchildren," he added. He started to sit down, but unexpectedly pivoted.

"Two million dollars for eleven acres is a lot of money, Hiram," he said.

"It's the focal point of the town isn't it? 'A prominent, historic spot?' I believe you said that, didn't you, Bill?" Hiram returned. And sly like a fox, he added, "But the fact is, a deal's a deal: I have a buyer on the front row who has a high-enough use for the land for me."

The Regulator wall clock chimed nine times. The three commissioners at the table put their heads together. People began to murmur. Some cautiously pointed at the windows where thick snowflakes brushed the panes. Others restlessly gathered their coats, sensing the conclusion of the evening ordeal.

"Well," Isabel rose from her seat with dignified finality. A hush blew through the room.

"Okay. Listen, people. We have an extenuating circumstance tonight—weather. Have you looked outside? We've got four inches of snow if we have an inch. The situation is this: I am in charge, and I have made a decision. We're going to postpone this meeting until after Christmas. By then we'll know the buyer of the property, whether it's the Crane's people, or someone else. And if we *don't have* another buyer other than Crane's, we'll hear their petition in January for upgrading the zoning from C-2 to C-1. Meanwhile, I'm going to suggest we adjourn right now, or we'll all have to spend the night here together, because we'll kill ourselves driving home in this blizzard. Understood?" There was a collective nodding.

"And even though the chairman's not supposed to make a motion," Isabel continued, "That's a motion! Do I hear a second?"

"Second!" The entire room spoke at once.

"Go home!" Isabel said. "Be careful!"

Frank collected his papers from the table and glanced at Isabel. Dressed as she was in her white collar over a black suit, Frank felt her pronouncement carried the power of a benediction.

Metal chairs creaked as men and women arose. The steam pipes clanked as if to say, "Hurry, Hurry." The men from Washington packed up their things hastily to exit, followed by a red-faced Hiram Venald. And, in the milling crowd, Bill Urbane pushed his way upstream toward Frank.

"I thought you said the county historical society people were going to pitch in on this zoning matter."

"Too little, too late," Frank said. "I sent the paperwork overnight to Washington, but you know how slow bureaucracy is."

Bill rubbed his chin.

Frank unloaded his props from his easel and slid them into an artist's portable case. He kept talking to Bill as he worked. "Really, as you know, the only visible historic structure on that parcel is the Circle Market. It's not picturesque, but it sits on fieldstones that go back to The Buck Stop. As for the foundation to the old church, well, I ran across those in some old books, but it would take a professional crew—archeologists, surveyors—to verify that they are what I'm reasonably sure they are. And those guys go slowly, at the rate of, say, one expensive soft-brushed foot every week or so. No, I'm not hopeful about getting a reprieve from the historians. It's you and your matching bid that give us a little time."

"Less than a week," Bill said. " I wonder how many people, if any, will chip in?"

"I aim to," Larry Layman said as he walked up beside the two men. He pressed a twenty dollar bill in Bill Urbane's hand. "All I got in my wallet at the moment," Larry shook his head.

"Thanks, Larry," Bill said. "I can't take it. But Isabel can."

"Oh, right," Larry said, folding the bill. He turned to go, but before he left he lowered his voice and said, "That Hiram is a real bucket of horse manure. The dollar comes first."

"You are being kind, Larry," Frank said. "Hiram Venald, I would have to say, is a greedy bastard, a real S.O.B. But we can't do much about that."

"Nope. A leopard doesn't change his spots," Bill agreed. "Let's go, the snow's getting worse. I wonder if we still have electric power at our farms." The men looked guardedly out the window.

"I'll get the lights," Frank said to Isabel, at the same moment Larry handed her the twenty dollar bill. She called "Okay!" to Frank, and, smiling at Larry, she put the bill inside a manila envelope alongside Bill Urbane's check and the Crane's twenty thousand in cash. Everyone moved toward the doorway. As Frank reached his hand toward the fluorescent light switches, he noticed the old stranger. *Funny,* Frank had a sudden insight. *The man's questions had generated the hope of an alternative to the Crane's sale.*

Frank saw the misshapen hat, the worn gloves, and the frayed scarf around the folds of the man's neck. The man stood in the hallway staring out a window.

"Do you have ride home?" Frank asked.

The old fellow turned, his blackish-blue eyes shining with—what? Excitement? Mischief? Distraction?

Maybe he's hard of hearing, Frank thought. "May I give you a ride home?" he asked. "My name's Frank Midland. We spoke a week or so ago, at the Circle Market."

The old fellow smiled and bowed slightly toward Frank.

"I remember." he said.

Frank blushed, remembering his sudden exit in pursuit of his wife.

The stranger continued. "Kind of you, Sir, kind indeed. I'm called 'Pap.' I do have a ride tonight. But looking out the window, I was just thinking."

"What's that?" Frank asked.

"I was just thinking, what a grand snow this is! How terrific a sleigh ride would be tonight!"

Frank was taken by surprise.

"Now that you mention it, it's a shame we got rid of those things," he nodded. "Kind of romantic they were, horses, bells, and all. My wife would love a sleigh ride again. She grew up on a farm in Vermont."

"Is she here?" Pap asked, his voice grating like that of a man who had smoked tobacco for a century.

"Yes. That's Jan, over there, talking on her cell phone."

The older man smiled, his gaze moved from the woman toward the window before him. He spoke to Frank in profile. "Well, if she loves a sleigh ride, you should take her on one!"

Frank chuckled. "I don't have a sleigh. I do have a tractor. But that's no sleigh."

"Would she go?" the stranger stared out the window.

Frank shrugged. "Nope, well yeah, maybe she would. A tractor's not a smooth ride, but it's a good ride."

"You should take her."

Frank grinned. "I should. You're right." Then he moved toward the door.

"I'll be heading home now. You've got a ride?" He wanted to be sure.

"I've got a ride." Pap tipped his hat.

37. Word Spreads

The next morning shone clean and bright, the tall nee-
dled pines and scruffy green cedar boughs drooped low,
weighted by white; the roadways—blacktop as well as
gravel—lay indistinguishable from land cut, in other seasons, by
ribbons of roads. As far as one could see, Peach County offered
itself as a placid rumpled ocean of ice.

With twelve inches across the mountains and valleys, in
its pastures, and within the town, Clearview's normal daily
school and work activities drifted to a halt. Over cell and telephone wires, however, the local news traveled fast.

Up early, Bill Urbane hiked a half-mile in his Gortex
boots crunching through the snow to his rural mailbox. He
pulled out the newspaper in a cellophane bag. He read his name
in an article headlined by twenty-six-point type:

"LOCAL MAN PLEDGES $1 MILLION MATCH
FOR LAND"

Back inside his warm, dry farmhouse he heard the
phone ring again and again, as people called to thank him for
his generosity. Francine took the calls and reminded each and
every caller that if he, or she, sent a check right away to Isabel
Charmin, they might claim it as a year-end tax deduction, since,

depending upon use of the land, the donation might be considered charity. Meanwhile, Bill kept checking his driveway and the television weather reports to assess the condition of the main highways for travel.

Terry Turner awoke from a cot at the television station where he had spent the night to report on the anticipated snowstorm. He glanced outside and swore in dismay because his satellite truck couldn't travel in the deep drifts for a live interview that morning with Mr. Urbane. And he cursed to himself that the newspaper had gotten the story first! How had that happened? He called Isabel Charmin and repeatedly got a machine on which he left message after urgent message. The gall of it! Here Terry was on hand for morning news but unable to get to the newsmakers! But—clever guy—he made do with a standup outside the TV building before the giant satellite dish and beside a glossy magnolia tree, its green branches glistening with Mother Nature's own baker's glaze. The backdrop made a sexy contrast to his blond hair and red Patagonia jacket.

Station engineers patched Bill Urbane's voice by telephone to the report, and the dignified gentleman's still photograph (a frame of archival video) moved in and out of Terry's shot in an electronic box. It seemed almost like live TV, one giant step above radio and a few leaps past newsprint.

Watching Terry from across town, and snugly wrapped in a fleecy turquoise bathrobe, Isabel Charmin checked her messages at the Chamber office from home. She kept putting off that call to the TV station. All morning, diligently writing down phone numbers and recording financial amounts, she sent donation reports to the newspaper and radio. Seeing the postcard-style interview with Bill Urbane prompted her to call Terry to report the tally collected toward Bill's pledge. Terry was grateful. It would be good for his noon report.

Meanwhile, the pledges were coming in to the Chamber quickly, but most of them were small—ten, fifty, two hundred dollars. One for ninety-seven cents in change came from the sixth-grade Sunday school class at the local Baptist church. By lunch time, Isabel was breathless: all this sudden extra responsibility, while the biggest seasonal event, the Chamber of Commerce Habitat Ball, loomed only two days away!

In neighboring Blackstone County, Myrtle impatiently thumped her hairdresser's appointment book in the palm of her hand as she paced her narrow, snowbound trailer. My, was she ever just all in a stew! Here it was, the busiest time for the beauty business all year, and every square foot of Peach County lay beneath a foot of white. Her insides churned. She needed to be, wanted to be, at her shop. And the women of Clearview desperately desired her to be there, too!

Jan Midland called Francine Urbane at 8:30 that morning. She dispensed with her customary how-are-you greeting and began, "We need a fitting, you know? How can we get hold of those ball gowns?"

Francine had already solved that one over her first cup of morning coffee.

"You have four-wheel drive right?" she asked. "The highways and main roads should be scraped by noon. Why don't you pick up Myrtle and Evangeline at the Blackstone Trailer Park and take them to Myrtle's shop in town? That way we can have a fitting with our seamstress, and women can get their hair done at the same time. I'll pick up Lucy along with some of my friends, also in a panic like I am."

"Okay," Jan replied, calculating the timing. "I think I can make it by then. That would give Myrtle about three hours for customers, and Evangeline time to nip and tuck our dresses. The daylight goes fast this time of year, and I don't want to drive after dark. Every year I feel I just can't wait for those long days of summer. But there's hope. You know that today is the shortest day of the year?"

"I thought of that," Francine replied, trying very hard not to relive the anniversary this day represented for her and for Bill. "Let's get moving."

So the plan of ferrying folks to Myrtle's Beauty Shop cranked into motion, and as the news spread, more and more townswomen carried one another there in trucks and vans and even with a few helpful husbands as drivers, via a tractor or two. By noon, the place was buzzing.

In the shampoo area of Myrtle's salon, Evangeline, who told everyone, "Just call me Eva," set up shop. She turned over a wooden orange box as a platform in front of a phalanx of glistening salon mirrors in which the women could see themselves. Then, kneeling with pins in her mouth, she made one or two custom adjustments here and there, marking Jan's hem to a flattering height above her dyed-to-match heels. She also added a few sequins to the back of Francine's full-length black gown.

Both Jan and Francine had been fitted when Lucy emerged from the bathroom where she had changed clothes. She stepped out into the busy shampoo room wearing her two pink gowns transformed into one. When she swished through the door, even the shampoo lady gasped. Her blonde hair, compliments of Myrtle's talented fingers, was layered in a crown of coils with wispy tendrils sweeping her soft white neck. Her amber eyes aglow, Lucy literally shimmered in the pale pink. The design was Jacqueline Kennedy's forte, a Chanel classic, with a matching short jacket over slimming, pink satin sheath, flowing from a strapless bodice to an ankle-length hem.

"Oh!" Jan cried. "Lucy! Never have I seen you so, so—"

"Perfectly gorgeous!" Francine exclaimed.

260

Myrtle beamed. But the seamstress reacted with dismay.

"Dear, dear, dear!" Eva fussed through her pins. Her nimble fingers began to pull in a half inch around Lucy's bodice, pinning it against her body. "What has happened here? Did I make such a terrible mistake?"

"No," Lucy twinkled. "After my gift day at Francine's country club spa, I've started walking and lifting hand weights. I've lost five pounds."

"Wow!" Jan exclaimed. "Just what Frank wishes I'd do."

"No comment," Francine said.

"No problem," Eva looked up and broke into a smile. "That's why they invented dress darts." And she deftly began adjusting the extra fabric as two narrow isosceles triangles to elongate Lucy's waist in a most becoming manner.

At that moment, Isabel Charmin rang Francine's cell phone. "Jingle Bells" played as a shrill ringer for a few seconds, alerting the room. Francine took the call and turned to the group, which still warbled with excitement. Her expression turned from delight to dismay. Then she said, "Okay, Isabel. Thank you for calling." She snapped her phone shut and looked at a sea of expectant faces.

"All this festivity for the Chamber Ball is so positive, but the news I have from Isabel about the Crane's matching bid is disappointing," Francine said. In the room that was, moments before, a beehive of activity, you could now hear a pin drop. Because one actually did drop, and Eva said, "I'm sorry," and reached down to pick it up. Here and there the salon customers stopped reading magazines, looked up, and listened. Hair dryer fans switched from "high" to "off."

"People have been sending in donations and calling to pledge," Francine sighed. "But what we have in confirmed cash—remember Hiram Venald stipulated 'Cash'—or its equivalent in gold," she turned her mouth in sarcasm, "is only fifty thousand dollars. And while that's good—great, even—it's not enough."

"Uh oh," Lucy said, holding her arms out to her sides while the seamstress finished pinning her gown.

"Hiram may get his way, after all," Myrtle grunted, holding a circular brush mid-air, and then she went right on teasing a client's bouffant style.

"You can't stop progress," another woman wagged her head, which glistened with layers of tin foil chemically lightening her blonde hair.

"Well, nevertheless, it's a display of community spirit," Jan murmured from the manicure table as she watched red polish transform her drab nails. "Too bad the spirit happens to be nine hundred and fifty thousand dollars short."

38. The Legend of the White Fawn

efore noon, December 21, Bill Urbane surveyed the partially melted snow on his Virginia driveway and declared the roads beyond it "fit for travel." But truth be known, it would have taken a twenty-foot blizzard coupled with a lunar eclipse to keep him from his mission. Their daughter, Anna, had visited friends in Washington, D.C., for a few days after the fall term at Smith. She was to arrive in Fredericksburg at two-thirty that afternoon, and Bill was to pick her up for their family holiday visit. It, for him, was the brightest moment of the season. From Thanksgiving to Christmas every year, the weight of sad memories tugged at his sides like stones in his pockets. As the days grew shorter, Bill felt himself spiraling downward into an ineluctable void, a black hole of despair.

In fact, four years ago on the morning of December 21 in a hotel in London, suffering from a hangover and self-destructive grief, Bill had swallowed a handful of tranquilizers, chasing them with enough scotch to poison a mule. Ironically, the mix had been his salvation; the quirky confluence of medicine and whiskey caused Bill to vomit so violently, the hotel maids who found him still slumped over the toilet bowl immediately notified superiors, who called emergency services.

On the shortest, darkest day of the year, Bill— semiconscious and still trying to empty what should have been an empty stomach—found himself strapped to a gurney and being rushed by ambulance to a nearby hospital. There, in an emergency quadrant, curtains hanging all around, he sensed someone.

"Having a rough time of it, my friend? The scotch I certainly recognize; the medication is less familiar," sniffed the elderly man in a white coat leaning over Bill's hospital bed, while holding his medical chart.

"It's Serax, a tranquilizer," Bill whispered, his voice made raspy by the vomiting.

"Ah, I see," the doctor responded, as if he'd just been given a clue as to why Bill might have downed that pharmaceutical cocktail in the first place. Yet the doctor's face was kind; he spoke familiarly.

"It's regrettable that anyone would ruin perfectly good scotch with such medicine," the doctor observed, "but what I find far more tragic is that you felt the need to do this to yourself. Unless, that is," he added looking directly at Bill, "you're now going to tell me it was an accident?" For Bill, the doctor's amiable bedside manner was at once reassuring and a cause for embarrassment. While the words assured Bill he would survive the clumsy suicide attempt, they also reminded him that he had a lot of explaining to do.

"I was depressed," Bill said, turning his head to avoid seeing the doctor's reaction.

"Depression is not a flaw in one's character, Mr. Urbane," the doctor said as he placed a stethoscope on Bill's chest. "It's an illness, and like all illnesses, it can be treated . . . but not," he added, tapping Bill on the forehead, "with thirty-year-old scotch and Serax."

Bill felt himself smile ever so slightly.

264

"We have people on staff here who are expert in such matters," the doctor offered, "you might want to consider talking to one of them. Having spent the greater part of my adult life mending people," he said, "I believe I am safe in saying, Mr. Urbane, that you, too, can be mended."

Bill shook his head sadly. He wanted all of this to be just a bad dream. He wanted desperately to wake up and find that he had never left his hotel room.

"Is there someone you would like us to call, your wife, a friend?" the doctor asked.

"No," Bill said, feeling ashamed.

"Listen old chap, we all have bad days, it's how we cope with those days that spells out how they'll end and trust me," the doctor admonished, "they don't have to be in a hospital bed."

Bill nodded his head and stifled what he knew would be an inadequate response.

The doctor again smiled, patted Bill's shoulder and said, "Hang in there old chap, you'll make it, I've treated far worse cases."

"Why?" It was the cry of a child, not the voice of a man.

"Why?" The doctor raised his eyebrows. "Why hang in there? Why, to see how it plays out!"

Bill groaned and shut his eyes. The doctor persisted,

"Listen, old boy, I've been around seven decades, seen wars, accidents, every trouble you can imagine. But life—you must stick with it. It has its compensations. You'll see."

He then turned to leave, but not before giving Bill one piece of unpleasant news.

"I'm afraid we may have to pump you out some more. I want to be sure that between us, we have completely emptied that stomach of yours."

Bill nodded, and then he lay still. He realized that tears were seeping from his eyes, staining shallow circles on the narrow, crisp mattress. He smelled the stinging odor of antiseptic, felt the crackle of the doctor's starched sleeve. Then he heard, "Relax, my friend, and open up. This tube is not pleasant down the ole esophagus, but it will do the trick."

Afterward, Bill fell asleep not to awaken fully for three days. On Christmas Eve Day, he heard the horns of automobiles and the ringing of church bells. There was an infectious vigor in the activity, and he bolted from his bed to yank up his hospital blinds. What he found outside the window was a rare sunny winter morning in London.

"This is a day worth living!" he exclaimed, turning back toward his bedside to dial his home. The little high voice that answered from a distant time zone said, "Hi, Daddy. It's Anna."

Having made good time on the Virginia roads, even with the inclement weather, Bill pulled into the brick two-story railway station in Fredericksburg, just in time to hear the blast of an oncoming train. He parked his car and took the steps to the upper tracks in twos. Then he watched the black chugging behemoth slow to a halt, disgorging its passengers, among them, his blue-eyed daughter with hair the color of honey.

"Hi, Daddy!" She handed him her suitcase from the steps of the train, jumped down, and hugged him in the holiday crowd of passengers.

"Merry Christmas, Baby Girl," he said.

"Baby Girl! Daddy! Here I am all grown up—a college woman—and still you call me that!"

"It's a term of endearment, nothing more," Bill smiled and wrapped his arm around his daughter.

"You've got snow here!" she said.

"Yes." Bill opened the car door and nestled her in the passenger seat. "And more is on the way."

"I love snow in the country, all clean and fresh. It's gotten all stacked and sooty in North Hampton."

"I special ordered a pristine snow just for you." Bill grinned as he slid behind the wheel.

"Oh, Daddy, even you couldn't do that." Anna folded her arms and sighed contentedly as she stared through the window, the windshield wipers rhythmical like the ticking of a clock. "Okay," she said, after a moment, as Bill pulled away from the train station, "catch me up on the news. What's happening in little old Clearview?"

"Actually," Bill cocked his head to one side as he watched the road, "a lot."

As he traced the rural highways, passing snowy cedars, leafless sycamores, and stalwart pines, he told her of the recent events, of life on the farm, new calves born in early fall, of the imminent Circle Market zoning petition, and the irked reaction of most town citizens. He relayed news of the upcoming Chamber Ball and its Habitat honorees, the seamstress widow and her crippled son.

To each story, Anna reacted, with an "Aw," or a "Really?" or "Hmmmm." But when he told her about the Christmas Swap, his daughter gaily clapped her hands.

"Hilarious!" she said. "Daddy, that is so cheesy! Did Mom agree to do it?"

"Francine has been a good sport," Bill said loyally.

"But having to wear the thrift dress to the Chamber Ball—what did she say about that?"

Bill rolled his eyes. "A lot."

Anna grinned. "I bet! Is she really going to show up in a thrift dress?"

Bill smiled wryly. "A thrift dress with a few adjustments that are quintessentially Francine."

267

"Hah! You go, Momma Girl!" Anna sang out, throwing her fist in the air. Bill laughed.

As they neared the farm, Bill was reminded of other local news. "We've had a couple of mysteries," he began.

"Oh?"

"Yeah, an old stranger showed up at the Market. He's harmless, we think. Just comes in, eats sandwiches, and drinks hot chocolate. Looks homeless, but he's gotten a job here and there, and he came to the zoning meeting and raised a few salient questions."

"Hmm," Anna said noncommittally. "You said a couple of mysteries."

"A white fawn," Bill said. "There are reports of a pure white deer, perhaps an albino, very rare, one in one hundred thousand births, right here in Clearview."

"You're kidding."

"No. There have been local television and newspaper stories on it."

"Have you seen it?"

"No. And it has eluded the newspaper and the local TV station. They've shown canned photos or file footage from national preserves, one in New York, one in Wisconsin. But not from Clearview."

"I bet it's beautiful."

"There's a legend about it," Bill offered.

"Tell me, Daddy."

"The story is attributed to the Chickasaw Indians of Oklahoma." Bill leaned his head back, reminding Anna of his nightly gearing up for the bedtime stories he had spun for her long ago when she still wore feet pajamas.

"Go on, Daddy," she urged gently.

"Well, it seems, once upon a time, in the season when

the air smells of acorns and the leaves are red and gold, a young man fell in love with a maiden named Bright Moon, who was the daughter of a Chickasaw chief. The brave was called Blue Jay, for some members of the tribe thought him aggressive and rude. Others said he was simply impetuous and headstrong. However, most agreed he was unusually handsome because of his solid shoulders and jet black eyes."

Here Bill grinned and Anna smiled, giving Bill a side-long glance.

"Just my type," she said.

"Well," Bill went on, "Blue Jay asked the chief for Bright Moon's hand in marriage, but the old man didn't really like the fellow. He considered the brave reckless and arrogant. Nevertheless, he knew his daughter was quite desperately in love, so he presented a challenge to the young brave.

"'Bring me the hide of a white buck,' the chief said, 'to win the hand of my Bright Moon.' Of course, the chief was confident that Blue Jay would fail. Such a find was rare in the forest. But, on the other hand, if the young brave somehow snagged the rare buck, then a white deerskin would make a fitting bridal gift as a wedding dress for Bright Moon. And, thought the chief smugly, it would bring honor to himself for having such a clever son-in-law."

"Sly fox," Anna interjected.

"Now, Blue Jay knew," Bill continued, "the insurmountable odds of finding a white deer; he sensed the chief's device. Nevertheless, one night, under the moonlight when the air still smelled of acorns and the red and gold leaves drifted from the trees, he met Bright Moon in a secret tryst. Blue Jay wrapped his arms around his beloved. He confessed that others thought him arrogant and reckless, and maybe that was so, but he was also courageous and smart. So he told the hopeful maiden,

269

"'I will travel far and wide, deep into the wilderness beyond the lands known to our tribe, to forests far away. I will find the white buck.'"

"As they parted from their fervent embrace, the brave left her with a promise: when he returned, he, courageous Blue Jay, and she, faithful Bright Moon, would be lovers forever."

"So romantic," sighed Anna.

Bill nodded. "And in the weeks that followed, Blue Jay actually found the white buck deep in the wilderness beyond the lands the tribe knew. He discovered the magical creature on a cool night when the air was frosted and scented with the winter sap of fallen pines, the leaves of the hardwoods, a layered carpet of red and gold, and the moon, full and bright. Silently, loading his sharpest arrow in his bowstring, holding his breath, Blue Jay drew the blade back slowly, slowly, until his arms quivered with the strain. Then the brave released his fingers, the bowstring snapped, and the arrow dove straight into the heart of the deer. The creature leaped into the air, contorted and gasping—but not dying. Instead, the white buck shuddered mightily, lowered his antlers, and charged Blue Jay."

Bill glanced at Anna. She was frowning.

"Alas, the body of Blue Jay, the brave hunter, was never found. Inconsolable with grief, it seems, Bright Moon never married."

"Ohhhh," sighed Anna.

"But, that's not the end of the story. Wait," Bill said. "One month after Blue Jay released his arrow on the night of the full moon, the white buck appeared to the maiden when the air was frozen and scented with pines and the land was white with snow. In the shimmer of the moon she saw the animal's magnificent shoulders and the passion of fire in its jet black eyes. And she knew her lover would never die.

"Every year thereafter, following the season when acorns fall as fragrant rain and the trees disrobe, Bright Moon looked for the stag. And, at the full moon, stepping out of winters of snow, he appeared—a consoling presence by her side. In this way, Bright Moon knew for certain, that in its luminous soul, the magnificent creature carried the heart of Blue Jay. And her own heart filled with joy. For she knew that he, courageous Blue Jay, and she, faithful Bright Moon, shared an abiding love to last for all eternity."

"Aw, Daddy, that's beautiful," Anna said. "I wish we could see it."

"The white fawn? It's been spotted on the Bennington Property that backs up to ours."

"I wish we could see it," Anna said again.

"Supposedly, even today, the white deer is sacred to the Chickasaws."

Anna's sudden reaction surprised Bill.

"Anything that beautiful and rare *is* sacred." She clenched her jaw.

Now, it was Bill's turn to say, "Hmmmm."

While it was just beyond four thirty in the afternoon, on this December 21, twilight descended, turning the snowy woods an eerie blue in the golden pink light of the setting sun. By the time Bill and Anna approached their farm, the opaque horizon had turned the color of smoke, and their automobile headlights dimly picked up the rails of the white board fence lining the gravel driveway leading to the Urbanes' immense Federalist home. Solitary candles glowed in each window. Bill downshifted the gear into four-wheel drive and moved slowly through the gathering dark.

Suddenly on Anna's side, there was a rustle of branches

beyond the bordering fence and a volley of deer sprang over one fence rail, sprinted across the driveway in front of the car, and cleared the other fence.

"One, two, three, and—Oh!" Anna cried. "Daddy! Did you see it?"

A white flash in suspended motion, lifted up, over, and away . . . .

"Oh! What a coincidence!" Bill said.

Anna was silent. Then she said, "Daddy, for a philosophy paper this term, I researched the work of Dr. Elisabeth Kübler-Ross on death and dying." Anna spoke slowly, "She calls coincidences by a different name—'God incidences.'" Then the girl turned eyes full of adoration in Bill's direction. "Thank you, Daddy, for the story about the fawn. I love you so much."

"Wow," Bill said quietly. And then he remembered the doctor's words: *See how it plays out. Life has its compensations.* Bill felt his eyes fill with grateful tears.

39. The Chamber Benefit Brawl

*E*ven in a small, rural town like Clearview, twenty-four hours passes quickly, especially when excited townsfolk are anticipating the most special event of the year. Each December, the Chamber of Commerce Ball introduced and reacquainted all businesses to one another in a splendiferous setting within the Alistair Hotel. The building, more than one hundred years old, had served as a Confederate Civil War hospital. Long since, it had been restored to welcome tourists who wished to visit the land of Thomas Jefferson and Robert E. Lee.

Tonight, December 22, everybody in and around Clearview wanted to be in one place: the Alistair Hotel. They wanted to arrive in limousines rented from Richmond and Washington. They wanted to disembark from their cars before its floor-to-ceiling candle-lit windows, gracefully ascend its marble stairs, and swirl through the resplendent twelve-foot double front doors.

They wanted to greet their self-consciously glamorous neighbors, many of whom were hard to recognize without baseball caps. They wanted to sail up from the vast entryway with its blazing fireplace, to glide toward the grand spiral oak stairway; to mount it slowly, step by step, looking back over their shoulders to wave at those below, then to pause on the landing for the photographer to snap a picture. They hoped to make a distinctive sweeping entrance into the elegant ballroom scented with holly and spruce, and lit with tiny lights overhead and candle sconces lining the walls. Such an atmosphere revealed everyone at his or her most flattering best.

A few miles away, anticipating this exceptional once-a-year event, Frank Midland wanted, more than anything else, to be on time. But his wife, Jan, could not let her eyelashes alone! Layers of mascara took what seemed hours. Jan, generally not vain, knew that her lovely eyes could be transformed to brilliance by eyeliner and dark lashes. They lit up her face until she, once again, became startlingly beautiful. And while he appreciated the effort, Frank judged painted beauty like he graded student papers. If perfectionism made them tardy, the effort didn't count. In frustration, he paced the living room beside the red and white Christmas tree. He watched the twins watching TV. He jangled loose change in his pocket.

At last his wife emerged, in a moss green dress with sheer long sleeves, and trimmed with a necklace of rhinestones, which led to her soft brown hair pulled back in a loose bun at the nape of her neck. Frank stood stunned. Ryan let out a wolf whistle, and Kyle greeted her with a Rebel yell.

"Oh, you guys," Jan blushed. Then she did a little dance singing the *West Side Story* tune, "I feel pretty, oh so pretty." The men laughed.

"Because you are pretty," Frank grinned. Maybe his wife scored an "A" after all. "And here is the limousine." He glanced out one of the front cottage windows. "Let's go. I'll get your overcoat. We have to pick up the Urbanes and the Laymans on the way."

When they climbed in the generous back seat of the

black stretch limo, well, who should be driving in a Santa Claus suit? The old man, "Pap."

"Why, hello!" Frank said. "I see you've got yourself another job. I didn't know you were a driver."

"I'm a driver," the crusty man nodded, stroking the beard stubble that had grown into a grayish white brush over the past few weeks. His Santa costume cap seemed to fit just right. *Suits him,* Frank thought.

"Too bad this isn't a sleigh, Santa," Jan laughed, arranging her moss green gown in a graceful swirl, pulling her coat over her shoulders.

"Too bad, indeed. I ordered one for you," the unpredictable Pap returned jovially, "but it hasn't arrived."

"Oh, hilarious!" Jan leaned her head back, giddy with glamour and gaiety and the magic of surprise. She pealed off gales of laughter as delightful as a ringing bell. Frank sat back smiling, just enjoying the sound. Even with two more stops beforehand, he thought happily, it looked as though they just might make it to the Alistair on time.

Anywhere in the South, there is nothing grander than a grand ball. In Clearview, Virginia, at an event such as the Chamber Ball, a woman of taste like Isabel Charmin knew how to rise gracefully to the occasion. At the tall front doors, over shining heart pine floors, dressed in her midnight blue gown with its flowing velvet sash, she greeted the guests under the resplendent lights of the Alistair entrance hall. Her sequins glittered; her smile sparkled. She enveloped the room like a giant bejeweled butterfly, in flighty warm welcomes and billowing embraces.

"You feel better just 'cause she's greeted you," Bill turned to say in such a way that only Frank could hear.

"I feel better once I get past her," Frank smiled. "I don't mean that unkindly. Watch out for the hearty kiss. You'll have ruby lips on your cheek all night."

They moved beyond Isabel's enthusiastic smooch and started up the magnificent stairway. Pausing at the landing before the upstairs ballroom, they turned, couple by couple, as the photographer below shouted "Next! Smile!" Bill Urbane turned after the camera flash to see his wife, standing as tall as five-feet, two inches could stretch, and as elegant as a ballerina onstage in floodlights of applause. She wore a black brocade sheath gown with silver and white flowers across the bodice, sewn in rhinestones and pearls, trailing toward the hem of her dress. Her dark brown hair held a small diamond clasp over her right ear. Bill shook his head in amazement. *It never fails. She makes my head spin. What a woman she is! And what a good sport. That dress came from a thrift shop!*

Francine sensed his stare and turned toward him for just a twinkling instant. She winked and held up her left hand flashing her sapphire and diamond wedding ring.

"C'mon, Bill Urbane, let's dance," she laughed. "You belong to me."

And I am so glad I do, Bill thought, clasping her hand and walking tall through the enormous French ballroom doors.

Larry Layman had not worn a tuxedo since his high school prom. He and Lucy had gone to a shop in town and rented one. He'd even cut his hair, which had become a scraggly hedge, the color of weathered hay bales. With a proper fitted suit and a shave, Larry looked at himself in the mirror, measured his chiseled cheekbones, stroked his hair across his brow, and wondered who he was. Folks used to say he favored Clint Eastwood, a ridiculous compliment in Larry's opinion, but one he secretly enjoyed. Lucy said that very thing for the first time in a long while when they were in the tux rental shop. She picked up a red bow tie teasingly and said,

"How 'bout red for Christmas, Mr. Clint?"

"Naw," Larry had responded, looking at himself in the store's three-way mirror. "I'll just stick to tradition and wear black."

"Well, you know what you like," Lucy said.

And that was true. And one thing Larry liked—even at a fancy party—was a real "settin' down" meal. Standing up, balancing a plate, trying to hold a napkin, a fork, and a drink was not his idea of eating. *Stall feeding*, he called it. But he had to say that, though you had to stand to eat it, tonight the food at least was good. He liked the fact that Isabel had ordered a lot of meat. He liked to chow down on things like chicken wings and meatballs and shrimp. He was headed back for seconds on the shrimp, reaching into piled pink mounds around a glistening ice sculpture of a porpoise curling a fluted wave. He didn't see another hand lunging toward the bowl, and his own fingers bumped it.

"Excuse me," Larry pulled back and looked up, noticing as he did that the pudgy hand in the bowl scrabbled around like a crab looking for the biggest shrimp.

"Excuse me, too, Mister, but I got here first," Hiram Venald glanced at Larry as he piled the shrimp on his plate. His mouth was smeared scarlet with cocktail sauce from previous plunders. "Well, I'll be," Hiram said, grabbing a linen napkin, putting it to his mouth. "It's ole Larry Layman. What a surprise. I wouldn't have known you'd clean up so good."

"And I wouldn't have known, until this moment, that you're so short, Hiram," Larry returned. "It's hard to go public without them two-inch cowboy boots, ain't it?"

"It *ain't*, Mr. Carpenter Boy." Hiram sneered at Larry's

uneducated speech. "But at least I get to walk around town with a brain—something you *ain't* been blessed with."

Smoldering with anger, Larry felt his temple throb, just like Eastwood's in an old-time cop movie. Somewhere in his memory he heard that leaded voice, saying, *C'mon. Shoot. Make my day.* But Larry gritted his teeth. Deliberately, he reached for a large curled shrimp from the mound piled below the ice sculpture. He dipped the solitary shrimp deep into the nearby bowl of thick cocktail sauce.

"You know what I think, Hiram?" Larry growled, and Hiram leaned in next to him, his full cheeks pulsing like a squirrel's.

"What?" Hiram gulped.

At that moment—squish! Larry plunged the sauce-loaded shrimp with the force of a dart, deep into Hiram's left ear, just hoping he'd hit an eardrum.

"You're a stupid weasel and a crook, too." Larry hissed, giving the shrimp a hari-kari twist. "You think I don't know you stole from me? I know it. Other people know it, too."

"You horse's ass!" Hiram sputtered, pulling away, shrimp bits flying like confetti from his mouth, sauce oozing like blood from his ear. He drew back, balled up his fist, and took a swing at Larry. He missed.

"Speak for yerself! You're the ass!" Larry hissed as he

dodged craftily. "I only plugged up one hole in that drafty body of yours. You got more—a lot more—holes!" Larry grabbed a handful of shrimp. He held them in the grip of his fist, tails poking out between his tanned fingers. He pushed his fist right in front of Hiram's nose.

"Here, Short Shirt! Have some more plugs!"

Reflexively, Hiram knocked Larry's hand sending the shrimp ricocheting against the iced porpoise. Larry spun in a circle and put up his fists. A few guests circled the men and began hollering.

"Don't!"

"Hold on, guys."

"Stop that!" Isabel's bellow broke through commandingly as several male guests stepped up and restrained the belligerent men.

"Shame on you, Hiram! And you, Larry." Isabel rushed toward them, her blue taffeta bustling, her thighs swishing. "I'll have you know this is a party to celebrate a worthy cause. It's open to ladies and gentlemen. If you boys can't act like GENTLEMEN, then you can leave! Right now!"

The men glared at one another. Hiram's head shone slick with sweat; his cheeks flamed. Larry's skin turned white; his right temple throbbed.

Lucy Layman ran up and grabbed her husband's arm. "Honey," she said, "let it go." Larry froze, relaxed, then shook off his male handlers, and stood straight. He looked at his pink doll of a wife, realizing how much this event meant to her. "Okay," he said. He gave Hiram a scorching look. "We just disagreed over the shrimp."

Hiram took the benign cue and shrugged off the hands that restrained him. He straightened his bow tie and suddenly brightened. "Shrimp ain't worth a roe," he joked. "*Roe,* get it?

Row and *roe.*" The crowd twittered nervously. A few people giggled. Hiram pulled his tux jacket straight as possible over his rotund shape and looked around for Stephanie. At the same time he stood as tall as his black patent dress shoes would allow.

"Now, not just anyone could pull a clever pun like that," he smiled smugly at Larry, while he mopped his ear with a napkin. He tapped his head with his other hand, "Smarts," he said. "I got smarts." When a visibly annoyed Stephanie flounced over to join her husband, Hiram took her arm, unable to resist another pun that suddenly occurred to him.

"C'mon, Honey," he said ostentatiously glancing back at Larry over his short shoulder. "Let's *row* our boat in a better direction."

Larry snorted his contempt and then guided Lucy in an opposite path through the crowd.

Across the ballroom through double glass French doors, the newspaper photographer had set his tripod. After fifteen years in photography as a career, Hank Bissell generally did not like what he called "society news," but this event was special. For one thing, it offered different fare. Most of the people he took pictures of every day were standing in blue jeans in wide fields clasping hands over some financial deal they'd made. Also, he often was tapped for those boring award shots, the ones with two people smiling, their hands holding an oversized check or an embossed wooden plaque.

But at the Chamber Ball, he got to shoot candid shots as well as pretty women; furthermore, the newspaper generally ran a splendid layout in which the publisher sprang for the extra expense of color. That dimension always brought Hank, not only compliments, but also extra assignments, many of them free-lance.

For these reasons, he was particular about the backdrops

he chose. Tonight, for the group shot, Hank selected the fireplace with the silver candelabra on either end amid fragrant pinecones and green holly bursting with red berries, the greenery accented with crisp red bows. He had taken candids in the crowd of women who flashed their smiles and men who jovially waved.

The shots in the parlor, however, were posed. Isabel helped to arrange them, and now she ushered up three middle-aged, attractive women and another quiet, slender woman Hank already knew: the Habitat House honoree. Tonight, she looked modestly glorious, like a candle. Her jersey silk gown draped beneath a sheer glittering cowl at her shoulders and fell in a soft swirl at her feet. At her back, the neckline drape, studded with flecks that caught the light, became a shawl, tied low near her waist.

From the start, Evangeline Holmes had caught his eye through his lens as one waif of a woman who would photograph well in just the right slant of light. That is why for his first newspaper article to announce the winner of the Habitat House, he captured her outside, on the porch of her trailer, with a background of wintry woods. He also shot her inside the trailer with her pitiable boy, Tom. And he'd taken care to light Tom's drawings just so, bringing them full frame with his macro lens so they'd show up in newsprint.

When Evangeline had been preoccupied, he'd also taken a soft-focus close-up of her face, capturing her thin, chiseled nose, her high cheekbones, and her lovely skin, almost translucent in its clarity. *Haunted beauty,* he thought, and his heart went out to her in a way he had not felt in many years. Since then he had wondered more than once about her husband. *Did she have one?*

Tonight Isabel wanted a separate picture for a separate story. She had talked with Hank's boss, the publisher, who had agreed that she had a fresh angle for an additional feature. Three women had bought second-hand clothes, and Eva, the "Habitat Seamstress," as she was beginning to be called, had transformed them as her own designs.

"Creative recycling, don't you think?" Isabel suggested.

"Of a sort," the publisher responded.

Now in the warm bath of assured flattering publicity, Isabel introduced each matron to Hank. He pointed his camera and began to take pictures of the women in quick succession, his flash filling the room with intermittent brilliance. *Flash! Flash!* Francine Urbane by the Chamber Christmas tree. *Flash!* A silhouette of Jan Midland beside the drapery of holly greens cascading from the mantel. *Flash!* A portrait of Lucy Layman beside a Queen Anne's chair, her arms in a pair of long white gloves, her stance as radiant as the night she was crowned homecoming queen in the Peach County High School football stadium.

As he began to arrange all the women together alongside Isabel for the group photograph, he saw from the corner of his eye that the French doors to the parlor suddenly opened. A tall blonde woman strode toward the group, her sheath dress as tight as a corset, her three-inch heels clicking across the heart pine floors of the Alistair dining room.

"Why, Stephanie," Isabel said, raising her brows to a pointed tent of surprise.

"I'd like to know why my picture has not been snapped this evening," Stephanie paused and prissily pursed her coated pink lips. "My husband, Hiram, donated a lot of money toward printing the invitations. Didn't you notice his company logo on each and every one? The green thumb? What's going on here? Don't y'all think I'm good enough to stand up beside you?" Her blonde hair was pulled high off her forehead to a rhinestone headband. It fell down her back in bleached curls.

The first of the group to react, Jan said under her

breath, "God, you think she'd know that 60s hairstyle is as dead as Jayne Mansfield."

Lucy spoke quietly through gritted teeth. "Them people is just trouble. Really, that's all they is."

"White trash," Francine said, nodding and smiling as if she had just paid someone a compliment.

Isabel heard the murmurings and took charge. "Ssssh," she hushed the women by her side. She stepped out of the line and took Stephanie Venald's arm with a firm, guiding hand.

"Stephanie, of course you are good enough to stand in line. I've been looking for you. I'm so glad you found us." She turned slightly toward Hank, squinting behind his tripod. "We'll take several shots," she told him. "Stephanie will stand next to me on the end here."

Stephanie sashayed to the line. She wore a metallic gold gown wrapped like a Christmas package, ribbon layer after ribbon layer around her frame. It was strapless and would have looked stunning on a younger woman. But the shiny fabric and the ultra high-style sheath outshone its model. Although Stephanie had remained thin, she did not, as a rule, exercise, and her underarms had begun to droop, creating small bulges of pink flesh over the stark strapless top. Jan leaned over to whisper to Francine, "Let's face it, control-top panty hose and bustier bras can only do so much."

"Not enough in this case," Francine said, still smiling straight ahead.

After several snapshots of the group, Isabel spoke up. "That one seemed to be good for the gown story, also," she said to Hank. Then she stepped out of the line. "Crop it," she murmured. Hank nodded.

Stephanie overheard the remark. "Crap it?" she said. "Crap it? What the hell does that mean, it's crap?"

"Crop," Hank replied. "Cut."

"Cut? Cut me out?"

"That shot is special, Stephanie," Isabel told her. "Has nothing to do with you. You'll be in the others. But the last picture is for a particular story about the gowns that Francine, Jan and Lucy are wearing. They're thrift shop gowns that Eva here, our designer seamstress, has made over. It was part of the Christmas Swap."

"Uh oh," Jan said out loud. "Here we go."

"A Christmas swap?" Stephanie's pink lips actually popped the final "P" like a champagne cork.

"That's right. These wives swapped into each other's homes," Isabel began energetically.

"A wife swap?" Stephanie's voice climbed. A crowd began to filter through the doors into the parlor.

"What's that about wife swapping?" someone said.

"Who swapped wives?"

Hiram stepped in. "Wish I'd been in on that one."

"Why that's just plain low-rent, trashy behavior," Stephanie huffed pompously.

You should know, Jan thought.

Francine interrupted, "It's not what you think."

"No, it's not," Lucy snapped.

Stephanie whirled toward her. "Well, Lucy, you started your swapping around a long time ago with the boys at Peach County High, now, didn't you?"

"Shut up, Stephanie!" Lucy clenched her fists.

Jan spoke a warning. "Lucy . . ."

"Will you ladies stop that? Right this minute?" snapped Isabel, her midnight blue sleeves raised like an avenging angel.

Hank Bissell stepped beside the tripod of his camera. He just knew a snarling catfight was on the way. He scanned the crowd. Thank goodness Larry Layman wasn't in sight. Probably outside smoking a cigarette. Maybe Frank Midland was with him. The professor was known to slip off with his pipe, now and then. Hank saw Evangeline visibly cringe, as she saw Bill Urbane, just at that moment, wheeling her son Tom through the glass doors. Tom's arms flailed in agitated circles. "Loud voices," she had told Hank at the earlier photo shoot in the trailer park, "always upset him."

Watching the boy's eyes grow wide as Tom looked at the women gathered around his mother, Hank had a premonition: something bad was about to happen. What? A convulsion coming on? The boy suffering a panic attack? Unexpectedly, there was a beat of absolute silence in the room. Then, as if in slow motion, Hank saw the boy open his mouth in a twisted "O." He heard a high-pitched keen, a swelling wail, as if an anguished lament for someone who had died. The cry pulsed with strangling guttural sounds.

Evangeline moved quickly. She leaned over to quiet her son. She positioned herself close to his face. She placed gentle fingers on his cheeks. But the eerie bleating persisted, louder, louder, provoking a frightened reaction, as if to an emergency siren, among the astonished guests. Some of the women began to scream. Some men, running from the ballroom into the parlor yelled, "What's the matter?"

Hank suddenly had an idea. *Distraction! I need to distract these people from the boy.* He quickly unfastened his camera from the tripod, looped the strap over his shoulder, and began to shoot. *Pop! Flash! Pop! Flash. Here. There. In that face. Of that group. Right in the middle, over toward the corner. Pop! Flash!* Light splashes filled the room in an arresting strobe effect. Every time he shot, Hank yelled, "Smile! Smile! This is for the newspaper! Smile!"

The crowd, after a few seconds, responded. It became a glutinous mass of faces. It squealed, retreated, and then just as quickly settled down, a shuttering pool of quicksilver. After all, every one of them—man and woman—wished to look his or her best in the newspapers! The mass finally congealed as one homogenous smile.

Isabel called to Bill Urbane, "Take little Tom and his mother out. Strike up the band in the ballroom! It's time for the award."

Bill offered Evangeline a handkerchief and she dabbed the boy's eyes as she spoke to him comfortingly. At last, she stood up. Through his lens, Hank could see the dark stains of tears on her gown; the boy's fingers had become entangled in her cowl neck, tearing it slightly. Evangeline looked beyond all of it, as if nothing had happened. Bill made a circle with the wheel chair. The mother, now holding her son's hand, began a stately walk beside him. People began to stream slowly behind the trio through the tall glass doors. Hank lowered his camera and sighed with relief.

Stephanie Venald sulked, hanging back. She turned toward Hank. She wet her strawberry lips, raised her right hand, and snapped her fingers in his face. "You know what, Mr. Picture-Taker? I wouldn't want my picture in the paper anyway with the likes of them snooty bitches. Wife swapping and thrift shop gowns! My dress is first class! Cost a fortune! I ordered it straight from Saks Fifth Avenue in New York City!"

And with that, Stephanie stomped out of the room in a tight metallic hiss of female steam.

Jan overheard the remark and raised her hands toward Hank in a gesture that said, "Go Figure." But she also noticed Lucy had become tearful because of the insults and the general tension of the evening, so she reached over and drew the younger woman next to her. "Don't let that floozy bother you. Her dress may be first class, but she has no class."

"And she *does* have a past," Francine stepped close and raised a dark eyebrow. "I've heard it's *perfectly awful.*"

Lucy blushed, Jan noticed. She turned her head toward Francine.

"Well, I don't know about you, Francine," Jan lowered her voice, but her tone was rueful, "but I can tell you that some of my past is *perfectly awful,* too."

Francine shrugged. "We've all had our moments."

"I'll just let her be," Lucy sniffed, lashes still wet with tears. Then she borrowed a tissue from Jan and resolutely blew her nose.

In the grand ballroom, the band was finishing "Joy to the World," a preliminary herald to the presentation. The carol attracted attention, and the guests migrated toward the band to sing in a crowded semicircle. At the last note, Isabel in her rustling taffeta claimed the standing microphone.

"Attention, attention. Thank you all for being here," Her voice rang hearty with well-rehearsed joy, the parlor scene banished momentarily from her memory. "What a special night . it is indeed. I cannot remember a more fantastic event to help our wonderful community of Clearview," she said. "Having fun?" The desultory crowd, still influenced by the strange scene in the parlor minutes earlier, clapped perfunctorily.

Isabel was unperturbed. She knew how to massage an audience. "Well, you all look glamorous, and this is a glorious night. Hey up there," she waved one of her blue satin arms toward the floodlit rafters. "You! Working the spotlight! Sweep this crowd, will you? Let everybody see each other! All these gorgeous, glittering souls!"

The spotlight washed around the crowd, turning colors, of flattering blush and blue, illuminating them like Oscar stars. The people grinned and bowed and laughed and waved.

One great boredom buster, Frank smiled, mouthing his empty pipe stem. It still was slightly warm. *What a crowd manager you are, Isabel.*

"But now!" Isabel's voice brought the key spotlight back to her own glowing face, "it's my great privilege to introduce to you the lovely, talented young woman who this spring—with hammer and nails like the rest of us—will be helping to build her own Habitat House. Evangeline Holmes and her son, Tom. Please, take a bow!"

Bill Urbane had positioned the boy in his wheelchair by Evangeline's side. Tom began a self-conscious flailing wave. Evangeline bowed slightly. Then Tom smiled a crooked smile. He began to clap his hands together.

"Yes, yes!"

The guests warmed to the boy, applause shaking loose from their midst.

Isabel clasped both honorees' hands for a moment; then she turned to gush further into the mike. "But I'm going to tell you a story about how this all came about, and why this year is the biggest financial success we've ever had!"

She paused a beat, and the drummer behind the orchestra hit a cymbal with a dramatic smash. People twittered and laughed as the sound faded behind Isabel's voice.

"Perhaps some of you have seen the television shows where people swap lives? They spend a day in another person's shoes."

Nods and murmurs of assent filled the room.

"Well, in Clearview, we've had our own little swap among the Urbanes, the Midlands, and the Laymans. C'mere Bill, and Frank and Larry." The men walked forward self-consciously. "These men," Isabel cradled them in her generous arms, "pledged money and talent toward the Habitat House on the condition that their wives swap lives for a day!"

Applause and laughter mingled briefly.

"Now, Francine and Jan and Lucy," Isabel crowed. "Come over here and stand by your men! Because that's what they did! They took on the challenge! They spent a day in each other's homes, helping out, living a different one-day life! All, mind you, for charity. For our community! And you know what?" Isabel paused again for the cymbal strike. She raised her arms, now in the arc of a Christmas angel. "Well, I'll tell you what! As a result, Clearview will have its Habitat House built by June!"

There was a deafening collective cheer. Whistles circled the ballroom. The three husbands bowed. Their wives nodded, smiled, and blushed.

Suddenly a piercing eye-level spotlight moved forward. Terry Turner from the television station was nudging the crowd with his cameraman, trying to get a front row shot.

"Ms. Charmin!" Terry shouted. "Ask them what they learned!"

"What?" Isabel was startled by the interruption.

"From the Christmas Swap—each one. What did they learn?"

"Why, I don't know." Isabel was momentarily flummoxed. She turned toward the ladies and said, "But I think they would be glad to answer that. Jan, you go first. What did you learn?"

Jan gathered her moss green gown hem and stepped closer to the camera mike. Zeke, the cameraman, caught the woman's luminous green eyes in an extreme close-up shot.

"I learned that sometimes when you try to teach somebody else a lesson, you wind up learning something yourself. In my case, I learned a new appreciation for my husband and I've realized a closer bond with these new friends." Jan smiled at the other two women and Zeke refocused his camera lens wide. Isabel held up her hands and began clapping. The audience clapped and cheered right along with her.

"Lucy?" Isabel asked.

Terry whispered, "Wide shot," and Zeke nodded and stepped backward, his camera light illuminating the small woman.

"Well, I'm not a fancy person," Lucy said, her gold hair glistening, her eyes the color of maple syrup, melting Zeke's camera lens with her warm gaze. "But I went to the Clearview Country Club not long ago on a one-day trip. And what I learned is, everybody's the same. Everybody's got problems. Everybody needs help. We're all the same, that way."

The crowd applauded again. And several of the men whistled and nodded, remembering afresh why they had voted for Lucy long ago as homecoming queen of Peach County High.

"Okay, Francine," Isabel laughed, "What did you learn from the Christmas Swap?"

Francine stepped to the mike. She paused. She smiled her amazing smile. She lowered her voice. "I leaned that with *less* pocket change, you have to be *more* creative," Francine said, and Terry Turner said, "Close up," to Zeke, who zoomed in on Francine's dazzling expression. "Anybody can spend money," she continued. "It is doing things with less money that brings out ingenuity. And fun!" She looked for her husband's face and winked.

"How about the men?" Isabel couldn't resist asking. The guests joined in. "Yeah, how about the husbands? What did they learn?"

Frank leaned his tall frame over the floor microphone, which had been set low for Isabel. "I can't speak for the others,"

he said. He looked up. "But what did I learn? Ah, I learned . . .
I learned . . . to do it, ahhhh—NEVER AGAIN!" The other two
men nearby reared back and laughed. They shook their heads in
agreement and shouted in unison, "Never again!" The crowd
exploded in delirious hoots and stomps and whistles.

Isabel's shoulders were shaking with mirth as she
turned back toward Terry and his camera.

"So now, I have to tell you, there's something else,
something you would never guess," Isabel said, enjoying every
instant of her quivering opportunity. All this footage, destined
for local airtime. The thought catapulted her to verbal jubilance.

"Francine mentioned being creative," she said. "Do you
see these exquisite gowns that they are wearing? Why, just look
at these gorgeous girls," Isabel bubbled over the microphone.
"Turn around ladies, show your stuff!"

Francine slowly pivoted, the sequins catching the chan-
delier lights. Jan stood at attention and bowed, her moss shade
an echo of the wintry greens. Lucy curtsied gracefully like Miss
America and waved a white glove. Then all three women waved.
Adoring men and women clapped from the thronged semicircle.

"Would you believe these are second-hand gowns?
Thrift shop clothes?" Isabel shouted.

"No!" the crowd shouted back in unison.

Isabel had reached heaven. She raised her right fist with
all its gold clinking bracelets falling together, "They are! They
are, they are! Thrift shop dresses!" She roared. "EXCEPT—"

And she grabbed hold of Eva's arm, "EXCEPT, our
lovely lady here transformed them! She remade these gowns,
knowing, even as she worked her needle and thread, that she
and her son, Tom, were literally being THROWN OUT INTO
THE SNOW!"

Gasps and oaths erupted, a menagerie of sounds.

"But Evangeline Holmes kept sewing—and believing—in the wonderful community spirit of Clearview."

"Hooray!" the guests cheered. Evangeline stood, drawing the spotlight to her as if she were Joan of Arc.

"But the good news that I want, most of all, to leave with you good people," Isabel said, "is this." Isabel moved closer to Tom's wheelchair. On the flat shelf before the boy there lay a package wrapped in brown paper. Isabel picked it up and propped it heavily on his chair.

Slowly, while the boy eagerly watched, she began to unwrap the package. The paper rustled, unfolded, and fell from her fingers to the floor. She held up a framed canvas, its back toward the crowd.

"Yes, in his own inimitable style, Tom has painted us a message," Isabel said movingly, without benefit of her microphone. "And this message, I'm proud to say, will grace the first floor hall before the door leading to the Chamber of Commerce office on Main Street."

"You want to see it?" Isabel loved suspense.

"Yes!

"Quit stalling!"

"Show us the picture!"

"Here you go," Isabel said, and slowly she turned the picture around. The ceiling spotlight centered on the frame. The crowded ballroom of guests leaned forward as one. Hank snapped a shot for his newspaper. Zeke zoomed in for a tight shot for the television story. There was murmuring and not a few gasps. There, before their eyes, within the feathery strokes painted by the young boy, was the familiar Blue Ridge that everyone loved. The rounded peaks stood in a whirl of clouds amid muted golds, blues, pinks, and whites.

"But the magic is not only in the mountains," Isabel

said. "If you look close, you'll see faces—the faces of people you know, or might think you know. They are emblematic of the people in Clearview who have come together to work as one." Isabel's voice choked a little. She looked down at the small brass plate on the lower edge of the picture frame.

"In fact, oh, I can't read it without my glasses, Tom," Isabel muttered. "So, tell us, Tom, you tell us your message."

The boy looked up at Isabel and out at the crowd. Some people standing nearby winced. Could the boy speak under these pressured circumstances? Would he start wailing again?

His mother stepped close beside and put her hand on his shoulder. "Tell us, Tom," Eva said.

The boy clumsily brought together his two thin hands in a tangled grip of brittle fingers. Holding them together tightly, he spoke in a voice twisted by hoarseness, but at the same time eerily clear.

"Together, One."

"Together, One!" Isabel cried, clasping her mammoth arms together over her head.

"Together, One!" cried the townsfolk reaching high, clapping their hands triumphantly together.

Together, One, the words swept around the heart pine floors of the ballroom, out the massive French doors, and up and through the twelve-foot windowpanes of the Alistair Hotel.

Together, One, the voices blended together, whirling toward the mountains, spiraling toward the stars.

40. Hank's View

I t had been a long night for Hank Bissell at *The Clearview Clarion*. During the tedious stretch between midnight and four in the morning of December 23, he had developed his photographs from the Chamber Ball and constructed the layout for the newspaper to ready everything for the day's edition. He had created a collage of pictures, pulling those of Isabel Charmin, the three women smiling in their thrift shop dresses, a shot that included Stephanie Venald, some crowd shots of attending guests, and one of Evangeline as the Habitat House honoree and her son, Tom.

The photos made a nice spread, and Hank was pleased. In the center, he had floated Tom's watercolor painting as a ghosted graphic, the mountains and shadowed faces of Clearview citizens rendered preternaturally timeless by the technique. He had no cut lines beneath the pictures other than one—an opaque banner scrolled below the collage. It read, "Together, One."

Now at ten after four, he was ready to go. The printing presses were running; he could hear the great drums rolling, generating a vibrating grind against the old brick building walls, as one fed to another, inking pages into sections, smacking out final edition after final edition for the next day. The sound reminded him of an old-time steam train, marking miles. As he gathered up the remnants of his efforts in the paste-up room, Hank realized that he was bone tired but also strangely enlivened. He took one last look at young Tom's picture, the boy's splayed hands outstretched, that crooked smile on his narrow face, and Hank remembered the last time he had shot that quivering expression.

He recalled the conversation with the boy about his drawings, and particularly the one of the white fawn.

"You believe it exists?" Hank remembered asking.

And Tom had replied, "Yeeeeeeah."

"Well, I wish I could confirm it. Seeing it is believing to a photographer. If I'm lucky enough to snap it, I'll get you a copy, okay, Tom?" Then Hank had smiled and looked up at Eva.

Once again, her angular beauty struck him. *She's transparent, like an icicle,* Hank thought. *She exists, but she's fragile. If I were to touch her, she'd melt.* She must have felt his gaze. She looked up. Their eyes locked. Hers were wells of gratitude; his were pools of yearning. He wanted to touch her face; instead he looked away and buttoned his camera case with a snap.

Since the visit he had thought of little else but the woman's face. Now, weeks after that moment, before the sun rose in the east window of The Clarion, Hank put away the newest edition's photos in a file drawer marked "Chamber Ball" for the picture morgue. He switched off the fluorescent lights in the paste-up room and ducked upstairs to his office to retrieve his camera. He prepared to shut down his computer. But, on impulse, he sat down in his desk chair, put in a few key words, including *white* and *deer*. He wanted to refresh his memory of prior research. Sure enough, albino deer were rare in America and also the subject of Indian lore. The white skin was favored, Hank read, for the buckskinned gowns of Indian brides.

Hank hit a few more keys and pulled up photographs of a preserved herd of forty white deer on the acreage of an old abandoned military base in Seneca, New York. Beautiful, they were, glowing from his computer screen: running, leaping, poised.

"Gosh, Bissell," Hank muttered to himself as he shouldered his jacket and his camera bag. "Wish you could get that deer." When he locked the front door to the newspaper office, he noticed at four thirty, that the horizon beyond the mountains was charcoal black.

41. Hiram's Shoot

Hiram Venald hated drinking too much because liquor always woke him up at four in the morning with a sugar rush, which left him turning and tossing for hours with his mind tracking all his problems. But tonight, after arriving home from the Chamber Ball, he forgot about the consequence of alcohol excess. In fact, even if he had thought about it, he wouldn't have cared. Tonight, Hiram knew he wouldn't sleep anyway. He was hopping mad about more than a few things. Why, in the past few days he—a capable con artist (and proud of it)—had been out-conned by Isabel Charmin over trailer park rent; he had temporarily lost the zoning designation to sell his land to Crane's on his terms; and, most disgusting of all, he had been broadsided with a sauce-dripping shrimp at the biggest social event of the year!

"That no-good redneck Larry Layman, all dressed up in a tie. He's a low-rent fool. Shouldn't let his kind or his slutty wife neither in high-class places like that." Hiram glanced at his own wife to see if she were listening. He leaned back against the kitchen counter, and he reached for the bottle of red jug wine that Stephanie had opened before the ball "to let it breathe."

He poured a cupful in a jelly jar glass and stuck the

cork back in the wine bottle, settling it beside the plastic poinsettias Stephanie had placed near the sink. Temporarily, Hiram had forgotten that he and Larry Layman had been born on the same street almost four decades before, the very same street opposite the "fancy houses," as Hiram called them, the ones on the other side of the railroad tracks cutting through Clearview.

Hiram blinked, watching Stephanie suddenly performing a most amazing acrobatic feat.

"Ugh!" exclaimed his wife, and she reached up, elbows cocked, groping for her back zipper; then she deftly peeled off the layers of her gold foil dress. Next, she stepped beside the fallen garment, pulled up her half-slip, and stripped off her panty hose.

"God, I hate those things!" she said in disgust. She kicked the hose off her feet and then scooped up the stockings and gown like a pile of rags.

Expensive rags, Hiram could not help but reflect.

Stephanie stood in her corset bra and slip and reached for Hiram's glass, taking a swallow.

"That's mine," Hiram growled.

"I know, Honeykins. I'm not taking much. After a night with all those society snobs, I'm beat. I'm going to bed."

And she had left the room, her bare feet slapping the hardwood floors, her rumpled dress and stockings floating behind her.

Hiram watched her go, and had a depressing thought: *As a younger man, I'd bolt after her. But not tonight.* He did not have the energy, or the desire; instead, Hiram felt the need to salve his wounded ego. He unbuttoned his stiff white tux shirt stained with remnants of blood-red cocktail sauce and dropped the shirt in the kitchen trashcan.

"Another expensive rag," he grumbled.

He picked up the wine bottle on the counter and sauntered into his den. He turned up the thermostat on the wall nearby to ignite some gas logs. The instant *Whoof!* and dancing blue flame cheered him a little. He found the sofa and hunkered down, pulling off his shoes and propping sock feet on the sofa table. "Don't put yer feet on the furniture," he could hear his wife's voice in his ear. But he wiggled his toes and slouched in his white T-shirt and tux pants, the suspenders hanging toward his knees, just watching the flames with his feet stacked on the furniture, big as you please.

"I own this furniture!" he spoke out loud to his wife, now snoring in the next room. He toasted the fire with his jelly glass. "Here's to me!" But the toast was ill-fated, splashing red stains on his stomach, reminding him once more of the earlier night's embarrassment.

"Never could stand that scrawny creep Layman even in high school," Hiram sipped the crimson liquid and smacked his lips, "And that Lucy Smith, even before she became Mrs. Layman, always did think she was better than me. Cheap hussy."

Hiram squinted, remembering how mortified he had been when Lucy chose Larry over himself as her escort to the senior prom after Hiram had bragged to everyone in high school about how crazy she was for him. And then—at graduation, before she began to show—he'd heard she'd gotten herself knocked up by that Larry creep!

Sorry piece of crap, that one, Hiram cringed. *Some humiliations you just don't ever get over.* He squirmed forward on the sofa and reached for the wine bottle on the coffee table, filling the jelly jar glass as he continued his private monologue.

"Someday, I'm gonna get even with everybody in the whole damn community. Then they'll respect me. 'That's Hiram Venald!' They'll tell their kids. 'He made this town rich!' And what will I do? How will I act?" Hiram lifted his glass toward the fire. "Well, I'll just snub my nose at every one of them! Yep. The whole sorry bunch. They'll see. They'll see. You don't step on a skunk, and you don't mess with Hiram Venald!"

With these sour hopes and sore thoughts as companions, sometime before midnight, Hiram reached for a plaid throw on the back of the sofa. His head spinning, he pulled the woolly comforter over his torso and fell asleep.

At four o'clock, right on the hour, he was awake.

"Damn kidneys!" he scowled and rolled over. "God, what a headache!" He turned slowly off the sofa and dropped onto the floor on his hands and knees. Wagging his aching head, he crawled to the nearest bathroom, off the hallway. For an instant he held on to the commode and pressed his face gratefully to its side, the cold ceramic surface cooling the fever pounding his brain. Then he grunted, rose up, and assumed a settled position on the seat, leaning over, his head cupped in his hands.

"Wonder where Stephanie stuck the aspirin?" he muttered.

Squeak, slam. Squeak, slam. The banging noise awakened his wife.

"Whatcha doin', Hiram? You'll wake the dead!"

"Well, I wish't I was dead. Got a damn headache and you've hid the aspirin. Where is the friggin' stuff?"

"Try the medicine cabinet, Hiram," Stephanie moaned. "And shut up!"

"You shut up!" Hiram railed, banging a few more cabinets. Then he stomped to the master bedroom bathroom and flung open the medicine cabinet door.

"Thank goodness!" Hiram said, pouring a few tablets in his hand and tossing his head back to down them. "Water? A glass? Nowhere. Oh, c'mon!" He bent down and ran the spigot, bumping his lip, reaching with his tongue for the stream of water.

"Damn it! Now I've got a fat lip!" He stomped back to

the kitchen. On his way, he passed by the gun cabinet in the hall. Oddly, it made him think of something: the white deer.

"Hell's Bells!" A slimy thought wound through the tunnels in Hiram's torpid brain. *He was up already, wasn't he?* Before dawn. Hunting season. Suddenly, he wanted that animal—the mysterious white fawn—to replace that old dusty buck at the Circle Market. What a great marketing gimmick! He could read the signs, the banners, the headlines, telegraphing one letter at a time:

WHITE TROPHY BUCK—SEE IT!
CLEARVIEW CIRCLE MARKET
HUNTER—"GREEN THUMB" VENALD
COME ONE—COME ALL!

"Buy something!" he chuckled, his mind running along. Not only would he pull in the locals, tourists, and such, but also his wife could show off that tight buckskin skirt she wanted so bad. He'd have that deer tanned in time for New Year's Eve.

Hiram giggled to himself. Then he turned and walked gingerly down the hall toward his home office, where in the closet, he found his hunting jacket and pants alongside a flame orange vest. A few minutes later in full gear, he was back in the den unlocking the gun cabinet. He heard his wife thrashing among the bed covers.

"Hiram? What in the world are you doing? Come to bed!" she wailed.

"Nope. Not doing that. Going hunting. Gonna shoot you a white buck skirt."

"A white buck skirt? You're drunk, Hiram. You'll shoot yourself."

"Nope. Not drunk. Not stupid neither."

Then he giggled. Stephanie could hear a knob turn, this time with the telltale squeak of the pantry door.

"Fool," she mumbled.

Hiram reached inside the pantry and fumbled around a lower shelf. He removed a pint of Wild Turkey and nestled it inside his jacket. He grinned. *To keep me warm.*

"Bye, Bye, Hon," he called to the bedroom. "I'm off to bag a deer!"

"Just don't *you* come home in a bag!" Stephanie yelled. Then she grabbed another pillow among the covers and buried her head. At last, her world was not only dark, it was silent.

42. Three Shots

*L*arry Layman groped for his rifle in the dark and eased out the kitchen door, gently closing the screen. The dark morning enveloped him in damp. This weather suited him; the winter season was his favorite, just for the way it smelled: leaves tampened into black rot; hickory nuts fallen and peeled open, their petaled husks dark on the ground; walnuts in pungent green turning to black, releasing an oily scent; and acorns—the musky, delicious smell of acorns. Even the snow this morning—invisible darts—struck his face with pleasant sprinkled cold.

He drove down the highway toward the Bennington Property where he had scored his doe a few weeks before. He'd set his blind there and left it, a rough structure of chicken wire and branches, not much to it. He didn't need it, for he didn't hunt like other men in a pack in the wilds for a week with a cabin for shelter and food and liquor and war stories for entertainment. He was a solitary guy; he hunted for sport, but also for food. The quota for each hunting season was six, but Larry felt lucky if he bagged two deer. It was all his family could eat anyway. Why not save something for the next guy?

Something flashed in his full floodlights beside the

road. A small buck, its beginning antlers just barely visible, stared into the automobile glare, his glance measuring what to do, to jump, or to turn.

"Turn!" Larry shouted inside the truck as he lowered his lights and hit the squealing breaks. The creature turned as if on cue and headed back into the cedar forest from which it came.

"Good!" Larry said, letting his foot off the break pedal. "Don't want no deer that way."

Hank Bissell knew that the large tract of private land, known as the Bennington Property, bordered the trailer park where Tom and Evangeline Holmes lived. The boy had told him that he had seen the white fawn more than once, and since deer mostly stayed within the radius of a mile from their home territory, Hank reasoned that the Bennington land likely was the most promising site.

But where? The tract was huge. Hank eased his black Jeep as if he meant to park among the house trailers. Then he shouldered his gear and began to walk in an easterly direction. Clouds moved in drifts overhead. He was glad he'd brought a weather hood for his camera and a slick parka for himself. As he walked farther into the woods, heavy cedar branches showered him, catching his arms, splashing his face. He brushed invisible spider webs from his eyes and made his way into the area called The Pines.

Nearing five o'clock in the morning, now, the dark clinched the light in a relentless winter grip. It reminded Hank why ancient peoples needed holidays to welcome the sun, and why, in modern times, winter needed breaking up with celebrations—Christmas, Hanukkah, and Kwanzaa.

Hank wasn't given to formal religion; he felt most reverent in the wilderness. And unlike many people, he did not fear the dark, nor the specter of death. Hank had seen his share of grisly deaths early in his career as a big-city photojournalist covering accidents, fires, and crime scenes. What did cause Hank to pause in his rare times of reflection was the idea of extinction; but then, he figured, obviously he wouldn't know anything, if oblivion came at the end. No, few universal fears beset Hank at night. What made him tremble was unremitting pain. As a kid, with his mother, he'd kneel by his bed and say his prayers, "Now I lay me down to sleep . . ." And when he got to the part, "If I should die before I wake," Hank would interject, "Make it quick!" As a boy he watched his father, made old in middle age, consumed by abdominal cancer, his ashen face contorting in spasms, vomiting blood in the bathroom on his slow journey to the grave. It was then Hank determined that suffering was the real enemy, not death.

A noisy squirrel chattered at Hank and scampered up an oak tree, scattering the photographer's morbid thoughts. Hank paused, watched him climb and disappear into a hole. "Home sweet home," Hank called, noticing at the same time that he could see farther in the lightening forest haze. Skimming the Blue Mountains, dawn glowed, thin as a lemon peel.

Hiram Venald stumbled into the stationary post-and-wire blind by accident.

"Why, Hell's Bells and Glory Be!" he roared. "Somebody's left this just for me!" He saw a small hunter's stool folded up, leaning against the back of the blind, and he helped himself to it and sat down. He looked through the contrived thicket of brush before him, delighted that he was hidden, feeling satisfied and safe. He put his rifle across his knees, reached into his jacket pocket, and pulled out some shells. He loaded his twelve gauge and snapped the cylinder shut. The chamber cock echoed with a shock in the woods.

"Damn it. Damn it," Hiram swore. "Should have loaded it back at the house. Stupid!" He was reminded of Stephanie's warning, *You'll shoot yourself.* And his retort, *I ain't stupid!* Well, loading a gun in a silent wood was stupid unless it was damn necessary. He'd scare off the deer. All of 'em. The white deer, too, the one he aimed to get that very day. Hiram reached into his jacket pocket for the Wild Turkey. Just what he needed. A few sips to calm his nerves.

Larry Layman was less than five yards from his blind when he saw the shadow of a bulky mass beside it. He spotted a flame orange vest, a parka hood, and the backside of a man hunched over as if asleep, his gun on the ground beside him. The man's head was resting against the blind.

What the heck? Larry thought. *So much for generous thoughts about the next guy.* Larry stepped backwards left and away. He stood in a pine thicket, listening as the crows began to call from overhead the news of a new day.

The light in the mountains turned from pale yellow to orange gold. Larry knew that bald fried egg of a sun would soon appear in the elbow of the hills, flooding the brown landscape in a ruddy, shimmering light as dust and pollen, wind and seeds joined in minute whirls. *Always an awesome sight,* he thought.

Yet, today, Larry had an eerie sense of foreboding. In addition to the sleeping hunter in the blind, there was a presence in the woods. He could feel it. He leaned his head into the pine branches, smelling the resin, feeling the wet, listening, listening. For what?

A twig snapped.

Larry slowly raised his rifle.

He thought he saw something moving to his right, farther east beyond the blind.

306

Another twig snapped. Larry shifted his eyes. Straight ahead, north, three rasping crows flapped up and away. The cedar branches in the same direction shook slightly.

Startled awake, the man in the blind sat up. Larry saw him wipe his mouth as if he had drooled on himself and then reach around for his gun.

A twelve gage, Larry noticed. *God almighty, did the guy expect to shoot a bear? A twelve-point buck? Where's the sport in a twelve gage? Knock out the side of a barn, no problem!* Larry scowled and held his own rifle steady.

He looked north, to his left, and saw the stand of cedars tremble again. Larry held still. The man in the blind shouldered his gun. He, also, turned slowly left to sight the cedars with the cross hairs of his gun. Larry recognized Hiram Venald. *Of all the lowlife to occupy his blind!*

Larry noticed Hiram swaying, even sitting down. *He's drunk.* Larry thought, disgusted. *He's dangerous.*

Another snap, straight ahead. The sun formed a diaphanous path, gilded shadowed bands through the pines. Larry looked down his gun sights and reflexively flinched with dread at what he now saw: the white fawn, slowly moving into the red and gold path of dampened leaves. It stepped cautiously, its pinkish white ears erect, its head aloft, eyes tentative like those of a nearsighted schoolboy. The animal's coat glimmered as a halo, and for an instant, Larry thought this scene must have been what gave rise to the unicorn myths of ancient lore. For, what Larry spied was not a horse, not a deer, but rather a vision on earth—a pure, spotless fawn, crowned with light.

Time froze. Larry watched, immobilized. Then his peripheral vision detected movement. Hiram's gun—it spun from right to straight ahead, right at the white fawn.

From the direction of the cedars, Larry heard a click. *A*

click? What? A safety release? The white fawn sprang back. Larry frowned. Hiram reared back and swore, shifting his seat to face east. Larry held his finger trigger-reader, pointing his rifle high and right where the click had come from.

Next, in a scramble of hoofs, the fawn ran a few paces. Then, incredibly, Larry saw it stop and turn and stare. Hiram saw it pause, too, and he hunched forward, shotgun ready.

"No!" Larry shouted and squeezed his right index finger pointing high.

Two shots exploded, and Hiram suddenly whirled around, the butt of his gun in his fat shoulder with Larry in his sights. He shouted.

"Layman, you slime ball! You messed up my shot!"

"Hiram!" Larry ducked. "Stop!" At that instant, behind Hiram a large black mass slammed into the hunting blind. Hiram's shotgun exploded again. Larry flattened himself against the ground. He could hear animalistic snarls and grunts. He looked up.

"What the heck—" Larry crawled toward the spot.

The men rolled into the sides of the camouflaged blind tangling themselves in honeysuckle vines, crushing pine branches, bending the wire, and all but flattening the structure.

"You bum! You old fool!" Hiram shouted. "It's hunting season!"

The struggle went on until Larry saw Venald face down in the earth with his arms tied behind with a honeysuckle vine. Larry turned toward Hiram's attacker. He was amazed to see the town stranger—old Pap—in a black wool jacket covered with leaves. He sat astride the hunter's back.

Larry could not help but laugh. He slapped his sides, "You okay, old man?"

Pap panted a moment. Then his face assumed a baleful

expression. "No way to treat a gift." He looked down apologetically at the muddy sleeves of the leaf-covered jacket Larry had presented as an offhanded present several days earlier. He flicked off a piece of pinestraw.

"Aw, man," Larry said, reaching for the other man's big hands to pump heartily. "You just saved my ever-lovin' life!"

Hiram sputtered in the leaves and began to shake his head on the ground. "I wanted to kill it. I wanted to kill it."

The burly man leaned close to Hiram's ear. His words came as gruff gusts of wind, each syllable weighing a separate breath . . .

"You don't just kill what you don't understand."

Larry drew back, astonished. The authority in that voice!

Hiram wagged his head back and forth. He mumbled something about needing a drink.

"This?" Pap held up the bottle of Wild Turkey. He unscrewed the top and tilted it toward the dirt.

"Wait," Larry said. "Give that to me." He looked down at Hiram. "You got half a bottle. You want it?"

"It's mine. Give it."

"Sit him up," Larry told Pap. The old man leaned his captive against a vertical post, a remnant of the fallen blind. Larry reached into Hiram's jacket pockets fumbling for the man's car keys. He pulled them out and held them before the drunken man's face.

"Hiram," Larry grunted. "We'll give you your liquor. But we're taking your keys and your gun."

Hiram spat out an angry, "No!"

"Shut up, Hiram! In your shape, you don't need to drive, and you sure don't need to shoot. We'll drop these things off with your wife. Stephanie can come get you, unless she wants to leave you here to rot—a feeling I can sure understand."

Hiram groaned.

"You want this stuff?" Larry held the open bottle before the man's nose.

Hiram nodded. He was suddenly very tired.

"Well, I'm gonna unscrew this lid and lay this Wild Turkey down. I'm sure you can sink low enough to get it out the bottle neck."

Hiram whimpered and began to use his legs to scrunch himself down from against the post toward the whiskey dribbling on the ground.

Larry stood up. He turned away to raise his eyes toward the direction from which, earlier in a path of ethereal light, the white fawn had revealed itself.

"Was it hit?" Larry asked Pap.

"Hope not."

"Me, too. I shot high. Some things should be left alone," Larry said.

"True enough. You don't just kill . . ." and the voice trailed off. At that instant Larry noticed something strange: the old fellow's eyes turned from black to blue.

Strangely moved, Larry asked. "Who are you?"

"Pap," the man said. "Just call me Pap."

Larry shook his head, puzzled; then he shouldered his rifle. "My truck's close by. You want a ride?"

"Thank you," Pap said, his eyes now hidden by forest shadows. "I have a ride."

Twelve hours later, as Christmas Eve morning seeped over the Blue Ridge, Hank Bissell finished his front-page layout. He'd made a Christmas present for Evangeline Holmes and her artist son Tom. By 9 that morning, he found himself on the other side of the vast Bennington Property, bordering Blackstone County, not far from the trailer park. He had eaten breakfast at the Circle Market where, on impulse, he purchased a single red rose wrapped in cellophane at the cash register, before Flossie's curious gaze.

Outside, on the wooden platform before the trailer door, Hank raised his hand to knock, and then paused, knowing it was awfully early, wondering if Eva might still be asleep. He was comforted to hear the sound of a sewing machine through the metal door. He tapped gently.

When Evangeline shyly opened the door, her beauty once again stunned Hank. She wore a soft blue flannel robe, and a pair of fuzzy slippers. Her hair was down around her shoulders in a fan, as if she'd simply run a quick brush through it after arising that morning. Hank stammered an apology for the early hour, said he knew he could not call as she had no phone, and explained he was stopping by before going to bed, having been up all night working at the paper. Then, feeling awkward, he thrust the package toward her along with the rose.

Evangeline put him at ease. "I have fresh coffee," she said. "Come in."

"Where's Tom?" Hank asked, watching her slender fingers as she grasped the coffee carafe and began to pour.

"Sleeping," she smiled. Then she directed him toward the back of the small quarters. The boy was snoring softly, his face turned toward the trailer window, his body small and still. Hank found it comforting to see the boy relieved, however briefly, from the palsied flailing he'd witnessed.

Evangeline opened the envelope with Hank's photograph of the white fawn and held it before her eyes for a long time. She said one word:

Beautiful.

It was all Hank could do not to gush, *YOU* ARE BEAUTIFUL! But he resisted. Instead, he found himself telling her about his work, how he loved the world through a lens, how capturing images made him appreciate detail. Evangeline had nodded silently, her eyes absorbing his as if she truly understood.

Before long, it was time to go. She stood in the cold on the wooden platform outside the trailer long enough for both of them to notice the light showing the day at its best.

After a moment, she spoke.

"The deer is crippled."

"Flawed," Hank said, "not actually crippled."

"Yet beautiful."

"Definitely that."

"But people say it should be shot."

"So it won't breed—"

"Some people look at Tom that way, as if he should be shot—"

"Horrible."

"They don't understand," Evangeline smiled wistfully. "Tom is—is—he's beautiful."

Hank had gone silent. He watched the sun winking behind dripping needles from the tall pines. He sighed, "I guess there is a lot in this world we don't understand: why there are crippled children and crippled deer." He kicked his boot against the wooden boards and kept his gaze straight ahead. "Sometimes," he started and stopped, not wanting to sound foolish.

"Sometimes?" Eva asked.

"Sometimes, I think we humans are incredibly nearsighted. We busy ourselves in one plane, while the universe revolves in another—a plane more vast in scope and more intricate in detail than we can even begin to comprehend."

After that, Hank felt something on his cheek, soft as a dove's wing, a kiss, followed by the quiet closing of the trailer door behind him. He stood on the platform in a wedge of filtered sunlight, wrapped in her vanished presence, facing a new day.

Twenty-four hours later on Christmas Eve Day, Hiram Venald downed three aspirin with a Coca-Cola in the final attempt to rid himself of a hangover that would not quit. He dropped wearily to his den sofa and pulled the The Clearview Clarion from the coffee table to his lap. He held it up before his face and blinked once, twice, three times. There, on the front page, was his target: the backlit photograph of the solid white fawn.

Hiram squinted at the picture to see the small attribution below it: *Photo by Hank Bissell.*

"Damn it! Damn it!" he exploded. "That newspaper photographer—Hank what's-his-name—got off the first shot!"

43. Christmas Pageant

C hristmas Eve at the Layman home began in chaos. Each
year the neighboring church, All Saints' Episcopal, hosted
a Christmas pageant, and for the fourth year in a row, the
Layman children were playing a part. At four thirty that afternoon,
Lawrence, Jr., stood before the full-length mirror in Lucy and
Larry's bedroom, trying to level out the rope that loosely held a
sheet draped to his head like a shepherd's. He grumbled to himself.

"This is the last year for this stupid stuff. I'm too old.
Fourteen. I look dumb." Meanwhile, before a small dresser mirror, Lucy wound a halo of silvery tinsel around her daughter
Linda's brow to simulate an angel's halo. Linda flashed a cheru-
bic smile at her sparkling reflection.

In the living room before the wood-burning stove,
Larry paced. He was smoking. "Just can't give up all my vices at
once," he had told Lucy resignedly earlier that month. But she
asked him to keep the habit outside, so now he stepped to the
front porch, noticing as he did, the smell of fresh paint. *My, how
that Francine Urbane took charge of my house.* He inhaled. *In less
than a day she transformed the place.*

"Aaaah, the power of money," he sighed.

But people with money weren't always attractive. He

had learned that. He'd watched the bossy way Francine had ordered the workmen around and reflected that he sure was glad she wasn't his wife. And that Jan Midland, why, you'd think she would have more sense than she obviously did. After Jan cooked the Swap dinner in their home, Larry had informed his wife that Mrs. Midland left a pile of dirty adult diapers open in a bag, smelling awful in the laundry area.

"Dumb!" Larry said. "I sure got the best of the three-some," he told Lucy. "I know that for a fact."

Lucy had responded with a bemused smile that had puzzled him vaguely at the time.

Now, he gazed distractedly across his front yard, where the immoble flamingoes pecked the grass, and wondered about tomorrow. He and Lucy had bought Linda lots of random things for Christmas. But were they enough? After all, Lawrence, Jr.'s gift was big. Larry's thoughts wandered to Christmases past. Thank heavens—the gifts this year did not need to be assembled! Those Christmas Eves of opening boxes at midnight marked "Made in China" or "Made in Japan" where screws were not included as specified, and screwdrivers the right size were missing from his toolbox anyway, and the plastic holes for the screws were too small, besides, for anything to slot together easily. Every Christmas Eve, Larry lost his religion in a litany of cursing. Lucy was amused at first; then she complained.

"Not the Christmas spirit, Larry," she whined. "This is supposed to be fun!"

"Not for me!" Larry glanced at the cuckoo clock, sensing it was nearly two in the morning.

"Think of the kids tomorrow, how happy they'll be riding these things outside, up and down the driveway."

"Today," Larry grumbled as the wooden bird jumped on a spring, opening a tiny door. *Cuckoo! Cuckoo!*

"Hear that? Tomorrow is today!"

Of course, invariably in the morning, Lucy was right. Christmas Days dawned with delighted squeals and the sounds of clacking "motors" from pedal bikes traveling up and down his driveway. This year would be different. After a small celebration around the tree tomorrow morning, he was taking his family to the Urbanes' for brunch, and also, for a surprise presentation to his son.

Larry snuffed his cigarette into the floorboard of his porch. Then he picked up the stub and automatically put it in his pocket. Homeowners complain if workers leave trails of cigarette butts in the yard. Larry had learned that. What he wished Lucy would learn is that if you don't empty the pockets of a workman's pants, you'll likely wash a bunch of nasty tobacco flakes in with everything else in the load. It could gum up the pipes, requiring a plumber. Expensive! Larry could not count the number of times she'd done that. Of course, when he complained, she observed that Larry might want to empty his butts along with his wallet and keys and change at night. So, that unpleasant discussion always ended in a draw.

He heard his mother call and returned inside the house. She needed help with her shawl. She was dressed and ready, a red bow on the handle of her wheel chair.

"I just can't wait to see the children in the pageant," she smiled. Something in her expression—excitement? Amusement? It reminded him of the young mother she once was, how enthusiastic she always had been for her children at Christmas. Impulsively, he leaned down, arranged her shawl, and kissed her tiny wrinkled forehead.

"You'll be waking up in a brand new bedroom on Christmas Day," he said.

"I have a very smart and talented son," she replied. "You got it done. I'm so grateful and so very proud."

At that moment, the angel, the shepherd, and the creator of it all, Lucy, burst into the living room.

"We're finally ready!" Lucy panted.

"It's quarter of five," Larry glanced at the cuckoo clock on the wall. "Let's go. You kids are pageant stars tonight."

"Oh," Lucy spun around in distress. "Linda, do you have the baby Jesus?"

The child angel put her hands over her tiny mouth. "Oh, no!" She fled the room, returning with a doll wrapped in a towel as swaddling cloth. "Now, I got him," the little girl pulled the towel edge under the baby's chin.

"Good thing," Larry said, winking at Lucy as he began wheeling his mother through the door to help her into the family car.

"You sure can't have Christmas without the Baby Jesus."

44. Silent Night

By nine that evening, the eighteenth-century grandfather clock had struck its mellow gongs, and Francine had refrigerated the remnant of the clove-and-cherry studded ham, her featured entrée for Christmas Eve dinner this year. She basked in her husband's unexpected compliments as she worked.

"Elegant, Franny. You have a marvelous sense of elegance that I don't see in other women. I believe it a special quality and very rare."

She smiled and left the kitchen to return to the dining room. She removed the linen napkins from the table, looping the three silver napkin rings lying beside them onto her fingers. She opened the felt-lined drawer in the antique bureau where she stored the silver flatware and the napkin rings. She noticed a solitary engraved ring inside. It was bright, however, for she had shined it earlier that day. Nevertheless, it lay hauntingly still, for it had not been used in a long, long time. She fingered it briefly, and then she placed the three others next to it. She pushed the silver drawer shut with a heavy thump.

Earlier that evening, her daughter, Anna, announced

from the entry hall that her date had arrived, and Francine and Bill had waved them off.

"Don't be late," Bill admonished the young couple. "You've got two weeks to see one another before Anna returns to Smith. Don't try to pack it all in tonight."

A tall, freckled-faced, red-haired youth named James smiled back. He was one of Frank Midland's architecture students at the university. He and Anna had met last year at All Saints' Episcopal as they walked out in the milling throng from the Christmas Eve service.

"Improbable place to meet someone cool," Anna said to her parents afterward.

Later, James had confessed, "Lucky for me, too."

During the ensuing school year the two had kept in touch, seeing one another on school breaks. Frankly, Francine thought the match was just about perfect. She had observed just that to Bill after the young couple left the house. Of course, he said what he always did, "Perfection is the enemy of the good. Nothing or no one is perfect. "But," Bill had added, "James is a pretty fine boy. In fact, it's hard to think of a better young man."

"Except one," Francine said wistfully, and Bill went silent.

Now seated together in the living room, a small amount of brandy in a pair of Reidel snifters, Francine leaned her coiffed hair back in her matching wing chair, drawn next to Bill's in an arc before the fireplace. She could hear the coals heaving and sighing. Bill's voice came pensively as if stirred by the sifting of the coals.

"I liked what the priest had to say in his message, at the five o'clock service tonight. You remember? The latest theory physicists have to understand the origins of the universe. He called it—"

"String theory?"

"Yes, that's it."

Francine nodded. "It's fascinating . . ." She tapped her fingernails against her crystal glass. "And amazing, really . . . the idea that all matter—down to its protons, neutrons, and electrons—everything, along with every force in nature, is composed of teensy, tiny, invisible, vibrating strings."

"Hard to imagine," Bill stared at the fire.

"Yes it is," Francine agreed.

"But they say it could explain where we came from, time, space, galaxies."

"Mmmmhum," Francine nodded.

"But what I liked, what really caught my attention was Reverend Matthews' bit about dimensions," Bill leaned forward, his elbows on his knees, a quiet earnestness in his eyes. "You remember? He said scientists suspect extra dimensions, more than the three we see in the world around us. Like the New Testament, 'In my father's house, there are many mansions.'"

"Yes."

"And then he said, 'What if *mansion* is just another word for *dimension*?'"

"I liked that, too. And he said the dimensions may be really close, 'at hand' as he quoted Jesus."

"Franny, I guess you and I think along the same lines." Bill settled back in his wing chair, and turned his head in her direction "Because string theory physicists—according to Reverend Matthews, anyway—think energy may escape from the dimensions we know, to leak into those extra dimensions we can't detect. Under special circumstances."

"High-energy circumstances. Terribly high energy circumstances, as I recall." Francine sipped her brandy. "Actually, he said like atom smashing."

"Right. So I was sitting in the pew thinking. 'What's

more high energy for human beings than birth? A strenuous passage like it is, to this world.'"

"Not only for the baby," Francine smiled ironically. "A tough one for the mother, too. How well I remember, with our two babies."

Bill blinked. He stared at the fire and continued with his line of thought. "Well, the idea of passages and high energy and birth led me to think about death, and how people who nearly die describe the experience of traveling a tunnel and seeing a bright light."

"And you think their souls just might be passing into a new dimension?"

"Well, I know this may sound far-fetched, but supposedly a soul weighs twenty-one grams."

"According to a movie with that name," Francine added skeptically.

"Well, it's said that people are twenty-one grams lighter *after* they die than *before*."

"Okay." Francine wrinkled her nose, wondering where all this was going. Physics was not Bill's normal preoccupation. She cocked her head at her husband and kept listening.

"So if the soul weighs something, then you might assume it is matter." Bill pressed on.

"Hmmm."

"And scientists tell us that matter changes shape, even becomes energy, but it doesn't disappear."

"So?" Francine whirled a final sip of brandy around the bottom of her snifter.

"So that is where the other dimensions come in—the ones where the soul might go."

Francine's eyes, sapphire blue, reflected the dancing

firelight. She sat somewhat transfixed by the deep discussion, the dancing fire, the brandy warming her veins.

"It's a comforting thought," Bill offered, clasping his hands, an enigmatic smile turning up the corners of his mouth.

"Yes, it is," Francine mused. "A comforting thought. That maybe those we love who have gone are close by . . ." She sighed quietly.

Outside, the night was star-strewn and windless. Later, Francine supposed it was the meandering thoughts Bill had spoken, or the soft wind gently rattling the windows that provoked her to break their shared vow of silence. But mostly it happened because she was afraid Bill might be growing dysphoric. So she changed the subject.

"You want to open a gift?" she asked, hoping the shift didn't sound as manipulative as it felt.

"Our open-one-gift custom on Christmas Eve?" Bill asked smoothly. After thirty-five years, he was used to her sudden, sometimes disconcerting shifts in conversation.

"Yes," Francine said. "Our under-the-tree stash is bigger this year than it's been in a long time."

"All those Swap gifts from the Midlands and Laymans.'"

"Yes. Why don't you open one of those?" Francine suggested.

Bill stood up and walked over to the towering tree, eying the package in a brown lunch bag clumsily tied with a piece of yarn.

"This looks like it needs opening," he smiled.

"That's from Larry's boy, Lawrence."

Bill picked up the small bag and returned to his wing chair.

"You know, Honey, silly as it sounds," Francine rambled on dreamily, "I had an unexpected thought in the middle of the Christmas pageant following the sermon. You know how mixed up the pageant was." Francine involuntarily giggled. "The child who played Mary dropped the baby Jesus and had to pick it up and put it in the fake manger—a bureau drawer—where the doll lay with its hands straight up. Remember?" She giggled again. "And Lawrence Jr.'s shepherd rope fell off his head, along with his sheet, because his little sister stepped on it from behind. Oh! It was funny! How he hissed, 'Dummy!' and Linda pulled off her halo, and she just boo hoooed."

Francine's shoulders were shaking now, and Bill's somber mood was lightening. "Then those two Jack Russell terriers got in a tussling match—the cows of the display—" She went on. "And then," she succumbed and laughed until her sides ached. Bill involuntarily joined in. "And then," she finished, "the sheep—that silly Bassett hound of the Midland's—what's his name?"

"Lamont," Bill replied, with a sideways grin.

"Lamont! Yes, goofy Lamont kept turning around biting at the fake sheep's wool covering his back and his sides until it shredded like snow all over the altar area. Oh, I thought I would die laughing."

"It really was funny," Bill said.

"But the situation made me think about *perfect*. You know the word you hate?"

Bill winced. Then he grudgingly nodded.

"Well, life is not like that, is it? It's not perfect. Not in the present, not in the past. Think about it. Mary, the mother of Jesus, gave birth in a barn. A barn, for heaven's sake! Her husband was poor, kind, yes, wise but uneducated. And they raised that boy . . ." her voice choked. "And then he died." Tears brimmed the corners of Francine's eyes.

"Cruelly and publicly. I don't know how she stood it," Bill said.

"They," Francine corrected. "Both parents stood it."

"Well," Bill said reflectively, "unending grief will kill anybody. You have to let it go. Go forward. I'm glad, at least, that we have Anna."

"And we *had* Andrew." Francine surprised Bill. She actually spoke the boy's name.

"And listen to me, please, Bill," she hurried on, "I want to go public about it."

"Why?" Bill jolted forward in his chair, his voice a croak of anguish.

"I want to start a foundation . . . a foundation to help physically disabled children to develop skills, practical, artistic, whimsical talents, I don't care what," Francine said, her voice charging through the tendency to weep. "Frank Midland tells me, with computers and education and physical therapy, the sky's the limit for those kids—kids like that seamstress's boy, Tom. Training and skill development, they are just things—things that cost money. But money is just a thing, too, and you know, Bill, how good I am at raising money."

"The sky's the limit." Bill tapped the gift in his hands.

"You know what I want to call it?" Francine swallowed. This was a risk. For the second time she was about to break a promise made long ago. "The Andrew Foundation."

Bill blinked a moment, startled by the pain behind his eyes. He began suddenly to fiddle with the yarn bow on the paper-bag gift.

"Franny, we agreed never to speak—" he began as he spread open the mouth of the bag and distractedly reached inside. He pulled out a square plastic case. He stared at the object in stunned silence.

Francine felt the air swoosh suddenly from the room. She saw Bill's face freeze.

"What, Honey? What is it?"

With long graceful fingers, Bill turned the CD in her direction.

"*Mannheim Steamroller*," he said with the weight of the world in his voice.

"Oh!" Francine cried. "Oh. I can't believe it. Amazing, the coincidence! The gift from Larry's boy was Andrew's last gift to us."

Bill tapped the disc, then laid it aside, leaned back, and sighed.

"He was bringing it to us for Christmas that year."

They sat there, the two of them, silent a moment. Then Francine picked up the disc and walked toward the CD player in a cabinet, which discreetly housed the television and other electronic paraphernalia. She turned back toward Bill as she snapped opened the CD case.

"You want to hear it?"

Bill spoke as if walking through clouds, "The last song is number eleven."

Francine put her hand to her mouth in a silent, "O."

"That's what Andrew said, Bill. Wasn't it? On the phone to us from Amherst. 'The best song is the last one, number eleven.'"

Bill nodded. "Silent Night." He sighed.

"Just once, Bill, please. Let's listen just once," Francine urged.

"Not tonight."

"Only tonight."

"This is a mistake." Bill shook his head wearily.

Francine slid in the disc and electronically selected the eleventh title. She went to Bill's side and knelt by his chair to listen, her hands curled like a kitten's on the arm of his chair . . .

Beats of silence fanned the air. Then gliding swanlike into the room, the shining strings of *Silent Night* soared aloft. As

Francine held Bill's arm, they felt the shimmering hues of humming voices, the shattering radiance of cymbals and the ringing droplets of xylophone. Violins and bells burst forth like a spray of shooting stars. The music swam to every corner, filling the cloistered atmosphere as if possessing an angelic spirit of its own. Celestial exquisiteness encircled the sorrowful couple, pulling them close to one another, hypnotized by the reaching fire and the simple, wondrous melody, the inspired new version of a beloved ancient carol.

As the music faded in a sprinkle of distant tiny bells, Francine took her husband's hand and spoke quietly. Both of their faces glistened with tears reflecting the flickering firelight.

"Bill," Francine whispered, "I'm glad we did that. I'm glad we finally heard it. Andrew's gift. It's—"

Bill winced. *Here comes that p-word. Perfect,* he thought.

She lifted her husband's hand and kissed it. "Precious," she said.

Taken aback, Bill struggled with his emotions. Then, without warning, the ice dam broke from his heart and his shoulders began to heave. He enfolded Francine in his long warm arms and sobbed.

"Andrew. Andrew," he said the word over and over. Finally, finally he could speak the name of his first-born, his son.

After a while Bill grew quiet. He drew back, turned his head, and gazed into the brimming blue eyes of his wife. "You are right, Franny." Bill nodded. "Lawrence's gift, here—ah, and Andrew's gift—is precious."

Francine smiled a tremulous smile. "And," Bill said as he reached over to place a long gentle finger under his wife's chin, "Andrew's mother is precious. Very precious to me."

45. Christmas Ride in a Green Sleigh

*I*t was nine-thirty Christmas Eve, and still the Midland's had not eaten dinner. Jan was exorbitantly flustered.

She had meant to tell Frank to program the oven in which the turkey was roasting to cut off while they were in church, but she had forgotten to mention it. And now, well, the thing was a crackling brown color—a bit crispy; furthermore, she had yet to make the creamed turkey gravy.

"I've taught you how to program the oven many times," Frank reminded Jan when she fussed at herself. "You can do it."

"I'm not good at electronics," Jan huffed. "You're the wiring brain in the family."

"Is that a compliment or an insult?" Frank raised his professorial eyebrows.

Jan inadvertently smiled. "It's a fact. Unbiased."

"Can't win either way, can I?" Frank said.

"Nope," Jan said ruefully, "but tonight, you have a reprieve—it's Christmas Eve."

"Aha!" Frank said.

Jan winked at him and looked toward the living room at the twins.

"That was a nice Christmas Eve service, wasn't it, boys?" she asked as she clanked through a utensil drawer to find the plastic turkey basting tube. She opened the oven and reached inside, squeezing the tube, filling it with fragrant broth and drippings. She sent a gurgling spray over the breast of the turkey.

"Now!" she nodded to Frank, who reached in with potholders and gently transferred the heavy weight to the top of the cook stove.

"Maybe it will be okay as crispy roasted turkey," she said. The bird, stuffed with celery, onions, apples, and pears, generated an aroma so delicious, the boys began to roll on the floor groaning as they had as children.

"I'm starving."

"Hurry up with that bird, Ma, will you?"

Kyle turned on his stomach and stared at the Christmas tree for a few moments. "You know, Frank?" he called to his step-dad. "This tree doesn't blink."

"Nope," Frank had left the kitchen for the den where he crouched behind the television, near the new shelves on which the DVD player, the satellite receiver, and the CD player rested comfortably, each in its custom spot. Frank was quite proud of this arrangement, and Jan had been thrilled. Larry Layman had put the basics in place and drilled holes for the wires to fall through leading to a central panel. Frank could easily reach them; Jan was ecstatic to have the tangled mess hidden. The burled walnut cabinet doors were due by the end of January.

Meanwhile, Frank had rerouted the CD player to send Christmas carols to speakers throughout the house. There had been a slight glitch and he'd leaned behind the television to get it right when Kyle made note of the tree. Frank grunted.

"No, Kyle, that tree doesn't blink."

"And it doesn't have *our* ornaments on it either," Ryan

said. "All our kindergarten and grammar school masterpieces with popsicle sticks and glue."

"Frank. Are you listening?" Kyle whined.

"Yeah, Frank,." Ryan chimed in. "I made you a God's Eye one year—you know, colored yarn on a cross of glued Popsicle sticks. You called it the badge of the 'Me Generation.' That's not hanging here either."

"Nothing of ours is on the tree!" Kyle exclaimed.

Frank walked over to the spruce laden with red balls, glistening with white lights and a few sequined ornaments. He stretched long arms, four fingers, two hands, delivering the "Peace" sign. Facing the boys on the floor, he arched his slender torso as if making an important proclamation.

"Peace and salutations!" Frank said grandly.

The boys looked at each other and rolled their eyes.

"Gentlemen, all of what you say is true," Frank began in overblown tones. "But this year departs from all others. You boys have achieved enough academic success to get your-selves off to a state university, leaving your mother and me mercifully alone."

Lamont barked. The boys laughed. They loved it when Frank went off on one of his professorial rants.

"So, this year, what we have, gentlemen, in honor of your absence—er—presence—is a theme tree! For the first time in her entire life, your mother has the tree that she herself, exclusively, has created!"

"A theme tree? Why am I gagging?" Kyle smirked.

"What's the theme? Red and white?" Ryan asked.

Frank leaned over and picked up the lumbering Bassett hound at his feet.

"Drum roll, Lamont," he said, nudging his dog. The pup happily offered a garrulous "Ruff!"

"Atta boy! This year's theme is—farm animals!" Frank turned sideways toward the tree.

"Farm animals? Like the manger scene?" Ryan asked.

"Like that Christmas pageant where Lamont kept shedding his sheep's wool?" Kyle snickered.

"Shedding? No! Shredding!" Ryan countered.

"That was hilarious!" Jan offered from the kitchen.

"Old Lamont, you know, you're no Bassett in sheep's clothing," Frank plopped the heavy pup on Kyle's stomach.

"Ooof," Kyle laughed. "Nosirreee. Lamont's the real thing—a genuine—a genuine—"

"Pig!" Ryan shouted. "Look, Lamont! There's no dog, but there is a pink pig—and, and—a sheep—with sequined eyes!"

"How can you have a farm without a dog?" Kyle asked.

"Without a Lamont!" Ryan agreed.

"If you guys don't let up," Jan called from the overheated kitchen, "I'm going to throw this crispy turkey out into the snow and let you go hungry all during Christmas!"

"Aw, Ma, we're just kidding."

"No we're not! I want my old gooey ornaments on the Christmas tree," Kyle said.

"I didn't think you'd care," Jan said.

"Care—why I have a baseball card with Hank Aaron on it. We always hung that along with—"

"Mine—of Pete Rose!" Ryan finished his sentence.

"We put yours on a lower branch," Kyle said like a know-it-all.

"You think you're cool, don't you, bro?" Ryan said.

"You can see why I wanted something peaceful—" Jan rejoined.

"Where are our ornaments, Ma? In the garage?" Kyle rolled up from the floor to a sitting position.

"Yes."

"C'mon, Ryan, let's go get 'em. It's not Christmas without our stuff on the tree."

"Oh, don't bring in all that mess," Jan called. "Frank, stop them!"

The two boys shoved playfully at the front door. There was a blast of cold air, then a few whirling flakes, and then a slam.

"Too late," Frank shrugged.

"No respect. I get no respect in this house!" Jan whisked flour into the gravy drippings.

"Now, Honey, calm down. I think it's nice. Let them find the ornaments and put them up. They are tying their lives to Christmas through the ages. Makes the event personal, you know? Traditional."

"Nobody ever did anything *new* that was labeled 'traditional.'"

"Well, we'll call this a *new* tradition then," Frank's tone was placating. "Honey, it is a nice tree. But I do think next year you should make a dog ornament. You know? Really." Lamont had waddled over to slump at Jan's feet. Frank looked down at him, pointedly. "Just so you won't hurt his feelings." Jan turned back to the stove. She knew she was supposed to smile. But something else happened—tears.

"Nobody thinks about *my* feelings," she sniffed, her long hair curling in the steam. Frank beside her.

"Sure they do," said Frank. "I'll show you. How long 'til the turkey's ready?"

"It's *over ready*," Jan said. "We're just waiting on the gravy to simmer and thicken a little more. I should take a cue from Francine Urbane. Order things at the deli and have them delivered."

"Except the food tastes delivered."

"You enjoyed the Tiramisu."

"Cardboard compared to yours."

Jan scowled. "Yeah, well, meanwhile, I get all hot and bothered with a million things to do: set the table, carve the bird . . . "

"Make that a million and one," Frank said, and he put his arm around her and squeezed her hip next to his frame, just like the old days. He felt her soften with his hug.

"A million and one . . .?"

"Yep," Frank said. "Put that stove on 'pause.' And put on your coat. And your scarf. And your hat."

Jan cut the gravy to simmer. She cocked her head to one side, listening to the low grumble of a running motor.

"Is that the tractor?" she asked.

"Nope," Frank said. "That's a genuine Santa sleigh."

"Yeah, r-i-i-i-ght," Jan said.

Frank ushered Jan outside into the dark night. From the front porch, she squealed, "Frank! How did you get lights to hang from the tractor?"

"Aw, Ma, quit talking and get on!" Kyle hollered.

"Yeah, Ma, just do it!" Ryan called.

Frank hoisted Jan up and she squeezed to the side of the one-seater tractor cushion. Sharing a tractor seat defied all safety rules, of course, but they had always loved a roundabout on the acreage of Double Nickel Farm. They snuggled together, Jan putting her arm behind Frank's shoulders, Frank placing one gloved hand on the tractor wheel, another on the gears.

Jan laughed into Frank's beaming face. "One of my favorite things—a sleigh ride!"

"That's right, Honey. We're going to take this John Deere sleigh through the snow. Does the star-spangled night I ordered up suit you well enough?"

"I like your star-spangled banner of lights," Jan said, pointing above her head.

Her eyes traveled across a graceful skein, gathering like an ivy vine stretching to the tractor rooftop. Far above, the vault of the universe expanded—a wheeling wash— billions of stars.

Frank followed her gaze toward the heavens. "I'd like to say, I wired them, too."

"Oh, Frank!" she exclaimed. "You are magical!"

"A wiring genius?" Frank winked.

"A magical Santa," Jan said.

"Well, I did have some help from a coupla' elves," he said. "Okay, boys!" he shouted. Frank pushed the tractor throttle up. The engine roared. He let his foot off the clutch. Just then, right on cue, the picket fence surrounding their home burst into a dazzling garland of lights. Frank laughed to himself.

Not bad! Not bad! Even Rich's of Atlanta could not have done better.

"Oh!" Jan exclaimed. "Oh! Oh! Oh!"

"I think it's correctly, 'Ho! Ho! Ho!'" shouted Frank.

The twins bolted from inside the garage where they had flipped the switch for the Christmas lights on the fence. They clambered up the steps, hanging over the porch railing, waving, next to a large cardboard box full—Jan just knew it—of all those old tacky handmade ornaments. She shook her head. The boys hollered. "Merry Christmas, Ma! Way to go, Frank!"

Frank lurched the tractor forward, "Funny," he frowned, hearing something odd. Despite the chugging engine noise, he could swear, as they circled the hill down from the farmhouse, he could hear sleigh bells.

Jingle, jingle, jingle . . . somewhere . . . somewhere . . .

Ryan turned to go into the warm house. "Did you attach that old horse sleigh strap to the tractor?"

"Sure," Kyle said. "Rigged it to the back on the bush hog. Frank couldn't see in the dark. I figure it will drive him crazy, hearing sleigh bells."

Ryan laughed. "Mom always said Christmas isn't complete without a sleigh ride."

"Well a John Deere tractor is sure no sleigh!"

"But it's a heck of a good ride!" Ryan said. He leaned over to pick up the box of Christmas ornaments. "By the way, my brother," he straightened up, "do you know how to carve a turkey?"

"Nope. Frank said use the electric knife. It's easier."

"Yeah," Ryan nodded. "He would think that—"

"Yeah, he would," Kyle nodded as he pushed open the front door. " 'Cause it's wired."

46. Christmas Eve at The Circle Market

Less than two miles away under the flickering fluorescent lights of the Circle Market, Flossie turned from scrubbing the stovetop behind the serving counter as a blast of cold wind swept in the front door. The hanging bells on the door handle jangled merrily.

Flossie scowled. *What time is it?* She glanced at the bright pink hands glowing from a green plastic wall clock. *9:45.* She pursed her lips. She had posted a sign saying she would close the market at 10 p.m., on Christmas Eve. She eyed the man in the black overcoat as he walked toward her.

His shoulders were sprinkled with snow, his black hat rimmed by white, and a red wool scarf snuggled his beard. Pap, the now-familiar stranger to Clearview, walked slowly, holding a bulging paper bag. Flossie stiffened. He had visited the market almost every day for the past three weeks, buying national newspapers mostly, drinking hot chocolate regularly, and eating a hamburger every few days or so.

She had never been afraid of him before. But he always came during daylight. His sudden appearance out of the dark made her uneasy. Flossie was an avid reader of mystery books, and this scene fit right in with most of them.

Oh, God, this is it. He's not a harmless old bum. He's really a serial killer! The notion sprang to mind. For an instant she considered ducking behind the counter.

"Merry Christmas," he said breathlessly. "Do you have any of that good hot chocolate of yours?"

"I'm closing early tonight, ya' know," Flossie said, exhaling. But she couldn't completely relax, for why was he carrying a paper bag? With what inside?

"A midnight brew?" she asked, staring pointedly at his gloved hand with the package.

"Oh, no!" he laughed. "Not tonight. Too much to do. But I did want to ask you if I might shine up Old Buck here." He set the paper bag on the counter. Flossie heard the clink of glass.

"Old Buck? You mean the trophy head?"

"Yes, he's needing some attention, I think." The man loosened his wool scarf and took off his worn hat, laying it on the counter. He unbuttoned his coat. Then he reached into the bag and began pulling out what looked like jelly jars filled with oil, and wax and shoe polish. "It won't take but a few minutes."

This guy is really a kook, Flossie thought. But she shrugged and said, "Well, okay. But don't ruin him. Even though he's dusty and kinda moth-eaten, people still like having him there. Reminds them of the old tavern on the place."

"I know that," the man nodded, his eyes smiling. *Strange eyes, from blue into black. Black as the night outside.* Flossie poured the steaming chocolate into a ceramic mug and then reached into the fridge for a can of spray whipped cream.

"Cream like usual?" she asked.

"Yes, Ma'am. And please don't be—"

"I know," Flossie looked up and smiled. "Don't be shy with the whipped cream."

In the time it took her to circle the cocoa cup to the

rim with white, the old man had found a stool near the door and climbed up to where he could reach the deer. He poured a little dark oil, which looked like molasses, on a rag. Then he dipped out paler, olive-looking oil, and then a small spray can of something that made the buck's head shine.

The old geezer is thorough, I'll say that for him, Flossie thought.

"Looks like you got some good products there," she observed. "You get them at the hardware store?"

"Nope," came the raspy answer. "Just a little this and that, potions I know about."

"Looks like it's workin'," Flossie noted. "I ain't never seen him shine up like that. Now that you wiped his eyes, why, they're shining like real."

"Why, of course he's real," the man turned and looked at Flossie as if she had a screw loose in her head. She returned the look. *I hope he's not dangerous, after all. Crazy dangerous or something,* she thought.

Finally, twisting the top off a metal tin, Pap took what amounted to a thick tar and wiped it across the buck's nose, restoring it to a wet glaze as if the creature had just run through the snow.

"That makes a big difference," Flossie said. "You want your chocolate? It's gonna be cold."

"Just about done," the man said, taking a final rag and stroking the trophy as if he were petting a large dog.

"You're a good soul," he said, looking right into the creature's glass eyes.

"Deer ain't got no souls," Flossie sniffed.

"Sure they do. All living things have souls."

"But he ain't living. He's dead as a doornail." Flossie jerked her head toward the buck, her hand on her hip.

Pap smiled and shook his shaggy white head. "Good souls never die," he said evenly. He gave his work a final flourish and replaced Flossie's garland of red tinsel and sprig of mistletoe across the antlers. He winked at the trophy, "Do they, Old Buck?"

Flossie raised an eyebrow. "Oh, boy," she murmured as she turned around and glanced at the green wall clock. Its fluorescent hands glowed 9:55.

"I'll be out before ten," Pap said, as if reading her mind.

"That would be good. I'm closing early, Christmas Eve and all," Flossie said, pushing his hot chocolate across the counter. "Got to bake a hen for my mother for Christmas Day. She's gettin' on up there in years, 'bout eighty-five now. Tonight I want to tuck her in bed. Maybe I can catch a Christmas special on the tube. Good music tonight, ya' know?" The man nodded and simultaneously reached in his overcoat pocket for his wallet. Flossie said, "Don't bother. This cup's on me. Merry Christmas. I'm gonna finish cleaning my stove."

The old man took the chocolate and gratefully sipped it, whipped cream coating his mustache. He drained the cup and set it on the counter with a satisfied, "Aaaaah." He licked his upper lip.

"Good as ever," he said. "I'll be going now. Merry Christmas. Take care of Old Buck for me, will you?" He smiled, his black eyes like flaming coals. He replaced his weathered black cap over his white hair and bundled his red scarf under his beard.

"Sure," Flossie said. She watched the fellow carefully replace his jars in the brown paper bag and pull on his gloves. With one hand, he picked up his package of potions and with the other hand, he wrapped his coat around his ample girth. He walked toward the front door. Flossie followed at a distance across the worn linoleum. The man went through the door and turned to tip his hat at Flossie through the glass. She gave a smile and a wave. He disappeared in the darkness. As the door hushed, she moved to lock it. She flipped the "OPEN" store sign to "CLOSED."

Wiping her brow with fatigue, Flossie walked back toward the kitchen and glanced at a shiny, newborn Old Buck. "Got life in you yet, ain't you, big boy?" she spoke to the deer. "And you look kinda purty with that mistletoe a-hangin' from your antlers." Flossie paused a moment in silent chagrin. *Well, this is one more Christmas I ain't been kissed.*

She turned to reach for Pap's empty hot chocolate mug on the serving counter. As she picked it up, she noticed something wet, stuck, in a square of sorts underneath. Paper napkin? She peeled it away from the counter and stared.

"Surely he didn't make no mistake?" she asked out loud. Then she felt the flush of gratitude all the way from her pointed chin to her hairline of orange-red curls. For underneath the empty mug, folded in thirds, Flossie found a one hundred dollar bill.

47. Christmas Morning

C hristmas morning, as he awoke to the venerable tones of the grandfather clock striking seven times, Wilburn Urbane bolted upright, guilts storming his mind like a swarm of Japanese beetles. All were omissions.

First, he had not followed up with the machine shop, which had picked up his tractor for service, along with the old dirt bike in the shed. Nor had he confirmed the bike delivery to his home before noon on Christmas Day. And finally, he had not called Isabel Charmin, as he promised, to determine the status of the matching sum to buy out Hiram Venald's property. But since he had not heard from her, Bill reasoned, likely the tract would belong to Crane's by twelve o'clock today. Greedy Hiram would be free to gobble land like mammon, ruining Clearview in his wake. The thought made Bill's stomach turn, and he reached for his robe. His bare foot hit the floor. Cold! He glanced at Francine, asleep in her hair bonnet.

"Got to keep that bouffant puffed up," he smiled.

He trailed down the hall, pausing at Anna's room. He could smell her perfume through the closed door. Estee Lauder's *Beautiful*, her fragrant favorite. Quietly, he turned the knob and looked in. *God, what a precious child*, he thought. *Precious*. The word he and Francine had rediscovered last night. Bill tiptoed in, leaned over, and smoothed his daughter's long, light brown locks twisted on the pillow like caramel taffy. He leaned down and kissed her creamy face.

"Hi, Daddy," she smiled, opening her blue eyes sleepily and then turning onto her side.

"Merry Christmas, Baby Girl," he said. "I'll go make us all some coffee."

He reached the kitchen before the King Charles spaniels had unwound themselves from the circle of one another in the laundry basket bed. He wished them, Merry Christmas, and then he scooted them out the back door to take care of puppy business. With the opened door came a breeze and the fresh scent of new snow.

"Gosh," Bill said, looking out across the tops of weighted bushes near the kitchen, "I bet we had three inches last night." He wiped a drift from the nearby camelia bush, which had grown tree-size under Francine's care.

"Soft powder, perfect for a snowman. Perfect." He laughed at himself and searched the pantry for the coffee filters.

Not far away, the digital clock beside Frank's bedside was blinking, indicating that the power had gone off during the night. Mercifully, it was back on, however. He reached for his wristwatch nearby, picked it up by its stretch band, and squinted at the dial. 6:50. Frank grunted, laid the watch back down, pulled up the down comforter, and rolled over among the pillows, which also enveloped his sleeping wife. He rose up to look at her. Her long brown ponytail was curled in a ragged knot, tied by a band. She slept on her side, her hands folded like an infant in the womb. He smiled thinking how Jan could be so tough one minute and so tender the next. He watched her breathing for a few seconds. He hated to wake her. But they were due at the Urbanes' today. Then he remembered something else—they weren't due until eleven that morning.

He lay back against the pillows and stared at the ceiling. He played in his mind the magic of Christmas Eve, the tractor ride, the late supper, and the special time he and Jan shared playing Mr. and Mrs. Santa Claus as they stuffed the twins' stockings by the fireside before midnight.

"I think I may go back to teaching, Frank," his wife had said. "Seeing how the boys' reacted to those grammar school ornaments and also being with little Linda Layman reminds me how joyful it is to work with young children."

"Joyful?"

"Yeah," Jan sighed. "They still believe in miracles."

"Well, I think that's a good idea," Frank had said. "You'd feel connected again as a teacher. You'd be in an environment where you'd contribute a lot, and people would recognize it."

He was surprised at how pleased she seemed by his remark. But what had surprised him even more was the package hidden in his bed as he slipped under the covers.

"What's this?" he leaned back against the bedstead and discovered a lump behind the pillows. He glanced at Jan sitting up in bed reading a paperback novel through her Coke-bottle-thick granny glasses. He retrieved a square package wrapped in dark green paper with a gold bow.

"Heavy," he said, and he stretched his legs out, noticing how good the flannel sheets felt. Jan pulled the billowy down duvet up over both their laps.

"For you," Jan said.

Frank pulled at the gold ribbon and green paper.

"Palladio," he read out loud.

"Italy," Jan said. "I know how you want to go there."

"To see the Villa Capri."

"And other works that inspired Thomas Jefferson," she added.

"Yeah," Frank held the picture book in his hands.

"Page 34," Jan urged excitedly.

Frank flipped the pages and stopped at a full picture. There it was, the structure Frank thought the most beautiful in the world, high on a hill, its four distinctive fronts lit by a descending Italian sun.

"Like a dream . . ." Frank sighed.

"Just what I wanted to talk to you about."

"This is a lovely gift, Jan. But talk? I'm so tired." Frank yawned.

"Just for a minute or two," Jan put her arms around Frank's elbow beside her.

"Dreams . . ." she began. "That's what lives are made of: dreams of love, of happiness, of lasting significance."

"Go on," Frank said.

"And you've had dreams . . ."

"Still do."

" . . .To look up your long-lost Italian relatives . . . to study Palladio up close and personal . . ."

"True."

"But you've put your dreams on hold to put the twins through college."

"Four years is not forever," Frank began. But Jan interrupted him gently.

"But it's a long time and I want you to know that I appreciate what you are doing s-o-o-o-o much."

"It's not—" he began again. But Jan unraveled her right hand, kissed her fingertips, and placed them on Frank's lips to silence him.

"So, we know that right now," she continued, "I can't buy you a trip to Italy. But when I go back to teaching, I can. I can save up. And I will. So this Italy book is a promise," she smiled.

"The promise of Italy." Frank grinned.

"And other dreams we'll explore together," Jan finished.

Frank stared at the villa in the photograph. Then, to his surprise, he felt his wife's fingers on his chin as she turned his face toward hers. She had taken off her glasses. She touched his lips again. Then she kissed him hungrily, the way she had once, twice, long ago . . .

Now, seven hours later, Frank smiled at the memory of the encounter following the kiss. He glanced over at the blinking clock and reached up to set it by his watch. Seven, zero, two. 7:02. He set the alarm for 8:30. Blissfully, he listened to Jan's steady sighs. He snuggled under the covers.

"What are you doing? What time is it?" his wife asked drowsily.

"Spooning," he murmured happily, aligning his body cozily behind hers. "Merry Christmas, Honey. We've got time. Go back to sleep."

Lucy and Larry Layman had been up until past midnight finishing Santa Claus duties and final Christmas wrappings to arrange under the tree. When from their bedroom they heard the cuckoo clock sing out at six, both parents groaned. Then reflexively they stifled their voices and lay ramrod stiff, listening, dreading, and not breathing . . .

Sure enough, their fears came to life.

Thump! Small feet hit the floor from down the hall. "Mommy? Daddy? Has Santa come?"

"Oh, Linda, he's probably not come yet, go back to bed, okay sweetie?" Lucy called. "Daddy's sleeping."

"No, he's not, Mommy. I hear him in the bathroom!"

"Darn," Lucy said, reaching for her robe in the bedcovers. Larry came back in the bedroom, a sheepish look on his face.

"Busted," he shrugged.

"Just what I was thinkin'," Lucy nodded. "You reckon we'll ever really get the chance to sleep until seven o'clock on Christmas Day. Ever? Ever?"

"Don't know. But we're up today for sure. I hear feet just a'runnin' lickety split to the living room."

"Put on your slippers, Linda!" Lucy hissed.

"What time is it?" Lawrence's voice chimed from the third bedroom.

"Hush, you'll wake Mamaw!" Larry called in a raspy whisper.

"Mamaw's awake," a wavering voice broke the darkness like the trill of a meadowlark. "Merry Christmas, everyone! I got myself to my wheelchair. I'm setting here just a'lookin' at this beautiful tree in the living room. Good news! Good news! Santa has come!"

48. Good Souls

Larry elected to take his pickup even though it meant Lucy and Mamaw rode with him in the front seat and Lawrence and Linda bundled up in coats and blankets outside in the truck bed. He figured, excited as they were, they'd stay warm. Furthermore it was not much over two miles to the Urbanes', and the pickup afforded the option of bringing home his boy's Christmas surprise. That is, if he had one.

Larry repositioned his baseball cap—his old nervous habit; then he put two gloved hands on the steering wheel. Snow lay ahead on the road. Lucy kept singing "White Christmas," and his mother gaily joined along. Larry kept thinking he should have called Mr. Urbane. But he felt strange about reminding a man of Bill's stature about a small detail. Larry remembered their last conversation about the bike.

"I've called Johnson's Motor Repair," Bill Urbane had said. "They picked up my tractor and the bike. Let me handle the mice damage to the bike that way. I'm not sure but what those blasted critters have eaten my tractor wires, too. They get in and build nests. Varmints. Cost me a bundle. I'm going to go out and get a barn cat!"

Larry had laughed. "Okay, Sir. Thanks." That conversa-

346

tion led to Bill's invitation to Larry's family for brunch. Of course, not having the bike at Larry's home Christmas morning had caused some confusion and disappointment. Larry and Lucy had wrapped a new dirt bike helmet from Santa.

Lawrence saw it under the tree, whooped, and went looking out the window for the bike. Lucy said lamely, "Well, you're a step closer to your goal you've been savin' for." Lawrence's face fell almost down to his bare feet. He just said, "Yes'm. But you don't expect me to wear this with my old bicycle, do you?"

Both parents had responded, "No, Son."

Mamaw saved the day with chirping hope: "Keep the faith—'the evidence of things not seen . . .'"

Lawrence just shook his head and said, "I'd rather see things."

Similar disappointment greeted Linda, who found Mamaw's crocheted pony blanket and no pony under the tree. The same assurance greeted her. "One step closer to a pony. Start savin' for a saddle."

"But what good is a saddle without a pony?" Linda had wailed.

Larry rubbed his eyes wearily. So much for a joyous Christmas morning. He knew a dirt bike awaited Lawrence at the Urbanes'; he also knew that no pony awaited Linda. Maybe he hadn't thought this Christmas through very well.

Meanwhile, he had opened a large box from Lucy and discovered, of all things, a rich royal blue terrycloth robe with a gold crest—Clearview Country Club. Larry had never held such a heavy bathrobe in his life.

"Put it on," Lucy urged. She had bought it with the Urbanes' gift certificate on her one-day trip to the spa. Larry felt slightly ashamed, like he was "puttin' on airs."

Lucy shook her head. "You're just as good as anybody. You can wear a robe as good as those folks who've struck it rich. Most of 'em inherited their money. We're earnin' ours." Then she pulled out a pair of jogging pants with the same crest. "These are gonna help me lose another five pounds," she said.

"Well, then we better throw out that frozen chocolate bundt cake from Sam's Club you got in the freezer," Larry smiled.

"I'm saving it to reward myself," Lucy smiled.

Larry's eyebrows went up.

"Oh, I know it don't make no sense. But it's a step to a goal, like Lawrence's helmet and Linda's pony blanket. Workin' on a dream like your Mamaw says." The kids looked at their mother askance.

"Is she kiddin' or what?" Lawrence asked his sister.

Mamaw, full of childish excitement over her new porch bedroom, kept bubbling. "Keep the faith. Dreams come true."

"With time, work, and money, I guess they do," Larry murmured. He told them to clean up the wrapping paper and bows; they were due at the Urbanes' in an hour.

Back and forth across the front windows of their Federalist home, Bill Urbane paced. "I should have called the repair shop," he said. "I should have set a specific time. I just said, 'before noon,' and of course, on Christmas Day, nobody is answering the phone."

Weeks ago, Bill had stressed repairing the tractor, but he said to please get the bike back by Christmas. Then he had dismissed both items from his mind, which had ricocheted between the Christmas Swap and the last-minute sale of the adjoining Circle Market property. *I wonder if I'm out a million dollars?* Bill asked himself again. *No. Isabel would have called and said we have the money to match.*

Bill heard a grinding noise outside. He saw the Laymans' pickup followed by the Midlands' SUV slowly coming up his long drive through the snow. The drifts billowed as light as flour.

"Francine?" he called. "They're here!"

She heard him from the kitchen, where she launched into preparation overdrive. Francine enlisted Anna in the feverish endeavor. "Cut the fruit up, darling, just chunks, will you? Put them in those carved-out pineapple halves."

"Here?"

"Yes, arrange the platter with lettuce and pile the strawberries and blackberries and blueberries."

"And pineapple?"

"Yes, all of it."

Francine turned to the top oven and cracked the door a bit, looking to see bubbles on the ham-ala-king.

"Aha, ready," she said, smiling with satisfaction. She reached toward the counter where pastry puffs sat in even rows on a cookie sheet. She slid those in the lower oven.

Then she turned her attention to a yellow mix in a large ceramic bowl.

"Scrambled eggs?" Anna asked, as her mother floated a pat of butter in the frying pan.

"Yes, and cheese grits, in that back pot," Francine said. "This is a down-home country breakfast. Or rather a fancy, down-home brunch."

"I cannot believe you have converted to grits," Anna wrinkled her nose. "Tasteless grainy corn. It's hardly fit for horses!"

"Silly goose," Francine said with affection. "Just because you grew up in Boston doesn't mean you don't have Southern roots. My mother, remember, your grandmother, was from Savannah, Georgia. You can't get much more Southern than that."

"I still think they're tasteless."

"All you need to add is enough butter and salt and milk. And cheddar cheese with a hint of garlic makes grits just magic."

"Well, I still think, as the saying goes, 'a horse eats corn.'"

"So do people," Francine said. "You watch how those Midland boys and the Layman kids dive into these grits."

"Yuk!" Anna said. Slowly, she turned the platter of fruitful labor around on the counter for Francine's critical gaze, "What do you think?"

"Beautiful!" Francine smiled. "Just perfect."

"It is colorful, isn't it?" Anna nodded with satisfaction.

"Why don't we sing a few carols around Jan's piano?" Francine suggested after brunch. "Will you play for us, Jan?"

"Just a little. I'm rusty, but I think I can remember "Jingle Bells," at least. Frank and I want you to know that we have appreciated your storing the baby grand for us."

"We're glad to keep it 'til Frank designs that farmhouse," Bill said magnanimously.

"After a song or two, we can gather in the den before the tree Jan decorated," Francine suggested. "I have some hot apple cider, some eggnog, and sweets for dessert."

" . . . A tree Mom decorated? Another theme tree?" Ryan asked.

"With farm animals?" Kyle smirked.

Jan shot them a silencing look. Frank succinctly came to her rescue. "Color scheme, yes, blue and silver. Theme, no. No farm animals."

Bill sensed a private family joke. "There's a nice fire in there," he offered.

Anna stood up to clear the table. As she did, she noticed little Linda take her finger and run it around her plate rim, scraping up the last little bit of grits with obvious relish. She smiled, remembering her mother's words.

Sitting beside her, Lucy saw her daughter's eager movement and tapped her elbow, whispering, "Don't do that!" The child snatched her hands toward her lap.

"You like grits, Linda?" Anna said, winking at her own mother.

Francine said, "Now, Anna."

"Yes, Ma'am," said the wide-eyed child.

"I don't," Anna wrinkled her nose. "But I *do like* to feed them to the neighbors' horses."

Linda's mouth sprang into a round little "O." She gasped, "Do your neighbors have a pony?" she asked.

"Sure. They've got a couple. They raise thoroughbreds mostly. I used to muck out their stalls, feed them, and even exercise them when I was in high school."

"You did?"

"Yep. They hire young people in the summers; the owner's wife teaches horseback lessons. Have you ever ridden a pony, Linda?"

"No."

"I have. Won some blue ribbons. I'll show you in my room." Anna winked.

Stunned, Linda stared at Anna and looked at her mother. Lucy raised her eyebrows. Mamaw perked up, suddenly aware. She didn't say it, thank goodness, but Lucy heard the echo of an Eastern meadowlark, *Dreams come true.*

After a few songs, Larry had asked Lawrence to fetch his helmet to show the group. Everyone seemed snug and comfortable in the Urbanes' den. In her tiny lap, Linda stroked a blue satin ribbon Anna had given her.

Whump! The front door blew open and Lawrence hurried in, hugging his helmet.

"Somebody's comin'," he announced. With that, the three adult men bolted from their seats, followed by everyone else. Through a front window they watched a cattle truck slowly make the turn and ease across the snow, making ruts with its massive tires. Bill glanced at Larry and winked. Larry felt like he was fourteen himself. Frank Midland smiled. So did Ryan and Kyle. They knew what was up.

The truck moved forward, ending in a wide circle on the pebbled drive. The door to the driver's side opened, and as everyone watched, an old man in blue denim coveralls, wearing a red and green plaid flannel shirt, stepped around to the rear of the trailer, his boots tracking the snow. He raised his hand.

"Merry Christmas!" he called.

"Why, it's the guy who saved my—" Larry gasped.

"The limousine driver," Jan blurted out.

"His name is Pap," Frank added.

"Santa!" Linda squealed.

Bill was the first out the door to pump the old man's hand. "Want some cider?" he asked. "Eggnog? We got plenty."

"No, thank you." The old man said cheerily. "Last delivery on Christmas Day." His grin shone through a beard as white as the snow.

"Who is Lawrence?" Pap asked, his eyes crinkling. Lawrence stepped forward.

"Me, Sir," he said.

"You been saving for a dirt bike?"

Lawrence nodded.

"Well, boy, you keep on saving. Put that money toward college. You got some generous folks for parents and some fine friends here." With that, he opened the double trailer doors, hinges clanking in the cold. The shivering circle of faces peered inside.

There, with its shiny red flanks and gleaming chrome, sporting a red bow, a dirt bike stood roped to the trailer sides. Everyone burst into a clamorous cheer. Lawrence, Jr., put his hands to his face, then spread his fingers to look between them to be sure the bike was real.

"You want to ride?" the driver asked.

Everyone ran back inside to gather coats. Pap reached inside the truck cab and pulled on Larry's black jacket. Regrouped outside, they seemed to make noise all at once. What a thrill it was to stand and shout and watch! Larry took the first spin, showing his son how to operate the bike. Then Larry became the first passenger, on the back of the bike with Lawrence driving. Next, the Midland twins took a turn each and then Frank. Bill stood aside watching them share the thrill, noticing how the snow, a tall white wake, billowed in streams behind the bike. The scene was familiar . . .

How I loved to create wakes of powder behind my son, riding that very bike, he thought. *In my mind, I can see it. Feel it . . . the throbbing engine muffled by the silence of the snow, Andrew's dark hair curling in a whipped frenzy, a blizzard in our faces, the warmth of his strong, young back against my chest . . .*

Bill blinked back the pain. He straightened his shoulders, cleared his throat, and spoke to the old man beside him.

"I don't know how you keep turning up like a bright penny the way you do," he said huskily. "But it seems you have a knack for bringing happiness."

"That I do," Pap agreed.

"Well, I want to pay you something," Bill said, reaching for his wallet. "This was a special delivery, for sure. And it's Christmas."

"Thank you. No, Sir. Happy to do it." The man reached his hand to stop Bill, inadvertently pulling up his own left shirt-sleeve by an inch or two.

Bill blanched, startled. He could swear that in the instant the red flannel cuff was pulled up, he saw a watch with the word, *Rolex*, on the face. *Couldn't be,* Bill thought. *Must be a knock-off, a fake, like vendors sell on the streets of New York.*

The old driver seemed to catch Bill's thought. He pulled down his sleeve and spoke with gravel in his voice.

"Time to go." He turned toward the running board of the truck, his hair against his flannel collar, ruffling in the wind.

Bill held the driver door as the old man grunted, climbing behind the wheel. Bill shut the door and waved a silent, "Thank you."

Pap paused. Then he rolled down the window and leaned out. Bill leaned forward.

"Don't worry about that boy of yours," he said.

"Oh, that's Larry's boy," Bill corrected. "Not mine."

"Your boy," the old man said. "Andrew. Don't worry about him."

Bill squinted his eyes as if having a hard time hearing what he thought he'd heard.

"He's fine." Pap nodded, turning the ignition key. The truck motor roared. Then he leaned his head out the window once more toward Bill.

"He's a good soul."

With that, the truck and trailer eased forward, down the drive, and slowly out of sight.

Bill Urbane shook his head like a man coming out of a dream. But this was real, he said to himself.

Still, he thought, his heart beating wildly, *the coincidences . . . a rare white fawn, a stranger turning up repeatedly like a shiny penny, the Rolex watch on his arm, a Christmas delivery, and the crusty old driver speaking his own boy's name . . .*

Bill heard the telephone ringing from inside the house. He ran through the front door, snow tracks on the Italian tiles, as he headed to the nearest extension. He hurried past the eighteenth-century clock, which was striking twelve times. For some reason, he knew, *he just knew*, as he breathlessly said, "Hello?" that the person on the other end was a jubilant Isabel Charmin telling him that his million-dollar land offer had a match.

EPILOGUE

EVERYONE IN THE COMMUNITY said it was just amazing
what a pretty spring it was that year, the most beautiful in about
five years, they all agreed. The redbud trees with their delicate
pink flowers, which usually preceded the white flaky dogwoods,
seemed to hold up and wait on them this year, and after two
weeks, when the blooms began to fade, Clearview experienced
what amounted to a heavy snowstorm of pink and white blos-
soms blowing all over town.

Bringing spring, the petals coated the backs of pasture
cattle and dotted the woodlands with lace trailing up the Blue
Ridge Mountains. Thick like a ticker-tape parade, the flakes
swept down Main Street, past Horton's Drugstore, and the Ice
Cream Parlor, and circled back toward the center of town. They
whirled across the front porch of the Circle Market, now remade
as a rustic tavern called The Buck Stop. Further along, they blew
in fragments up the steps and around the tall columns of a solid
red-brick school with an Italianate roof and Palladian arches
connecting its several buildings. Standing there, you might have
heard the sound of children's voices singing, as the bell in the
school tower chimed twelve.

Today was May Day, and anybody who had children, and
many who didn't, turned out to see the little ones dance with
shimmering pastel ribbons around a central decorated pole. The
ceremonies for May Day, the anniversary day of the founding of
The Andrew Academy for the Creative Arts, began at one o'clock.

When she heard the academy clock tower strike, Lucy

Layman closed the door to her Main Street business, glancing happily at the painted letters on the glass door: "Clearview Home Cleaning Service." She'd chosen the flamingo as a logo; she had a sign painter draw it "real big" on the front glass where its bright pink color attracted attention from the street. She had business cards printed to match. She made it a point to leave a card at every customer's house. Soon, new customers handed them off to newer customers. Those pink flamingo cards began to migrate all over Peach County. Lucy was beginning to wish she'd called her business, "Flamingo Home Cleaning Service." *'Cause that's how people remember it,* Lucy thought. Funny how each time she left Mrs. Urbane's house, the older woman laughed after Lucy's shining, scrubbing, and vacuuming. Then invariably she'd wave from the front door,

"Well, I've been 'flamingoed' today, Lucy. Thank you!"

Lucy walked past a few shops on the way to her car. She noticed with satisfaction another sign, small and discreet, in the yard of a remodeled older house on Main Street. Another motif—that of a swirled thread piercing the eye of a needle— illustrated the windows beyond the front porch: "Eva's Dressmaking Designs."

Meanwhile, across town near the outskirts, Larry Layman pulled his truck away from his latest project while a framing crew waved him on as they pounded the rafters of still another new home. Clearview had zoned a few subdivisions at its fringes. Larry was constructing several homes with his own team and he was hard at work on a Contractor A license in night school.

At the university, Frank Midland told his architecture students that there would be no quiz today, as his class was cancelled that afternoon. He climbed in his new SUV and raced across town. On the passenger seat of his vehicle, the blueprints of the main farmhouse he had designed for Double Nickel Farm lay rolled up and fastened with a rubber band. *I'll walk it tonight,* he promised himself. Beside the plans, Frank's glance caught something else—the travel agency pamphlet: two round-trip tickets and an itinerary for a week in Italy. Yesiree—promise kept! Frank grinned and rolled down the windows to belt out an Italian aria alongside Pavarotti singing from a compact disc in the dashboard player.

Meanwhile, within the halls of the Andrew Academy, Jan Midland lined up her class of nervous, giggling fourth graders along the halls. "Stand tall," the teacher reminded them. "We'll be marching in just a minute. And sing loud. It's May Day!"

At home, Francine Urbane positioned a silver ribbon on a plaque for "Best Creative Effort," one of many she had wrapped for the ceremonies. She called out to Bill that they didn't want to be late.

"No, Ma'am," Bill answered his wife, putting a period with a fountain-pen flourish on a speech he had written. And the couple dashed out the door together.

In the green quadrangle behind The Andrew Academy, Isabel Charmin, posed behind a podium and enthusiastically read the names of this year's winning students with talents that ranged from finger painting to sculpture and from essays to dance. Bill Urbane stood up to address the celebratory crowd, his gaze settling briefly on Evangeline Holmes, sitting next to her new husband, photographer Hank Bissell. With triumph in his tone he began to tell the Once-Upon-A-Time Christmas story five years before when a small group of people exchanged places, when a rare white deer moved through the surrounding forests, and when the community unknowingly attracted the attention of a mysterious benefactor who was inspired by the town's united purpose, "Together, One."

In the interim burst of applause, Hank Bissell took Eva's hand. No one knew but the two of them . . . .. No one knew of the amazing drawing Tom produced on that long ago Christmas morning. No one but they had seen the feathery chalk of a scene the boy had sworn he'd witnessed: a bearded old man in the woods, his arms cradling a solid white fawn. Nor did anyone know of the sketch they found a year later: the delicate charcoal of the rock ledge behind Eva's trailer on which the mysterious stranger and a young boy—free of his constraining chair—sat quietly, the boy's hand—very still—upon the back of the fawn.

"It was Tom Holmes," Bill Urbane continued, his voice swelling, "one of our earliest students, who first made us realize how talents trained, despite infirmity, can transform our world. And while Tom, sadly, is no longer with us in flesh, he is with us in spirit." A gathering applause from the audience washed over Bill, who felt a conviction that swept him toward his conclusion.

"There are many dimensions to life: some we understand; others we don't understand." Bill lifted his eyes, his gaze sweeping across the upturned faces, "One thing we know: Tom was a good soul."

Then Bill finished with an affirmation he had come to believe, "And good souls never die."

Later that night at The Buck Stop, Flossie leaned over *The Clearview Clarion,* lying on the counter near the cook stove. She opened a piece of bubble gum and read the quote of Bill's words out loud.

"You know, I've heard that before," she said, popping the gum into her mouth. "After that bum, the stranger, named Pap? After he brushed up our trophy buck here on Christmas Eve years ago, he said the same thing that's in this paper, 'Good souls never die.' And, you know? Since then, this Old Boy's been different. I ain't crazy, honest. But sometimes, when I'm shining up that buck like I did the other day, dusting and such, well, I'll tell you something. I do believe that buck winked at me."

"Nah," shrugged Hiram Venald, putting down his empty coffee mug on the counter. "You're dreaming."

"I ain't," Flossie said. "You want more?"

"Naw, I've had enough." He slid his short round body the remaining distance of a foot from the counter stool where his feet dangled above the floor. "I can stay awake as far as the next county."

For, that's where Hiram was heading—to Blackstone County. He left the tavern and put a two-inch, patent-leather cowboy boot on the floorboard of his brand new extended cab truck. He lit the stub of a smoldering cigar pulled from the ash-tray and rolled out of the parking lot, looking forward to cross-ing the county line to view his brand new seven-thousand-square-foot home sitting astride one of the foothills of Virginia. Why, in the valley below it, part of the deal and right in view, stood the brand new vaulted red and black arms of a brightly lit Crane's station. His development plan didn't make it in Peach County where the snooty folks of Clearview held sway, but Hiram didn't care. He just jumped the county line and vengefully built the spread where everybody who traveled that far into the hills could see it.

"Can't stop Green Thumb Venald! I'm a rich man now, and gonna be richer! Hell's Bells and Glory Be! I won! I won!"

His wife, Stephanie, did not quite share Hiram's view of victory, however.

"I don't like the way it smells up here when the wind shifts," Stephanie had said to him one recent evening as she stood on the balcony of their home wearing a gold silk blouse, her bleached blond hair blowing in the mountain air. She had on her favorite pants, white leather, stretched tight like bungee chords, the pants Hiram gave her as a consolation prize for missing his shot at the white fawn. And, of course, for coming to get him lying drunk in the woods that day a few years back.

"The smell, my dear?" Hiram accepted a triple-olive vodka martini from his wife and hoisted it toward the mechanical view below his home. "Why, that's a smell . . . better than apples or tomatoes or avocadoes or any fruit or vegetable known to humankind. That, my Stephanie, is the smell of oil—the ripe, rich smell of money!"

Later that night, after he had watched the sun retreat over Double Nickel Farm, and he had kissed his wife goodnight, Frank Midland closed the back door to his home. He had, as was their custom, walked with the lugubrious, elderly, nearly blind Lamont on his evening doggie rounds. As usual, Frank spoke as if the Bassett understood the King's English.

"Hate to bring you in from this lovely spring night. But I've got to gather up some papers and get my briefcase ready for tomorrow, old boy," he said. "Need to find one of my architecture books." The dragging hound looked sorrowfully at his master and padded after him into Frank's office. Frank leaned over and lit his pipe. He loaded some papers in his flapped briefcase pockets and then scanned his bookshelves. There it was. He hadn't referred to that particular book in several years. He pulled it from the shelf and a newspaper clipping fluttered out and landed on his desk nearby.

"Hmm," Frank said. "What's this?"

"*BILLIONAIRE ESCAPES ASYLUM,*" the headline read. And Frank nodded to himself, remembering. He scanned the article once again, stopping at the words of an attorney representing the eccentric, old, filthy-rich geezer who had fled from a mental hospital in northern New York around Christmas a few years back.

"His family says he's a kook," the attorney was quoted as saying. "He's throwing money away, so they say. But the fact is, his doctor says he's sane. So, if he's a kook, you must realize, he's a legitimate kook with cash!" Frank peered closely at the picture of the "insane" billionaire.

"That's him," Frank chewed his pipe stem. "That's Pap." And Frank removed his pipe and laughed out loud, the same way he had after the Christmas Swap five years ago, when he had read to Jan the article he had discovered on that December 26 in *The Washington Post.*

"A kook with cash," Frank looked amusedly down at Lamont, who gazed lovingly up. "Someday that's what I hope they'll say about me."

Lamont doggedly, in his inimical way, agreed.

By eleven that spring night, the temperature had cooled to fifty and the wind had died down. The Big Dipper hung low over the Blue Ridge, its starry bucket poised over the town of Clearview.

Flossie was ready to close up shop. She had her purse and her keys. The coffee pot was ready for tomorrow. The cook stove was turned off, the cash register was locked, the old newspapers stacked in the recycle bin. She went toward the front door and turned off the lights. On impulse, leaving, she turned to "Old Buck," and said,

"Night, night, good soul." She pushed the shop door to with a key, and she walked out into the silent night where all the townspeople lay sleeping in their beds, where all the Main Street shops were tightly shut, and where the windblown flower petals on the sidewalks lay inert.

Yet within the quiet darkness of the new-old tavern called The Buck Stop, on the wall above the service counter, visible through glass windows that overlook the arc of the circle that centers Clearview, two mellow gold orbs of clear, animated light shone steadily, eternally reflecting the celestial sheen of distant stars.

.jam

Author's Notes

Reference is made in this book to the work of Dr. Ellisabeth Kübler-Ross, M.D. (1926-2004), a Swiss-born psychiatrist, author of many books, including the groundbreaking work, *On Death and Dying*. I had the privilege of conducting a television interview with Dr. Kübler-Ross in February of 1988, at her farm in Highland County, Virginia.

The story told by Bill Urbane to his daughter, Anna, in this book draws on and modifies a Chickasaw legend about a white stag, a brave warrior, and an Indian maiden. American Indian lore abounds in legends about the world, its origins, and its inhabitants. An artfully recounted version of the tale, entitled,

"Ghost of the White Deer," may be found at the website: *http://www.ilhawaii.net/~story/lore128.html,* by Stonee's WebLodge, 1997.

Quotes from Goethe and Einstein are drawn from assorted readings; that of Brian Greene is from *The Fabric of The Cosmos*, Vintage Books, a Division of Random House, Inc., New York, © 2004

Music noted within the novel refers to:

"Silent Night," as described, is from *Mannheim Steamroller Christmas,* by Chip Davis, prolific composer and founder of American Gramophone, LLC. The multiple-million-selling musical compilation features astonishingly original arrangements of traditional carols.

Home page: *http://www.amgram.com*

Brad Paisley's country song, "Celebrity," is the title number from his CD, *Mud on the Tires*. The lyrics offer an entertaining spoof of comtemporary America's fascination with notoriety and fame.